T0322321

Circus of Mirrors

Circus of Mirrors

JULIE OWEN MOYLAN

MICHAEL JOSEPH

PENGUIN MICHAEL JOSEPH

UK | USA | Canada | Ireland | Australia
India | New Zealand | South Africa

Penguin Michael Joseph is part of the Penguin Random House group of companies
whose addresses can be found at global.penguinrandomhouse.com

Penguin
Random House
UK

First published 2024
001

Copyright © Julie Owen Moylan, 2024

The moral right of the author has been asserted

Set in 13.5/16pt Garamond MT Std
Typeset by Jouve (UK), Milton Keynes
Printed and bound in Great Britain by Clays Ltd, Elcograf S.p.A.

The authorized representative in the EEA is Penguin Random House Ireland,
Morrison Chambers, 32 Nassau Street, Dublin D02 YH68

A CIP catalogue record for this book is available from the British Library

HARDBACK ISBN: 978–0–241–65152–0
TRADE PAPERBACK ISBN: 978–0–241–65153–7

www.greenpenguin.co.uk

This book is dedicated to the courage
and resilience of women.

Of two sisters,
one is always the watcher,
one the dancer.

Louise Glück

Berlin, August 1961

Annette was sitting in the dark, smoking a cigarette. She could barely make out the hands of the clock on top of the sideboard, but she could hear it ticking. Outside was a violet sky and the promise of a new day. She hadn't slept at all. She wasn't sure that Leni had either. The apartment was still draped in a bitter silence – but the dull yellowish glow of a bedside lamp shone from under the bedroom door, and Annette thought that she could hear her sister moving around: the gentle tread of her footsteps and the creak of the floor.

Crushing out her cigarette in the glass ashtray, she walked over to the window. Outside, the streets were empty, and she felt completely alone. Running her fingertips across the side of her face, Annette winced. It felt sore and tender – a bruising reminder of just how much her sister hated her.

She had nobody now. She'd lost everyone she'd ever cared for. Annette felt sorry for herself, even as she realized that it was probably her own fault. Hot tears spilled down her face as she contemplated her future. Where could she go? There was nobody waiting for her. Wiping away her tears, she cast another glance towards the tiny pool of light.

There was something she should have done years ago.

It was probably too late to make any difference now. But Annette needed to at least try and explain things.

She took a tentative step towards the bedroom door before hesitating just outside with her hand raised. Finally, inhaling a deep breath, Annette gently tapped on the door with her knuckles.

There was no answer, yet she was sure that her sister was awake. She waited for a few more seconds, her hand hovering in the air, unsure of what to do. Then Annette knocked again – and, this time, she didn't wait for an invitation.

PART ONE
Berlin, August 1926

I

Dieter's finely manicured fingernails made gentle tapping sounds on the side of his tin cheek as he surveyed the state of his desk. Leaning back in his wooden chair, he lit a Turkish cigarette and exhaled. The cloud of smoke curled menacingly in the direction of Herr Keks – a small white cat that was fast asleep on top of a large pile of bills. The bills lay stabbed through the heart with an enormous steel hat pin to stop them escaping into the random piles of paper that were scattered in all directions.

He rubbed anxiously at the edges of his face – the place where the tin met the skin. He had left the rest of his cheek on a battlefield in Belgium. One moment he was a man in his prime, with not unattractive features – and the next minute a violent explosion had blown him off his feet, the skin on his cheek melting away as if it had never existed, leaving him with nothing but a bloody pulp. Now, at nearly thirty-five years old, Dieter was so very tired of his face. The raw skin was kept hidden away under a tin mask, which was painted with a single brown eye, to replace the one he'd lost – his left. Most of his mouth remained intact, but the left edges of his lips had gone, too, replaced by a rather strange painted smile.

This gave Dieter a peculiar way of speaking, and meant that people never quite knew whether he was really smiling at them as his metallic brown eye stared blankly and his painted lips were permanently turned upwards – as if he were privy to an amusing joke that he refused to share.

Now, his good eye blinked furiously at both the sleeping cat and the pile of unpaid bills. The cigarette he was smoking made his throat itch, and he coughed, first delicately and then as if his life depended on removing the smoke from his lungs. Eventually, Dieter leaned forward in the wooden chair, which creaked ominously under his weight, before spitting a small yellow ball of mucus into his empty coffee cup.

Herr Keks woke grumpily, jumped down from the desk, raised his tail in a haughty fashion and disappeared through the open door. The door to Dieter's office was always left ajar, but it was meant only for the cat to come and go – not, under any circumstances, for people to use. Especially women.

The girls of the Babylon Circus, with their tears and tantrums, their fights and jealousies . . . Dieter let out a long, miserable sigh at the thought of them. Dancing girls, singing girls . . . *Why was his life so very difficult?* It was, he thought, because he was always surrounded by women. Dieter preferred the company of men. They were less likely to complain or cry. He still shuddered at the memory of the time one of the dancers had sobbed all over his shoulder. He had patted her on the back of her head – with rather less affection than he reserved for Herr Keks when handing him a small piece of fish.

Outside his office, Dieter heard a shriek of loud screeching laughter that he recognized as Berolina. The Babylon Circus employed a range of 'artistes', mostly sweet singers and girls who might dance with the 'guests' until later on in the evening, when the lights were lowered and the dancers took over the stage. The final part of the night required girls like Berolina. Loud, skilled at strangely exotic tricks, and mostly naked.

A riptide of amusement echoed once again right outside his office door and on through the dark brown passageway leading down to the dressing room. For reasons that escaped Dieter, given they had a perfectly good room with a door that closed, the corridor was always filled with girls fixing their feathery headdresses or hoisting their silk stockings, smelling of face powder and perfume. Several of the dancers liked to stand around smoking there, although Dieter was sure he had told them a million times to go somewhere else and stop cluttering up the passage with their smells and laughter and complaints.

They were always complaining. It was too hot or too cold. The customers were too mean or too rough with them. There was never one day where these girls were happy for the entire shift. He coughed again, a light rattling machine gun that ended with nothing except his fist pounding his chest. He wasn't a well man. They could at least afford him a little peace in his life.

Dieter adjusted his tin mask again. The edges felt tight today. They irritated him, making his skin red and inflamed. His cough irritated him. Berolina's laughter irritated him. It was too early in the evening to feel this irritated. There was a whole night ahead.

He glanced at the bills on the desk. Now the cat had vacated his position, Dieter could clearly see the amounts demanded. He would need to put the prices up again. Lately, once the customers had paid their three marks to enter the club, they were content to ogle the dancers yet refused to buy more than one bottle of champagne for their table, which caused him great distress. The mark-up on the champagne was enough to pay if not all the bills on his desk, then at least a good number of them, if only bottles were bought. He would have to speak to the girls about enticing the guests to drink more . . .

Berolina shrieked with laughter again. Dieter chewed angrily at the inside of his mouth and crushed his cigarette out in his mucus-filled coffee cup. 'What could be so funny that people need to keep on laughing?' he muttered out of the part of his mouth that still worked. He should fire them all. Annoying creatures. But then what? No girls meant no customers. *But why couldn't they just be quiet?*

Suddenly, a loud, heartrending scream replaced the laughter and was swiftly followed by an anguished cry. It wasn't Berolina this time, but Adele, who was howling, 'NO!' over and over.

Dieter got to his feet. His knee hurt from an old shrapnel wound when he tried to sit or stand. The aching made him rub at his right leg as he set off in the direction of the wailing. He would tell them to shut up or be sacked on the spot. He was the manager after all. They should listen to him and show more respect.

By the time he reached his office door a cacophony of wailing and crying was pouring out of the dressing room, the howls of anguish increasing with every step he took. Dieter muttered swear words under his breath, cursing his lot in life – the girls and their noise, his aching knees, the sore point at which the tin mask rubbed against his left cheek. Oh, his life was all pain today . . . He just wanted five minutes of peace and quiet.

Dieter shuffled along the empty passageway, shaking his head and preparing himself for battle. He was only one man and they were many, but there had to be silence today or his head would burst with pain.

The door to the dressing room was wide open. Every surface appeared to be covered with sobbing half-naked women.

'WHAT IS GOING ON?' Dieter roared at them out of his lop-sided mouth. A now weeping Berolina turned to face him. Her large breasts were covered by only the smallest of silver stars, while a ballet skirt of the thinnest pale green gauze parted dangerously to show the milky white of her legs. She fixed him with a serious glare, her eyes quite pink now from sobbing. 'Rudolph Valentino *died* . . .'

Dieter slowly shook his head. Valentino. The loss of a movie star famous for parading around in silly costumes meant nothing to him.

'Well, this caterwauling won't bring him back,' he snapped before slamming the dressing-room door shut on the women who tormented him so. Muttering to himself, Dieter strode purposefully back towards the safety of his office – only to find his path blocked by yet another agitated young woman, who appeared to be waiting to speak to him.

'I . . . I'm looking for work. I can wait on tables . . . or whatever you need.' She looked up at him with wide, pleading eyes. The girl looked no more than eighteen or nineteen years old – no doubt she would be just as annoying as the other women at the Circus. He grimaced slightly as he considered the matter.

As it happened, his cigarette girl had quit suddenly that week and he did need to replace her. Dieter looked this young woman up and down disapprovingly.

'I'm very reliable,' the girl added hastily. Taking in her nervous demeanour and shabby cotton dress, he let out a deep sigh.

All he wanted was five minutes to himself. Yet, as he raised his one good eye to the heavens, Dieter understood there would be no peace for him today.

2

Leni could not take her eyes off the man with the peculiar tin face as she waited for him to make a decision. Half of his face could have been handsome, except that his mouth was pushed to one side by the tin mask that covered the place where his cheek and eye should have been. This tin mask fitted across the bridge of his nose and sliced up between his eyes to the top of his forehead. It looked to Leni as if it was very uncomfortable.

Returning his gaze to her, he suddenly asked if she was a *quiet* girl. Leni rightly assumed this answer might be the key to any future employment and so she smiled broadly, assuring him that she was well known for being as quiet as a mouse. This answer seemed to satisfy the strange man.

'The girls will tell you where to go. I pay on Friday nights and not before.' The man spoke as if he was being constantly harassed for money and then made a wild waving gesture with his left hand. Leni nodded obediently, having spent all day fruitlessly searching for work. She needed money desperately, and if the only way she could earn it was to be a cigarette girl in this strange place, then that's what she would do.

'Come with me . . . you can start tonight,' he called out as he walked away at such a pace that Leni found herself practically running to keep up.

As she scurried down the passage after him, Leni saw a

young man coming from the opposite direction. He wore a navy suit with a white shirt and a dark red tie. His light brown hair was neatly slicked back, yet one strand fell on to his forehead. As the young man drew closer, he called out cheerily, 'Good evening, Dieter,' and then smiled as he noticed Leni hurrying along behind. She slowed her pace a little, in order to smile back at the young man, who stopped briefly in the middle of the corridor and nodded a greeting at her. 'Fräulein . . .'

Leni found herself staring after him as he continued on his way, watching him go until Dieter turned and barked at her, 'Hurry up!'

She could not take the chance that he might change his mind, and so she raced along a dark passageway until they reached a room that was filled with half-naked girls.

There was no room in the dressing room for another person, but somehow Leni squeezed into the throng of bodies. They were all in various stages of undress, besides the most elaborate headdresses that seemed at odds with the simplicity of what adorned their bodies – which was not much. Strategically placed spangles and feathers covered the worst of it, but there was still plenty of naked flesh for the customers of the Babylon Circus to admire. Leni felt instantly inadequate. These girls were real performers, their faces painted extravagantly, and all but their most intimate parts on show.

'This is . . .' the tin-faced man announced; then he hesitated and glanced at her.

'Leni . . . Leni Taube,' she offered, smiling up at him, pleased to have got what she'd come for. She would work hard, and tomorrow she would get paid, and all would be well. Then she tried her broad smile on the other women, but they didn't seem very interested.

The man sucked at his teeth, seemingly reminded of a name that was of no significance to him at all. His finger went to his tin cheek as if he'd also forgotten the mask covering whatever lay beneath, and then continued addressing her, abandoning his attempt to attract the girls' attentions.

'Anyway, they will show you what to do . . .' He pointed across the room. 'That's Irma, who helps out with cigarettes when we're busy, but she runs the cloakroom so most of the time you will be in charge of making sure everyone has what they need. Understand?'

Leni nodded, making herself as small and quiet as possible so that he had no reason to fire her before she'd even begun.

'Berolina, stop that sulking and get the cigarette tray for . . .' Clearly, Leni's name had already floated out of his mind. He waved a hand in her general direction as a girl wearing nothing but silver stars over her breasts gazed sorrowfully at her.

With that, the tin-faced man walked away, leaving only a gasp of cold air where he had once stood. One of the girls kicked the door shut after him, and Leni stood there feeling awkward and abandoned. The Babylon Circus felt like a strange, exotic land. But she thought of her sister, Annette, and took a determined breath.

She would do this for her.

3

'Leni? Over here . . .' One of the women signalled towards the tiniest gap at the end of a makeshift dressing table that ran the entire length of the wall. It was really just a couple of planks of wood nailed together, propped up at one end with some kind of metal box to stop them collapsing, and it looked as if the lot might come tumbling down if anyone leaned too hard on it. The planks were covered with a thin red cloth on which the girls had laid out the mysterious paints and potions, creams and perfumes that transformed them from ordinary Berlin girls into exotic creatures that came alive at night.

She squeezed past a girl who was doing some sort of stretching that involved contorting her leg so high that Leni was sure she would injure herself. She tried to keep out of the way, wrinkling her nose at the sickly, spiced air redolent of stale cigarettes and the scent of violets.

Once inside the room, Leni quickly realized that what seemed to be taking up most of the space at the far end was a black iron rack of costumes that glittered and swayed every time someone walked past them. She stood in front of them, feeling out of her depth and wondering what on earth she should do next.

'Wally . . .' The girl who had called to her thrust out her hand and gave Leni a most formal handshake considering she was only wearing a belt of sequinned stars and a hat shaped like the moon. Her bare breasts and arms were covered in a dark paint, presumably meant to signify the night sky.

Leni shook her hand and smiled. 'Leni.' The girl took this as encouragement to take charge, giving a shrill whistle that stunned the chatter into silence.

'Everyone, this is the new cigarette girl – Leni. Make some room for her.' Wally smiled and began pointing around the room, indicating the nearest women. 'That's Berolina, Adele, Margot, Marta, Greta . . . oh, and that's Christa.'

Christa was the girl with her leg extended up towards the ceiling, dressed in a layered ballet skirt of the same pale green gauze that Berolina was draped in. 'She trained at the Bolshoi Ballet but her family had to leave Russia when the Bolsheviks took over,' Wally whispered as the Russian girl gave Leni a shy smile.

'And this is Irma.'

Leni glanced down to see a small dark-haired woman dressed all in black who looked at her coolly. The woman didn't smile at all, so Leni just nodded a polite greeting and waited for someone to show her what to do.

Irma swept aside the row of costumes to reveal a sort of shelf underneath them. On the shelf lay a deep silver tray with several compartments, while attached to the back of it was a thick red velvet cord which would allow it to be carried around her neck.

'Here you are – this is your tray. You have to see Dieter to fill it. There should be a uniform around here some-where. I have some special tables that I take care of when I'm not in the cloakroom. You keep to your tables and I'll keep to mine. Got it? Now hurry up and get changed.'

Irma looked her up and down scornfully before turning her back and walking away. Leni felt a pulse of panic that this girl seemed to have taken against her already, but there was nothing for it except to get ready for her shift.

Compared to the other girls, Leni felt overdressed in her loosely fitted blue cotton frock and sensible shoes. She hadn't been expecting to take her clothes off in front of these women and felt strangely nervous. She was about to ask where she should put her things when Berolina chirped up, 'You can hang your street clothes over there.' The girl gestured to the other end of the dressing room and a series of large silver hooks on the wall behind the door. Each hook held a selection of faded summer dresses and threadbare underwear that had seen better days.

Leni was handed a black fringed dress and a tiny gold top hat by Wally, who fussed about her, holding the dress against her body. 'This should fit you . . . If it's too big, then I've got some pins. It's what the last girl wore. And you can make up your face here.' The girl swept a hand across the red cloth to move a jumble of jars and coloured tubes out of the way, leaving a small part of the dressing table clear for Leni. 'Dieter likes it if you wear a lot of make-up. He wants his girls to look healthy, he says.'

'Oh, I don't have any make-up.' It dawned on her that she was completely unprepared for this kind of work as she stared anxiously back at Wally, who at least seemed kind.

'Don't worry. I can lend you some until you get on your feet.' The girl quickly handed her a blue velvet bag that gathered at the top with a strip of navy ribbon. 'Here you are – use mine. Now get yourself ready and then you can see Dieter about your cigarettes and things.'

Managing to squeeze on to a rough wooden stool and stake out a small area for herself, Leni swallowed hard. A flutter of shyness flooded over her at the prospect of changing into her uniform in front of these other bolder women. She was not a particularly bold woman. She wished she was curled up under a blanket with her sister, telling stories of how things used to be – rather than here in this strange place.

Leni loved to tell Annette about their lives before their mother died. Three years ago, they had been part of a large, bustling family, but now that family was kept alive only in their late-night stories. Influenza and tragedy had taken them all, one after the other, until Leni was left alone with her sister depending on her.

As she glanced around, feeling increasingly anxious, she desperately wished her mother was still with them and could tell her that everything would be all right. But Leni only had herself to rely on now. She had to make this work.

Shrinking down on her stool, Leni slowly slipped her feet out of her sensible shoes and unbuttoned the front of her blue cotton summer dress. She felt desperately awkward, yet the other women weren't even looking at her. Instead, Leni found herself staring at them as they transformed themselves in front of the brightly lit mirrors.

Marta, a thick-set blonde, was busily draping herself in the same thin pale green gauze ballet skirt as Christa, while Berolina set about reattaching a tiny silver star that had fallen off her breast. Greta, Adele and Margot were balancing hats made of half-moons on their heads, and hiding the rest of their bodies under transparent robes of inky blue gauze.

Having wriggled out of her clothes and underwear, Leni

set about trying to squeeze her body inside the black uniform. Her hips slid inside easily enough but the dress was
designed for a much taller woman, and Wally needed to
step in with her trusty safety pins, gathering up loose
material and holding her modesty in place.

'There you are. All pinned together. You'll need to sew
this as it won't hold forever, especially the way some of
those hands keep grabbing at us girls . . .' She made a clawing movement using her fingers as pincers before moving
away to cadge a cigarette from Marta.

Leni dipped her hand inside the blue velvet bag and
picked out a small pot of bright red cream. She rouged her
cheeks until they glowed like fresh apples. She then powdered her nose and the parts that the black dress didn't
cover between her breasts, before combing her curls out
so they framed her face. Taking a moment to inspect herself in the mirror, Leni exhaled a quiet sigh of dissatisfaction
at what she saw: fair hair, which needed a shampoo if she
were honest, large blue eyes, an unfortunate chin she'd
inherited from her grandmother Rosa; but her nose was
good, if a little shiny. Her smile was definitely her best fea-
ture, she thought, although it had become rare these days.
She dabbed at the sheen on the tip of her nose with a dirty-
pink powder puff. Underneath the make-up, her face was
pinched with worry, and if she looked closely, Leni could
trace weary purple shadows beneath her eyes.

Attaching the little gold hat to her hair, she stepped
back. To her surprise, her reflection looked much older
than her nineteen years. A different and more sophisticated
creature entirely.

She was ready.

4

Dieter stood to one side of the club and gazed out at his creation. The stage was completely black. All around him, the walls of the Babylon Circus were covered in enormous silver and gold mirrors, allowing the lights to reflect and dazzle. As Dieter hated seeing his own reflection, he'd bought the kind of mirrors that were found in fairgrounds. He thought it funny that everyone looked as distorted and strange as he felt when he saw his own reflection. It was a circus of mirrors.

Earlier, the chandelier hanging from the centre of the ceiling had been lit, casting white drops of light all over a rectangular wooden dance floor, where men in tuxedo suits grabbed at sweet-voiced girls. Dieter paid many of these sweet-voiced girls to keep his customers company if they were alone. The men shuffled them around the room to the sounds of the tinny orchestra on the stage, their hands sliding lower and lower on the backs of the girls' silky dresses. At this stage of the evening the dancing was fairly refined: it even had a slight air of sophistication. The scene could easily have been mistaken for an innocent tea dance.

However, the minute the dancing was over, the chandelier lights were extinguished and a whisper of anticipation spread through the room. It was now almost pitch black, the only light coming from tiny golden lamps that glowed from each of the wooden tables.

Gathered around each dimly lit table were the 'guests' – mostly men, but occasionally they were accompanied by their female friends. These women wore expensive dresses embroidered with things that sparkled, even when the women themselves did not. They often appeared bored, only laughing when one of the rich men who had brought them said something, when someone brought more champagne, or a silver tray of gin rickeys suddenly appeared at the table. These occasionally amused women sipped at their glasses as they watched the men watching the dancing girls.

The 'guests' all wore masks which they were given upon entry to the club. Black for the men, and white for the women. It was an extra touch that Dieter had thought up one day, allowing some degree of anonymity for his customers, and ensuring that they could drink and carouse without worrying about being recognized. The reputation of the club had spread owing to this, and now many important people liked to come to the Babylon Circus. There were a number of rooms in the basement that Dieter was willing to sell a key to, allowing special 'guests' to be further entertained by the girls on his payroll. He allocated only half an hour for each entertainment. Any longer and he would have to interrupt proceedings, as a queue would have begun to form, and that upset the peace and order of the club.

Leni stood just behind Dieter, peering nervously over his shoulder, unsure of what was happening as the lights went out and the dancers left the floor. She'd never seen anything like this place. The shimmering dresses, the glittering lights, the strange, distorted shapes in the enormous mirrors before everything went dark. It was another world entirely.

Her cigarette tray was filled to the brim and the thick velvet cord tugged at her neck. The black fringed dress was split up the side and showed off the entire length of her legs, making Leni keep tugging at it with her right hand, while dispensing packs of cigarettes and cigars with her left. She'd got into a nice little rhythm when suddenly everything had been plunged into darkness and the atmosphere began rippling with an anxious exhilaration.

The customers paid her little attention now as they spied hints of the dancers waiting to take to the stage. Margot and Christa were both in the wings, visible only by the glowing orange-red tips of their cigarettes.

Dieter walked to the centre of the stage and clapped his hands for silence.

'Ladies and gentlemen, welcome to the Babylon Circus cabaret . . .' He drooled a little as he spoke due to the tin mask pinching the edges of his mouth and wiped it away quickly, not wanting anyone to see. The audience applauded wildly in anticipation of the forthcoming attractions. Men inched forward in their chairs, their mouths hanging open, small drops of spittle gathering at the corners of their lips. Hungry for what was about to unfold. Their women friends giggled nervously, unsure what to expect from the infamous cabaret.

Leni could see Irma walking slowly around one or two of the tables carrying her cigarette tray, before stopping in front of a small, silver-haired man. Irma turned her back and then slowly raised the edges of her black dress to the man, briefly revealing a garter on her right thigh containing tiny packets of white powder. Each packet was fastened to the garter and from where Leni was standing, they looked like little white pillows. The silver-haired man selected his little white pillow and hastily shoved a handful of cash on to Irma's cigarette tray. Leni stared open-mouthed as it suddenly dawned on her what was inside the little packets.

Slinking into the shadows, she watched as the young man she'd seen earlier took his place at a black piano just below the stage. His face seemed earnest and filled with concentration. It was a nice face, a boyish face, yet he wasn't a boy any longer.

Under the dim lights, his cheekbones were sharply drawn and his jaw determined. Leni traced her eyes across his lips for a moment. He looked down, staring intently at the piano keys. She focused on his lips again. They were full, and Leni imagined them to be soft. She thought him handsome, but more than that, his face seemed too gentle to fit in the madness of the Babylon Circus.

The eager chatter of the crowd hushed as the young man gave a delicate cough. His long, elegant fingers plunged on to the keyboard, making a sharp sound that brought the Babylon Circus to a nervous silence.

As the pianist began to play, Leni saw the moon and the stars in the night sky taking up their places on stage along with an assortment of planets. Christa stretched her long legs out and, standing on tiptoes, began an elegant ballet routine, the lights catching her naked body under the green gauze of her gown. From time to time the gauze parted in waves, teasing the crowd with a clear view of a naked Christa and then hiding her away again. Marta danced around her while Berolina did the splits at the front of the stage, raising her arms and allowing her enormous star-spangled breasts their full moment of glory under the spotlight.

Leni had never seen anything like this. The men in the audience stared wildly at the girls gyrating and removing bits of coloured gauze.

Berolina was now lying on her back with her legs forming a large V shape in the air, causing the crowd to cheer madly. Leni stood, transfixed by the dancers and everything about this strange place, until Dieter gave her a hearty shove on her back in the direction of a customer who had run out of cigars. She reached the table just next to the spot where the young pianist sat playing something from Holst's *Planets*. He looked up as Leni approached, and then, as the planets spun and the moon and stars appeared under the spotlight, their eyes met . . .

5

When the final customer had made their way out of the bright blue door that marked the entrance to the Babylon Circus, the women removed their feathers and spangles, returning their tired bodies to threadbare underwear and cotton summer dresses. Leni changed back into her clothes slowly as she could hear the pianist talking to Dieter outside the dressing room. They were discussing music and other pleasantries. Then their voices dropped to a whisper and she could no longer hear what they were saying. Hastily buttoning up her dress, Leni squeezed past Berolina and Wally, calling out goodbyes over her shoulder as she hurried into the passageway.

Dieter and the pianist seemed surprised to see her as she mumbled 'Excuse me' on her way to the street door. The tin-faced man scowled at her, but the pianist merely smiled and wished Dieter a good night as he made his way towards the door, with the rest of the girls following quickly behind him. The pianist held the door open as the dancers filed past him and Leni hesitated, pretending to look for something in her handbag, until she was the last one out.

She found herself standing on the pavement at the same time as the pianist, nervously shuffling her feet as one by one the dancers walked away, dun-coloured cloche hats pushed down on to their heads. They whispered to each other about the supper they had left for their husbands or their plans for the next afternoon, before scurrying away like mice who had been uncovered by daylight.

Leni and the pianist walked along Jägerstrasse, not quite together yet not separately either. Not a word was spoken, yet for once she didn't feel stupidly shy. They walked slowly, their steps mirroring each other. Finally, Leni broke the silence.

'I don't know your name,' she whispered softly.

'Oh yes, of course. Forgive me. Paul – my name is Paul. You are Leni, I think? I heard the other girls call you that.'

'Yes, that's right. Leni . . .'

On the corner, she could see a stocky, fair-haired young man leaning against the window of a wig shop while smoking a cigarette. Leni didn't think much about it until she heard Paul mutter something under his breath. As they reached the corner, the man looked up and called out, 'Ahh, there you are – I've been waiting.'

Paul sighed. 'This is my brother, Otto . . .'

The man gave her a surly look and, before she could open her mouth, he draped an arm around Paul's shoulder and led him away, whispering urgently and gesticulating as he went.

Leni felt a flash of disappointment that she hadn't had the opportunity to talk to the pianist, and then wondered why she had wanted to. This was her job. She didn't need to become entangled with handsome piano players.

Quickening her pace, she began walking briskly along Friedrichstrasse until she reached the edges of Kreuzberg, where she allowed herself to slow down a little. Halfway along Lindenstrasse, she saw the blue and gold sign for a shop that sold all manner of exotic birds and their feed.

Next door to it was an old apothecary filled with large stone jars of peculiar-smelling ointments, and in between the two shops was a small alleyway. Leni slipped quietly down the alleyway to the rear of the shops, before arriving at an abandoned courtyard that contained a dying brazier burning the last of its coal.

In the corner of the courtyard was a pile of old wooden crates stacked up high against the wall. Between the crates, someone had left a small gap in the centre that was covered with a threadbare grey blanket acting as a roof.

Leni dropped down to her knees, taking care not to ruin her only pair of stockings, put her thumb and forefinger in her mouth and gave a soft whistle. From deep inside the darkness, underneath another grey blanket and a thick army coat, came a little creature of tangled fair hair and a small yawning mouth. As the creature shifted, the sleeves of the old army coat draped out to the side, as if a soldier had fallen to the ground and now was unable to get back up again.

'Did you bring something to eat?' the creature mumbled before pushing her hair out of her eyes and finally revealing herself to be a girl of around six years old.

'No, but I got a job. And tomorrow, I'll get paid, and then you can have whatever you want.' Leni crawled between the crates and settled herself under the blanket next to the girl. She smiled as she saw her sister outlined by the glow of the dying brazier. Her wild tangled hair covered an angelic little face, all wide eyes and a tiny plum of a mouth. Her face, for all its beauty, held a petulant expression of unmet demands – yet when she smiled, Leni couldn't refuse her anything.

'But I'm hungry now. I haven't eaten anything since breakfast.' Annette pouted a little.

'I know. But I told you, I had to find work today. We'll get something in the morning and then, once I've been paid tomorrow, we can have a feast on Sunday . . . whatever you like.'

'Why do we have to wait until Sunday? Can't we go tomorrow or Saturday?'

'I have to work, Nette. It's my day off on Sunday, so we'll go then.' Leni wriggled herself into a comfortable position under the blanket and closed her eyes.

'Do you promise?'

'I promise. Now, go to sleep.'

'Tell me what we'll eat for our feast?'

'I'll tell you tomorrow. Goodnight.'

'Can we go to Aschinger's?'

'Yes, if you like. Annette, go to sleep.'

'Can we have pea soup and sausages?'

'Hush . . . I have to sleep. Goodnight, Nette.'

There was a moment of peaceful silence as the sisters lay side by side with only a few thin blankets between them and the hard cobbles of the courtyard, before Annette piped up, 'Leni . . . I'm cold.'

'Come here.' Leni held out her arm and gathered the child to her. Annette giggled. It was their usual bedtime routine, and Leni smiled at it. She felt the warmth of her sister's tiny body wrapped around hers.

'Tell me the story of when I was born . . .'

It was a well-trodden tale of a stormy night, her mother lying in the upstairs bedroom, while down below the family waited nervously. There were complications; their father had run to fetch the doctor. Annette liked to hear the part where she had bawled at the top of her lungs and everyone had laughed with relief. Leni exaggerated it for her benefit until, pleased to have heard the part about her arrival in the world being celebrated once again, Annette settled quietly.

Leni kissed her sister gently on the top of her head until her own eyes flickered shut. She began to think about the Babylon Circus, which in turn led her to wonder about the pianist.

Curled into the side of her, Annette was not yet asleep. She stared up at the threads of the grey blanket that formed her night sky and imagined eating all of her favourite foods – one after the other.

At the Babylon Circus, Dieter retired to the rooms above his office. Once the last of the girls went home, he was left completely alone with just Herr Keks for company. Taking a small piece of his fish supper, he gently placed it in the cat's dish for him to nibble at. Closing the door to his rooms, he walked over to the window and opened it a crack. At his feet the cat purred contentedly while Dieter scratched at the side of his tin face and wondered what tomorrow might bring.

Loosening his tie, he lit up a Turkish cigarette and poured a small glass of absinthe for himself out of a green bottle that he kept on a silver tray beside his armchair. Then, sitting down on the leather couch underneath the window, Dieter let out a long, complicated sigh and, with a swift movement of his hand, pulled the tin mask off, leaving the charred meaty pulp of his face to feel a cool breeze from the open window.

Swallowing the absinthe down in one gulp, as was his nightly routine, he finally allowed himself to think about kissing his pianist.

6

Leni woke at first light to the sound of rain pattering down and a sliver of fat raindrops trickling through the grey blanket roof. Tucking the army coat protectively over a sleeping Annette, she sat up, leaning her back against a wooden crate . . . and began to worry.

She worried a lot these days – about the next meal, finding a warm bed, and of course about her baby sister. Often, she had thought how much easier it would be if she were alone. A single woman had many ways to make a living in this city. There would always be a dry bed if she were willing to do the things that would make that possible. Yet, as she watched her sister sleeping peacefully, the gentle rise and fall of her chest, Leni knew that she could never abandon Annette. She was all that Leni had left of her family.

One day, three years ago, Leni had insisted that she and their mother go out to get some fresh air. It had not been long since influenza had turned to pneumonia for her father and brothers, taking them one by one. Her mother had been overwhelmed with the grief of it.

Later on, she thought how lucky it was that Annette had had a cold that day, and had been left behind with a neighbour. Leni and her silent, stone-eyed mother had walked for an hour, going through the motions of window shopping. She'd pointed out pretty things, and her mother had nodded blankly before moving on to the next shop, without saying a word. Leni had been distracted by a shop window, hesitating in front of brightly coloured summer dresses. Her mother had left her sight for only a moment . . . the briefest moment, she was sure of that.

As Leni had turned to check on her, she'd heard the rumble of a tramcar. Later, she would not recall seeing her mother walk in front of it, but the passers-by who witnessed the 'accident' all said she had not appeared to know that the tram was there. Leni was very sure she had.

She tried to picture them all when they were strong and healthy. Their home, the laughter – how happy they had been when Annette was born. A late surprise baby for her mother who had believed her childbearing days to be over. The rain eased slightly and Leni shivered but she didn't want to pull the army coat off Annette, who looked so peaceful sleeping next to her.

The coat had belonged to her father. Leni thought of him, of waving him off to war when she was a child. The parades and the excitement. She remembered all the handsome young boys who had gone with him. Shining faces in their brass buttons and helmets. Most of them had not returned from the battlefield, and the others were so terribly wounded that she would see them begging in the streets for food. Their limbless bodies and scarred faces terrified her. They had ceased to be fresh-faced boys, heroes that she might marry when she grew up, and had turned into the ghosts and monsters of her nightmares. Her father had returned unscathed, which made his death only a few years later feel especially cruel.

Leni reached out a hand and gently stroked Annette's hair, wiping it away from the child's face. She frowned. All she needed was a full week's work and then she would find them a dry bed, no matter how terrible. Anything was better than this. This morning, she would take Annette to get their weekly bath at the public bathhouse, then she would go to work and get paid.

Leni hoped the nice waiter in the café by the tram stop was working today so she might exchange her sweetest smile for some hot chocolate and rolls. Poor Annette felt the hunger so much more than she did these days. Leni had got used to it. Anyway, it wouldn't be for much longer. She would work hard at the Babylon Circus and earn enough money to set her and Annette up, no matter what she had to do to get it. She flushed a little as thoughts of the handsome pianist flickered through her mind unbidden. His polite manners and friendly smile . . .

But he was one more thing to think about, and Leni had no room in her mind for extra thoughts. She felt as if she were carrying the whole world on her shoulders at just nineteen years old. She should be going out dancing and being told off by her mother for wearing too much lipstick. Leni could barely remember the days when she did such things. It felt as if she'd been responsible for her sister forever.

As her mind grew cloudy with misery, a fat raindrop smacked on to the top of her head and when Leni put her hands to her face to wipe away the rain, she found that a sly teardrop had taken the opportunity to glide down her cheek.

7

'It's six pfennigs if you want the second towel,' the old woman said impatiently. 'Fräulein, if you please, there are people waiting . . .'

Annette didn't like her and eyed her spitefully while her sister scrabbled around in her purse, trying to find the extra cash but coming up short. She scraped her feet noisily over the tiled floor and scratched furiously at the neck of her dress. She liked being with Leni, but dreaded bath-time – the horrible vinegary smells and the rough towels against her skin. The air was always thick with a steamy heat, and the old woman who worked here had a wart-covered face that frightened her. Maybe she was a witch, Annette thought as her sister gave up on trying to find the money for an extra towel. Sighing, she realized that she'd have to share a rough towel that scratched her skin and was already damp from Leni.

'We'll manage with just the one towel.' Her sister grabbed the thin grey-white piece of cloth from the hands of the attendant and began walking towards the cubicle doors.

'Number four is free,' the wart-faced woman called after her.

'Thank you!' Leni replied cheerily as Annette scuffed her way slowly behind her. The tiles squeaked under her shoes and she liked the sound they made. Leni gave her a stern look to make her stop, before shoving her through the open door of the number four cubicle. Annette eyed the green-tiled walls and the enormous fat bathtub. On the wall was the clock that timed their visit, ticking down the minutes so there was no time to linger. Next to the clock was a large metal hook for their clothes.

Her sister closed the door and leaned over the tub, removing a wiry black hair before she filled the bath with their allotted inches of water.

'I'll go first.' Leni set about undoing buttons and pulling off clothes while letting the hot water splash into the enamel bath.

'I always have to use your water and your wet towel. Why can't I have my own?' Annette whined and sat down on a wooden chair that was placed next to the tub, precisely because so many people shared their weekly bath. The unfairness of not being older and able to have fresh bathwater and a clean, dry towel brought a tiny frown between her eyes, yet there was no way to stop her sister, who was already naked.

'Because I need to go to work, and anyway, I have to pay for it. When you pay for it then you can bathe all day long and dry yourself with clean towels.' Leni lowered her body into the steaming water, exclaiming over the temperature. Annette didn't want her to add more cold water as it would make her own bath tepid. Bad enough that it would be greasy and grey with soap scum floating on top of it. She pulled a face as Leni's white goose-pimpled skin turned bright red with the heat, watching as she leaned back in the bath, the water barely covering the curve of her sister's hips.

'When I grow up, I shall have all my bathwater to myself . . . and I'm going to eat whatever I want to . . . and

I'm going to go everywhere in the world.' Annette nodded emphatically as she spoke, but Leni just dipped her head under the water, leaving her to squeak her shoes across the tiles again.

Annette inspected her sister and tried to imagine herself in this grown-up state. She stared down at the flatness of her own chest and compared it to Leni's full breasts. It seemed impossible to imagine, and anyway, it was years away. She scraped a fingernail along the side of the bath as her empty belly growled.

'I'm hungry . . .' Annette slipped her bare feet out of her shoes and tried to make her toes touch across the grouted lines of the tiled floor. Leni began to lather the small green cake of soap into her hair.

'I told you – I'll get paid tonight, so on Sunday we can go to Aschinger's and you can have your pea soup with sausages.'

Annette licked her lips at the prospect of such a feast. 'And for dessert can we have Berliner Luft?'

Berliner Luft was a light lemony mousse served with a raspberry sauce that Annette had eaten only once – for her sixth birthday – but it had become the dessert by which all other desserts were measured in her mind. It was so light in your mouth that they named it after the air.

'Yes, anything you want. This won't be for much longer, Nette. Next week, I can rent a room for us. Everything will get better, you'll see. Now hurry and we can go to the little café next to the tram stop where the nice waiter works. He will probably let us have some hot chocolate and bread if we ask nicely. I could pay him tomorrow.'

Annette cheered up at the thought of breakfast and

leaned over the bath to pour handfuls of water over Leni's soapy head. She was determined, however, that any hot chocolate and bread rolls should not replace the promised feast. 'But we can still go to Aschinger's on Sunday, yes?'

Leni picked up a handful of warm water and splashed Annette's face with it. 'Yes, we can still go. Now – quick, before the timer goes – get undressed.' And with that Leni emerged from the grey soapy water, making Annette squeal as she scattered thick droplets all over the cubicle.

Outside, the warm sunshine dried their hair as Annette felt her dress sticking to her body. The nasty towel had been wet and made little difference to her damp skin. As she skipped along in anticipation of some kind of breakfast, Annette reached for Leni's hand. She liked holding on to her sister, and if Leni was in a good mood she might tell her more stories before she went to work.

Her legs were beginning to ache slightly from walking when Leni suddenly leaned down and pointed along a side road. 'That's where I work now.'

'What's the name of the street?' Annette asked as she liked to know exactly where her sister might be at any given time.

'Jägerstrasse.'

She silently repeated it to herself for a moment, committing it to memory. Then she had to abandon her concentration to focus on catching up with Leni.

Her sister walked on so quickly that Annette struggled to keep up. When she grew up, she vowed she would remember that some people had very small legs and it was hard to walk at the same pace as people with much bigger ones.

'What's the name of the place where you work?' she asked, waiting to file it away in case she should ever need to know. When their mother had first died, Annette had been overcome by fear that something would happen to Leni, waking up in a blind panic if she didn't know where she was. These days, her sister made sure she always knew where to find her, and that made her worry less, although not entirely.

'The Babylon Circus,' Leni replied before dragging Annette across to the tram stop and then into the café where the nice waiter worked.

'A circus? You work in a circus! Are there clowns? Or elephants?' Annette's little mouth hung open and her eyes grew wide.

'No, but there are dancers wearing magical costumes and a man with a tin face,' Leni said with an excited expression.

Annette digested this information for a second. Thoughts of hot chocolate and bread rolls left her mind as she imagined all kinds of wonders. Her sister worked in a circus — surely it was only a matter of time before Leni would take her there . . .

8

Leni arrived at the Babylon Circus flushed and slightly out of breath, having run to escape a sudden shower that had threatened to wreck her hair. She'd left Annette back in their courtyard with strict instructions not to move from their little home.

As she timidly entered the dressing room, the other women nodded in recognition but didn't pause in their conversations about what they had done that day, or intended to do on Sunday. Sundays were what they lived for. A whole day to stay in their street clothes, to walk in the park, or maybe go to Wannsee and take a boat ride. The conversation about how best to use their Sunday began as early as their Monday evening shift. A dream to keep them going through another week. Leni, listening in, found herself wondering what the pianist did on his day off.

'Leni, have you got my face powder?' Wally picked up a small silver pot from the dressing table while Leni stared up at her somewhat confused. She'd been so busy dreaming about the pianist that she hadn't noticed Wally standing there.

'Oh . . . sorry . . .' Leni felt flustered. She needed to concentrate on her work. She had to get Annette off the streets as soon as possible. She pushed all thoughts of Paul to the back of her mind and stared at her reflection in the mirror. She looked a little pale. Leni reached inside the blue velvet bag to get out the pot of rouge before applying it in generous quantities. When she was satisfied that her face was transformed into a more worldly and elegant creature, she slipped into her black dress that was still held together by safety pins and firmly attached the little gold hat to her hair.

She took a deep breath and stood up. She was just about to reach down under the costumes to collect the empty cigarette tray when the dressing-room door suddenly burst open.

In the doorway stood a woman, her hair cut into a razor-sharp dark bob, swaddled in a coal-black sable coat that reached past her ankles. On her feet she wore gold shoes with little ribboned bows on the toe. Something like a small brown monkey clung to the side of her neck as if it were a scarf – and Leni was surprised to realize that it was in fact a real creature. The monkey nibbled nervously at a purple grape while whimpering into the woman's neck.

'Anita!' the women cried in unison as she stood in the doorway, swaying slightly. Anita tried to speak, but all that came out was a series of indistinct words – and as she raised her arms to greet the other women, she stumbled a little, causing the monkey to fall from her neck. The creature scrabbled about the floor for a moment, before becoming distracted by Christa's left leg stretching all the way up towards the ceiling. The monkey squealed and in one leap it clawed its way up the leg as if it were a tree branch. Leni watched in horror as Christa let rip with a piercing wail and a stream of Russian words. The monkey chattered hysterically but still it clung on to the girl's leg.

'Come here, darling . . . come to Mummy,' cried Anita. The monkey eventually scampered away to hide under the dressing table while Anita clutched at the doorframe to stop herself toppling over. 'Oh, look, now you've frightened him.' Her mouth twisted as she slurred her words and sniffed loudly. Reaching inside her sable coat, Anita tugged at her silver necklace. At the end of the long chain around her neck was a little silver globe which the woman proceeded to flip open with her thumb, scooping up a tiny mound of white powder from inside it to place on her little finger. Surveying the room with an unfocused stare, she sniffed violently until the mound of white powder disappeared up her left nostril. Wiping under her nose with the back of her gloved hand, she threw her head back, letting out a peal of laughter and raised her arms to the ceiling. 'I have a new creation – a special performance like no other. Tonight, I will show it for the first time . . . isn't it *so* exciting?' Anita's arms lowered as she squinted at Leni. 'You – I don't know *you*.'

Leni's mouth flapped open but no words came out.

'She's the new cigarette girl . . . We didn't think you were coming back. We heard you were in Paris with your new husband,' said Irma.

'Did you hear about poor Rudolph Valentino?' whispered Berolina mournfully.

'Oh no, poor Rudi . . . There is too much death. So much death – Paris is death . . . Berlin is *life* . . . This is art.' Anita rambled on quietly until her pet monkey made a break for it across the floor of the dressing room, causing the girls to start screaming, shooing the creature away from their limbs. She bent down and opened her arms, making sweet babyish noises. The monkey deemed it safe to return, and in one bound wrapped his tiny arms around her neck, making chattering sounds of pleasure in her ear. Leni's eyes widened as she stared at the strange monkey-clad woman, while noting that the other girls seemed entirely unperturbed by her antics.

Dieter appeared in the doorway, scowling. 'Why is there screaming? Come now, ladies, we have "guests". It is time to entertain. Big smiles now . . . and *quiet* . . .' His one dark brown eye leered as he inspected the moon and stars and all that lay between. He barely glanced at Leni in her badly fitted black dress as his attention finally rested on Anita.

'Oh no . . . Anita, what are *you* doing here? Not the monkey. He shits everywhere.'

Anita unfurled the creature from her neck and attached it to the metallic side of Dieter's face. 'Now you are two shits together.'

She stumbled again before righting herself and drawing her shoulders back, standing proudly before them. 'No matter . . . I must get dressed for my performance.' Anita took a step inside the dressing room and then, in one swift movement, she let her coal-black sable coat slide elegantly to the floor.

Leni gasped. Underneath the fur coat, Anita was wearing gold body paint to match her shoes. Every part of her was painted except her face.

Apart from the long silver chain that dangled from her neck, Anita was completely naked.

9

Dieter stood to the side of the stage, his one good eye staring anxiously into the blackness where Anita shuffled into position wearing nothing but gold body paint. Thankfully without the monkey, who was currently locked in the wig cupboard, sheltering in some long blonde curls that belonged to Wally's second-act performance, in which she played a doll that comes to life and parades around the nightclub making strange doll-like gestures at her customers.

A single white spotlight lit the stage and there was an audible gasp as Anita appeared with her golden back to the audience. Everything below her waist was hidden by the darkness. Only her shoulder blades and arms shimmered under the lights.

Leni was busy serving cigars to a group of men on the front table as she spied Paul out of the corner of her eye: he was taking his place at the piano. Her stomach gave a little flip of excitement at the sight of him. He was wearing the same suit and dark red tie as the night before. His face was solemn as he bent over the keys and began to play a series of long tinkling notes. The men paid for their cigars and she was able to move back into the shadows where she could see the stage . . . and observe the pianist a little.

Anita turned her head as her fierce little eyes picked out the tables. The long tinkling notes became more urgent and she began to make circles with her hands, wider and wider. The spotlight dipped, teasing the customers by showing the back of her golden legs and shoes but not now reaching up as far as the tops of her thighs. Then the light flared, fully illuminating the golden back of the naked Anita as she writhed and danced on her spot, her arms forming patterns and her hips gently swaying.

Leni watched with her eyes growing wider by the minute. She had never seen anything like it. The stumbling drunken woman was gone and in a split second transformed to a golden goddess, her arms conveying her message to the silent crowd.

She began to build a wave of movement, her head reaching from side to side, her arms wide now, clawing at the air. Her feet slid effortlessly to the sides until her golden legs parted and she thrust her bare bottom towards the crowd, garnering a murmur of anticipation. The music swirled and spun in time, reaching a climax, at which point Anita began to turn to face the crowd. One arm covered her painted breasts, while the other lay across the tops of her thighs, just about covering what the crowd strained to see through her fingers. She raised her chin, her eyes surveying the crowd, waiting . . .

On her cue, Paul released his fingers from the keys, so that only silence would accompany Anita on her final movement. This was her moment, her liberation – a golden triumph. Her body was her art. Her dance was her song. She was an artist. She was a free woman . . .

Suddenly a loud, coarse laugh ripped through the room. Dieter frowned and the girls behind him gasped as a man sitting at one of the front tables threw his head back and laughed again. Leni couldn't see what he was laughing at.

Was it Anita, or something else? Anita's head twitched in annoyance, but she completed her turn, unfolding her arms from across her body like tired wings as her eyes searched the room for the culprit. A woman in a silver dress, wearing an elaborate jewelled white mask and sitting just behind the man, giggled and then, unsure that this was the right thing to do, clamped her hand across her mouth. The man muttered something to her under his breath and the table next to him began to laugh, their shoulders shaking with amusement until one of them slapped at the table top with the palm of his hand in time with his own laughter.

Anita stood stone-like, glistening with gold paint, and then she dropped her arms to her sides and glared at them. Her naked body was fully revealed but now nobody knew quite what to do. The crowd did not dare applaud. Paul sat there looking unsure as to whether he should play something to disguise the laughter or carry on sitting in silence. He stared helplessly at the side of the stage where Leni was also staring helplessly at the golden Anita. Dieter smothered an irritated cough and then the club fell silent again.

Regaining her composure, Anita folded her arms in front of her and resumed her dance. Everyone expelled a long grateful breath until the man called out to Anita. Leni couldn't make out what he'd said, but just the very fact that he'd spoken was enough. She could see Anita's head jerk upwards and then, before anyone could stop her, the golden naked woman leapt down from the stage and walked slowly towards the man at the front table. Her eyes were locked on his; a strange smile lit her face. With one bound Anita stepped on to an empty chair and then up on to the table. The man's mouth opened and snapped shut again as he wondered what she was doing. The crowd began to cheer as Anita bent over, exposing everything that wasn't golden to them. She plucked a bottle of champagne out of its ice bucket; raising the bottle in celebration, she took a long swig, and then another. The cheers grew louder; people banged their approval out on the wooden tables, making a terrible din while the laughing man stared up at her, his face wild with anticipation and fear at what might happen next.

She carried on drinking his champagne, smiling benignly, her eyes beckoning him to lean closer to her and then, just as he did so, Anita bent her knees wide, raised one golden foot on to his shoulder and released a long yellow stream of piss all over his shirt front. The club erupted in howls of laughter, gasps of disgust, the banging of tables and then the scraping of chair legs as the man staggered to his feet.

He screamed at Anita, calling her all the names under the sun, but she wasn't done yet. Anita took a bow and then raised the champagne bottle high above her head.

'Anita – NO!' Dieter shouted. As Leni watched on in horror, he began to run towards her, but it was too late. Anita lifted her right arm high into the air and brought the now empty champagne bottle down upon the man's pink, balding head. He slumped backwards into his chair, his black mask slipping down under his nose as blood began to pour from his scalp. Dieter grabbed hold of Anita, dragging her off the table and towards the door that led back to the dressing room. Anita was waving to the crowd and bellowing, 'He didn't see the funny side . . . and he loves to laugh. Such a shame . . .'

As Dieter carried the squealing woman out, he shouted

at the girls, 'What are you waiting for? DANCE!' Then, as he spied a shocked Leni doing nothing, he hissed, 'YOU – get him cleaned up.'

She quickly grabbed at one of the thick white table-cloths, dragging it from a table and frantically dabbing at the pools of piss on the man's shirt front and the blood on his face.

As she stood there with the soiled cloth in her hands, she glanced up to find that Paul was watching her. Their eyes met across the room, just as they had the night before. For a brief second Leni felt her breath leave her body as they stared at each other. Then there was the slightest twitch of their lips, and they began to laugh.

10

The rest of the night passed uneventfully. As the finale, the dancers of the Babylon Circus performed a peculiar flower ballet where each woman wore a large red rose-like hat while the smallest of glittery green leaves covered their breasts. Around their waists were satin chains made out of pink silky petals that shifted precariously as they danced. Berolina formed the large bud at the centre of the flowery ballet, while the other girls each formed a petal. As Berolina did her customary splits at the end, the other girls discarded their satin costumes while keeping their backs to the baying crowd. The lights went out, plunging them into darkness and the night drew to its close.

Leni hurried to get back into her street clothes, eager to collect her wages and feed Annette. They both desperately needed to eat a proper meal before much longer. Even she was beginning to dream about Nette's feast at Aschinger's on Sunday. She carelessly hung up her costume and buttoned up her dress, grabbing her bag just as Dieter entered the dressing room carrying a clutch of little brown envelopes. Finally, she would have some money. There was unlikely to be much of it given that she'd only worked two shifts. But at least they could eat, and next week they could rent a room, and Leni could stop worrying so much.

Dieter called out her name and handed her one of the envelopes, which she buried deep inside her handbag.

Relief flooded through her veins now she'd been paid and she rushed towards the street door, almost colliding with Paul as she did so.

'That was quite the evening . . .' he said, grinning at her as they fell into stride together. It seemed perfectly natural to walk alongside him and he seemed to take for granted that they would leave together.

'Yes. I hope that man will be all right. There was a lot of blood,' Leni replied.

'I'm sure he'll be fine, if a little sore when he sobers up. Anyway, how are you settling in?'

'I'm getting used to it, I think. I worked in a café before this so it's very different,' she said shyly while studying his face out of the corner of her eye. The little strand of hair had flopped on to his forehead again and for a moment she felt the urge to reach out her hand and sweep it back into place.

'A café? And you left to come here?' His question didn't seem unkind but Leni felt the need to try and explain.

'The woman I worked for died from a heart attack. It happened quite suddenly. One day I had a nice job waiting on tables – the next day the café had closed down. She was a lovely lady.'

Leni thought of Frau Keppler and how kind she'd been after her mother had died. Since the café closed down, she'd spent days searching for work but to no avail until she'd wandered into the Babylon Circus. Their landlord had run out of patience before she could find another job and Leni had returned home from another fruitless day searching to find Annette sitting on the doorstep surrounded by their belongings.

'Oh, I'm sorry. You must find all this a little strange.' He seemed genuinely concerned, fixing her with a tender stare as he spoke.

'Yes, it's quite a change!' she said, laughing softly.

'It's not always as bad as tonight . . . but things tend to happen when Anita turns up. She's famous for it.' He smiled at her – a warm grin that made his entire face come to life. It *was* a very nice face, she decided.

Paul had a way of looking at her intently, his dark brown eyes studying her face as she spoke. The way he concentrated on her gave Leni a strange fluttery feeling inside.

She couldn't think of one sensible thing to say and so she walked alongside him, saying nothing but thinking very carefully about his full soft lips and warm dark eyes. As they approached the corner of Jägerstrasse, there was no sign of his brother Otto lurking on the corner and Leni found that she was glad about it.

On finding that they needed to choose a direction, she hesitated before glancing up at Paul. A small sheen of sweat glistened on top of his lip and she realized that he was nervous. This surprised her, as he'd seemed so very comfortable chatting away to her. Something about discovering his nervousness made her feel instantly less shy with him.

Leni pointed along Friedrichstrasse. 'I'm going this way . . .'

She hoped that he might be going in the same direction, and felt a flush of relief as he nodded eagerly and said, 'Oh – then I can walk with you . . . if that's all right?'

'Yes, perfectly all right.' She gave him a shy look, hardly daring to meet his eyes again. They were such nice brown eyes, too . . .

Leni had very little experience in talking to young men. She'd seen other more forward girls giggling and flirting but she didn't know how to do such things. Her words were always careful and considered and most young men didn't seem terribly interested in what she had to say. Paul paid such great attention to her words that she felt as if a light were being shone upon her. It was both lovely and disconcerting.

'Do you live near here?' he asked gently.

'Not far . . . Lindenstrasse.' Another nervous silence descended. 'Do you live in Kreuzberg?' she finally asked after they had walked along for some minutes without any conversation between them. He had given no clue as to which direction he preferred to walk in and Leni wondered if she crossed the street whether he would just follow her all the way home.

'No, I live with my brother over on Münzstrasse,' he said and then, apparently realizing he had revealed himself to be walking in entirely the wrong direction, mumbled quickly, 'But I like to walk around the city at night.'

Leni felt her mouth form a secret half-smile as she suddenly understood that he had walked out of his way to carry on talking to her, even though they were not particularly talking at all. A fizz of delight rippled through her as she realized that the handsome young pianist liked her.

'Have you worked at the Circus for a long time?' Leni asked, feeling more at ease now she knew he was only there for her.

'No, not really – I was at another club before this, but Dieter pays a little better. I'm hoping to join a proper orchestra one day,' he said hastily as if he wanted her to understand that being a nightclub pianist was not the extent of his ambitions.

'I wish I could play the piano . . .' Leni mused. 'I can't do anything so clever.'

'My mother taught me to play when I was very small. I've never wanted to do anything else. It's always been my dream to be a concert pianist but it's very difficult, particularly these days. I'm grateful for the work, of course, but I can still dream . . .' His voice tailed off wistfully and Leni gazed up at him, recognizing the flicker of sadness that crossed his face. Then he smiled again and she had to look away as she was blushing.

'What about you – what do you dream of?'

The question took her by surprise. Nobody had ever asked Leni about her hopes and dreams. She wasn't entirely sure that she had many of them, or that they were of any importance – yet this man who was practically a stranger made her feel she could confide in him.

'I've always wanted to travel. When I was very young my father used to tell me stories about all the different countries in the world. He worked on ships when he was a boy. I would imagine what it must be like to see countries that are so very different from ours . . .' The words rushed out of her so quickly that Leni was surprised to find that she did still hope to travel the world. Her dreams hadn't died – they were just sleeping, and this man had uncovered them with his questions.

They walked on for several minutes, holding polite conversation, but as they neared Kreuzberg, Leni felt her heart quicken. She didn't want him to come as far as the courtyard with her, for that would be too humiliating, and yet she didn't want their walk to end. She liked being with this gentle, polite man who was interested in the things she liked or didn't like and who gazed at her as if what she thought was of great importance to him.

His hand went to his little strand of hair and swept it back off his face. She noted that he did this from time to time but it made no difference, as within a few seconds the tiny strand of hair would flop forward once again. She smiled to herself as she thought how boyish it made him seem.

But, as they strolled through familiar streets, Leni wondered how to bring the evening to a close while retaining the promise of more. It was too complicated for her to work out and she found that in answer to his perfectly ordinary questions, she grew sullen and mute.

Finally, in the distance Leni could see the turning to Lindenstrasse – and a horrible burning shame began to seep through her. The blood pulsed in her ears as she tried desperately to think of something entertaining to say while not wanting to walk much further with him. *Imagine if he were to find out that she was sleeping on the streets. What would he think of her?*

I I

Leni certainly didn't want anyone at the Babylon Circus to know about her circumstances, but she especially could not bear for Paul to find out. Gnawing on her bottom lip, she tried to think of things she might do to avoid him uncovering the truth as he pretended not to notice that she'd stopped speaking.

'And do you live with your family?' he asked and then looked away as if he felt he might have gone too far, although it was a perfectly ordinary question.

The memory of her mother flashed through her mind and made her feel sad – the house they'd shared was always so clean and neat. A warm fire in winter and good food on the table. She would be horrified to think of her hungry daughters sleeping on hard cobblestones with only a grey blanket to shelter them. Leni suddenly felt a ripe pang of humiliation. Her mother would never have allowed them to end up on the streets. She had let everyone down.

Her bottom lip trembled a little and she had to fight to stop herself becoming tearful.

Leni wasn't quite sure what to tell him about herself and so she stammered out her answer, feeling rather foolish. 'Umm . . . Yes . . . Do you?' was all she could manage to say. Her throat felt thick with emotion as her mood turned sour. She'd basked in this man's attention but now she felt uncomfortable. It was surely safer not to invite any more scrutiny.

He didn't seem to notice, or possibly he mistook her reticence for shyness as he continued to smile at her as he spoke. 'Yes. My brother Otto is a little older than I am. There's only the two of us now . . .'

He paused and then continued, 'So, you live in Kreuzberg with your family. That's really all I know about you. Tell me about them . . .'

Leni felt a blind rush of panic as Paul fixed her with his tender stare. She couldn't bring herself to explain all the terrible things that had happened to her family, having shut it all away. His attention had forced an opening that left a gaping wound and now she wanted to stop him studying her. The silence went on a moment too long and she couldn't stand it. She had to say something.

Suddenly her mouth opened and she found, to her horror, that she was talking. 'Yes, we all live together. There's my baby sister Annette, and I've got two brothers, twins, Josef and Ferdi. My mother and father too, of course. Do you have family here? Oh, you said already – just your brother?' She spoke rapidly, her lies tumbling over each other to escape her mouth.

She should have stopped herself yet, somehow, she couldn't. Leni carried on describing the tricks that her twin brothers played on their sisters and the delicious food that her mother loved to cook for them all.

In spite of herself, she painted pictures with her words of these headstrong young boys waiting for their mother to ladle out soup while she laid the table and her little sister carried the bread. Being petted and fussed over in this happy household. Her story grew more and more animated until she abruptly became aware that they had finally reached the turning on to Lindenstrasse.

A nervous dread rose in her chest as she looked around at where they were standing. She didn't want him to walk any further along the street with her as they would soon arrive at the little bird shop and the turning for the abandoned courtyard.

The night was ruined and it was all her fault. She paused outside a large house and her tone became brisk. She'd behaved like a fool and her cheeks burned with embarrassment – for a moment she was glad of the darkness that hid her shame.

'Well, thank you for walking me home. I'm sorry if I talked too much,' Leni said, trying to end the evening in a cool yet friendly way. Her tears had been stifled and all her emotions locked away safely once again.

'Oh no . . . I liked listening to you talk about your family. You're lucky to have them. I miss mine, but Otto and I keep each other company. It was very nice to talk to somebody who isn't my brother – I don't really know anyone at the club very well.' He laughed softly and Leni noticed the way his eyes crinkled at the edges as he did so.

She felt that same liquid warmth inside her again and, for a brief moment, wished that she could let this young man get to know her. Her mind churned with confusion.

'But now you have a long walk home . . .' Leni said anxiously.

'I don't mind. I told you I like to walk.' He was looking at her so tenderly that Leni wished that her life might be different. That she didn't have to think about her sister and their terrible situation. She imagined a version of herself that was free to get to know this man but then, with a brief nod of her head, she shook away the thought.

'Well . . . goodnight then.' Leni extended her hand in a businesslike manner and Paul took it in his, clasping his fingers around the warmth of her palm.

'I'll see you tomorrow night at the club?' he said gently, as if they were making a date rather than agreeing they would both go to work the next day.

The touch of him made her breath quicken and Leni wriggled her hand free, her eyes lingering for a moment on his soft full lips. 'Yes, I'll be there.'

'Then we will meet again . . .' Paul looked at her, his eyes filled with warmth and maybe, just maybe, a slight longing – Leni wasn't sure as she stood watching him reluctantly walk away. His shoulders seemed to sag a little as if he were disappointed in some way, and for a moment she considered calling after him, but it was too late.

She couldn't imagine why she had told him such terrible untruths about her family. There would be no way to pass it off as a mistake. She'd been desperate that Paul wouldn't find out they were sleeping amongst wooden crates, but that was no reason to make up an entire family who no longer existed.

She had been so silly. Confusion swirled inside her. It was better not to get close to him, and yet . . .

She liked him very much and there was nothing wrong with having a friendship. Even though they had only just met, there was something about him that made her feel cared for. She hadn't felt so cared for in a long time. Couldn't she have something just for herself?

*

When Leni was sure that Paul was on his way back home, she began to run past houses and tenement buildings, boarded-up shops and restaurants that had closed many hours before. She wanted to get back to her sister – to her life, as quickly as possible. Only when she saw the familiar red bricks of the courtyard did she finally slow down, gasping for breath.

She leaned against a wall and pictured Paul making his way home across the city. With a pang of regret, she realized that he hadn't asked her to make plans with him for Sunday when he'd have known that neither of them had to work. She sighed. Maybe he didn't like her in that way and she was having these ridiculous thoughts for no good reason.

It was probably for the best. She had to take care of Annette anyway. She'd promised her a feast and some fun. Maybe they would go to the park together.

But the thought of her sister only brought the reality of her lies crashing down again.

Leni felt her eyes fill with tears. She was so very lonely for company her own age and this man seemed to like her . . . at least a little bit.

Maybe they could be friends. Maybe it wasn't too late to unpick the lie . . .

No. It was better to stay away from him. She needed this job. Leni took a determined breath. She would be polite, but other than that, she would keep her distance.

12

She was late for work. Creeping past an already irritated Dieter, Leni sighed and squeaked out an apology. It wasn't even her fault. Annette had cried so much at the prospect of her leaving for work that she'd had to bribe the child to be quiet with a pink sugar mouse and a story about the time their brothers had made her a paper doll out of old newspapers. Still Nette had clung to her tearfully until the promise of her feast tomorrow eventually made her calm down.

As Leni had left Annette behind wrapped up in the army coat in the courtyard, she hoped it would not be for too much longer. However, being late for work put her in grave danger of not having any money to rent a room next week. She rushed into the dressing room, tearing at the buttons on her dress and eager to get back into Dieter's good books as soon as possible.

Once her face was powdered, her hair brushed into loose waves and her short black dress suitably adorned with the loaded cigarette tray, she tiptoed down the passageway that led to the stage, pausing only to smooth her hair before taking a step into the nightclub. The doors weren't open yet, and Leni was relieved to find that she had made it just in time.

As she pushed open the little red door, she could hear a piano note being struck over and over again. Then a tune played hesitantly. From her vantage point Leni could see the back of Paul's head bowed over the piano, one hand on his forehead and the other striking at the keys. Pressing back into the shadows, she studied him carefully for a few seconds. He seemed a little sad, and Leni longed to go over to him but at the same time she was hesitant. Things were so complicated in her life . . . and yet she liked him very much. For a moment she imagined how it might have been . . . Her brothers teasing her because she'd brought home a boy . . . Her mother asking him to stay for dinner. She'd make Leni's favourite dish – roast pork and maybe a honey cake to eat afterwards.

The thought made her sad and the problem of whether to approach him or not made Leni stay where she was, watching him carefully from her vantage point as the expressions on his face changed with the music. She'd arrived at work that evening determined to keep her distance, but there was something about him that kept drawing her in. A gentle aching for his smile beaming down on her, for the way he studied her answers and listened to her so carefully. It felt intoxicating to be so understood and Leni wanted to feel the intensity of his attention once again.

This time she would behave properly and explain that she'd babbled like an idiot about her family. She would tell him the truth . . . after all, she didn't need to tell him they were sleeping in the courtyard. Next week she would find a room for her and Annette and then he would never need to know. For now, she would just explain that her family were dead – then she would wait to see if he wanted to make a date with her. Yes, it was really quite simple now she thought about it.

Leni took a deep breath and stepped forward so she could be seen by anyone who cared to look. But still he didn't turn around – he hadn't noticed her coming in. She didn't want to call out and so she stood there feeling quite stupid.

The problem was eventually solved by Irma appearing at the cloakroom and calling out for Paul to play something cheerful. He immediately snapped out of his melancholy and began to play a Cole Porter song that she liked, his fingers flying over the piano keys and the tiny lock of hair flopping over his face in the way that made Leni want to reach out with her fingers and press it back into place.

Once he had finished playing, Paul looked around and his eyes came to rest on Leni's slightly anxious face. He smiled, a timid smile . . . she took a deep breath and smiled back at him. Taking half a step towards the piano, she rehearsed the words that she might say to him.

Her mouth opened to speak but just as Leni plucked up the courage to say something, she was interrupted by Dieter rushing through the nightclub to open the front door and let the 'guests' inside. 'Come, everyone – we are open for business,' he cried out in his strange lop-sided way.

13

Annette could feel the gnawing hunger in her belly. She hadn't eaten a thing since Leni had bought her some hot chocolate and a bread roll for breakfast . . . and now it was dark. She lay on her empty belly, with her elbows propping her up so she could see anyone approaching. In her pocket was the sticky remnant of a pink sugar mouse that Leni had given her before she went to work. She nibbled at the tiny pink mouse, trying to make it last but now it was very nearly gone. The sugar had all dissolved in her mouth and her stomach ached for more food.

It was too early for Leni to come home, but how Annette wished that she would hurry. In the corner of the courtyard, she could see a fat brown rat scurrying along the wall. She wrinkled up her face into a frown. She hated rats. They scared her. The creature disappeared into the blackness and her thoughts returned to tomorrow's feast.

Annette's mouth watered as she imagined a bowl of thick pea soup and then the bite of a sausage. The delicious meaty taste and the grease sliding down her chin. She rubbed a hand across her mouth as if the food had suddenly appeared on her tongue but her stomach clenched and she let out a groan.

She tried to remember a time before this, when they had a mother who baked and roasted things that were served on plates, but it was so long ago that she could no longer see her mother's face in her dreams. She used to be able to see her clearly and hear her voice but lately she'd faded from Annette's memory. The only face she ever thought about was Leni's, her sister who was so much older than her that she had to all intents and purposes become her mother.

Wriggling around under her grey blanket, she traced out the splinters of the wooden crates with her fingers. They felt rough on the outside but soft on the inside, having soaked up the rain for several hours. The grey blanket above her head was dripping rainwater, and it would take ages to dry out again.

A dangerous thought flitted through Annette's mind. She had been told to stay where she was . . . *exactly where she was*. Leni was always very clear about that. But she surely couldn't expect her to just lie there in the rain. It didn't seem fair that Leni got to spend her nights at the circus while she was lying here on the hard cobblestones. She began to imagine dancers with wings flying through the air and a magician in coloured silks wearing a tin face. A place of wonder and enchantment – and probably food.

Suppose . . . The supposing began, and grew into a plan.

Annette crawled out from under the blanket and the army coat, pulling them carefully out of sight and rolling them into a bundle that she tucked right at the back of the wooden crates, as she'd seen Leni do. She shivered a little since she was only wearing a thin cotton dress and a pink cardigan that was covered in dirty streaks from crawling in and out of the crates. If she began to walk towards the bathhouse, she would see Leni coming home, and then she could remind her to buy something to eat. The plan seemed so very clever to Annette as she stared up at the evening sky that thankfully showed no further sign of raindrops.

She began to walk away from their little home amongst the wooden crates and towards Leni. She would be so pleased to see her. *She was sure about that.*

14

The girls of the Babylon Circus were dressed as strange dolls for the evening's performance. Instead of the satin-pink flower petals, each girl was made up with wide unblinking eyes, rosy cheeks and smiling red lips. The dresses were pink gauze, split halfway down the front and up the back to give generous views of the parts of them that were definitely human to the audience. The women were joined together at their left ankles, a stream of blue ribbon attaching each doll to the next one. They danced in a line, mirroring each other, their arms waving and their free legs lifting as high as they would go. Eventually the dolls became untied from each other, roaming freely around the dance floor, picking out particular customers for their strange doll-like attentions. The crowd loved it. They cheered and roared their approval as the girls joined back up in a line once again, only this time high-kicking their legs into the air in unison before ending the show in a series of elaborate splits, with arms aloft, that inevitably saw the pink gauze dresses fall to their waists.

The spotlights went out and as the stage became dark, the girls rearranged their dresses and scrambled back to the safety of the dressing room.

Leni gathered up her cigarette tray and plastered an inviting smile on her face. As she passed by the dancers leaving the stage, she saw Dieter pull two of his regular girls to one side, whispering in their ears and then pointing out a thin, pale-faced man with a monocle placed in his right eye. He was the only person in the nightclub without a mask. He didn't appear to care who saw him. The man didn't smile, nor had he made eye contact with the women as they walked past him, but somehow a selection had been made. The two women nodded as Dieter uncurled his hand to reveal a small door key which one of the women pocketed.

Leni had no idea what the key was for, but before long the two girls were politely ushering the unsmiling monocled man down the staircase at the back of the cloakroom.

As customers poured champagne or ordered more cocktails after a performance, it was Paul's job to keep them entertained with a selection of popular tunes. Dieter didn't want them cluttering up the dance floor as that would mean an annoying delay before the next show, so each tune was chosen to be just entertaining enough, without encouraging the patrons to do anything except drink and smoke.

As Paul played, Leni wandered amongst the tables offering customers the contents of her silver tray, her smile inviting them to tip her generously, for neither she nor Annette had eaten since breakfast. She was trying to save her money to give her sister her feast tomorrow and there wasn't much left from two night's wages. Never mind. Next week things would look a lot better for them.

The piano music came to an end and the stage was lit by a bright white spotlight once again. From time to time, Leni caught a glimpse of Paul watching her as she flitted in between the tables while the customers with their elaborate masks demanded more cigarettes or cigars. She tried to catch his eye but, each time, he had already looked away.

The club was busy this evening with large groups of men from out of town. The men's eyes were concealed by the masks but their mouths were all set in red, sweaty faces. These were men who had never missed a meal in their lives, men for whom money was always available, who could buy whatever they needed. They were not men who understood the word 'No'. They smacked their lips together as they shouted encouragement to the dancers or even the waitresses. Asking for favours – to see things that nobody else could see. Leni tried to ignore them.

She moved swiftly, pulling out matchbooks and cigars, dispensing change. Often if she lingered just long enough the man would become distracted by another round of drinks arriving, or the sight of Berolina and Wally dressed in neat, navy-blue sailor dresses that barely covered their hips doing back bends on stage, and Leni could drift away pocketing the change in a small compartment under the matches.

When Berolina and Wally had got halfway through their next act, Leni noticed the two girls come back up the stairs. Then, a little while later, the thin, unsmiling man followed, going immediately to the cloakroom to collect his hat, before heading towards the front door.

One of the girls seemed unhappy about something and the other kept patting her gently on the shoulder as they walked back towards the tables. As they passed by Dieter, he opened the palm of his hand and then closed it quickly as the key was returned to him.

*

Leni was allowed to take a break once during her shift, but only for ten minutes. Not a minute longer. Tonight, she had vowed to save her ten minutes up all evening, even when her feet hurt or the velvet rope of the cigarette tray caused her shoulders to ache under the weight of it. She waited until the end of Berolina and Wally's act, when a sharp-tongued comedian called Ernst arrived to entertain the guests.

As Paul stretched out his arms and moved his head from side to side to relieve the tension in his neck, Leni was ready to move. He got up from his piano and walked slowly out of the nightclub towards the dressing room.

Abandoning her cigarette tray by the side of the stage, Leni slipped through the red door that separated the night-club from the backstage area and walked quickly towards the dressing room. Opposite the dressing room was the street door that led to the alleyway at the side of the club where the girls would often take a break to inhale some fresh air. Leni assumed that Paul would be outside on his own, as everyone else would be getting ready for their next performance.

The street door was slightly ajar, and Leni could see him leaning against the wall of the Babylon Circus smoking a cigarette in hasty puffs. He was staring up at the night sky, clearly lost in his own thoughts. His hand swept his hair back off his forehead and Leni smiled at the sight of it. She decided that she would very much like it if he asked to walk her home again. This time she would be on her best behaviour and clear up all the previous 'misunderstandings' between them.

She stepped outside into the alleyway, pausing only to

glance at Paul and pretend to be surprised that he was there.

'Ah you had the same idea, I see?' she said, trying to keep her voice light. Her casual enquiry startled him a little but when he looked up and realized it was her, he looked pleased.

'Fräulein Leni ... I haven't seen much of you this evening ... How are you?' His mouth formed a gentle searching smile and Leni felt her breath catch in her throat.

'I'm well, thank you. It's very busy tonight,' she replied.

'Yes, there's some kind of conference in the city, I think. There are a lot of men here from Frankfurt. Would you like a cigarette?' He pulled a crumpled pack from his jacket pocket and Leni took one reluctantly as she didn't really smoke, yet she wanted desperately to keep the conversation going. Paul struck a match on the wall of the club, cupping his hand around the tiny flame and offering it to her. She inhaled, stifled a cough and then blew a cloud of smoke out of the corner of her mouth. Rather than risk another lungful, she held the cigarette between her fingers, and pointlessly flicked the ash every few seconds.

'It's such a lovely evening,' she offered shyly, unable to bring herself to look him straight in the eye until she was sure where she stood. 'I love the summer ...'

'Yes, the warm nights are very pleasant. I like to be outside.' For a moment the two of them became shy again, hesitant strangers, but then Paul broke the silence: 'And I like to walk around the city ...'

Their eyes met and this time Leni didn't look away. His face broke into a broad smile at the sight of her and Leni felt a spark of joy blossom inside her chest.

This time she would do things properly. She would tell him the truth about her family and they would become friends – and maybe a little more than friends. She found that she was hopeful – for the first time in a long while. It was an unfamiliar feeling that made her giddy with anticipation. Yet he didn't say anything further, or suggest walking her home again this evening. His smile was warm – but silent.

She toyed with her cigarette and stared down at the ground. He crushed his cigarette out under his shoe before clearing his throat as if he were about to speak.

All of a sudden, the street door opened wide and a familiar voice said, 'Leni, there you are. Dieter is looking for you . . .' Irma sighed as she spoke, her tone implying that Leni had somehow wasted her time. She gave them both a sly glance before disappearing back inside the club.

Leni looked over at Paul. But he was already following Irma back inside the Babylon Circus.

15

Annette, having walked what she considered to be a very long way, tried to spell out the words on the street signs but with no luck. She knew how to spell simple words like milk and bread but street names were not part of her education. She passed by the bathhouse and then racked her brains trying to remember where Leni had pointed. Was it that street or further down the road? She couldn't remember the name of the street. It was on the tip of her tongue but the word escaped her. She knew that it must be nearby but how close she wasn't sure. Annette had to keep stopping to ask people where the circus was. Nobody had heard of any circus, but people kept suggesting that she try further along Friedrichstrasse and only once did she have to run away from a woman, who asked why she was out so late on her own.

Some gaudily dressed young women paraded up the street, having a fine time giggling and chatting to passers-by. Annette wondered if they knew how to find the Babylon Circus. Leni might be wrong. A circus might have clowns or lions and tigers. Maybe her sister hadn't seen them yet. After all, she'd only just started working there. Her mother had taken them all to see the circus once. Annette remembered an elephant that could stand on a tiny stool on one leg. He'd worn a funny red hat which made her laugh. She would ask these young women if they knew if the circus was nearby. It was very hard to hide a circus, for there would surely be a large striped tent set up somewhere around here. Annette searched for signs, tracing the words with her fingers, as circus was a word that she knew how to spell. But she couldn't see anything resembling it at all.

She stopped to rub at her toes. Her shoes pinched her feet having walked such a long way. It couldn't be much further.

As the gaudily dressed young women were getting closer, Annette rehearsed the correct thing to say. The taller of the girls was wearing a blue straw hat with red cherries decorating the upturned brim. Annette's little stomach grumbled. She had stopped at a water fountain to drink from her hands but Annette was so desperately hungry now and the smells of food on the street were making it worse. She wondered if the cherries on the hat were real, and whether the woman might share one or two with her. It seemed a funny place to keep your cherries, though.

She approached the cherry-hat lady and tugged at her elbow to get her attention. The young woman looked down, surprised to see her.

'Good evening, young lady. What can we do for you?' The group of girls began to giggle, wanting to get on with their walk, but Annette had blocked the way of the woman in the cherry hat.

'Do you know where the circus is?' she asked. Her voice rang out, clear and determined.

'The circus? Are you running away to join the circus, little girl? How funny . . . There's no circus here. You need to go home to your mother now. Go on . . .'

Annette didn't like the way the women seemed to be

mocking her. They were sniggering behind their hands. She didn't have a mother or a home and the loss of both stung her as the young women carried on giggling to themselves. Suddenly she remembered the name of the street.

'Is this Jägerstrasse?' Annette asked.

'It's down there.' The woman pointed back in the direction she'd come from. 'Now run along.'

Annette didn't move. 'Are they real?' she said, pointing to the cherries.

'What? My cherries? No, silly, they're not real ... Off you go now.' And with that the woman in the cherry hat patted Annette on her head and trotted off to join her friends.

She walked down the street that the cherry woman had come from, searching for a circus tent. She sighed wearily. Leni couldn't be far away. Annette spun around on her heel trying to avoid the cracks in the pavement. Good luck could only be hers if she didn't stand on a crack. Taking a deep breath, she squinted under the street lights, before her eyes suddenly made out the word circus over the top of a bright blue door.

16

The girls of the Babylon Circus were taking their final bow of the evening, having finished off a long night's work with a bawdy routine that involved them pretending to be milk-maids trying to fill their enormous glasses with milk. At the end of the routine the girls had run out into the audience, sitting on the laps of the men and making crude milking gestures with their hands.

Then Paul hit the long notes signalling the end of their routine, and they had raced back into a line to take a bow, kicking up their legs and giving the customers one last titil-lating glance at them, the crowd whooping and cheering until the girls disappeared through the stage door.

As the dancers ran back to the dressing room to get changed and the lights came on to signal that customers should go home, Leni fiddled about with the velvet strap on her cigarette tray pretending that there was a problem. Paul closed the piano lid, slowly gathering up his sheet music.

The customers finished off their drinks under the full glare of the lights. Everything that had looked enticing moments ago – the lights, the painted walls, the strange distorting mirrors, the darkened stage – were now revealed as rather ordinary and quite tawdry. The spell was broken. They drank up quietly and set about gathering coats and hats from the unsmiling Irma in the cloakroom.

Leni adjusted the velvet strap on her tray again, and waited.

Paul folded his sheet music and put the bundle under his arm. He took nervous glances in Leni's direction until the two of them were quite alone, and then he spoke.

'I am considering taking a long walk. Maybe towards Kreuzberg . . . if you would like some company?'

He gazed down at her and this time Leni allowed herself to look directly at him. She took in his boyishly handsome face, his dark eyes, his lips.

'I would like that . . . very much. I'll just get changed.' A fizz of excitement bubbled inside her.

'I'll meet you at the street door then.' He nodded politely, but began whistling a happy little tune as he walked away.

Leni's heart was singing as she raced back to the dressing room. He wanted to walk her home again. *He must like her* . . . This time maybe, just maybe, he would ask her what she was doing tomorrow. Of course, she would buy Nette her feast first of all, and then she might at least have an hour or two just for herself . . . should he ask her to meet him.

They might go to the cinema or to the park to sit, or have a picnic. The list of possibilities floated through her mind, each one seeming luscious and ripe with potential. She practised saying his name in her head as if he were an examination that she needed to pass. *Paul . . . Paul. Leni and Paul . . .*

Leni hummed a happy tune – one that she'd heard Paul playing earlier in the evening. She opened the dressing room door, seeing a familiar throng of bodies. Berolina was already in her street clothes and the girls were laughing and joking over something. As Leni squeezed her way past Christa, she looked straight ahead and her heart sank. Her wonderful plans lay in ruins. For there was Annette, sitting happily on Berolina's chair, eating an orange. The girls were fussing around her, and her sister was lapping up the attention, her hands filled with thick orange peel and the sticky juice smeared across her chin.

17

Annette could still taste the sharp tang of orange in her mouth but, having finally eaten something, her stomach had woken up demanding more. Before she could suggest this to Leni, she'd been quickly ushered out of the dressing room while her sister buttoned up her summer dress as they hurried along the passageway. She tried to keep up with Leni but her legs just couldn't cover the same amount of ground and she ended up falling further and further behind, causing her sister to stop walking and chastise her for being so slow.

Leni had not seemed altogether pleased to see her, even though the other girls in the circus seemed very nice. They made a big fuss over her although when she'd asked after the lions and tigers, one of them giggled and patted her on the head in a way that she didn't like. Another girl gave her the orange and Annette had not known quite what to do with it. She'd pressed it against her nose and mouth, inhaling the sharp scent until the girl had snatched it back and torn part of the peel away to show her what to do. She'd liked the taste of it, the sweetness and the slight pop of the flesh before the juice filled her mouth.

'Leni, wait for me . . .' she cried as her sister halted before the street door.

'Come on, quickly. You shouldn't have come here,' Leni hissed. She was angry with her and for a moment Annette regretted disobeying her. As she scurried after her sister, she could see a man leaning against the door waiting.

Leni stopped to talk to him allowing Annette to catch up with her in time to overhear her say, 'I'm sorry – I have an unexpected visitor.'

The man looked down at her and smiled. 'Ah, I see . . . and who is this little visitor?' His smile was friendly, but Annette could tell he wasn't pleased either. Nobody wanted to see her this evening. She was beginning to regret having left her grey blanket and her army-coat bed.

'This is my sister, Annette, who should be at home in bed.' Leni sounded cross, but as they didn't have a home or a proper bed, Annette couldn't understand why she should be.

Suddenly, while both Leni and the strange man carried on talking, Annette spied another man, this one with a tin face. She let out a gasp of horror, running quickly to grab hold of her sister's hand. He didn't seem magical at all. The man with the strange tin face glared at her with his one eye, making Annette terrified. There was no sign of any lions or elephants. In fact, nothing was like any circus that she remembered.

There were no clowns or animals at all. The whole place disappointed her, although the orange had been lovely. Her tiny teeth gnawed at her bottom lip nervously. Annette tried to hide herself behind Leni's legs until they escaped the tin man and the three of them were finally out on the street.

The man kept walking alongside them, smiling and talking as if she weren't there at all. She tugged at Leni's hand until her sister hissed at her, 'What is it?'

Annette tried to whisper but Leni wouldn't lean down so she could talk to her without the man listening in.

'Nothing . . .' she replied but gave Leni a sharp look so that her sister would realize that Annette didn't want this strange man to accompany them. But however much she screwed up her little face and pulled at Leni for her attention, her sister continued strolling along while exchanging shy glances with him. With some disgust, she dropped Leni's hand in a cold sulk, walking along on her own, scuffing her feet along the pavement, and only turning her head from time to time to make sure that Leni hadn't abandoned her.

18

Leni was relieved that Annette was quietly dragging her feet along by the side of her and Paul. He had taken the sudden appearance of her sister in his stride, cheerfully suggesting that they all walk together so that he could carry on talking to her while they made sure her sister got safely home. The fact that there was no 'safely home' for Annette was something that Leni wasn't sure how to explain in front of her sister, given that she had painted a picture of such an idyllic family life only the night before. She had fully intended to tell him the truth about her family – but now she couldn't say a word, not with Annette there.

And anyway, even if she could find a way to tell him, he would surely be put off by the thought of having to drag her baby sister along everywhere they went. No, she wouldn't explain things tonight – better to get to know each other and lead up to it gradually.

As they carried on walking, talking about nothing significant, Leni tried to work out what to do once they got to Lindenstrasse. There was something about Paul that made her want to stay with him for just a little longer. They were strangers and yet she felt as if they'd known each other for the longest time. He also seemed determined to carry on talking to her, and so she allowed herself to continue walking onwards, towards the courtyard that held their pile of wooden crates. She told herself that on the very next corner she would stop walking and say her goodbyes ... and then the next street lamp ...

He was not so shy this evening and chatted away as if they were old friends, telling her stories about the club he'd worked at previously. Leni felt so happy just strolling along on a warm summer's night, listening to this man trying to entertain her. Even when Annette turned to pull faces at her, Leni didn't stop walking, although she knew that she should.

On they went, past the café where poor Frau Keppler had taken her final breath ... past the house where her brother Josef had gone to visit the friend who had turned out to have influenza. Within days both her brothers had come down with it: sick and feverish, their eyes glassy and unfocused. Leni shook her head to get rid of the memories and moved closer to Paul.

'So, a whole Sunday to do nothing. What bliss ...' she murmured.

'And the weather will be nice, I think. What will it be for you – a picnic with your family perhaps?' Paul spoke gently, but Leni was unsure what she was supposed to say in return. *Was he building up towards asking her out, or merely making conversation?* She cursed the silly rules of courtship where you couldn't say what you wanted or what you really thought about things.

'I haven't made any plans yet ... What about you?' Underneath her casual enquiry, Leni's heart was thudding against her ribs as she waited for his response.

'Nothing very exciting, I'm afraid. I have to sort something out for my brother Otto.' Paul sighed as he spoke, and Leni hoped it was because he would prefer to be with her. 'He's always in some kind of trouble.'

'I see,' she mumbled while using her hand to give Annette a gentle steer back to the other side of her. She silently cursed Otto for his troubles but then Paul's hand gently brushed against hers. Leni glanced shyly at him and smiled. Their fingers touched briefly as the gap between them narrowed. She felt her heart leap with excitement for a moment until Annette suddenly wriggled free, shoving between her and Paul, making him laugh as she did so.

'Hah. This young lady is bored with us, I fear. Quite right too.'

Annette's face glowed with triumph as she grinned up at Leni with her sweet gap-toothed smile. Leni rolled her eyes and felt the weight of disappointment pressing on her. Paul had moved away from her. She didn't know what to do or say, and besides they were very nearly at the courtyard. She couldn't under any circumstances take the chance on Paul finding out that she was sleeping under a pile of wooden crates. The humiliation would be more than she could bear.

She could see Annette skipping ahead, her face gleeful at having vanquished her enemy and sure that she was about to have her sister all to herself again.

An idea started to form inside Leni's mind . . . She had to be quick, but maybe, just maybe it would work. All she wanted was five minutes alone with Paul, without her sister distracting them – so if there were to be words spoken or arrangements made, then they could unfold without interruption.

She could already see the familiar red bricks of their

courtyard in the distance and knew that it was now or never. She couldn't allow him to walk any further with them.

Leni called out to the skipping Annette, 'Nette, go straight indoors and no more dawdling . . . you should be in bed.' Her sister scowled at her until Leni gave her a threatening glare. Her little mouth flapped open but as Leni's eyes widened, so Annette's mouth snapped shut again.

Leni gestured towards their courtyard. Her sister screwed her little face up into a sulky pout, but reluctantly trudged away, leaving her alone with Paul.

'I'm sorry about Nette . . . she's like my little shadow sometimes.' Leni smiled up at him, noticing how straight his teeth were. He had such a nice face and she just wanted to stare at it and listen to his soft voice say the most ordinary things to her.

'Oh, it's quite all right. I used to follow Otto around when I was young. I'm sure he thought I was quite the nuisance at times. Won't your mother be worried about her though? It's very late for a little girl to be out.' His eyes changed from the warmth of his smile to an earnest concern and Leni couldn't decide which expression she liked better.

'Yes . . . it's very late,' was all she could say.

'I should be going . . .' Paul said, yet he didn't move and she felt the gap between them narrow slightly. All around them was silence. Leni could hear the sound of her own breathing. She could smell the slight dusty warmth of his skin. Another step and Leni imagined she might feel his breath on her cheek. She stood quite still, not wanting to shatter the silence between them. Praying that Annette wouldn't cry out for her.

His eyes were fixed on hers and his soft full lips parted. She wasn't imagining it. He was standing closer to her. She could feel the heat radiating off him. He was so very close now . . .

Leni watched as his long pianist's fingers reached for her cheek, before gently guiding her face towards his. The air between them shifted as she closed her eyes and felt the soft, tender pressure of his lips touching her mouth. He was kissing her . . . and she was kissing him back. His lips were so warm and his mouth seemed as familiar as her own. The kiss lasted forever – and for a split second.

Her breath came in jagged bursts as she felt him draw away and their lips finally parted. Her eyes inexplicably filled with tears as she gazed up at him. Paul smiled shyly – a questioning smile, and she answered him with her own. Then his arms wrapped around her tightly and he kissed her again.

This time so fiercely that Leni never wanted it to end.

Berlin, November 1926

19

Dieter was worried about his heart as he stood by the window in his office with Herr Keks rubbing around his legs demanding food. There was nothing medically wrong with his heart, or at least not that he knew of. It was rather that the days felt grey and lonely to him.

November had arrived with its merciless rain and days that never really grew light and, even though Dieter could hardly enjoy a summer's day, he missed them all the same. The sunshine made the tin mask fiercely hot, burning his skin if he wasn't careful. And so, Dieter remained indoors. Given that most of his evenings were taken up with running the Babylon Circus it gave him the rather ghostly appearance of a man who did not get enough fresh air or indeed any fresh air. But at least in summer he could see a blue sky and a sunny day through the window, even if he did not particularly like to go outside.

His days felt strangely joyless at the moment. Everything was exactly the same as it had always been. The Babylon Circus opened at eight o'clock every evening except Sunday, and closed in the early hours of each morning. The same guests arrived in their black or white masks, drank the same cocktails or bottles of champagne and watched exactly the same dancing girls as they had during the long, hot evenings of the Berlin summer. But no – something was not quite the same. And that something concerned the pianist . . .

Dieter reached inside his jacket pocket for his silver cigarette case. He had lined up an entire row of neat little cigarettes earlier that morning. It seemed a shame to ruin his neatness, but nevertheless he plucked one from the case, placing it in the corner of his mouth where he still had intact lips and felt around in his pocket for a book of matches. Herr Keks mewed softly as Dieter struck a small flame and exhaled a cloud of sweet-smelling smoke.

'Ahh, at least you love me, Herr Keks . . . as long as I feed you.' He moved back to his desk and opened the drawer, taking out a little cold sausage that he had bought for his supper. Tearing off a small chunk with his fingers, he watched as the cat gobbled it down. Herr Keks leapt up on to the desk, purring his comforting rumble, coming close to Dieter's face as he sat down with his hands cupped around his chin.

Footsteps outside his door made Dieter almost hope for company yet he really didn't want to talk to anyone. He brushed the cat away as he prepared himself to go through the week's accounts. The wooden chair creaked under his weight as he shifted his body trying to get comfortable. Yet he couldn't settle.

Outside in the passageway he could hear voices. Soft murmurings that were unlike the usual loud squawking from the performers. A man's voice . . .

Dieter pricked up his ears when he realized that it was the pianist. He couldn't stop himself thinking about Paul lately. Even when he was supposed to be checking on the 'guests' he often found himself lingering by the side of the

86

piano and watching the boy's serious face as he immersed himself in the music.

Getting to his feet, Dieter walked slowly to his office door and then out into the passageway. It was empty. After a long moment puzzling to himself, he pushed open the little red door and wandered into the nightclub, catching a glimpse of his body in the large silver mirror on the wall. His strange, distorted, grotesque shape amused him for a moment. The club was empty and there was no sign of the pianist. He'd disappeared into thin air.

Dieter was sure that he'd heard his voice – maybe he was imagining things.

Then, just as he turned back towards the little red door, he heard another softer voice – a woman's voice . . . Rubbing at the edges of his tin mask, his skin flaring with irritation, he followed the sound of the murmurings, creeping towards the cloakroom.

As he reached the corner of the room, there, by the side of the cloakroom, was *his* pianist. With his arms wrapped tightly around the cigarette girl.

Dieter heard himself gasp as if someone had thrown iced water over him. The sight of them kissing, the girl then straightening the pianist's necktie and smoothing down a strand of hair that had fallen playfully over his forehead, made Dieter reel with shock. He backed away, shaking his head. For a moment, he was furious. But then – how ridiculous. 'His pianist'. He wasn't *his* pianist at all. He was just *the* pianist.

Dieter had rarely loved, and when he did, it was furtive and secret. The moment that Paul had started work at the Babylon Circus, he'd found himself beginning to wish for something. The wishing was so delicate and quiet that it had taken him a long time to understand it. It was contrary to everything that he believed about himself. But at that precise moment, Dieter knew somewhere deep inside him had been hope . . . and now it was gone.

20

The café had become their regular meeting spot since those golden days of late summer, when they would sit around in the Tiergarten, eating ice-cream and feeling the warmth of each other's arms. Café Krause on Alexanderplatz had long wooden tables, friendly waiters and the added advantage of being a short walk from Paul's apartment. They sat in the corner next to the window so they could watch people coming and going, eating bowls of soup with dark bread and talking about their plans for the future. Now, in the chilly winds of November, Leni shivered as she took off her coat and hung it neatly on a wooden coat stand just inside the door. She smiled as she saw Paul heading for their usual seats, securing them for her because he knew she liked to look out of the window. It was late afternoon and the sky was violet and threatening rain. The café smelled of boiled cabbage and the heat of damp bodies.

Leni pulled out a wooden chair to sit down before leaning across the table to kiss Paul.

'It's so cold already and it's not even winter yet,' she complained.

He immediately took both of her hands in his, blowing on them with his warm breath and rubbing them until she stopped shivering. 'Let's order hot chocolate – my treat.'

Paul toyed nervously with the fingers of her left hand across the table and then cleared his throat to speak.

'I thought maybe next Sunday, I could meet your family. After all, it's been three months. They must wonder why you keep disappearing and who you're meeting?'

Leni's face grew pale and the smile froze on her lips. 'They would love to meet you, of course . . . but unfortunately my mother . . . isn't feeling very well at the moment. I'm sure she would prefer to meet you when she's better . . .'

'Oh, I'm so sorry. Please give her my best wishes. I didn't know your mother was ill.'

'Yes, she's been ill for quite some time. Anyway, I like it when we go to your room . . . if Otto is busy . . .' Leni swiftly changed the subject, knowing full well that Paul would be distracted by thinking about his brother.

Otto spent Sunday afternoons at his political meeting. He was a young Communist, or at least he had been until Lenin was replaced by Stalin instead of Trotsky. Now he seemed to be set upon antagonizing the local Communist leaders with his constant sniping and criticism of the 'revolution' and how in his opinion they had squandered it. He had no time for the Social Democrats, calling them 'bourgeois' and worse than those silly National Socialists. The Social Democratic government always seemed to be having problems of some kind. People arguing. Frequent newspaper headlines about the government collapsing, written as if it were an invalid. Leni didn't understand any of it, except that Otto was frequently angry and constantly getting into trouble. She had only met him once properly – a brief meeting in the room he shared with Paul. Otto had barely said a word to her. He'd struck her as rather arrogant and full of his own importance, blathering on about his 'cause', and when she hadn't understood what he was talking about, he'd looked her up and down in such a disdainful manner that Leni had taken an instant dislike to him, although she hadn't said as much to Paul.

In their early days, she had loved going to work at the Babylon Circus, knowing Paul would be there, and that afterwards he would walk her home. But those nightly walks had turned into lazy Sunday afternoon dates in the Tiergarten and sometimes they would go on to the Gloria-Palast to see a movie. Now, Sunday afternoons were her favourite time of the week.

By the end of September, they had abandoned the movie theatre and lying around in the park to spend their days in his small room on Münzstrasse. As soon as Otto went out to his weekly political meeting, Leni and Paul would spend long Sunday afternoons lying entwined in each other's arms, watching the sun casting shadows on the walls. She had not as yet slept with Paul, since Leni wanted to be quite sure of a future together before she took that step, but his long, urgent kisses were quite enough to sustain her.

Their afternoons always ended the same way, with Leni having to tell her usual lie about family supper before rushing back to the gloomy little room she now shared with Annette just across the street from their abandoned courtyard. The landlady, Frau Vogel, was a widow and had split her own apartment into two rooms with a shared kitchen and bathroom; she was friendly enough, having taken quite the shine to her sister.

When she finally returned home to their room, Nette would greet her with a frosty stare and it would take promises of treats with endless stories to make her be sweet again.

It was all worth it to spend those stolen hours with Paul, though, feeling the curves and sharp bones of his body. His smells and sounds were becoming as familiar to her as her own. Sometimes she allowed him to unbutton her dress a little, planting kisses along her shoulders, until Leni couldn't think about anything except the pleasure she felt, and would feel for the hours ahead of them.

Afterwards, when she was buttoning up her dress, a lake of sadness would begin to swell up in her chest and she'd wish she could tell him that she'd lied about her family. But it was too late. She'd meant to tell the truth every night he'd walked her home, and then she was sure she would tell him on that first Sunday when they lay down in the grass of the Tiergarten, feeling the sun on their skin, their fingers barely touching but the heat travelling between them regardless. Every time, something had stopped her. Now, it had gone on so long that Leni knew she could never tell him the truth.

Her gloomy thoughts were interrupted by the friendly waiter bringing two cups of hot chocolate and placing them neatly down on the table in front of them.

'Cold enough for you? This should warm you up.'

'Thank you,' they both said at once and then giggled shyly across the café table. Leni cradled the cup of hot chocolate between her palms, taking hesitant sips. It was too hot to drink and so she sat and waited.

'Will Otto be at his meeting this afternoon?' Leni whispered hopefully.

'I think so. We're not really speaking. We had a fight . . .'

'What happened?'

'I think he's in trouble.' Paul's face clouded over. 'Some

men turned up at our apartment looking for him. They weren't the kind of people you want to fall out with.'

'What did they want?' Her good mood evaporated as she suddenly realized how worried he was.

'They didn't say . . . It wasn't anything good. My brother takes too many risks with the wrong people. I worry that he's gone too far this time . . .'

He took a mouthful of the hot chocolate and, finding it burned his mouth, exclaimed with pain.

'Oh, your poor mouth!' Leni looked concerned but Paul just shrugged.

'It's nothing. Anyway, enough about my stupid brother for one day. Let's finish these then we can go back to my place.'

'And you'll walk me home afterwards?' she said softly, putting all thoughts of Otto to one side.

'Unless my poor mouth is not up for kissing this evening.' Paul's eyes crinkled with laughter and Leni looked at him and her heart felt full. She was happy. Her job at the Babylon Circus had brought her nothing but good luck. She had a room to call her own, she earned enough to feed and care for her sister, but most of all she had someone to love her . . .

Annette tried so hard to keep her eyes open but the hours had ticked by without Leni coming home. She was probably with *him*.

Everything had started to go wrong the night that she'd gone to the circus only to find Leni with that annoying man. Annette had stood there in the dark watching them giggling and laughing together – sticking her little pink tongue out at the two of them even though they couldn't see her.

When that man had leaned closer to her sister, a bleak future had begun to open up in her little mind. Annette had felt sick at the sight of them. She wanted Leni to herself . . .

That night, as she'd watched them kissing with her little chin wobbling and large salty tears splashing down her cheeks, Annette had decided that she hated him.

Sleep weighed down her eyelids. After a long wait for her sister to come home, Annette wriggled down amongst the blankets, curling up under the weight of the old army coat and put all thoughts of the annoying man away. It was cosy and warm sleeping in a proper bed again. Eventually, she'd closed her eyes – only for a minute, but the next thing she knew it was morning and Leni was lying beside her.

Annette clambered over Leni's sleeping body to reach her clothes. Tiptoeing across the floor in her bare feet until she reached the table, she picked up a knife and clumsily sawed the ends off a loaf of bread. Sitting cross-legged on the floor, she carefully chewed them, weighing up whether or not she should wake her sister.

Swallowing the bread, Annette began struggling into her school clothes, pulling the musty-smelling woollen over her head and fastening her pinafore dress. Leni finally insisting that she go to school each weekday was a punishment that she did not care for. The other children were not friendly and Annette could not work out why.

On her first day, she'd stood quite alone as they all seemed to know each other, forming small groups without her or sharing desks. She'd been placed at the very back of the room without anyone to keep her company. Annette was used to being alone, so that didn't bother her so much until the children were allowed outside to play for a short period.

The playground was just a scruffy yard at the rear of the school but the girls gathered on one side and the boys on the other. Annette tried to position herself close to Hildegard Knopf, whose family ran the local bakery. She knew her well enough to mumble a greeting, yet now Hildegard with her neatly braided hair was standing in the centre of a group of girls. They were playing some kind of game with chalk on the ground. Annette crept closer, a nervous sweat trickling down her back.

She couldn't go any further without saying something. Her mouth felt parched, and her voice cracked a little as she spoke. 'Can I play?' The words had barely left her mouth as the girls turned to inspect her. Annette bit down on her bottom lip, her little chest taking jagged breaths.

Hildegard Knopf tossed one of her neat little braids over her shoulder and frowned at her.

'No, we have the correct numbers for the game. There's no place for you.'

The rejection was so swift, so coldly delivered that Annette could feel tears stinging her eyes. A flush of burning shame crawled up her chest and spread over her face, making her cheeks pink. She turned away before Hildegard could see her cry. Wiping her eyes with tiny fists, Annette hurried back into the schoolroom, sniffing away her tears.

Passing by Hildegard's desk, Annette felt a rush of fury flooding over her, replacing her shame. She opened the desktop, finding amongst Hildegard's schoolbooks a small knitted doll in a blue hat that was barely bigger than Annette's hand.

She grabbed the doll, running out of the classroom and into the toilets. Locking the cubicle door, Annette threw the tiny doll into the toilet bowl, watching it float face down in the water for several seconds. She could hear the tramp of feet heading back into their lesson and so, taking a deep breath, she pulled on the long metal chain.

Annette had watched in horror as the doll became wedged. The noise of the other children approaching made her panic, and she leaned over the toilet bowl, praying for the doll to disappear as she pulled at the chain again and again – but no water came out. Eventually, Annette fished the doll out of the toilet and hid it on the floor behind the toilet pipe, and then scurried back to the schoolroom before she was missed.

The teacher called the class to order. Annette slunk back into her seat all alone at the back of the room. 'Please take

out your letters books. We will practise our handwriting.'
The sound of wooden desk lids opening and thudding shut
again was interrupted by a high-pitched wail as Hildegard
discovered her doll was missing. The teacher interrogated
Hildegard: Why had she brought a doll to class? When had
she last seen it?

Hildegard couldn't remember exactly. The teacher grew
exasperated as Annette watched with wide eyes, her heart
thumping inside her chest. Hildegard was instructed to
check that she hadn't in fact left the doll at home that
morning and not to make a fuss. The girl sank down into
her seat, her cheeks now taking on a familiar pink flush.
Annette couldn't contain her delight and her lips formed a
cunning smirk.

It had been a brief moment of triumph, as the rest of her
school days had remained miserable. Now, a familiar feeling of dread swelled inside her chest as she prepared
herself for another day sitting on her own at the back of
the classroom with nobody to talk to. Annette took a lingering look at her sleeping sister and wished she could
stay home.

Leni stirred as Annette slammed the door shut behind
her. If she didn't hurry, she would be late for school. As
the noise of the door woke her sister from her slumber,
the little jolt of it closing knocked a tiny knitted doll off its
perch on the windowsill.

22

Leni loved to watch the girls in the dressing room as they painted their eyes and lips, listening to their chatter. Tonight, they were trying out a new routine where they dressed as cats. Their noses were replaced with tiny blobs of black paint with whiskers drawn around their mouths. Around their waists they strapped a belt to which was attached a tail made out of mismatching pieces of fur while on their heads they wore sparkly pointed ears. Everything else was covered in a sheer gauze that was dyed to match their ears and tails.

She had thought they looked amusing, having sat out front as they rehearsed with Paul at the piano. He'd played a jolly tune for the beginning of the routine as the girls strutted around the stage making little cat movements, each one shaking her tail at the audience and pretending to lick her paws. Then the music slowed to a sultry beat as the girls swayed and shook their bodies before jumping down from the stage to find welcoming laps.

Now, with their faces painted and the costumes on, they were all very amused at themselves. Berolina was of course leading the laughter as they swished their furry tails towards each other, but even Irma was more friendly than usual.

Leni slipped out of her coat and little woollen hat before unzipping her dress and shivering into her costume. The thin black dress and little gold top hat did not change with the seasons and so until the customers arrived and the rooms began to warm up, Leni felt cold and wished she had a cardigan to wrap around her bare arms. Once the customers began dancing, they generated heat trying to keep up with the latest craze. This made the Babylon Circus smell of the sweat and fire of their bodies as they danced faster and faster. The tinny orchestra with their bloodshot unfocused eyes played at ever-increasing speed until the dancing crowd started to disperse, their throats parched, their skin glistening with sweat, and their bodies warm with desire.

Shivering, Leni fixed her little gold top hat to her hair and dipped her head under the velvet cord of her cigarette tray, making sure that it was sitting comfortably on her neck before she loaded it with a range of cigarettes (American, Turkish, German), then the cigars (small cigarillos, thick long cigars), and glittering matchbooks inscribed with the name of the Babylon Circus. She kept the left-hand side of her tray for small crimson posies that men liked to buy for women.

Checking her look in the dressing-room mirror, Leni was satisfied. Nothing could spoil her good mood that evening, not even the scowling Dieter who barged into the dressing room bellowing at Leni to get to work. She'd got so caught up with watching the girls paint their faces that she'd forgotten the club was already open and she was missing.

'*What am I paying you for?*' he roared at her. His tin mask moved slightly with the effort of his shouting, exposing the smallest piece of his cheek. What lay beneath was horribly scarred, and rubbed raw by the tin mask so it appeared red and inflamed. Leni tried not to stare but she couldn't take her eyes off Dieter's face. His hand moved quickly to adjust the tin mask, covering everything up and storming out of the dressing room, his mood now worse than before he'd entered.

'What is wrong with him tonight?' Greta sighed, wearily fixing her headdress and flipping the tiny pointed ears so they were straight.

'You know what Dieter needs?' Berolina whispered before making grinding movements with her voluptuous hips to demonstrate. The sight of her made Leni giggle as she hurried up the passageway towards the bright red stage door.

Irma was already doing her rounds with the cigarette tray and her garter filled with tiny pillows of white powder wrapped around her right thigh. Leni heaved a sigh of relief. At least customers wouldn't be complaining to Dieter that they'd had to wait too long, although Irma might have ended up with a pocketful of Leni's tips by now. She took her place to the side of the tables at the front of the stage, ready to respond to a hand waving in her direction. From time to time, she would do laps of the room, swaying gently in between the tables saying good evening to her regulars and waiting for their notes to fall in her tray. Standing to the side of the stage gave Leni a chance to weigh up the room, to understand which men she should fear and which ones would tip well. After three months she was quite expert at telling the difference.

She had only made one mistake, on a Saturday evening not long after she'd first started working there. She had been captivated by the girls on the stage, watching their doll routine with wide eyes while standing somewhat shyly in the shadows, when the thin-faced unsmiling man wearing a monocle in his right eye walked up behind her. Leni hadn't realized he was there until his hand reached over her shoulder to select a packet of cigarettes from her tray. As he did so his fingers grazed her breast and Leni jumped away, slapping his hand without thinking about who he might be. In one movement the man pinned her to the wall of the Babylon Circus, his hand around her throat. '*Silly girl . . .*' he hissed in her ear before walking away without paying for his cigarettes. After that Leni had avoided his table.

The orchestra finally stopped playing and the out-of-breath couples made their way back to their tables, the men downing chilled bottles of champagne while the women fanned themselves with their hands before ordering long, cool gin rickeys.

Leni walked slowly around the tables waiting for Paul to come in and sit at his piano. Ernst the comedian was telling jokes, and although there were still a few minutes to go before the girls would be on stage there was still no sign of Paul. By now, he would usually be there, arranging his sheet music and waiting patiently.

She searched the room with her eyes but he wasn't anywhere to be seen. Whispering to Irma that she'd be 'back in a minute', Leni unhooked her cigarette tray and made her way out of the red door towards the dressing room. There weren't very many places that Paul could be if he wasn't in the club itself. There was only the dressing room, Dieter's office, a toilet with a rusty old tap over a sink, and the street door leading outside. She tiptoed down through the passageway praying that Dieter would not come out of his office and catch her. The dressing-room door opened as the girls were ready and about to take their places. The toilet was empty, its dark brown door left open. That only left the street door. Leni took a deep breath and twisted the door handle.

23

Paul was lying on his back, his mouth open and a trickle of blood dripping down his chin. Leni raced towards him, flinging herself to her knees and cradling his head in her lap.

'Paul, what happened?' she cried.

He lifted his head, trying to wipe the blood that was dripping on to his white shirt. 'It's Otto . . . he's in trouble again. Some of his "friends" were delivering a message . . .' He yelped in pain as he moved. 'Help me up . . . I have to go on,' he mumbled but then fell back down to the pavement again.

Leni used the hem of her dress to wipe his face and tried to get him to sit up. Part of her wanted to run inside and scream for help but, having seen how angry Dieter had been earlier, she didn't want to take a chance that Paul would get into trouble.

After a few moments, he was able to struggle to his feet. Trembling, he draped his arm around Leni's shoulders to support himself. Every movement seemed to cause him agony and his bloodied face contorted in pain as they shuffled together back inside the club. She managed to pull him towards the rusty bathroom, kicking the door shut and looking around frantically for something to wash his face with. There wasn't anything so, propping Paul up against the sink, Leni slipped out of the toilet door and into the dressing room. She grabbed Wally's dirty pink powder puff and raced back to find Paul.

Slowly she dipped the powder puff under the rusty old tap and wiped the blood from Paul's lips. As soon as his face was clean, however, a small stream of blood slid slowly out of his mouth and dripped off his chin. 'It's no good. I can't stop it bleeding,' she said, an edge of panic in her voice.

'Find something I can put in my mouth to stop the blood . . .' Paul was ghostly white and looked as if he might faint at any moment but his eyes were determined as they urged Leni to help him. She raced back to the dressing room, searching for anything that might help, when, suddenly, she had an idea.

Ernst finished with yet another stale joke just as Paul sat down at the piano and arranged his sheet music ready to begin playing, his mouth swollen with a rolled-up piece of gauze that Leni had ripped from one of the ballet skirts hanging on the costume rail. She had done her best to dab the blood spots from his white shirt but with no luck. At least he had his back to the audience so they would never know.

Dieter arrived at the side of the stage, waiting for Ernst to get to the end of his joke, take his applause and depart. He eyed Paul and whatever was going on with his swollen mouth but the girls were shuffling into the wings of the stage and the performance was about to begin.

Ernst took his bow to muted applause while Dieter warmly welcomed the 'guests' and announced the beginning of the cabaret. Paul struck up the opening chords of the music for the Cat Ballet routine and the girls readied themselves for their entrance.

Leni quickly attached her cigarette tray around her neck and made herself busy before Dieter could see her. Her dress felt damp against her leg and she realized that the hem was soaked with Paul's blood. There was nothing she could do and so she served her posies and cigars and hoped nobody would notice.

Berolina and Wally were the first girls on to the stage, swishing their little cat tails towards the audience, then bending from the waist and posing with their fingers on their whiskers. The other girls rushed on stage to join them and Leni slowly sidled over to where she could see the piano to make sure that Paul was all right.

He was grimacing with pain; his face looked ashen. At least she had managed to stem the blood for now. Of course, it could bleed through her makeshift bandage and trickle down his chin at any moment. Leni watched Paul playing and felt a rush of love for him surge through her. She longed to wrap her arms around him and plant kisses on his face until he was healed. Instead, she avoided Dieter's stern gaze by hurrying away to serve the customers, dispensing a matchbook to one table and a handful of cigars to the next. Leni's money bag grew fat with cash and she took a moment to go over to the bar where she handed over all her Reichsmarks, filling up her change purse with some coins knowing they would likely end the night in her pocket if she was lucky. Paul played on, until the little cats leapt from the stage and landed in the warm laps of the men seated at the front tables.

24

'What did those men say about Otto?' Leni's stomach churned with anxiety. Paul's face was a mask of pain and she had insisted on walking him back home rather than risk him walking all the way to Kreuzberg. He'd protested, but by the end of the night he was too weak to put up much resistance and so they walked along arm in arm, in an unfamiliar routine.

'I don't know. It all happened so quickly. I was smoking a cigarette and one of them asked me for a light. Naturally I obliged. They asked me if I was Otto's brother, and I said yes . . . Then one of them hit me and I fell down . . .' He groaned a little as if he was in pain. 'Another man kicked me in the ribs as I lay there and said, "Where's Otto?" I didn't know and I wouldn't tell them anyway. So that was that. They must have heard people coming down the street because they all ran off.'

Paul was leaning a little on her as they walked and, from time to time, Leni stopped to ask him if he was all right. Each time the answer was unconvincing and she glanced up at him to inspect his face. His mouth had stopped bleeding but he'd hit his head when the men knocked him down, and Leni was worried he might have concussion.

They trudged through the Berlin streets that were still darkly filled with men and women selling anything people wanted to buy. On one street young boys draped themselves seductively on street lamps whispering to men who walked past; on the next street broken-toothed women stood with their young daughters, lifting their filthy dresses to show what was on offer and pushing their daughters forward should any man hesitate in front of them.

Turning on to Münzstrasse, Leni eyed the 'Münzis', the hordes of pregnant streetwalkers lined up, available for the service of men who could afford them. Business was slow, as the street was still full of bored desperate women with painted faces. Leni watched as one or two of the more heavily pregnant girls rubbed at the small of their backs, stretching out their shoulders, their faces filled with des-pair as they wished they could go home to a warm bed. She hurried past them, trying not to meet their eyes, holding tight to Paul.

On they walked, until finally they reached his building. The street door was locked at night and so Paul scrabbled about searching his pockets for the key. 'You must stay. It's late and you can't walk all the way home by yourself now. Otto and I can sleep on the floor and you can take the bed. I'm sorry about all this. He's such a hothead. I'll have a long talk with him tonight and put things right.'

Leni doubted that any number of 'talks' would do any good with Otto. She sighed and said, 'I have to get home. They'll worry about me.' In reality she was rather more concerned that Annette might decide to go out searching for her if she didn't arrive home soon. 'I'll help you up the stairs first.'

Paul said no, but as soon as they were inside, she noticed that he didn't refuse her arm when she offered it. The walk had taken a lot out of him and he had to keep stopping as they climbed the stairs. Eventually they reached his room and Leni quickly opened the door.

The room was in darkness apart from the glowing embers of the pot-bellied stove that ate too much coal and gave out too little heat. Leni and Paul both stood in the doorway, staring around the room. Drawers had been pulled open, mostly emptied and then abandoned. The closet held only Paul's clothes. The bed was empty . . . and Otto was gone.

25

The Babylon Circus was holding a 'Carnival Night'. This was a special evening where all the girls were required to dress as 'Birds of Paradise' in bright colours complete with feathered plumage. The bar served rum cocktails and the tinny orchestra played songs from Cuba and Brazil for the girls to dance to. There was an air of celebration as Dieter walked amongst the guests, making sure everyone had enough to drink or smoke. He took extra care of those guests he recognized as important – minor government officials or third-rate movie stars.

He found himself smiling and laughing, enjoying the carnival atmosphere. Even Berolina's incessant laughter couldn't irritate him that evening and for the life of him he couldn't work out why. Each time his eyes drifted over to the piano where Paul sat with a sombre face, waiting for the performers to take their places, Dieter was relieved to find that he felt almost nothing. The sadness had lifted.

There was something about pianists that was so very delicious though – their long fingers and earnest faces. Yet he would no longer allow himself to be ruled by his emotions. The world could be a dangerous place for men like him and the only way he knew to safeguard himself was by making money. If he couldn't be happy then at least he could be miserable in comfort and who knew what the future might bring?

Every day the world became a little darker around them – and Dieter was determined to look after himself. This pianist was just another boy and he was a rational man. The answer to Dieter's problems lay in the fact that he did not currently possess enough money for happiness, or for comfort, but he would make a plan. That would make everything better.

As he slipped out of the bright red stage door and down the passage to the dressing room, ideas floated in and out of his mind. Changes he might make to the Babylon Circus – things he might charge more money for. Dieter liked to solve problems and this was just a simple matter of mathematics. He had X and he needed Y. 'Yes, that's it,' he muttered to himself as he rapped on the dressing-room door, yelling, 'Stage please, ladies.' He didn't bother to enter the dressing room. He had no wish to see any of the performers. In fact, Dieter thought he might slip upstairs to his apartment and begin work on his plan immediately. He walked briskly towards his office, wanting only to climb the stairs that led to his private rooms. He was already looking forward to the first gasp of his cigarette and the way the absinthe would hit the back of his throat. Dieter didn't know what form his plan might take as yet, but he was sure if he could just get a few moments of peace and quiet that something would occur to him. After all, plenty of people in Berlin made fortunes at the expense of other people. Why shouldn't he be the same?

He had fought for his country and what good had it done him? Nobody would employ him amongst 'decent people', with his face looking as it did. And so, he would take what he could get. He deserved something in compensation for the lack of love in his life. At this thought, his mind conjured up a picture of Paul, but Dieter quickly pushed it away. Striding into his office, he ran up the stairs and entered his private rooms. Making his way to his armchair, he reached down to the cigarette box that he kept on the small table next to it. Lighting up one of his Turkish cigarettes, Dieter exhaled a puff of sweet-smelling smoke and then poured himself a glass of absinthe from the familiar green bottle.

He sat back in his chair and tried to think of a clever idea but the more he tried to think of one, the more his mind went completely blank. He was about to reach for another glass of absinthe when out of the corner of his eye he spotted Herr Keks curled up into a ball under the table.

'Ah there you are, Herr Keks. We are going to be rich – just you wait and see. Little man, you shall have the finest fish every day. No more scraps for you . . .'

Dieter abandoned his cigarette on the rim of a large glass ashtray, before leaning across to pat Herr Keks, running his hand over the silky white fur and murmuring sweet compliments. But Herr Keks didn't respond. The poor cat lay there on the floor, cold and lifeless.

With an anguished groan, Dieter fell to his knees, bending over the little body and stroking his white fur as if it might bring his only companion back to life. Picking him up, he cradled the cat to his chest. He couldn't bear to lose him. Tearing the tin mask from his face Dieter began to weep for his lost companion, for his lost love, and most of all for himself . . .

Later that evening Dieter gave Herr Keks a suitable burial in a neat little box weighed down with stones which he then floated into the river. Things would be different now, he swore to himself. He would set about making so much money that nobody could ever hurt him again.

He was like the city in essence – always shifting loyalties and able to reinvent itself. Dieter watched the little box sink beneath the water and felt a new steely determination. He vowed that there would be no more piano players for him – nothing but work.

He would begin his new plan immediately by raising all his prices . . .

26

Back at the Babylon Circus, the Carnival night was in full swing. The dance floor was so crowded that it seemed impossible to squeeze one more person on to it. There was hardly room to move at all and once the orchestra began to play a Charleston, arms and legs crashed into each other until eventually some of the customers returned to their tables to wipe the sweat from their brows and drink several more rum cocktails.

Leni could barely get past the small tables to offer her wares as women were seated in men's laps or generally draped across their dates. She could see Irma doing a roaring trade with her tiny white packets and such was the extraordinary atmosphere that the customers tore them open right there in the open, snorting up the contents and offering the leftovers to anyone who wished to try. People were glassy-eyed and babbling nonsense to each other. Their laughter became shrill and hysterical. Leni carried on doling out packets of cigarettes or offering matchbooks to them. This evening, nobody cared about their change. They threw their Reichsmarks on to Leni's tray as if they were millionaires and money was of no importance to them.

The orchestra finally finished playing and Ernst took his place on the stage, telling his rotten jokes. Leni checked to make sure that Paul was at his piano, which he was. His wound had begun to heal but he still had several bruises and some painful ribs that, when anyone enquired, he put down to a clumsy fall. There was still no sign of Otto and she could tell that Paul was worried. This situation was beyond his brother's normal scrapes.

There was a brief lull while customers drank and smoked, readying themselves for the rest of the evening's entertainment. In the wings of the stage, Leni could already spy the brightly coloured feathered headdresses and skirts on the dancers. Apart from the blue and green feathers in their hair, and the tiniest plumes forming a skirt, the girls wore only long beaded necklaces across their breasts. Each necklace would be removed during the course of their routine before Berolina and Wally would leap from the stage and allow selected customers to 'pluck the feathers' from their specially made skirts.

Ernst began a stale old skit that used one of the customers as the butt of his joke. It wasn't particularly funny and Leni imagined everyone laughed heartily only out of relief that they weren't the one being singled out. As Ernst took his applause and the lights dimmed, Leni cast another anxious glance over at Paul to make sure he was all right. To her surprise she saw a tall, muscular man who she had never seen before moving towards the piano.

Leaning over Paul, he placed two great meaty hands on his shoulders. It looked to Leni as if the man was holding Paul down in his seat, yet at the same time he appeared to be smiling and speaking softly as if they were old friends. The second that the lights dimmed to signal the beginning of the cabaret, the man patted Paul lightly on his shoulders and walked away.

There was no sign of Dieter to introduce the girls, so

Paul began to play, but his face wore an expression of shock. He hit a wrong note and then another, before gathering his wits and nodding towards Greta in the wings to signal he was ready.

Leni was itching to rush over to him and find out who that man was and what he'd said but there were too many people between her and the piano. She tried to see where the man had gone but there was no sign of him now. He'd disappeared into the crowd.

The girls paraded out on to the stage, fluffing their feathers and high-kicking their legs. Paul played on as they shook their necklaces at the audience, another string of wooden pearls being thrown away every time the song hit a crescendo. Paul played faster and faster until the girls were naked from the waist up. They twirled and jiggled at the customers, fluttering their arms like birds as Berolina and Wally jumped down from the stage, shaking their feathers at the drunken crowd. Paul slammed the piano keys urgently as the two women allowed men and women to pluck off their feathers with their teeth. The atmosphere in the room was febrile and Leni watched the customers snarling and shoving to get closer to Berolina and Wally.

The crowd were too rowdy and getting out of control. What had started as the usual flirtatious game became ugly and violent until the skirts were shorn from the two women. Berolina lost her temper and began screaming at the crowd to stop touching her. Paul eventually slammed the lid of the piano shut in protest as Berolina and Wally scrambled back up to the stage before fleeing to the safety of the dressing room. The rest of the girls took a muted bow and raced after them.

The silence had a sobering effect and gradually the masked customers reverted back to their normal behaviour as Ernst began his second routine of the evening. Leni squeezed through the crowd, pushing people out of her way until she reached Paul.

'What happened? Who was that man talking to you?' she demanded. Paul got up from his stool and grabbed Leni by the elbow, escorting her into the shadows at the side of the stage.

'Hush . . . keep your voice down.'

He loosened his grip on Leni's arm but as she put her hand up to stroke his face, Paul took hold of it. 'That man was another Red. They're looking for Otto. They say he stole money from them. It's the same men who came for me last night. They won't stop until they find him and they think I know where he is . . .' He dropped her hand and his shoulders sagged, his face crumpling in misery.

'Do you know where he is?' she whispered, not really wanting to know the answer.

'No. I thought he would have turned up by now. I don't know where he's gone and I wouldn't tell them even if I did. He's my brother after all. He's an idiot but he believes in his cause, in his revolution . . . If he took their money then it wasn't for himself.'

'Will they come back . . . for you?' The thought, once it had entered her head, took root and flourished. They wouldn't find Otto. He was long gone. But they would find poor gentle Paul sitting at his piano each night at the Babylon Circus, and they would hurt him if he didn't help them.

Paul shrugged. 'Probably. When the man asked if I'd heard from Otto, I told them he was away visiting family this week, but they aren't patient men. They'll know that I've lied to them.'

Leni felt a horrible sinking feeling. For months she'd been so happy and in love that she'd barely listened whenever Paul had mentioned Otto. He was just an inconvenience to her. She'd only cared if he was at his Sunday political meeting so that she could be alone with Paul. Now she saw how foolish she'd been. Otto could be in serious trouble and those men had already hurt Paul once. They would come back.

'What will you do?' Her voice sounded sharp, but she could hear the fear behind the question. She couldn't bear the thought of anything else happening to him. Paul put the palms of his hands either side of her face; the intensity of his gaze made her heart sink as she knew what he was about to say.

'I might have to leave Berlin.'

'Leave? But you can't . . .' Leni could feel tears stinging her eyes at the thought of losing him.

'I might have to. If Otto doesn't sort whatever this is out quickly, they could kill me, Leni. I won't be able to stay here.'

'There must be another way . . . There must be something . . .' She could hear her voice becoming wild and agitated.

'There isn't another way.' His eyes searched her face, pleading with her to understand. Leni threw herself into his arms. Behind them Ernst told his rotten jokes, picking out targets in the crowd, and the audience roared with dark laughter.

'You can't go. You can't leave me . . .' The thought of

going back to her life before Paul felt unbearable. What would she do without him?

'I don't want to . . . You could come with me?' Paul's voice was low and urgent now. His face darkened with fear.

'Me? I . . .' Leni couldn't find the words to explain how she felt. Could she go with him? Was that even a possibility? A thought of Annette quickly flickered through her mind but she dismissed it. There must be some way to make this work. She would never want something to happen to Paul but leaving Berlin, together . . . could they?

'Yes. There's nothing for us here. We could go together . . . Please say yes . . .' Paul's eyes lit up with the prospect of his new plan.

'Where would we go?' Leni felt a rush of excitement bubble up from deep inside her. She'd always dreamt of travelling the world, and now she had the chance to do it. She could be bold . . . she could do this. They could do this together.

'I don't know. Anywhere away from this place and those men . . . Spain, maybe? I know some people in Madrid who work in clubs there. They could find us work?' His voice was eager – desperate. 'What do you think?'

Leni could see the strain written on his face. The worry about his only brother and the fear that she would say no. Reaching out her hand, she stroked his face tenderly with her fingers. She weighed his words in her mind. Every part of her ached to say yes to him. Then something was released inside her and Leni knew she couldn't let this man go no matter what it cost her. She would do whatever was needed to keep them together.

Throwing her arms around his neck, Leni planted kisses

on his cheek and hugged him to her. Holding him so tightly, afraid of what might happen to them if she let him go.

'Yes . . .' she whispered.

'So, you'll come? You will?' Paul held on to her for a moment before standing back to look at her, kissing her hands one at a time as she beamed at him. 'I'll take care of you, I promise. My friends in Spain – they'll help us. We'll need to leave soon – probably in just a few days. If you agree we could speak to your family tomorrow . . . I want them to know that you'll be safe with me.'

As soon as Leni heard the words, a wave of reality flooded through her.

Running away was one thing. But how could she possibly tell Paul that they would have to take Annette with them?

27

Annette lay on the floor of Frau Vogel's apartment studying with some fascination a pair of wooden legs complete with black shoes that were painted on the feet. The wooden legs in question were propped against an armchair and slightly crossed so it seemed to Annette that an invisible woman was sitting there with only her wooden legs on display.

The legs belonged to their landlady, Frau Vogel, who had moved over to her kitchen table using a small wooden wagon with four red wheels, and now, having hoisted herself up on to a chair, was busy pouring coffee for Leni. The two women were speaking in hushed tones but Annette was content to let them have their silly secrets as long as her sister was where she could see her.

She stretched out her left arm and gently stroked the black shoes, before running her little fingers up the wooden ankle as far as the shin. There were stockings painted on to the legs that finished just below the knee. Annette tried to pinch the wood between her thumb and forefinger to make sure they weren't real.

Since they had moved into their new room, Leni had befriended the landlady, Frau Vogel, often running up and down the stairs to fetch things for her, while the old woman reciprocated by taking a daily interest in their welfare.

Frau Vogel was always nice to her, offering liquorice

sticks or other treats if she had them spare. Leni said she was probably lonely as her family lived a long way from Berlin and didn't come to visit, and lately, she had taken it upon herself to look after Annette while Leni went to work. Annette didn't mind this arrangement as, apart from her fascination with the wooden legs, Frau Vogel had a parrot she kept in a cage that could say 'Hello' and 'How are you today?' The parrot's name was Bruno after her late husband, as Frau Vogel said that he reminded her of him.

Annette yawned. Leni would be leaving soon for work and she would have to go to her own bed across the landing. Frau Vogel would leave her front door open so she could hear anyone coming up the stairs. From time to time, she would roll her legless body on its little wooden wagon across the landing and peek around their door to check that Annette was sleeping or at least tucked up in bed. She was sure that her sister had asked her to do this to make sure that Annette didn't turn up at the circus again looking for her.

Suddenly, the wooden legs toppled over, crashing to the ground and causing Leni and Frau Vogel to stop talking and check what she was doing. She wanted to pick the legs up to see if they were heavy or light. Giggling to herself as she imagined making them dance as if they were part of a puppet show. She must have laughed out loud because Leni frowned at her from across the room.

'Don't touch Frau Vogel's things, Nette,' she said harshly.

Frau Vogel chuckled and waved a hand in Annette's direction. 'Bring them here . . .'

Annette scrambled to her feet, gathering the little wooden legs in her arms and resisting the temptation to walk them across the floor, possibly making them dance at the same time. The old woman took them from her, pushing her fat pink stumps into the tops of the wood and strapping them in place. Annette watched her open-mouthed, wanting to ask questions but not wanting to get into trouble with her sister.

The two women went back to their coffee and gossip. Annette, deprived of her only entertainment and bored, crawled under the kitchen table to imagine herself in a dungeon, a princess who needed rescuing from a monster ... The drawl of the conversation made her sleepy; her eyelids felt heavy and she curled up on her side using her hands pressed against her cheek as a pillow. The two women laughed about something and then the sleepy drawl continued. Annette felt the heat from Frau Vogel's stove warming her back as she lay on the floor. Occasionally her eyes flickered open and the black shoes were shuffling and dancing a little under the table. She smiled.

'Oh, the little one is sleeping ... like an angel ...' Frau Vogel said. Annette thought about correcting her, but was too sleepy to open her eyes. Then Leni spoke.

'There was something that I wanted to ask you. Privately. But you mustn't say anything to Nette.' On hearing her name, Annette's eyes flickered open.

'Of course – you know you can ask me for anything, Leni. You two are like my own family now. I've grown very fond of you both.' Frau Vogel patted Leni's hand with her own.

'I have to leave Berlin for a little while. I was wondering if you could look after Annette for a few weeks ... maybe even a little longer, until I send for her. Once I have regular work again, then she can come straight away, but it would be better for her to stay here until I'm settled ...' Leni's voice dropped to a whisper although Annette could still hear her perfectly.

'I'll be sorry to lose you, but of course, the little one is welcome to stay here with me and Bruno. I'll be glad of the company. A woman has to make her own way in this world, Leni. You're not her mother. You're too young to be worrying about a child. Leave her with me.'

Annette's eyes opened wide and her mouth twisted into a grimace. This was why they were here in Frau Vogel's apartment. Not because she was some nice old lady who wanted to look after her, but because Leni was planning to leave her here. Her little mind raced to make sense of it, and then it hit her.

It must have something to do with *him*.

Annette knew now that his name was Paul, but as far as she was concerned, he was still the 'annoying man' to her. She hated him. Bad enough that he should take her sister away every Sunday afternoon, so that they never went to the park or the zoo to see the animals. She wished that Leni had never got the job at the circus, even if that had meant they'd have carried on sleeping amongst the wooden crates in the courtyard. At least they'd had each other. Now Leni was leaving her behind. Everyone that she'd ever loved would be gone. She thought of her mother and tried to remember her face, but it was no use. All she had left in the whole world was Leni. Leni couldn't leave her, not even for a little while.

An even darker thought grew like a weed in Annette's mind. It was all well and good that her sister said she would send for her. But suppose Leni didn't ever come back? *What would happen to her then?*

28

The following evening, the door to Dieter's office was tightly closed and nobody was allowed to go inside. He was not speaking to anyone, nor was anyone allowed to speak to him. The Babylon Circus was eerily quiet. The tables were mostly empty. One or two men sat alone sucking on large cigars and waiting to be entertained. Girls who expected to be paid handsomely for their services were standing around the dance floor with sullen faces while the little orchestra played. One or two of the women passed the time by dancing with each other but everyone seemed bored and listless.

There was no sign of Dieter, nor did he show any intention of appearing in the club that evening. The sad news of Herr Keks's demise had spread like wildfire through the dressing room with most of the girls expressing their sorrow.

Only Berolina with her loud raucous voice exclaimed, 'It's only a cat, for goodness' sake . . .'

Unfortunately for her, at that precise moment Dieter had taken it upon himself to visit the dressing room but upon hearing her words, he had scowled furiously, shouting, 'Raise all the prices by another mark, immediately,' before turning on his heel, and marching back to his office.

Berolina had even tried knocking to apologize, having

been persuaded that her job might depend on it, but Dieter had not opened the office door.

Leni was also in an anxious state, waiting for Paul to arrive for work. She had come in early, getting dressed and taking her place in the club with her cigarette tray as usual. Given that the place was mostly empty, with Dieter locked away in his office, Leni had taken the opportunity to keep popping outside to see if he had appeared.

The clock in the dressing room said he was late and with every minute that passed Leni began to imagine Paul lying in the street, beaten to death by the same thugs who had set upon him the other night. Now she'd spoken to Frau Vogel, she was desperate to know that he was all right and to tell him they could leave together. She would finally get to travel and see a different country. And she would be with Paul – but where was he?

Having driven herself to distraction to the point where even Irma had remarked on her coming and going, asking if she had an upset stomach, as if nothing else could explain the number of times that Leni put on her cigarette tray and took it off again.

Finally, just as Leni was pretending for the umpteenth time that she'd forgotten something in the dressing room, the street door opened and in walked Paul, looking weary but at least in one piece. Leni was on her way back into the club when she caught sight of him, and her thoughts immediately filled with relief that he was alive. She rushed to embrace him, feeling the chill of his winter coat under her hands as she held on to him.

'I was so worried – where have you been?' she cried.

'I had to take a different route.' He didn't say why and Leni knew better than to ask.

'I have to get back inside. I'll get into trouble.'

'Leni . . .' As she turned to walk away, Paul caught hold of her arm and gently pulled her towards the street door. 'I can't wait much longer . . . Those men will run out of patience if Otto doesn't come back soon. When I lied to them, I said he was due back this weekend. At the time I thought I was giving him a head start, not setting up trouble for us. But when I got home last night there were two men standing across the street. I didn't recognize them but I swear they were watching my building.

'I kept my room in darkness and tried to spy on them from the window but they didn't move. Just stood there staring up at my window. The week's nearly up – they'll pay me another visit soon, I'm sure of it. Did you speak to your family?'

'I told them – I explained everything. There's no need for you to do anything. We can go with their blessing.' Leni gabbled away her lies.

'I should speak to your father – it's the right thing to do. After all, once we're settled . . . well . . . he would want to know that we plan to get married . . . that's if you wanted to . . . ?' His voice was hesitant, shy, yet underpinned with a steely determination. He waited nervously for her to say something. They had never spoken of marriage – yet when Leni heard him say the words, she knew it was what she wanted. All her dreams were coming true. She would be with the man she loved. They would travel together . . . Somehow, she would make things work so that Annette could be with them.

'Maybe we could get married before we leave?' Leni heard Paul's words and felt a bittersweet joy that he should want to be with her. His face was so earnest and he was so keen to do all the right things – none of this was his fault. She imagined how proud her father would be – he would like Paul; she was sure of it. They would sit together by the fireside talking seriously while she waited with her mother in the kitchen. Then her father would summon her and give them his blessing. Leni felt the loss of him keenly. They would never have his blessing. She needed to tell Paul the truth – but to tell him the truth now would be to break his heart. To let him know that she wasn't the woman he believed her to be . . .

She loved him so much yet it was all moving too quickly – she hadn't even told Annette about leaving Berlin, and now time was running out. Her stupid lie had caused her nothing but trouble. Getting away was one thing, but eventually she would have to send for Nette and then what would happen? He loved her – she knew that – but taking on her six-year-old sister was surely too much to ask of him . . . yet what else could she do? And what would Annette say? How could she explain things to her?

'Married?' Leni felt a dull ache of worry about the situation they were in. 'But surely there will be time for all that later on. Maybe my family could come and visit when we have somewhere to live in Spain. If you suggest a marriage now my mother will want a wedding here and that will delay us . . .' She chattered on and on. The lies lying like ashes on her tongue. Her heart breaking a little as she spoke. 'We should go as soon as possible. We can think about everything else once we get settled.'

He would never know – she would make up an illness, a tragedy. It was the truth after all. Then she would send for Annette when they were settled and everything would be fine. She would bribe Nette not to say anything. Spain might be nice . . . Annette might like it there. There were oranges: she would tell her about the oranges.

'If you're sure . . .' Paul was studying her face intently.

'Quite sure. But when should we leave?' Leni's heart sounded a drumbeat inside her chest as a wave of panic flooded through her.

'Sunday. We'll meet at five o'clock outside here. There won't be anyone about at that time and it's only a short walk to the train at Friedrichstrasse. Is that all right? It will be better if we wait until it's getting dark, I think.'

Leni nodded and reached her hand out to stroke his face, pushing back the tiny strand of hair that always managed to escape to kiss his forehead.

'Oh, my love, you look so worried. Do you regret letting me walk you home that first night? I have caused you so much trouble . . .' Paul said softly.

'No! I want to be with you . . . whatever the cost.' That wasn't a lie. Leni felt the truth of it beating inside her, accompanying her heart's rhythm.

Paul leaned down and kissed her. She could still see his bruises. His poor face – his lovely face. She could not imagine a day without seeing this face. They would go to Spain. They would wake up next to each other every morning and fall asleep in each other's arms every night. She couldn't let him go to Spain without her. Frau Vogel was right; she was much too young to care for a child. She loved Annette but she also deserved a life of her own. She had to explain things to her sister and then later on, when they were settled, she would have to think of something to tell Paul. The future would work itself out.

But, at this moment, she needed to think of some way to make her leaving right with Nette . . .

29

Annette greeted the cup of steaming cocoa with a sullen glare. It arrived with a tablespoon of cream on top accompanied by a cup of coffee for Leni as the sisters sat either side of the small café table without saying a word to each other. She stuck a finger in the cream and then licked it off. The cocoa was too hot to drink quite yet but the cream tasted light and delicious.

Leni, opposite her, was staring blankly at the clock on the wall and barely touching her cup of coffee. After Annette had overheard her sister plotting to leave her behind with Frau Vogel, nothing had happened – until today, when she'd insisted on bringing her here. She dipped her little finger into the cream once again and then slurped it greedily into her mouth, all the while occasionally giving Leni a cold, sulky stare.

Her sister tapped the tiny spoon absent-mindedly against the coffee cup as she bit down on her bottom lip. Annette took an anxious breath and inspected her sister from under her eyelashes. Eventually Leni looked down and began to speak.

'Nette . . . I have something to tell you and you have to promise me that you will be very grown up. You're not a baby any more, and this is important.'

Annette swallowed hard. It was true, then. Leni was going to leave her behind with Frau Vogel. Her little face screwed up into a furious glare as her bottom lip began to tremble. She could feel sobs thicken her throat and then rage swirling around inside her belly and pushing up through her chest. A white-hot fury bursting out of her mouth as she yelled at Leni, 'You're going away with *that man*. You're leaving me . . .'

Annette eyed her sister angrily while the shock of her words had struck Leni dumb for a moment. Her mouth opened and her eyes grew wide.

'How did you know? Did Frau Vogel tell you?'

It pleased Annette to see that she had surprised Leni. For a moment she felt triumphant and her anger began to subside, crawling back down into her belly as she grew quiet. They stared at each other across the table. She didn't want her cocoa now – the cream was dissolving into lumpy puddles across the top of the cup. It had lost its delight for her and all she could think about was Leni leaving her behind. The anger had given her a brief moment of relief but now a series of mournful tears began to drip silently down her cheeks.

'I . . . I heard you talking . . . when you thought I was asleep. *Why are you leaving me?*' she stammered, her eyes turning into large, wet pools pleading with her sister.

Leni couldn't look at her – she had a guilty look on her face and kept taking furtive glances towards the clock on the wall. Eventually, as Annette's tears turned to racking sobs, Leni reached her hand across the table and said softly, 'I'm not leaving you. It's just for a little while, until I can find us somewhere to live – until I can get work. Then I'll send for you . . . I promise.'

Annette jerked her hand away but then suddenly felt the

remnants of her anger collapse inside her. All that was left was a deep, aching void of hurt. She had no one apart from Leni and now she was going away – maybe forever.

'But why? You've got a job and we've got somewhere to live . . . Why do you have to go away?' She sniffed sharply, wiping away her tears but her little red face was still screwed up in anguish.

'It's too complicated to explain, Nette. If there was another way, I would do it. Please don't make this difficult for me. It won't be for long, I swear.' Her sister's voice broke as she got up from her chair and moved around the table. Annette felt the weight of Leni's arms wrapping around her, and for a moment she wanted nothing more than to give in and allow her sister to hold her.

But an ugly thought floated to the surface of her mind. *It's that man. It's all his fault.* Annette struggled away from Leni, refusing to be held. Her little body was fierce and rigid. She wanted to drum her fists against her sister's chest and make her go back to how things used to be before *him*.

Leni moved closer to Annette again, and gathered her up. Stroking her hair, she whispered to her, 'Don't cry, Nette – please don't cry . . . I'll send for you as soon as I can.'

Annette felt a dam burst open inside her. The pain of losing her mother . . . and now Leni. She opened her mouth and wailed, 'NO . . . I don't want you to go. Don't leave me . . .'

'But Frau Vogel will take good care of you – and you have your friends in school now? You'll hardly miss me at all. And we'll be together again before you know it . . .' Annette felt Leni's arms tighten around her and she could see tears filling her sister's eyes now.

Still she couldn't stop sobbing – stuttering out her plead-ings: 'I don't have any friends in school. I only have *you*. I hate it there.' Her words came in shuddering bursts and then her little head fell on to her arms as she wept. Her chest heaving with misery as she gulped down tiny breaths.

She could hear Leni's voice cracking as she said, 'It won't be for long . . . Please, Nette . . .' Leni patted Annette's tiny hands to offer some reassurance, but she pulled away from her touch in a cold fury.

'It's that man, isn't it? You're going away with him and leaving me here . . .' Her body heaved with sobs. She would never forgive Leni for choosing that horrible man instead of her.

'He's a nice man, Nette, you'll see. We'll be together – all of us. We're going to Spain – imagine that. You can pick oranges off the trees in the streets. As many as you like . . .' Leni was trying to make it better but Annette wouldn't be consoled.

'But why do I have to stay here? I want to come with you!'

In truth, she had no wish to be either in Spain or any-where near that annoying man, but she was determined that Leni would not leave her behind. She could tell that her sister was softening and she fixed her with a watery gaze. 'Please, Leni, let me come with you.'

Her sister dabbed at her eyes, her face a picture of misery now. Annette kept on looking at her. 'Please . . . please . . .' she whispered.

Finally, Leni's face softened as tears splashed on to her cheeks, and she said:

'All right, Nette . . . I'll tell him that you have to come with us now.'

30

It was her final shift at the Babylon Circus. A curious sense of sadness came over her as she took off her black costume for the last time and hung her little gold top hat on its hook. She hadn't said a word about her plans to Dieter and the others. At times it felt as if she was carrying so many secrets that she couldn't stand it. Then there was the matter of work – Paul was sure to find something being a pianist but what would she do once they got to Spain? Leni began to worry, chewing over her limited choices. Of course, there was always the possibility that once Paul knew the truth about her family, he would no longer include her in his plans and she would be back at the Babylon Circus working away but without him.

The girls were all chattering as usual about their plans for Sunday trips to the cinema or family lunches, but she wasn't listening. Since Leni had promised Nette that she wouldn't leave her behind, she'd felt nothing but agony at the prospect of losing Paul. Now, having barely spoken a word to anyone all through her shift, she had to find a way to tell him the truth – and she had to do it tonight.

Leni bit down on her lip – deep inside she felt a turmoil of regret that she hadn't done it sooner. It was quite possible he would prefer to go alone and she wouldn't be able to blame him. Yet tell him she must, because leaving Nette behind just wasn't possible.

They'd been through so much together and the child was so young. Leni could see that she'd been selfish – thinking only of her future with Paul. She had to take her responsibility seriously and tell him everything so they could take Nette with them . . . The thought that he might choose to go without them once he knew the truth made Leni feel sick to her stomach but the sight of Annette sobbing so violently had broken her heart. She felt torn between the two people that she loved most in the whole world.

As she walked towards the street door, Leni turned to take a last look at the Babylon Circus. The mayhem of the dressing room with glittery costumes stuffed everywhere you looked. The smell of powders and perfumes. The cackling laughter of Berolina.

Taking a deep breath, she hurried towards where Paul was waiting, only to find that it was pelting down with rain. Gusts of wind rattled down the alleyway as raindrops bulleted off the concrete.

Paul took her hand and squeezed it gently. 'Not the night for a slow stroll home, I fear . . . Never mind, tomorrow we will be on our way to Spain and hopefully an end to this cold, damp weather.' He gave her a rueful look. Leni grimaced at the rain. She really needed time to speak to him but they would be soaked through if they stood around for too long in this weather.

'Paul, I need to talk to you about something,' she said softly.

Immediately his expression altered. 'You haven't changed your mind? Please tell me you haven't?' He looked so serious that she regretted beginning this conversation, lodged as they were in the doorway of the Babylon Circus.

'No . . . of course not. There's just something I need to talk to you about, before we leave . . .' Leni whispered, almost afraid to air the words.

'Then let's go to my room. We can be alone there – and talk properly.' He had that earnest look she loved so dearly and Leni couldn't help but nod her agreement.

She clung on to him as they raced through the streets, rain drilling into her face. With every step, she felt she was getting closer to the moment where everything might go wrong.

As soon as Leni and Paul reached his room, a strange, nervous silence fell over them. The thud of their footsteps on the stairs echoed through the stairwell. Even the sound of the key turning in the lock seemed too loud.

Once inside, he set about adding lumps of coal to the stove, trying to encourage some warmth into the room. Then he peeked out of the window, checking the street below. 'At least it's too wet for Otto's little friends this evening,' he said with some relief, drawing the thick curtains across the windows so that the room was lit only by the flames of the stove.

Leni stood in the doorway, dripping fat raindrops on to the floor. Her coat was soaked and her hair plastered to her face as she shivered violently.

'Look at you – you're freezing.' Paul came towards her and she buried her face in his shoulder, inhaling his faint tobacco smell, his earthy scent, the fresh perfumed tang of his hair cream – she loved these familiar aromas. Reaching up, she stroked his face with her fingertips until he kissed her, with the same fierceness that had taken her by surprise the first time.

'You should take off your wet things. I'll get you something dry to put on. Then you can tell me what it is that you're worried about.'

Leni was too cold and wet to protest. Her teeth were chattering as she pulled off her coat and dress, rolling her mud-splashed stockings down her bare legs and allowing Paul to hang her things around the stove.

'I have some brandy. That will warm you.' Paul reached into the cupboard, pulling out a dark bottle and two dusty glasses. He wiped them with his damp shirt and filled the glasses a third of the way up. She took a glass from him, her hands trembling with cold. Pulling the blanket from the bed, he wrapped it around her, rubbing her arms to stop her shaking. Leni took tiny sips of brandy, all the time watching the flickering coppery flames of the stove and wondering what she should say.

Out of the corner of her eye she could see that Paul had removed his own wet coat and shirt. She watched him – the outline of his muscles. The smoothness of his skin and the small patch of dark hair at the base of his stomach. The brandy rushed through her blood, making her flushed with warmth.

She could feel him standing just behind her, even though they were not touching. Leni wanted to touch him – wanted Paul to touch her. So many times, they had kissed in this very room, always knowing there would be an end to the kissing.

Even on those occasions where a button or two was undone and his mouth felt hot on her skin – even then, Leni had always known she would rebutton her dress and leave before anything could happen. It was unspoken between them, and Paul had never pushed her to stay, or go further than she wanted to.

Tonight felt like an ending of some kind. A new life awaited them – but what kind of a new life? He put a hand on her shoulder. His fingers splayed across her skin and she turned to face him. *Tell him now!* she told herself . . .

Yet the moment she turned and saw his face all she could do was reach for him. She didn't want to say anything. Just for now, she wanted to feel like this. For a moment, they stared at one another. Then Paul kissed her with such intensity that she felt light-headed.

They broke apart, and not a word was said, yet they separated and undressed – with their backs to the other. Leni folded her petticoat and placed it neatly on a chair. Her hair was still hanging damp around her face, yet her trembling had stopped.

When they were both left in only their undergarments, they slid quickly under the covers of the bed. If he'd breathed a word, the spell would have broken – Leni would have returned to everything that was troubling her. But he did not speak and neither did she.

They lay there pressed together, breathing softly and then the unwrapping began . . . Slowly and tenderly, Paul removed her underwear and then his own, until they lay on their sides gazing at each other. He reached out his arm and gathered her in to him once again. Leni felt his warmth wherever their skin touched. Their fingers entwined . . . their mouths hungry for each other.

Her hands caressed his shoulders, tracing his arms with her fingers, feeling the sharp bones of his hips under her touch. Then he kissed her with the same fierceness as before, pulling at her, exploring her as if she were a foreign land.

When he pressed himself inside her, she found herself crying. It was almost too much to be so loved. To have something so precious for herself. These things they were doing in the secret silence of his bed – she wished for them every day. She wanted to wake up next to Paul, reaching for him as they were both still half-asleep. Waking each other with their kisses. She wanted to crawl into his bed at night for these kisses to soothe her.

At that moment, she didn't care about life outside of this room and the stove with its coppery flames. When he pulled her towards him again, she couldn't tell her body from his any longer, or his pleasure from her own. She craved him like air.

As dawn broke, Leni stood by the door buttoning up her winter coat, her mind rehearsing the things that she needed to say – as her mouth opened and then closed again. She watched Paul fastening his shirt, telling herself that what they had done in those tangled sheets bound them together forever. Whatever she said to him now wouldn't matter because he loved her . . . and she loved him.

And yet Leni didn't speak, not even when he smiled up at her – his face so full of warmth that she could never leave him.

'Today is the beginning of our new life – just the two of us,' he whispered softly.

The words landed like blows: *just the two of us*. Oh, what could she do to make everything right? Leni felt a keen agony welling up inside her.

I am a liar, she wanted to say. Her mind methodically gifted her with the stories she had made up and presented to him as truth. How could he ever forgive her? They had been together for months and she had kept up the pretence.

She thought of Nette and how her sister had wept until her little body was exhausted – but still the truth wouldn't leave her mouth. Her lips quivered as tears prickled her eyes. She couldn't bear to lose him. She felt as if she were being torn apart having to choose and it was all her fault. If only she hadn't told such a stupid lie in the first place – and to let it go on so long that Paul would surely feel as if she'd made a fool of him.

Then he was standing right in front of her with such an anxious look on his face.

'What's wrong? Oh, don't cry – please don't be sorry. Here . . .' He offered her his handkerchief – a pale, blue square of cheap cotton and she dabbed at her eyes with it.

'I'm not sorry,' she managed to say. Yet even as she spoke, tears carried on falling down her cheeks.

'Leni, what is it? Tell me what's wrong?' He looked at her so tenderly that she thought her heart would break.

Now was the moment to tell him, she thought. But she said nothing.

As he wrapped his arms around her, she could hardly bear the thought of losing him. 'I'm only crying because . . . I . . . I love you so much.' she whispered, her voice barely audible.

'You would tell me if you'd changed your mind, wouldn't you?' His soft brown eyes fixed on her – searching her face for reassurance.

'I haven't changed my mind.' She smiled tearfully but he didn't seem persuaded.

'Then I'll meet you as we agreed – outside the Babylon Circus at five o'clock?' His voice was more urgent now – desperate that she go through with it.

'Yes . . . of course.' Leni tried to sound cheerful for his sake. 'Five o'clock.' Wiping away her tears, she kissed him gently on his lips. As she got to the door, she realized that she was still carrying his blue cotton handkerchief, 'Oh, you should take this,' she said tearfully.

'Keep it – I'll see you later on.' He smiled but his face contained such concern that Leni felt a sharp pain tearing at her insides. She had not told him the truth, and now she would have to leave Nette behind, which would break her sister's heart. It wouldn't be forever but how could she possibly explain that to her after she'd promised that she wouldn't leave her?

'I'll be there . . .' she said and then turned to walk away.

31

Annette picked at the wooden floor with her fingers, scratching her nails over the surface. She was sitting cross-legged, watching her sister folding her things neatly into a small bag. Leni closed the straps on the bag and then sat down on the edge of the bed they shared.

'Don't be cross with me . . . Come and kiss me and say goodbye properly.' She sighed, but Annette continued to sit stubbornly on the floor refusing to speak or even look at her.

'Nette, you know I have to go now. Please . . .'

Leni had crept into their little bed in the early-morning light, without saying a word or curling up with her arm around her as she usually did. Annette had known then that she was leaving her. As they lay side by side, she could hear Leni crying softly, until finally she'd fallen asleep. Annette didn't like it when her sister cried, but she really didn't want to be left behind.

When her sister woke up, she had started packing things in her little bag. And no matter how sweet Annette had tried to be, or how many tears she'd cried, Leni had carried on.

Annette scraped the top of a splinter of wood with her thumb and sighed. She'd tried everything she could think of to make Leni change her mind. Pointing out how old Frau Vogel was – at least fifty years old. Asking what would happen if she got sick . . .

Leni just gazed down at her with a sorrowful look on her face and repeated how they could think of it like a little vacation – counting the days until they would be re-united. Annette didn't want to count the days. Leni had promised her, and now she was letting her down. And all because of *him*.

She knew that Leni was upset and part of her wanted to crawl into her lap and throw her arms around her neck. Yet her rage wouldn't let her. It felt like a ferocious animal in her belly. It would claw at her sister if she came close to her. The little bag was packed now, and each strap tightly fastened.

'Come here, Nette . . .' Leni said softly, but she wouldn't. She couldn't go near her or the ferocious animal would escape from her insides. She wouldn't even look at her sister. Good riddance to her. If she didn't want to stay then Annette wouldn't beg her now. It was too late for that.

Leni stood up, and walked over to her. She would not say goodbye or allow herself to be held. If only that man hadn't come between them. If only her sister hadn't gone to work at the circus. The ferocious animal began to rage inside her.

Kneeling down, Leni planted a fat kiss on top of her head. 'It won't be for long, Nette. Won't you even hug me to say goodbye?'

Annette stubbornly picked away at the splinters on the floor and said nothing. She heard Leni sigh and she sounded so miserable that for a moment her rage began to fade a little, leaving behind a great well of sadness.

Annette shook her head defiantly and then watched from the corner of her eye as her sister reluctantly walked out of their door. Leni hesitated in the doorway. 'I'll write, Nette . . . as soon as I can. Goodbye. Be good for Frau Vogel.' She didn't look up but she could feel Leni's eyes on her. Then her sister was gone.

The moment Leni left the room, Annette could feel hot angry tears filling her eyes again. Her chin wobbled and she began to feel sorry for her stubbornness.

Just outside the door she could hear her sister talking to Frau Vogel on the landing, and then the sound of her footsteps going down the stairs. She was leaving her.

A horrible thought crossed her mind. Suppose Leni didn't come back and they never saw each other again? Suppose something happened to her? After all, her mother had gone out one day and never come home.

Annette couldn't bear it. She had to say goodbye. She scrambled to her feet and raced out of the door. As she got to the top of the stairs, she cried out, 'Wait . . . Leni!'

The moment that Leni heard her voice, she turned around on the stairs and her face lit up with delight. Annette watched as she put her bag down on the step, and stretched her arms wide for her to run into them. *Leni still loved her . . . she would never abandon her for good.* Annette clattered down the steps, wanting to be held tight. Leni would make it all right in the end. She always did.

One more step, and she would be safe in her sister's arms. The girl bounded on but just as she reached Leni, her little foot stumbled and she pitched forward. Screaming as her hands clutched at thin air, she grabbed out at anything to save herself tumbling down the stairs, before colliding with Leni.

Annette eventually came to a halt as she gripped hold of

the banister. The shock of her fall squeezed the air from her lungs as she lay there on the stairs, panting for breath.

Frau Vogel stood at the top of the stairs staring down at them. A horrified look on her face. Her mouth hanging open. 'My God . . .' she kept repeating over and over.

Everything seemed to be happening in slow motion and Annette couldn't make any sense of it until she finally lifted her head.

Looking down, she could see Leni's crumpled body lying beneath her in the stairwell.

32

Leni was propped against the stairwell surveying her leg, which was lying at a very strange angle to the rest of her body. She couldn't think properly and when thoughts did come, she felt dizzy. She couldn't stand up, and yet she couldn't stay here on the stairs. There was a lot of noise – screaming . . . yet it wasn't her. She closed her eyes and shook her head, trying to make sense of things. She was going somewhere . . . and then she wasn't. She couldn't feel her leg at all yet it shouldn't be bent like that. It was then Leni realized that she couldn't move her leg either.

Someone was shaking her arm now . . . her sister's face again, shouting words at her. Leni lay back against the wall and thought that she might be sick. Her head felt strange as if she couldn't keep any thoughts straight at all. Suddenly everything became clear and she gazed up to see Annette's terrified face bending over her.

'Leni! Leni . . . !' she was shouting.

'Hush now . . .' Her thoughts became less jumbled as she took in her bag on the step above her. She must have fallen over it. She was going somewhere; she had to meet someone. Paul!

Leni tried to pull herself up but the moment she moved the pain flooded through her, making her cry out in agony. She had to get up . . . he would be waiting for her. She tried to move again but it was hopeless. The pain was excruciating. There was no way that she would make it to the Babylon Circus. Paul would be waiting. What would he think if she didn't show up? He had no idea where she lived – he'd simply think she'd changed her mind. He'd leave without her.

Grasping hold of Annette's hand, Leni pulled her closer. 'Nette, you have to do something for me.'

'Yes?' Annette's voice was barely audible and the girl's face white with shock.

'You have to go to the Babylon Circus and tell Paul what happened. Tell him to wait for me. Please. It's important. Can you remember the way there?'

Her sister nodded her head. 'I think so.'

'Promise me you'll go straight there and you'll tell him what's happened?' Leni squeezed Annette's hand so tightly that the child grimaced. 'Go – quickly. Frau Vogel will get help for me.'

'You won't die, will you, Leni?' Annette began to snivel into her sleeve again as her tears flowed down her cheeks.

'Silly goose . . . I'm not going to die. I've just hurt my leg. Now run and tell Paul.' Leni looked into her sister's eyes. 'Listen, Nette, this is important. Tell him not to leave without me. Tell him to wait. Promise me.'

'I promise . . .' Annette whispered.

Annette ran as hard as she could and when she couldn't run any longer, she walked as fast as her legs would carry her until she finally reached Friedrichstrasse. It took her a little while to find the sign for the circus again as she kept getting confused, but then she saw the bright blue door at the front and set about walking around the building to the alleyway until she saw Paul standing next to a battered old suitcase by the street door.

The annoying man walked towards her, leaving his suitcase on the ground by the door.

'Where is she?' His face looked puzzled and Annette tried to think of what she was supposed to say, but all Leni had said was to tell him what had happened. She tried to work it out but the image of seeing her sister lying at the bottom of the stairs made her feel upset again.

'Has something happened?' the man called out.

'Leni's not coming . . .' she shouted at the top of her voice, not wishing to get too close to him. The annoying man edged forwards so she took a step backwards. He looked sad and Annette tried to remember what she had to say.

A tiny flame of fury whirled inside her chest. The ferocious animal began clawing at her insides. This man had ruined everything. It was all his fault, so he *should* be sad. Leni was her sister – he wanted to take her away, and now she'd fallen and hurt herself. Annette remembered: she was supposed to tell him not to leave without Leni. To wait for her.

After weighing it all up for a long moment, Annette jutted her little chin out, quite determined, and said, 'She said that you should go without her.'

Once the words were out of her mouth, the child hesitated to see what the annoying man might do. A guilty shame flushed over her, and a spark of terror at what she had just said.

'Did she send you to tell me that?' His voice cracked as he spoke and Annette felt a pang of regret, chewing on her bottom lip while she decided what to do next. Would she get into trouble? She didn't care.

He moved towards her – kneeling beside her, with his hand on her arm. 'Is that all she said?' he asked.

She stared right into his eyes. And he stared at her – a strange, pleading look that made her feel funny. A peculiar sick feeling rose from her belly. But she wanted to stay with Leni. He had no right to take her sister away. Pursing her lips, she scowled at him and took a deep breath.

'Yes. She doesn't want to go with you. You must leave without her. That was all she said.'

His hand released her arm. Annette turned on her heel, and ran all the way home.

PART TWO

Berlin, June 1947

33

'Well . . .' Berolina said to no one in particular, as there was nobody else there. Pursing her lips, she stepped further into the Babylon Circus and began to survey the damage. Twirling the key around her finger, she silently cursed at the number of things that needed fixing.

The stage had collapsed to one side, while the dance floor was full of shattered glass from the broken mirrors. The whole place had been locked up for so long that it smelled damp and musty. In the distance, she could hear the faint scratching of rats in the walls.

Berolina made a list in her head of things that would need doing.

Stage – unusable. Then we won't have performers, she thought, removing the idea from her imaginary list. Just a dance floor will do.

The chandelier was missing and a thick rope-like cord hung down from the ceiling with its frayed end curling miserably. Fine – they would have oil lamps or candles.

The tables were all gone – taken for firewood probably, along with the piano. She sucked her teeth and pulled a face . . . then people will just have to stand. And that would mean more of them could get on to the dance floor, which in turn meant more money for her.

The walls were bare – stripped of all their silver and gold finery. A coat of paint would fix them. She knew some willing helpers . . . and a Russian major who might be useful to her in terms of getting permits and supplies.

Berolina's war had been difficult. Age had not been kind to her once she could no longer perform as she used to. When the Babylon Circus closed down, she'd moved in with her sister Clara, finding work where she could. It was a hand-to-mouth existence, and for the first time in her life she'd found herself struggling to make money.

Berolina had never felt 'shame' before – she'd taken off her clothes and on occasion entertained clients in the basement rooms of the Babylon Circus doing whatever they'd asked of her without question. It was only once her other sources of income had dried up that she discovered the true meaning of the word. In the winter of 1942, she had resorted to selling gossip and other information to the authorities. Some weeks she had nothing to sell and so she had made things up – stories of betrayal, or meetings that had never taken place. She was paid handsomely but the consequences of her endeavours became increasingly hard to live with. People were rounded up in sleek black cars by men in dark hats and long coats.

Berolina pushed it all to the back of her mind. She'd done what she'd needed to do to survive. No different from anyone else. And yet the stink of it surrounded her whatever she did these days, filling her thoughts and giving her nightmares as all those innocent people lined up in her dreams to accuse her.

Once the war ended, she had firmly attached herself to the first high-ranking officer she'd come across – a Russian major called Mikhail – providing him with both information and nightly comfort. Since then, things had improved.

And then one day Berolina had walked past the Babylon Circus; eyeing the crumbling walls strewn with bullet holes, she'd thought of a plan to secure her future.

'There is always a way . . .' Berolina muttered to herself as she stood in the centre of the dance floor, crunching broken glass underfoot, thinking of the nights that she'd spent up on that stage with the girls she'd known so well.

She knew where Wally was living, but as for the others – they had scattered in all directions. Poor Greta had died in one of the camps, she'd heard . . . Berolina remembered her dancing in her little half-moon hat with her skin painted inky blue as if it was yesterday. Her footsteps echoed across the dance floor as the memories came flooding back to her. The old songs . . . the dance routines . . . the costumes.

She wondered about Dieter and where he was now. He'd simply disappeared two nights before the Babylon Circus had been closed down by the Nazis. Nobody knew what had happened to him but furious rumours swept through the city. That he'd been arrested – and killed. That he'd bribed some official and managed to escape to London. Truth was, nobody knew if Dieter was alive or dead. The city was full of stories without neat endings. Some people with rather complicated lives were not unhappy about disappearing into the chaos of post-war Berlin. The others . . . well, Berolina didn't want to think about them, especially the ones she was responsible for sending to their fate.

As she reached the cloakroom, Berolina was surprised to find that one of Dieter's old fairground mirrors was still hanging on the wall, in its beautiful silver frame. Stepping in front of it, she watched herself become transformed into a strange misshapen creature – short and round with a peculiarly long face, her eyes popping out of her head.

'Hah . . . what a beauty!' she said to herself.

Maybe the mirror might provide some amusement for her customers if she could ever get this place reopened. Yes . . . she would hang it up by the dance floor.

Taking a last look around, Berolina gave a soft whistle at the amount of work that needed doing. And then she nodded in agreement with herself.

She was going to reopen the Babylon Circus. And this time, she would be in charge.

Berlin, August 1947

34

Annette was going out dancing in a dead woman's dress. She had never met the woman in question, but when Marta had sneaked her into the remains of a bombed-out house to show her the treasure she'd found, Annette had grabbed the chocolate-coloured crêpe silk dress in one hand, and an old fox-fur stole in the other. Now, as she slipped the dress over her head, all she could think about was dancing the night away.

For the next few hours, she could have fun without anyone to bother her or tell her off. Sweeping her fair hair back off her face, Annette pinched her cheeks a little. Sticking a hairgrip behind her ear, she allowed her hair to fall tantalizingly over one side of her face. She liked to look mysterious – maybe with a touch of Dietrich. Annette didn't have the kind of face that seemed mysterious though. Her blue eyes were too wide and open for that. She was pretty – but definitely not mysterious.

Just as she was pinning her hair, there was a sudden snap and the electricity went off. Through the bedroom door she could hear Thea's familiar hungry wail. Annette sighed but carried on fixing hairgrips to her curls, even though she could barely see her own reflection in the little mirror hanging on the wall. The child's cry became louder and more urgent as she added a dab from her ancient pot of rouge to her cheeks and lips, smacking her bottom and top lip together for effect.

When she was quite satisfied, Annette sat down on her single bed and cast a miserable glance over their tiny bedroom. The plaster was crumbling off the walls and a monstrous crack had appeared across the ceiling. The entire house had been badly damaged by the bombing but as it had retained some intact rooms it was deemed inhabitable. With barely enough space for two single beds and a makeshift crib on the floor, they'd been effectively billeted in a house that was falling apart, sharing with at least four other families at any one time, including the awful Hildegard Knopf and her mother. Annette thought back to the lovely bedroom she'd had all to herself in Leni and Karl's house – until a bomb had turned it to dust. Her rose-coloured bedspread and matching curtains. The polished wood closet filled with her nice dresses. All gone. Now she was stuck here. And Annette hated everything about it.

There was another apartment upstairs with two other families sharing and an old lady who lived downstairs even though half of her apartment was open to the elements, having lost the outside wall completely. Annette found it peculiar that they all had keys to the front door when you could just walk into the building through the gaping hole at the rear of the house. It was as normal as anything else these days.

She was glad that she was going out dancing tonight. At least she didn't have to sit in her tiny room all night eyeing that crack in the ceiling – although sitting in the kitchen with Hildegard Knopf and her family was a much worse option. Annette felt increasingly sorry for herself. What had she ever done to deserve this life? And there seemed to be no way out of it for her.

Suddenly the door to the bedroom flew open and Leni stood in the doorway with a furious scowl on her face and Thea nestling into her shoulder. The child was just eighteen months old with a shock of curly hair and eyes so dark they were almost black. Annette grimaced at the sight of them.

'We've gone over the power ration again. The man's just been to check. We'll have to use less. The Knopfs are complaining that it's our fault – that we use too much. Did you bathe in hot water again?' Leni said. 'You can't keep doing this, Nette.'

'I used an inch or two at most. I have to bathe sometimes. Just light the candle.'

Leni carefully placed Thea in the makeshift crib by the side of her bed and searched around on the bedside table to find the matches. Striking the little orange flame, she proceeded to light a stump of candlewax that sat in a saucer.

A glimmer of light cast gloomy shadows around their bedroom. Leni sat down wearily on her bed before making sure that Thea was settled next to her. Her sister began cooing over the child. Singing little songs, pulling silly faces to amuse her until Annette couldn't bear to listen to it any more. She got up and began smoothing out the wrinkles in her new silk dress.

'Where did you get that?' Her sister was getting that tone in her voice which Annette hated.

'I found it,' she replied defiantly as Leni gave her another sour, questioning look.

'I suppose you're going out again tonight? Don't you care what people say about you?' Just as Leni spoke, a hungry cry filled the air. 'Well, aren't you going to see to her?'

'No. I'm going to meet Marta and we're going to Clärchens Ballroom, if you must know. And if by people you mean the Knopfs, then no, I don't care at all . . .'

Thea's cries grew louder until they became a frustrated roar, her face turning red as her little fists clenched in fury. Before Leni could say another word, the sound of a broom handle rapped hard on their bedroom wall and Frau Knopf yelled, 'Your baby is crying!'

'Yes, thank you, Frau Knopf,' Leni called back to her before rolling her eyes at Annette and hissing, 'I'll see to her . . . but, Nette, you have to look after Thea. She's your daughter . . . I have enough to do around here. I spend half my day in a bread queue as it is, plus I have to work.'

Annette carried on smoothing out the wrinkles in the chocolate-coloured dress before slipping her feet into her worn-out shoes. She was going dancing, and if Leni was lucky, she would bring home cigarettes that they could trade for flour and sugar. Maybe other things too. Her sister would soon stop complaining if she got some extra food, or even chocolate.

'Don't wait up,' she snapped. Then, picking up her handbag, she walked out of their bedroom and down the hallway to the front door. These rooms must have been cherished at some point. The elaborate wood carvings on the walls and the thick velvet curtains all spoke of quality and comfort. Now, you could never be alone. Someone was always watching what you did, and she was desperate to escape from it.

As she opened the apartment door, she could hear Leni singing in the soft sweet voice that she reserved for the child. Whenever her sister spoke to her these days it was always harshly. She had developed a kind of rigid stoicism which demanded that everyone around her keep to the rules. Annette never saw her sister cry or look miserable. Leni simply got up every morning and did things. She never stopped moving until she fell into her bed exhausted at night. The sight of Annette not doing things usually brought on yet another lecture. Very occasionally, Annette wondered if Leni still thought about that man, Paul – and what might have become of them if she hadn't fallen down the stairs that day. But mostly Annette didn't want to think too much about whether her sister was happy.

She sighed and then scowled as she caught sight of Hildegard Knopf coming up the stairs.

'Good evening, Annette,' the young woman said, without a hint of a smile on her lips.

'Good evening, Hilde,' Annette replied and breezed past her, rattling down the stairs as fast as she could go so there was no chance of a conversation. She had not changed her opinion of Hildegard Knopf since they were in school together and, in general, she disliked the entire Knopf family, since they were always complaining about her. If it wasn't the noise she made, or the child made, then it was the amount of electricity they used . . . It had been two long years, and there was no end in sight because there was nowhere else to go.

Annette had hated the war, but she found the peace in some ways worse. Being told where she could sleep, what she could eat and how to live her life. The one thing that made her happy was the prospect of going out with her best friend Marta. It was the only time she didn't feel haunted by the waste of her youth and everything that had happened. Dancing so hard she forgot her troubles, and if they found some stupid men willing to part with their cigarettes or rations – all the better. Life was divided up into 'haves' and 'have nots' these days. Being on the right side of that line was the only thing that mattered.

She pulled open the thick wooden front door before slamming it shut in an act of deliberate defiance, even though chunks of plaster fell off the walls every time she did it.

Once she was out of the house and away from the tedious nagging of Leni and the moaning of the Knopf family, Annette paused for a moment and exhaled.

Standing on the pavement, she gazed at the devastation surrounding her. She had lived in this part of Berlin since she was a child, first with her mother and father, then with Leni sheltering under wooden crates in the old courtyard, and afterwards with Frau Vogel. Then Leni had married Karl and they'd moved into his neat little house over on Zimmerstrasse where Annette had been allowed to pick the colours for her very own bedroom. For a long time, she'd loved having both Leni and Karl to look after her.

Then the war had come, and they'd lost everything . . .

Annette shivered at the thought of it. She hated to think about the past. There was only the future now – whatever that might be.

It was easier to forget what had happened to them all when she was inside the apartment, but outside on the street, all she could see were shattered buildings. Jagged broken structures with hollow rooms. Piles of rubble instead of houses and cafés – and just around the corner, the burnt-out remains of the bakery the Knopfs had run for so many years. It was all gone. Some streets were completely missing—an ocean of space where once there had been bustling shops and apartments replaced by the lonely rumble of a tramcar and the shrill ring of bicycle bells as people tried to get from one part of this broken city to the other. The streets had been blasted to dust and the people left to pick up the pieces. Everything she'd ever known was destroyed.

She lived in a city of broken things now. Annette took a deep breath and straightened her shoulders – she was not going to be one of them . . .

35

Outside Clärchens Ballroom, Annette could see the tall, gangly figure of Marta already waiting for her. As she approached, her friend's face lit up and she gave her a broad smile.

'That dress fits you so well. The dead woman must have been the exact same size!' Marta threaded her arm through Annette's and pulled her towards the doors of the ballroom. Annette didn't want to be reminded of the woman who had once gone dancing in the chocolate-coloured silk dress. Besides, it was hers now.

The ballroom was a large, high-ceilinged room with a chandelier hanging down from a thick cord and a crown of little lightbulbs casting their glow. There were two square windows and dark wood panelling on the walls.

Moments later they were dancing together, all the time searching around for possibilities. There were very few men there tonight and no soldiers at all. They were surrounded by women of about the same age or younger – all practising their dance steps with each other. Annette grew impatient. After an hour of dancing, she'd only had one dance that wasn't with Marta, and gained precisely zero cigarettes. It was a waste of a night out.

'Let's go somewhere else. There's nobody interesting here.' Her smiling request hid a petulant tone but Marta readily agreed.

'All right, but it will probably get busy just as we go somewhere else and then some other girl will have all your cigarettes for the night.' The two girls giggled and squeezed past the other bored groups of women to head back out on to the street.

'Where shall we go?' Annette pleaded with her friend. 'I'll be in such a bad temper if this evening is ruined. I want to have fun. I had to argue with Leni to get here and it will be too much if it's a dead loss.' Marta was used to her little ways and they walked for a while arm in arm, with the girl making sympathetic noises. Annette wouldn't be consoled. 'Come on, you know everywhere in this city . . . there must be somewhere we haven't already tried.'

Marta frowned, a tiny crinkle appearing between her eyes, and then she stopped in the middle of the street, 'I know – they've just reopened that old nightclub over on Jägerstrasse, the Babylon Circus. It's a dance hall now. Let's go there!'

Annette grew quiet at the mention of the Babylon Circus. An uncomfortable memory shifted at the back of her mind but she shrugged it away.

'Isn't there anywhere else we can go?'

'We could try the American camp. They might be holding a dance . . . Otherwise, we'll be having a quiet night,' Marta suggested.

'No, I don't want to go all the way out there.' Her lips formed a small pout as she tried to find a solution. Annette loved her friend and asked nothing from her except that she would be up for anything that might be fun. They had been starved of fun all through their best years.

She had only been nineteen years old when the war had

started. Instead of having fun, meeting nice boys and having a beautiful wedding, she'd been hiding from bombs. Now here she was, eight years older, with nothing to show for it. All her best years used up and thrown away.

Annette was tired of being hungry, she was tired of living with the Knopfs and she was tired of not having any nice young men to take her dancing. She wanted to get away and begin again – a fresh start somewhere else – but there was fat chance of it happening while she was stuck in this city of rubble.

Marta grinned at her, trying to cheer her up. 'Well, what do you say?'

'Let's go to the Babylon Circus. But it had better be fun.'

36

Leni lay back on her bed with Thea on her lap. The little girl babbled away, grabbing handfuls of Leni's hair and then shrieking with laughter. Leni loved the warm heft of Thea's little body against her chest. The smell of her, the softness of her skin, the tiny miracles of her toes. She kissed the pale half-moons of her fingernails one at a time, which made the child giggle. But as the stump of the candle spat wax, Leni glanced across the room at Annette's unmade bed and felt a surge of bitterness.

Every day her eyes opened and she was immediately alert, worrying about something, her anxiety ticking away inside her like a clock. Mornings brought a deep restless panic so strong that often Leni would have to lock herself inside the bathroom until the feeling passed. She found herself worrying over potatoes or the matchbook-sized pieces of meat which were all she had to feed them with. Lining up for hours to come home with a rock-hard loaf of bread that tasted like acorns. Their rations were impossible to survive on and the black market expensive to navigate. There was very little left to sell these days. The men who hung around on Potsdamer Platz had taken everything of any value over the last two years, offering them small amounts of marks and gathering up their precious memories. About the only thing she had left now was her gold wedding ring and it wouldn't be too much longer before that went the same way.

She made endless lists in her head of things to do — today and the day after . . . The lists made her feel better, as if she were in control of her own destiny. She got up. She dressed. She found ways to stretch the food into meals for them. She went to work and came home again. She was reliable. She looked after them all. Leni would not break . . .

Wrapping the child up in her blanket, she began making up tales of little girls who became magical princesses or slept for one hundred years. There was always a happy ending for Thea although she was too young to understand it. Eventually the child's eyes flickered and gently closed. The sound of her breathing made Leni feel instantly calmer as she laid the child down in the makeshift crib which had once been a large drawer. She loved watching the little girl sleeping peacefully. It gave her a reason to get out of bed in the morning. She was determined to make a future for this child even if her own mother would not. As her reward she asked only for a bright gurgling smile at the start of a brand-new day.

In the beginning, the crib had been beside Annette's bed, but night after night, as the child began her plaintive wail, her sister would ignore it. Fearing the wrath of the Knopf family, Leni had taken it upon herself to move the crib across the room, so that she could reach down and take the baby into her bed, comforting her cries with a finger to suck on. The child melted her heart and allowed Leni to ignore the dust and rubble of her city. When she went out she thought only of what they needed to carry on living for Thea.

She couldn't understand why Annette didn't seem interested in her own daughter. She was the sweetest little girl, and yet Nette left everything to her. Whoever the father of the child was, he'd disappeared. Another soldier no doubt . . . her sister couldn't stay away from them.

The war had changed Annette – she'd grown harder. Maybe they both had.

Leni tucked her feet under her and tried to see out of the bedroom window. It was a cloudy, moonless night and she felt her loneliness keenly. On the table by the bed was a photograph taken on her wedding day in 1928. A look of quiet resignation on her face; a pretty dress and flowers. She'd been twenty-one years old, which was considered to be the perfect age for a bride. At her side was Karl, wearing the same grey serge suit that he wore for his job as a banking official, his square jaw and elegant nose looking somewhat at odds with his thinning hair and mournful eyes.

She didn't know if he was alive or dead now. Did she want him to come back?

It was a question she couldn't answer. The memories of him . . . wearing his long underwear at all times even in the heat of summer. Rolling on top of her in a hurry to dispense his dry, papery kisses on her cheeks. Rarely did he kiss her on her mouth. His hand searching in his underwear for his soft white penis, followed by the agonizing wait for the moment that she would be required to surrender. Leni was not allowed to touch him, to aid his conquest in any way. She was a bystander in his brief moment of pleasure.

Karl wasn't brave. He had only gone to war because in the end they had sent everyone. He went missing after a battle. There was a chance he was in a prisoner-of-war camp, but it had been two years since the war had ended and there was still no word. She lived inside a no-man's-land – neither married nor free to do as she pleased.

She'd never loved him: it was a marriage of convenience for both of them in many ways. She couldn't imagine that he was dead, though. Some nights Leni wondered if in fact it was not she who had gone missing.

As Thea gurgled peacefully in her sleep, Leni quietly opened the drawer of her bedside table, hesitating, as if she didn't want to go any further. But she couldn't stop herself.

Underneath her official documents and personal papers, tucked away at the back of the drawer, there was a faded blue handkerchief folded neatly into quarters. Reaching for it, she pressed it to her face as if his fingerprints might still be present. She'd meant to throw it away so many times, yet she couldn't bring herself to do it. It was her only memento of the last time she'd seen him.

This had become her nightly routine. Leni wasn't altogether sure if she was trying to find traces of Paul or the girl who'd once cried into it.

Last night she'd dreamt about him again. She had never once dreamt about Karl. Her dreams were becoming more vivid, and passionate. She was being kissed with that old fierceness. She knew it was Paul who was kissing her but she couldn't see his face clearly. The feelings that haunted her at night departed the moment she awoke, leaving her with a strange numbness and confusion.

When she tried to remember the intimate details of his face and his body, she couldn't picture him. She had loved him so much . . . but she no longer felt love. Leni no longer felt much of anything, except when she held Thea in her arms. Only then did she experience a small flicker of delight – a warmth spreading through her. A joy at seeing that beautiful little face with its serious black eyes. Thea brought her such comfort, although part of that comfort was the fact that she *could* still feel something.

Leni folded up the blue handkerchief and pushed it to the back of the drawer. She was a different person now. What had happened to the girl who wanted to travel the world and loved someone so much that she was willing to give up everything for him? Part of her had died the day she'd discovered that he hadn't waited.

At first Leni had not believed it. *He wouldn't leave without her.* Yet Nette had sworn that Paul wasn't there and he had never tried to contact her. At first, she'd worried that those men had caught up with him, but when she was finally able to go out searching his neighbour had confirmed that he'd packed his suitcase and left Berlin. She had believed for a long time that he would come back for her. Waiting like a child for some sign. But he didn't come back. And so, she married the first man who asked her.

Leni's heart was not broken – people say they are broken-hearted, but her heart was still beating strongly in her chest. She could feel its rhythm. It could not be broken if it was working as normal. She had survived. Married Karl so she would always have a roof over her head and enough food on her table. Mainly, Leni had married him so she could provide for Nette, and he was good to them both. Caring for her little sister as if she were his own child. Taking her to Rausch's to buy her pralines and being endlessly generous if Annette needed something. He was a kind man and she had taken to married life, busying herself with tasks and lists of things to be done.

No, Leni's heart was not broken – she just could barely feel anything at all.

37

'You wanna dance?' The American was tall, not really handsome but had an open, friendly face. Annette inspected her catch for the evening: hazel eyes; strawberry-blond hair that was slickly parted on the side. His face was peppered with large brown freckles and when he smiled at her she could see that he had very large white teeth with tiny gaps between them as if each tooth had been individually placed.

Annette turned on her most dazzling smile. 'Yes, thank you . . .' Her English was becoming well practised with a basic but free-flowing vocabulary that suggested her willingness to dance, to accept cigarettes and smoke them later and to be generally amenable to acts of friendship. She disliked hanging around with American soldiers but there were few other choices this evening. Besides, they had things that she needed . . . and all she had to do was smile and flirt to get them.

Marta had disappeared into the crowd with one of his friends. There were only three American soldiers in the Babylon Circus and they had their pick of Berlin girls to dance with this evening. Annette was surprised to find them there as they were in the Russian sector, but occasionally soldiers would cross over to see what pickings were available elsewhere. She clenched her teeth and tried to look as if she was having a wonderful time. They liked her better if they thought she was grateful.

The music changed to a ballad, sung by a young woman who posed shyly in front of a small orchestra in the corner of the room. She gazed out at the dance floor, which took up the rest of the space. There were no chairs or tables to sit at and people stood around the sides of the floor when they weren't actually dancing, chatting or making eyes at someone they hoped to dance with. As usual it was mostly women, waiting or shuffling around the dance floor together. On the wall was a large mirror in a silver frame and Annette was amused to find it was one of those old fairground mirrors that made everyone look strangely distorted. She eyed her own reflection – her wide popping eyes and tiny legs – and giggled to herself. Everyone looked so very odd that she couldn't help but laugh. For a brief moment Annette wondered if Leni had ever stood there looking at herself in the strange mirror and giggling. She couldn't imagine her sister doing such a thing.

When the three Americans had found their way inside the club, there had been a flurry of anticipation. Annette had checked her face in her compact mirror and deliberately refused to make eye contact with the soldiers until they were standing next to her: begrudging them her company but at the same time needing spare cigarettes or extra rations desperately. She hated this game – and herself for playing it.

'Shall we . . . ?' the soldier asked as the music changed to a slow ballad, waiting until Annette nodded before placing his arm gently around her waist and clutching at her hand with his fingers. Pressed against him, she could smell the waft of his cologne, the fresh soap smell of his skin, the hint of mint on his breath . . . he was so very clean and perfumed. Muscular under his uniform, well fed and exceedingly polite in everything he did. Asking her permission to dance, to hold her closer, and paying her compliments over the dead woman's silk dress.

'You like dancing?' he said softly in her ear.

'Yes, I go dancing most nights . . . for a long time there was no dancing here but now there is . . .'

'What's your name?' His lips were almost touching the tips of her ears as he spoke and Annette nestled slightly into his neck, knowing that's what he wanted.

'Annette . . . Annette Taube.' She stood back for a moment to smile up at him and then let him pull her closer.

'I'm Glenn Forester Junior. Nice to meet you, Annie.'

Annette was not sure how she felt about being called Annie but she said nothing. She could be Annie if that's what was required of her.

The song ended and they walked arm in arm back to where Marta and the other two Americans were standing. One of the men had bright red hair, like flames on top of his head. He kept up a stream of chatter, most of which they couldn't understand as he spoke too fast for them. Glenn put his hand over hers, which meant that she was unable to remove her arm. She felt trapped, which she didn't like. He nodded towards the red-haired man. 'This is Gene and this guy here is Bennie.' Bennie had slung a casual arm around Marta's shoulders – stretching up awkwardly as she was much taller than he was.

'Would you girls like a smoke?' Glenn released Annette's arm and pulled a crumpled pack of Lucky Strikes out of his jacket pocket. She carefully took a cigarette out of his packet and slipped it into her purse for later. He didn't seem surprised, which told Annette that she wasn't the first Berlin girl he'd offered his cigarettes to. Marta copied Annette, allowing herself to bend slightly, so that Bennie could hold her more closely. The two women exchanged a look between them. These men would have to do . . .

The red-haired man, whose name Annette had already forgotten, wandered off, spying a small blonde that he soon whisked on to the dance floor, swinging her around and around as if she were a doll.

'Oh, I love this song. Let's dance, please . . .' Annette smiled sweetly and Glenn took her arm straight away, leading her back to the dance floor. This time she allowed herself to be held so tightly that she could barely breathe. His hand on her back pressed her body against his and his fingers clasped around hers. She sighed . . . there was no escape now, only the matter of what she could get out of him for her trouble.

Over his shoulder, she could see a woman that she recognized from somewhere. Annette couldn't place her immediately: a stern-faced woman in her fifties with greying hair swept back in a bun. She was wearing a bright red velvet dress and watching everyone from the edge of the dance floor. A memory floated up to the surface of her mind – the night that she'd come to the Babylon Circus, waiting for Leni to finish work, and this woman had given her an orange. Annette stared at her to make sure: the woman was older, but she was sure that it was the same person. The woman's eyes flickered over her and then a grimace appeared on her face as she looked at the American disapprovingly.

Annette didn't care what she thought. She was doing what she needed to do.

Glenn's fingers splayed across her waist. 'Do you live around here?'

'No, but it's not too far away.' She smiled eagerly, knowing that all he wanted was to be alone with her. And she would need a lot more than one cigarette for her effort . . .

38

'Annette, wake up . . . WAKE UP!' Leni shouted at the top of her voice. She didn't care if the Knopfs could hear her. Her sister was sprawled face down on top of her single bed, still wearing the chocolate-coloured dress. Her arm hung down the side of the bed with her fingertips almost touching the floor, while her fair hair was strewn across the pillow that her face was buried in. There was no sign of life.

Leni shook Annette violently by her shoulder until she finally stirred, pushing her hair out of her eyes in a way that reminded Leni of when she was a child.

'Come on, sleepy head. Thea needs feeding and I need to get to work.' Her sister groaned and gradually sat up, swinging her legs over the side of the bed so that both feet were firmly planted on the floor.

'Can't you feed her?' she muttered as Leni thrust the bawling child on to Annette's lap. 'Wait a minute . . .' Leaning across, she reached down into her handbag. Scrabbling around inside it for a few seconds, she proudly retrieved three cigarettes. 'There you are . . . see what you can get for them.'

Leni placed the cigarettes carefully in her pocket. It would be an enormous help to get a little extra but she couldn't stop herself from being sour. 'What did you have to do for them?' she asked suspiciously.

'Nothing. Not *that*. I was just dancing and then he drove me back to my front door. We may have stopped off once or twice on the way . . .' Annette grinned. Her face looked rather smug and Leni felt a blast of irritation surge through her. Nette behaved as if this was all a game sometimes, while she had to figure out how to feed them all on the tiny rations they got. Swanning in and out of the apartment demanding food, as if Leni could magic it out of thin air. Maybe she could trade the cigarettes for a little bit of extra flour. They were running desperately short.

'You mind that you don't get into trouble, the way you're carrying on – out every night, doing God knows what . . . Remember what happened to you last time, and we can't afford another mouth to feed.' Leni was not unaware of her own hypocrisy. She didn't mind accepting the proceeds of Annette's nights out, yet still wanted to tell her off. She couldn't help herself. She felt crushed by worry at times and yet Nette seemed to do as she pleased.

Leni clamped her mouth shut. It was true that they couldn't afford another mouth to feed, but even as she thought it, she looked at Thea and couldn't wish her away. Her little smile caught at Leni's heart and she felt a rush of love flood through her. 'Aren't you beautiful? Yes, you are . . . yes, you are . . .' she cooed. 'Nette, you'll need to get the bread today – don't forget.'

'All right. Anyway, as it happens, we went to the Babylon Circus last night.' Annette rearranged the child on her lap somewhat reluctantly.

'It's open?' Leni felt her heart pitter-patter and then exhaled, knowing that it no longer mattered. The club had been shut down several years ago. Leni hadn't so much as walked by on the same street since the day she'd left, but something was lit within her just hearing the name again.

'Yes, it's open. It was full too. We danced all night and then a *nice* American soldier brought me home. I might go out again tonight—'

'And what about Thea?' Leni snapped.

'What about her? You like taking care of her – and I don't notice you refusing the things I bring home. It works better this way.' Annette's tone was soft, wheedling now.

'Nette, why won't you look after her?' Leni sat down on the edge of Annette's bed and held Thea's tiny hand between her fingers. 'She's a lovely little girl.'

'Because if I stayed home, we'd have no cigarettes to trade . . . Anyway, I'm no good with babies. You've always been better with her and she prefers you.' Annette plonked the child down on the floor and flopped back against her pillow.

'Of course she doesn't prefer me – *you're* her mother. And what about her father? Maybe he might help us in some way . . .' Leni looked at her sister for a moment, regretting her outburst. There was a sharpness about Annette's features that hadn't been there before. Hers was still a pretty face but there was a darkness to it now, which gave it a meanness. Leni worried about her too. 'Nette, are you all right?'

Annette sat up on her bed and fixed Leni with a distant stare. 'None of us is all right . . . Look around you – how could anyone be all right living like this?'

For a moment, Leni wanted to curl up with her sister the way they used to when they were younger but instead, she swallowed hard and pursed her lips. 'I'm late. Don't go back to sleep.'

'I won't.' Nette's lips formed into a little pout.

Leni kissed her sister gently on top of her head and squeezed Thea's hand before walking out of the bedroom. Her mind raced with thoughts of the Babylon Circus. It surely wasn't possible that Paul had returned. Yet Leni remembered her dream from the night before and, somewhere inside her, she felt a flicker of hope . . .

39

Frau Knopf complained when she asked her to look after Thea while she went out for the afternoon, but her greedy eyes lit up the moment that Annette produced a cigarette from her handbag. She'd felt no guilt about withholding the fourth cigarette from Leni – she'd earned it. And as she'd sat watching Thea playing in her makeshift crib, she'd wanted to scream with boredom.

The child didn't look anything like her, she didn't behave like her and Annette felt nothing at all when she held her – except a slight revulsion. She had to get away from these rooms and this creature who cried for her . . .

Having bribed Frau Knopf, she put on her old yellow cotton dress and took herself off to the cinema. They were showing *Gone with the Wind* again, which Marta had already seen, returning from a date to rave about how handsome Clark Gable was. Annette didn't care much about Gable – she just wanted somewhere to hide for a few hours.

Settling herself in an aisle seat, Annette waited for the newsreels to finish. She hated the news and so amused herself by looking around to see if there was anyone that she recognized or who might be useful to know. She was out of luck on both counts so she waited patiently until the opening credits began to roll.

Annette warmed to Scarlett O'Hara as she sat on her porch flirting in her pretty white dress while declaring how bored she was with all the talk of a war. She recognized how she'd behaved as a girl – flirting and dismissing all the gloomy talk of politics and fighting. After all, it was nothing to do with her.

By the time Scarlett descended into faded ugly dresses, tearing roots out of the ground to eat because she was starving, Annette couldn't bear to watch her struggle. The feeling of hunger was such a familiar one. She loathed feeling hungry. It made her feel small and desperate, as if she were a child again.

During the interval, she had nobody to talk to and, for the first time, this bothered her. She didn't like being alone with her thoughts and yet . . . if Scarlett could return to her life, to her beautiful dresses, after a war had stripped her of all she held dear, then maybe – just maybe – so could Annette. She felt a flood of emotion. A tiny sliver of hope that there could be another life for her and all she had to do was find the key to it.

As Scarlett happened upon a plan to marry an unsuspecting man who could take her away from everything and provide for her, Annette found that the idea had lodged deep inside her mind and would not let her go. She knew exactly what she had to do to save herself.

Why not get married? She would marry an American soldier and get out of this broken city forever.

People began to leave the cinema as the lights came up but Annette carried on sitting there staring at the blank screen, deep in thought. She weighed Glenn Forester Junior up in her mind: his politeness, his manners . . . even on the journey home, he'd behaved as a perfect gentleman when they'd stopped to kiss occasionally. Although he'd wanted her, when she had politely refused him, he hadn't sulked or gone looking for another girl.

More than that, he was the kind of man she could wrap around her little finger. She hadn't given him a second thought once she'd hopped down from his jeep but now, she pondered on the prospect of Glenn Forester Junior and what she might have to do to seal the deal. Was it even possible?

There had been a sixteen-year-old girl who had married an American soldier and gone to live in California. Annette couldn't recall her name . . . And more recently she vaguely remembered Marta reading something out of a newspaper about the rules changing – that it was now easier for German girls to marry their soldier sweethearts. Annette did not think of soldiers as sweethearts, so she'd not really been paying attention, but now she began to wonder if it was possible for her . . .

A new life – she couldn't even remember whereabouts Glenn Forester Junior had said he was from. Maybe she hadn't asked him. All she'd cared about last night was getting enough cigarettes for Leni to trade and dancing until she'd had enough. But America . . . a land filled with possibilities. Enough food to eat and a place to live that was clean and that she wouldn't need to share with a bunch of awful people. Annette got to her feet. She needed to find Marta and get ready for their night out. If there was a chance that Glenn Forester Junior was going to be at the Babylon Circus that night, then so was she.

40

Leni scrubbed at the burnt bits on the bottom of the pan as she finally got to the end of her dish-washing shift at the Café Bauer on Wilhelmstrasse. She washed dishes there until her hands were red and raw, the skin on her fingers pruned by the hot water. Then she would wipe grease pocks and crumbs up from every surface, leaving the kitchen spotlessly clean.

The owner, Herr Bauer, paid her somewhat reluctantly at the end of every week, as if this were a temporary arrangement and he hoped not to see her return. Yet, return she did, every single day, hanging her coat on the peg and tying her apron around her waist. Leni hated her job, but it was work and she needed the money – plus she had discovered one small perk.

She was not allowed to go into the storeroom where the food was kept – cans of meat or bags of flour and potatoes. Herr Bauer kept the room under lock and key, guarding his supplies for the café and a thriving black-market operation that they weren't supposed to know about. He would only allow Walter, the cook, entry and only then if he couldn't fetch what was needed himself.

Walter Keller was older than Leni but by how much she couldn't tell. She guessed that he was at least fifty years old, but he could have been sixty, she supposed. A large man with gnarled features and a shock of greying black hair, he gave Leni the impression of an old grizzly bear. He dragged his left leg behind him as he walked – the result of a bullet wound, he said.

He was also a man who couldn't survive an hour without a cigarette. And, as he could never get hold of enough cigarettes, he was particularly susceptible to bribery.

If Leni offered him the precious cigarettes that Annette brought home, Walter would find a reason to go into the storeroom when Herr Bauer was too busy to accompany him. After an agonizing wait, he would return, pressing a small tin of canned meat or a handful of potatoes into Leni's hands.

She secreted them away in her handbag with her heart racing, desperate not to be caught and lose her job, but equally desperate to have the chance of some extra food.

Today, Herr Bauer was busy chatting to some acquaintances at their dinner table where it was quite likely that he wouldn't want to be disturbed. It was nearly the end of her shift and the café would be closing soon. Leni wiped her hands on the tea towel and signalled to Walter that she had something for him. She raised three fingers and Walter nodded, making his way out of the kitchen and limping over to where Herr Bauer was enjoying a glass of beer with some old friends.

Leni watched anxiously from the kitchen door, giving a sigh of relief when Herr Bauer fished about in his pocket for his keys. Walter limped back towards the kitchen and disappeared into the storeroom, returning with a brown paper bag, which he handed to her. When Leni peeked in the top of the bag, she saw that it was just a few teaspoons of sugar.

'For three cigarettes, Walter?' she said sternly.

'Leni, I can't just take anything . . . he won't miss a few spoons of sugar. Now, quickly, put it away before he comes looking for his keys.' Walter put his finger to his mouth to silence her and walked out of the kitchen.

Having put the sugar in her handbag, she plunged her hands back into the grey, greasy water and finished up the final pan. Anything else would wait for her next shift.

The clock struck nine o'clock and Leni took off her apron, hanging it neatly on the back of the kitchen door. She was done for the day. Her back aching and her feet burning with pain, she took her handbag and crept out of the back door, finding Walter leaning against the wall happily smoking one of his cigarettes.

'Wait a minute, Leni,' he said, reaching into his coat pocket and pulling out a single white egg. 'Here you are . . .'

She wrapped her fingers around the delicate shell and looked up at him. 'But isn't it for your supper, Walter?'

'This is my supper,' he said, gesturing to his cigarette and waving away her concerns. 'It's only an egg.'

Leni carefully placed the egg inside her bag and gave Walter a grateful smile. 'Thank you.'

He shrugged before stamping his cigarette under his foot and walking back inside the café, mumbling his goodbye.

The sun was setting at the end of the street, casting a golden orange glow over the rubble and collapsed houses that surrounded her. It made them look as if they were on fire and for a moment Leni had a familiar feeling of dread at the thought of it. She began to walk away, but not in the direction of home.

Even though her feet hurt after standing for so many

hours at Herr Bauer's kitchen sink, Leni carried on walking. She didn't grasp exactly where she was headed yet her body contained a knowing all of its own. By the time the American uniforms had changed into Russian uniforms she'd realized what she was doing – but it was too late to turn back.

The bright blue door was long gone, replaced by a wooden door that had been painted with thick black paint. The front of the building was charred and cracked, and when Leni looked closely at the wall, she saw it was riddled with bullet holes.

She made her way around the side of the club to the street door, pausing in the same spot where she'd found Paul lying beaten on the pavement as a wave of memory rushed over her.

Suddenly, she could see his face quite clearly in her mind. The sharp angles of his cheekbones, the determined lift of his chin, his deep brown eyes . . . his full, soft lips. The last time she'd stood there it had been raining so hard – and they'd run through the streets back to his room . . . Her eyes filled with tears and she put a hand to her mouth, afraid that she might cry out.

The street door was ajar. Leni reached out her hand, running her fingers over the wooden door, then she took a deep breath and stepped inside . . .

41

Leni could see from where she was standing that the dressing room in the Babylon Circus was gone. The floor was covered in bricks and shards of glass. The wall where she'd spent months rouging her cheeks in a mirror and watching the dancing girls change into their costumes had collapsed, and a wooden beam hung precariously across the entire length of the room.

The passageway itself was untouched and painted the exact same dark brown colour that it had been all those years ago. At the end of the passageway was the door to Dieter's office, and beyond that the red door which led to the stage and the rest of the nightclub. The paint was dirty and peeling now.

Leni walked slowly towards Dieter's office door, not sure what she was hoping to find. Inside she could hear women's voices and a laugh that sounded so very familiar to her. The door flew open and, to her amazement, there stood Berolina.

The woman standing in front of her looked quite different to the Berolina that wore silver stars glued to her breasts and a gauze ballet skirt loosely tied around her naked waist. This woman was in her fifties, with grey hair tied back in a stern bun. Her dress was sombre and she wore a necklace of some glittery substance that didn't look valuable. Her face was lined and weary as she frowned at Leni.

'I know you . . .' she said and then she laughed again – it was the same old Berolina. 'You're Leni – the cigarette girl who ran off with our piano player! What are you doing here?'

'We didn't run away . . . that's not what happened,' Leni stuttered and felt a pang of disappointment. If Paul had returned to the Babylon Circus, then Berolina surely would have known that. Her face fell and she stood there staring at the floor, trying to think of a reason for her presence.

The woman waved her hand to dismiss any explanation, and opened the office door wide. 'Come on in and have a drink. We are open for business, but it's quiet tonight.' Gesturing to a thin, dark-haired young woman standing just behind her, she said, 'You remember Wally? This is her daughter, Monika. She helps me out with the accounts and keeps things orderly around here.' The young woman nodded before making her excuses and heading out of the office. As she pushed the stage door open, Leni heard a blast of piano music and a woman's voice soaring to the end of her song. There was the general chatter of a small crowd before the door closed firmly behind Monika.

Leni followed Berolina into the office, taking the chair that was offered while the other woman sat behind the desk and poured two glasses out of a large bottle of Russian vodka.

'So, you're running this place now?'

'Yes, I reopened it. There was nobody else who was interested so I said to myself, why not? All those people who want to go dancing need somewhere to go. Why should Clärchens have all the fun? I've got a few contacts, so I pulled some strings and here we are. As you probably saw when you came in, there's bomb damage. The stage has gone but we managed to patch up the worst of it and make it one big dance floor. It wasn't a direct hit so luckily most of the building is intact. Just like us, eh?' And with that she let rip with a loud cackle.

Leni smiled and took a sip of her drink. She felt unusually pleased to see Berolina. They had never been friends but she'd made Leni welcome and now she was a pleasant reminder of happier days.

'What happened to Dieter?' She glanced around the room, trying to remember the young girl who had once stood in this office terrified of his peculiar tin face. This place was full of ghosts . . .

Berolina shrugged. 'One minute he was here and the next . . . gone. There were rumours the Gestapo had picked him up but the truth is nobody knows.' The woman looked away, unable to meet her eye. Draining her glass of vodka and quickly pouring out another one. 'Another drink?' Berolina offered but Leni shook her head, and Berolina continued, 'So, what brings you here?'

'I heard this place was open again and I thought I'd take a look . . . It reminds me of happier times, I think,' Leni said wistfully.

'Yes, they were good days . . .' Another burst of laughter exploded from the woman's mouth, but when Leni looked closer, she could see that Berolina's hands trembled slightly as she poured out her vodka and the raucous laughter didn't reach her eyes. There was a darkness hidden in her face. Leni suddenly realized that there was nothing to find here.

'I really should be going – it's getting late.' She got to her feet, feeling rather foolish now.

Berolina swallowed down the glass of vodka and gazed up at her. 'It was nice to see you again. Maybe we could track down the other girls and get together. Talk about old times.'

'Yes – maybe we will do that . . .' Leni gave her a tight smile and knew that she would never see her again. The Babylon Circus was just a dream filled with ghosts of the past.

As she walked away, Leni heard a loud, cackling roar of laughter floating down the passageway, even though Berolina was all alone . . .

Berolina spent precisely thirty seconds thinking about the cigarette girl once Leni had left the club. She had a lot on her mind today as she refilled her glass to the brim with vodka and sat back in her wooden chair with her feet on the desk.

By the time she'd given backhanders and a cut of her profits to her suppliers and to her Russian major, there wasn't all that much left for her. The bills were mounting and for the first time in her life Berolina managed a small amount of sympathy for Dieter. She'd always imagined that being the boss was easier than having customers trying to pull off your spangles – yet it turned out that everyone had their problems. She wondered about him for a moment – whether he was still alive. Then she went back to downing her vodka and thinking deeply about her future.

Today, her problem was making more money. She wished that the club was in the American sector, as they had money to burn. Although she'd seen one or two of their soldiers on her dance floor recently, it wasn't really a place for them to visit. Her Russian major wouldn't like it if she encouraged them. Maybe she should tell the American soldiers they weren't welcome? On the other hand, they had spent a lot of money on those girls last night and she couldn't afford to turn that down.

Mostly she had locals – and they didn't have a pot to piss in . . .

It was just her luck that now she was in charge nobody could afford to pay.

Berolina took a long sip of her vodka and wondered about hiring performers. Maybe she could charge extra for some kind of a cabaret show. Although these days people just seemed to want to dance until they couldn't think about the state of their lives any longer.

And, as her own dancing days were over, she had nothing to do except think about things . . .

42

'But you must remember, Marta ...' Annette sighed, because her friend was being singularly unhelpful on the rules and regulations for marrying American soldiers. They were sitting on a makeshift bed in an overcrowded living room. As a single woman, Marta did not qualify for a room of her own in the house she shared, and the bed was mostly made up of old cushions and spare blankets. Annette was sprawled across it, staring impatiently at her friend.

'You can't marry a soldier . . . then you'd go and live in America and we wouldn't be friends any more,' Marta complained.

'Or you could marry one too and then we would still be friends . . . but somewhere else.' She gave her a pleading look.

'Honestly, I can't remember. It was probably in *Neue Zeitung*. I read it without thinking anything of it.' Marta shifted her legs so that she was more comfortable as she filed a broken fingernail.

'But you mentioned it to me!' Annette was growing increasingly frustrated now.

'I was just chatting – I wasn't expecting you to go and live in America with some GI you found on a dance floor. What's got into you?' Marta's pretty face darkened as she considered the possibility of losing her best friend, and for a moment she vigorously inspected her nails.

Annette sighed. 'There is nothing left for us here. I lost the best years of my youth to a war and now I am losing what's left of it to the peace. I'll be stuck in that shitty apartment with the awful Knopfs forever. I'm tired of rations and scrimping . . . and . . . and . . .' She ran out of words. Her mouth clamped shut and she bowed her head.

Marta threw down her nail file and stared at her. 'Oh, Nette, it won't be like this forever. Things will get better, you'll see.'

Annette knew she meant well but she wasn't in the mood to be consoled. 'So will you come with me tonight?' she asked softly.

'Of course. If you're determined to do this then let's go and find you a husband.' Marta leaned across and hugged her friend. 'On one condition . . .'

'What's that?' Annette whispered as she laid her head on Marta's shoulder, feeling grateful for her loyalty.

'You have to find me one of his handsome friends so that we can live in the same street in America. We will be fine American ladies . . . *speaking English all the time*.' Marta put on an exaggerated accent and they both burst out laughing. Annette felt her bad mood lift and the petty squall was over.

'Shall we swap dresses?' Annette had her eye on Marta's old blue silk dress that made her eyes shine.

'Oh, you just want my blue dress, don't you?' she said in mock annoyance.

'I have to look my best. After all, I am the bride . . .' and with that they both collapsed in fits of giggles.

43

The orchestra at the Babylon Circus struck up another slow ballad as Annette and Marta inspected each man coming through the door. There was still no sign of Glenn Forester Junior or indeed anyone else who might be a suitable candidate for a husband.

Annette sighed while Marta tried to make her feel better. 'Nette, do you want to dance?'

'No. I don't want him to walk in here and find me dancing with you. I'd look like I was waiting for him . . . Let's go and talk to those boys over there.' She gestured in the general direction of a gang of pimple-faced youths who looked around eighteen or nineteen years old.

'But they're children . . . not even grown-up men. Where did all the men go to in this city?' Marta sighed quite dramatically.

'They went off to war . . . and here we are,' Annette snapped. Her evening wasn't going as planned and it was a waste of Marta's pretty blue silk dress. Her grand plans had fallen at the first hurdle and she felt an eruption of fury deep inside her. He hadn't turned up and, even though they didn't have a date exactly, Annette had been sure that he was keen to see her again.

'Don't turn around . . . he's just walked in the door.' Marta looked as if she were involved in some complicated espionage, the way she furtively glanced over Annette's shoulder while maintaining a casual air.

'What's he doing?' she hissed but Marta just stood there staring at the door.

'Well . . . good evening, ladies . . .' At the sound of his voice, Annette composed herself, settling her face into a welcoming smile as she turned around to see Glenn Forester Junior standing there.

'Oh, hello . . .' She could hear the note of falseness in her greeting but Annette pressed on regardless. 'Nice to see you again. Glenn, wasn't it?'

'That's right, Annie . . . I remember your name.' He grinned at her and she grinned back. She was Annie now.

'Is Bennie with you?' Marta piped up from behind them.

Glenn shook his head. 'No, just me tonight.'

Annette felt a sly smile spread across her face. His friends hadn't wanted to come back here, so he'd come alone. Because he wanted to see her.

'It's good to see you again, Annie . . . I kind of hoped that you'd be here.' Glenn sounded sincere and his face lit up. It was the face of a man that had never missed a meal or known any real troubles in his life. His smile was so open and trusting. They lived in such different worlds.

Chattering away, he was overly talkative this evening. A thought didn't enter his head without leaving via his mouth.

He seemed permanently puzzled by Berliners – all these normal people serving him drinks and offering him dances, yet his mission had been to defeat them all and he'd succeeded. Annette viewed him cautiously. Defeat had thrown her back to that world of hunger and homelessness. Bombs raining down on them night after night. Rations that kept them hungry. Her belly was so used to being empty that she couldn't remember a time when it had felt full.

Maybe the Christmas when she and Leni had drunk wine and eaten such lovely food. They'd had no idea what 1945 might bring them and so they'd celebrated together, hopeful of an end to war. But when the end had come, there was only hunger and chaos; the Berlin she'd known as a girl was gone. Within days of the war ending, Leni had developed a horrible fever and it had fallen to Annette to take care of them.

One day, as she'd queued for water at the pump in the street, a stringy old horse collapsed and died. Before she knew it, her neighbours were racing out of their houses holding knives, tearing at the flesh – rejoicing at the prospect of a hearty meal. She didn't recognize the same neighbours who always smiled politely and wished her a good day. They had all become desperate and savage. Before she knew it, Annette too was on her knees tearing at the dead horse with her bare hands – a strange lump of bloody flesh her prize.

She had been so very young and stupid when war had broken out. It had taken her many months to understand that it would go on and on. Yet life continued – they had food and work. It was only in defeat that she was thrown back to the days when she had been so hungry as a child. At first, Annette had demanded things to eat – unable to accept what little rations they were given. It wasn't fair . . . they shouldn't be treated this way. Yet her anger had faded and now she ate whatever Leni was able to cook without complaint. There was nothing and so she wanted nothing.

'You're very quiet tonight. Oh . . . am I in the way here?

I mean, are you waiting for somebody?' Glenn suddenly looked embarrassed, as if he'd been very sure of himself but now that Annette had become silent and thoughtful, his mind had raced to the most obvious reason: that there was another man and this was a competition for who might take her home.

Annette gathered her wits and fixed him with a beaming smile. 'I'm very pleased to see you. Sorry . . . sometimes I don't know what to say in English.'

'OK then . . . so what about a dance? We can dance in any language, I guess.' Glenn chuckled at his joke and Annette laughed along. He put an arm around her waist and guided her to a spot on the dance floor. Once there he pulled her towards him as if this was the moment he'd waited for and she allowed herself to be pressed against him. Inhaling the fresh soapy smell of him and dreaming of a day when she could wake up in a land without ruins or memories of things that Annette didn't want to remember.

44

As Annette was pressing herself against Glenn Forester Junior on the dance floor, Leni was furiously walking away from the Babylon Circus. She couldn't imagine why she had gone back there or what she'd hoped to gain. Was she really so stupid that she thought Paul would be sitting at his piano waiting for her as if the years had not passed? He had left her without saying a word . . . he could be any-where in the world. Even dead. The thought of Paul not existing caused a spear of pain to pierce straight through her heart. Yet if he'd loved her then he would never have abandoned her the way he did.

Anyway, she was a married woman – Karl could be alive. He might come back and here she was mooning around over a boy that she'd loved twenty years ago.

There was as much chance of going back to Paul as there was of Leni getting a job as a cigarette girl. She was forty years old . . . her face was that of a hopeless stranger.

Leni quickened her pace, desperate to get home, to hide her shame away. What was she ashamed of? She couldn't really name it – maybe that of being hopeful for a moment? Of wanting things to be as they were all those years ago? It had been such a brief period of happiness when she would run to start her shift at the Babylon Circus, knowing that Paul would be there, anxious to see her. She felt angry with herself, with the world. Part of her felt as if she'd never been given a chance of real joy. Something had always got in the way.

No – the past was just a dream she'd woken up from. She was a middle-aged woman, with responsibilities. She was married . . . or a widow. People needed her – Thea. Her thoughts turned to the sweet-faced little girl who reached for her at night rather than her own mother. That would be enough for now.

As she turned the corner, continuing to chastise herself for her stupidity all the way along Friedrichstrasse, Leni walked straight into Walter coming from the Café Bauer.

'Leni! I thought you'd be at home by now.' He stood there looking at her, a cigarette dangling from his mouth.

She smiled politely while inwardly hoping he'd walk away from her. 'I had an errand to run. I'm on my way home now.'

'I'm going that way, too . . .' he said, pointing along Friedrichstrasse.

Leni sighed softly but plastered a polite smile on her face. The two of them walked along in silence for a few minutes. He reminded her of an old bear she'd once seen in the zoo. Everything about him was large and lumbering. The way he towered over her; his enormous hands scratching at his face as he tried to think of something to say. Eventually they reached the corner of Lindenstrasse, and to her relief he said, 'I go this way,' pointing to the right of her.

She nodded, feeling glad that she could get back to mentally delivering stern words to herself about her silliness earlier. 'I'll see you tomorrow, Walter.'

'Yes . . . good evening, Leni.' He gave her an enquiring look as if he had something on his mind before strolling away.

A short while later, she slotted the key in the lock of her front door and wearily climbed the stairs. It was late and all she wanted was to fall into her bed. She didn't want to feel Paul's kisses in her sleep, or, in fact feel anything at all. It was better just to get on with things. There was no room for hope or dreams in her world. She would cook her little gift of an egg and share it with Thea – building the little girl's strength. The past was gone . . .

As Leni opened the apartment door, she could hear Frau Knopf shouting at someone, and Thea crying. Leni hurried over to pick up the child from the kitchen floor where she was unhappily waiting for someone to notice she was there.

'What's going on?' she demanded while scooping the child up in her arms.

Frau Knopf was screaming at Hildegard and her daughter was shouting back at her. She soon gathered they were both unhappy that Annette had not come home when she said she would, leaving them to look after the baby.

Leni exhaled a miserable sigh. Hushing the crying child, she gave the Knopfs a stern look as she walked into her bedroom. She would not apologize for her sister.

Thea stopped crying and snuffled gently into Leni's shoulder as her aunt closed her bedroom door, and burst into silent tears.

45

It was a warm, humid evening when they came out of the Babylon Circus, nice enough for a walk, but Annette happily climbed into the front seat of Glenn's jeep. At first, she sat upright, watching him as he drove through the devastated streets of Berlin towards her apartment. They spoke haltingly about things they liked. He loved baseball and the Christmas lights of New York. He had an older brother Wes, who he admired, and a baby sister, Shirley, that he adored. 'Shirley would love you, Annie . . . she's always wanted a sister. Me and Wes are just disappointing to her.'

He laughed as he spoke but Annette liked the idea that he was slotting her into his life. Finding space for her. Letting his sister meet her – at least in his mind.

She shuffled closer, laying her head on his shoulder, which seemed to please him.

'What's it like in America?' she asked softly.

'America? I haven't even seen it all. Never been outside of New York except for army training. It's big . . . You'd like it though – I mean, you're a city girl. There're a lot of places to go dancing.'

He really didn't give her much to go on in terms of details, but Annette was careful not to push too hard or seem too needy. She knew better than to act like some of the girls she saw in the dance halls – throwing themselves at anything in uniform, making it clear that everything and anything was on offer. Turning up each night of the week with a different soldier. There were posters scattered across the city warning soldiers about the dangers of Berlin girls. It was humiliating but Annette was past caring. No wonder the Americans referred to them as 'Veronika Dankeschön' after venereal disease.

Marta had needed to explain that to her a long time ago but Annette was determined not to be a 'Veronika'. She was going to be a 'Scarlett', and slowly, slowly, get what she wanted.

'I think you would have liked Berlin – I mean before . . .' Her voice tailed away. She couldn't explain her city to him. It lay in ruins at his feet but it was not how it was in her mind. In her mind it was always beautiful and proud, full of impatient Berliners hurrying towards their future. Glenn could never understand. He had never hidden in cellars and then crawled out to see his city burning. Never woken up one day to find all the places he'd visited as a child were gone and all the people dead.

He carried on describing the beautiful buildings in New York – glass and chrome towers that touched the sky. The jeep crept along a street lined with burnt-out houses – everywhere you looked was rubble. Annette imagined that a giant had become angry with them, smashing his enormous fist down on their city – over and over again. These buildings used to be beautiful too, she thought . . . but she said nothing.

Glenn finally found a deserted spot in front of several houses with their front walls lying in piles of brick and dust. You could still see the wallpaper in the exposed rooms:

floral prints or dark crimson with gold leaves. She'd drunk cups of coffee in some of those rooms. Waited for friends to get ready or run errands for old ladies. They were all gone.

The people who'd lived there had lain under those bricks for a month after the soldiers came. The stink of them rotting, polluting the June heat. While Leni was recovering from her fever, it was Annette who had held a handkerchief over her nose and gone out to collect food and water, gagging over the putrid stench. Standing around for hours waiting for newspapers to be printed. Desperate to know what was going on. The Russians had taken all their radios. They knew nothing and were told nothing. They were hungry for news.

Annette took a determined breath and snuggled closer to Glenn Forester Junior. He pulled out a pack of Lucky Strikes and lit two of them. Annette wished that he hadn't – for now she would have nothing to trade the next day. He must have seen the expression on her face because as he handed her the cigarette, he said, 'Here, you keep the pack. I've got a spare.'

Annette greedily pocketed the Lucky Strikes and enjoyed the luxury of actually sitting back on a warm summer's evening, smoking American cigarettes. She'd seen men fighting in the street over discarded cigarette butts. People collected them, emptying out the tobacco to make new ones. Glenn would never understand what she'd been through. It was the only thing she liked about him. She wanted to live in his world, where you could walk to a store and buy fresh milk and steak. Where every day was filled with peace and the buildings touched the sky and didn't always remind you of the past.

She wanted to leave Berlin so badly that she would do anything.

Glenn flicked his unfinished cigarette into the street. Annette watched it fall, knowing that he would expect to be kissed now – yet she carried on smoking her cigarette until there was no tobacco left.

He waited impatiently, playing with her hair and placing his army cap on her head, adjusting it to admire her. She saluted him and they both laughed.

Glenn's body seemed too large for the jeep. He wriggled in his seat, trying to get his hips into a position to lean over her. Finally, he placed a hand under her chin, gently forcing her face towards his. He kissed her once on the mouth before stretching across to kiss her neck. His lips moved swiftly up to her earlobes, and Annette found herself pinned to the seat unable to move in any direction other than towards Glenn.

Eventually, she kissed him back, posing herself so that she looked both attractive and willing. His body pressed harder against hers as his hands ran up and down her waist. His tongue was in her mouth now, thrusting it open, and Annette tried to force herself to let him stay there – for that was what he wanted.

His fingers went to undo the buttons on her dress, clumsily tugging at them, until the front fell open. He reached his hand inside to caress her breasts, then pulled one free of her underwear so that he could press her nipple between his thumb and finger. His head moved towards her chest as he took her nipple into his mouth – sucking on it in a way that reminded her of a child. Annette neither liked nor disliked what he was doing. She only wanted him to desire her, to feel so crazy about her that he would want to take her away with him. This was the price she would pay.

She tried to think about how to reach this man in some way – to make him see that she wasn't just another fling with a 'Veronika'.

Should she pull away reluctantly, or let this happen? Annette weighed up her options, deciding in favour of giving more of herself to get what she needed.

She distracted him away from her naked breast by pressing her mouth to his and whispering to him, 'Not here . . . I know a place . . .'

Glenn, recognizing the invitation quickly, leaned back in his seat and turned the key in the ignition. He exhaled, a quiet gasp of pleasure as Annette tucked her breast back inside her underwear and leaned in close, planting kisses on his neck – instructing him to turn left and then again.

'Here . . . stop here,' she whispered. Her voice sounded thick and heavy as he came to a halt next to the pile of rubble that used to be the bird shop and the entrance to a very familiar abandoned courtyard.

'What is this place?' he asked.

'It's nowhere – there's nobody here. It's just more private, that's all.' Annette hopped down from the jeep before she could change her mind. Taking Glenn by the hand, she pulled him towards the courtyard. The buildings surrounding it were shattered and broken. Large white stones lay in the corner where once she'd slept safely amongst the wooden crates.

She closed her eyes and wrapped both arms around his neck. His kisses became more frenzied. His boots crunched against the small stones and broken glass on the ground as he followed her lead, pushing her against the only wall that was left standing.

She wriggled free. In the corner was a doorway and Annette headed towards it, leading him into the open stairwell with a determined look on her face. Her breath came in great juddering bursts as she contemplated what she was about to do. Sitting on top of a step, she stretched her arms out and lay back across the staircase.

'Here . . . here is good.' Annette looked up at Glenn. The building had partially collapsed and through the roof she could see the night sky. It looked the same as the last time she was here. Everything was the same except her. Then she closed her eyes and waited.

Glenn sat beside her for a moment, stroking his hand up and down her leg. 'Annie . . . is this OK? I mean . . . I've never really . . .' His voice tailed off – he was embarrassed.

She felt as if she were one hundred years old. He was such a child compared to her. Annette eyed him curiously and then nodded.

He ran his hand all the way to the top of her thigh. Then, when she didn't push him away, he fell on her hungrily, bundling her dress up to her waist. His hands pulling at her roughly . . . but not, she thought, violently.

Then his body was on top of hers, murmuring words that she didn't understand into her ear. He made a strange groaning sound and Annette made herself open her eyes and look up at him, just as he thrust inside her.

She stared at him blankly – his eyes were closed as he began to move urgently. She liked that she couldn't see his eyes. She didn't want to see them.

She willed her body to respond so that she might feel

something resembling pleasure but all Annette felt were silent tears gliding down her cheeks. Glenn carried on thrusting into her, his hands pushing her further back on to the step, until he finally exhaled a long groaning sigh and sat back on the stairs.

Neither of them said a word for several seconds. She pulled at her dress, covering herself; Glenn fastened up his trousers and straightened his uniform. Reaching into his jacket pocket, he pulled out a fresh pack of Lucky Strikes and offered her one. She accepted the flame of a match and sat up on the step, feeling raw and exposed. She could feel the stickiness of him leaking out between her legs and realized that he hadn't used a condom. She was almost pleased about it. *If she got pregnant then he'd have to marry her, wouldn't he?* Sitting in silence, she took long thoughtful drags of her cigarette. He placed an arm around her shoulders and kissed the top of her head.

'You're beautiful, Annie. I don't want you to think that I don't appreciate you.' Glenn seemed bashful, almost sheepish now that it was over. She could almost laugh at his politeness. Seconds ago, he was deep inside her body – and now he was a perfect stranger again.

Annette smiled at him and then stood up. 'We should go. It's late and that will mean trouble for both of us. It's been a lovely evening . . .'

She gazed up him meaningfully but Glenn didn't meet her stare.

'Sure . . . I'll take you home.' He stood up and walked away with his hands in his pockets. Annette wondered if it was so he didn't have to hold her hand or put his arm around her again. She was not going to give up that easily.

She practically ran to catch up with him, threading her arm through his as they strolled back to the jeep. Annette rehearsed things to say in her mind. Things that would make a difference – to make him feel as though he had to see her again.

'You know, I had a fiancé before the war and he was my first and only. He died . . . You don't know what it's like to be so lonely and you seem so nice. Talking about your family like I would ever meet them . . . it just made me feel I was part of a family again. There's only me and my sister, you see . . . I'm talking too much. I'm sorry. You probably don't even want to take me out on another date now . . . I know you think all Berlin girls are the same . . . but it's not true. I'm not *that* kind of a girl . . . I just want a home and a family, the same as any other woman.'

Her lies were whispered softly but with a steely determination behind them. When Glenn stuttered and mumbled his apologies – He would never think that. He could see right away she was a nice girl – she gazed forlornly down at her feet and then dabbed at a few non-existent tears until he could do nothing other than apologize for his actions over and over again.

As they climbed back into their seats, Annette laid her head upon his shoulder, gently stroking the length of his arm. 'Maybe we could go dancing again tomorrow . . . that's if you'd like to?'

There was a slight pause before Glenn spoke. 'Well, I'm on duty tomorrow but I could meet you on Saturday.'

'Really?' She sounded genuinely pleased . . . but not necessarily for the reasons that Glenn Forester Junior might have thought.

'Yeah ... let's go dancing. I'd like to see you again – you're a special girl, Annie. I'll meet you outside that place at eight?' He sounded as if a decision had been made.

'Eight o'clock. Then it's a date ...' Annette sat back in her seat, feeling relieved. She'd passed the first hurdle.

46

When Leni opened her eyes on Saturday morning, she was surprised to find that her sister was already wide awake. Annette was sitting up in bed with her arms tucked behind her head, staring blankly at the bedroom wall while Thea whimpered in her crib.

'You're awake early,' Leni muttered as she placed her bare feet on the wooden floor and rubbed the palms of her hands over her sleepy eyes. Taking a deep breath, she exhaled loudly and slowly got to her feet.

Standing for a moment at her bedroom window, she eyed the dark rainclouds that were gathering above them. Down in the street she could see people scurrying about. A woman was trying to manoeuvre a wheelbarrow loaded with her possessions around the neat piles of bricks at the edge of the pavement. Leni watched her struggling along the street until she was out of sight.

'It's going to rain . . .' she said to nobody in particular. Annette had not even acknowledged her presence. Turning away from the window, she reached for her old red wool dressing gown which hung on the hook on the wall. 'Better get this little girl some food . . .'

Sliding her arms into the sleeves of her robe, Leni bent down to pick up Thea before the child began to cry for her breakfast. Annette was still sitting in her bed, gazing at nothing and not listening to a word that her sister was saying.

'Nette!' Leni could hear that her tone was exasperated already and she'd only been awake five minutes.

'What?' Annette replied, seeming startled to find her sister standing over her.

'Nothing – what has got into you this morning?' Leni didn't wait for an answer as she was already halfway out of the bedroom door, beginning her usual sing-song chatter to Thea.

The kitchen seemed cold for the first time that summer. Autumn would soon be here, she thought, and then would come the struggle for enough coal or wood to burn to stop them all freezing to death.

Last winter she'd had to go out to the forests at the edge of the city to gather wood. Dozens of women were there, wrapped up against the freezing cold, chopping at trees until they could return home with bulging bags of logs strapped across their backs. Even then, it was never enough. The bitter cold and the hunger . . . the meagre rations they'd been given. She hated to think about it.

Leni boiled some water for coffee. Walter had managed to fill a bag with several large spoonfuls of Maxwell House, in exchange for four of Annette's Lucky Strikes, and although Leni was trying to eke it out, that morning she'd decided she deserved a cup of coffee to begin her day.

Dividing up her meagre breakfast of bread with a scraping of butter to allow Thea to fill her tiny belly first, Leni sat down at the table, settling the child at her feet on a blanket. Sipping at the strong, black coffee, she felt a sudden yearning for the carefree days when she would sit around cafés drinking coffee or hot chocolate.

No – she would not think about those days, and she

would not think about Paul. She was young then – and now she was no longer young. Love comes and love goes. That is life.

Leni nodded her head firmly as if making a silent agreement with herself. There was only the future now. She had to think about the child . . . and Annette.

They needed to make plans for winter, since they could not possibly survive another one like last year. She couldn't bear to think about it. The old people said it was as bad as the 'turnip winter' of 1916. That's what they'd called it back then, although they said you would be lucky to find even a turnip to eat. Nothing much changed in this ever-changing city.

What was the point of a peace that let them all freeze or starve to death anyway?

Leni drained her coffee and stood up to wash her cup and plate. She dried them carefully and placed them back inside the cupboard that belonged to her and Annette. The cupboard next to it was for the use of Frau Knopf and Hilde. Annette liked to peek inside from time to time, but Leni was not interested in what anyone else might have. She only cared about keeping what little she had managed to get for them.

Scooping up Thea, she blew raspberry kisses on her fat cheeks, making the little girl giggle with delight, then swirled them around the kitchen as if it were a dance floor, waltzing around and around until she was dizzy. Thea loved feeling the whisk of air on her face as they went faster and faster. The child shrieked with pleasure, her little fists pounding the air as they danced.

Eventually Leni became breathless and collapsed into the nearest chair with Thea on her lap.

In the distance she could hear the rap-rap of someone knocking on the street door downstairs but as Leni wasn't expecting any visitors, she carried on squeezing Thea's little hands and tickling her under her arms – delighting in the child's laughter. She treasured these moments with the little girl.

Some days she could almost imagine another world, one where she had married Paul. Somewhere in a land far away from the horror of war, they'd raised a little girl who looked just like Thea. Leni stopped herself, interrupting her imaginings to gently pat the child's little back – an indication that playtime was over for now.

The kitchen door opened and Hildegard Knopf stood in the doorway with a polite smile on her face. The girl was already dressed in her work clothes: a scruffy dress and a headscarf wound around her hair. She reported to work every day to clean rubble from the broken buildings – chipping the cement from the bricks so they could be reused.

It was backbreaking work, standing out in the heat or the cold, handling so many bricks that her hands would be bruised and bloody by the end of the day. Hilde had been a proud Party member before the war had broken out and this was her penance, Leni supposed.

She was not so proud now.

'Good morning, Hilde,' Leni said in a manner that suggested she was not particularly inviting conversation.

'Good morning. There's a man downstairs asking for you, Frau Müller. I asked him to wait in the hallway.'

Leni felt nervous. It was too easy to get into trouble these days, to be reported for things that you might or might not

216

be guilty of. Her mind went immediately to Walter and Café Bauer. Her mouth still held the taste of the stolen Maxwell House.

'Oh . . . I'll be right down. Thank you.' Dismissing Hildegard with a nod of her head, she walked swiftly back into her bedroom. Leni couldn't think who would be calling on her at this time of the morning but she wasn't going to run down the stairs without getting dressed first.

'Here – take the baby, Annette. There's a man downstairs wanting to speak with me.'

'Who is it?' Nette was alert to trouble and didn't even complain when Leni handed her Thea.

'I don't know . . . Stay here.' She could feel her heart racing and her hands trembling as she tried to do up her buttons. Slipping her bare feet into her old work shoes, Leni smoothed down her hair until she looked like a respectable older woman – and not the kind of person who might be trading cigarettes for food in her workplace. Then, taking a deep breath, she walked slowly out of the apartment and down the stairs.

As she turned the bend in the stairs, Leni caught a glimpse of a man pacing the hallway. He had his back to her but she could see that his clothes looked shabby and probably lice-ridden – they were no better than rags. And he carried a small knapsack over his shoulder.

Not a government official or some kind of police officer, then, Leni thought with some relief. She ran down the final steps until she was just a few feet away from him.

Hearing her footsteps, the man turned around. His face broke into a relieved smile.

Her mouth opened and then closed. She shook her head in disbelief. It couldn't be . . . yet it was.

'Karl . . . ?'

As she spoke his name, Leni suddenly realized what she had known all along. She hadn't wanted him to come back to her.

Berlin, November 1947

47

It had never occurred to Annette that she might have to find somewhere else to live until that summer morning, when her brother-in-law Karl had walked back into their lives. The apartment was overcrowded now. He had a make-shift bed in the kitchen as there wasn't room for Annette and Thea to sleep anywhere but their bedroom. Leni had explained all this to him but lately Karl had made it increasingly clear to Annette that she was a grown woman with a child to care for, and not his problem.

Her sister, meanwhile, seemed to spend all her time at work or out of the house. When she was home, Leni cooked Karl's meals and washed his clothes but other than that she would not resume her duties as his wife, because there was simply no room for them to do so. Annette knew she was in the way and had taken to bribing Frau Knopf with cigarettes and chocolate to look after Thea while she spent her time in pursuit of Glenn Forester Junior.

Her plan so far had not yielded much fruit. They met twice a week to go dancing in the Babylon Circus before returning to the same spot in the courtyard for some urgent yet brief sex, but other than that she was no closer to getting married than she had been before they'd met. Annette desperately needed something to happen between them to force his hand. But what?

Whenever she'd even hinted at other Berlin girls getting

married, it didn't seem to occur to Glenn that this could also apply to her. He was sweet to her, calling her 'his Annie' and keeping her well supplied with Lucky Strikes and chocolate bars. This had at least allowed her to contribute to the household and Leni had traded them for pats of butter, coffee and flour.

But now the weather was growing colder, Annette knew that Karl would not want to go on sleeping in the kitchen with nothing but a thin blanket to cover him. If the winter was as bad as the previous year, they simply could not go on living like this.

She'd asked Marta if she knew of anyone with any rooms at all but everywhere was full to bursting with people who had lost their homes. Now they crowded into apartments and houses so devastated by bombs that they were unsafe to live in – although people still did so.

There was nowhere to go . . . except America. But she couldn't see a way to get there.

The Babylon Circus was full and there was barely any room to move, let alone to dance. People kept bumping up against the orchestra, causing them to lose their place or hit the wrong notes and yet more people kept coming through the door. Everyone seemed to be smiling as if they had so much to celebrate. Annette couldn't understand it at all.

She was pressed right up against Glenn as they swayed in each other's arms. There was no room to take a step to the left or the right. She was hot and cramped and in an increasingly bad mood.

'It's so crowded in here tonight,' she complained. 'People keep elbowing me.'

'We could get out of here, I know a place . . .' Glenn looked furtive and she couldn't imagine where this place might be.

At that moment, a group of glassy-eyed girls with their dates barged right into them, giggling as they did so – causing her to stumble and cry out as her ankle was kicked in the crush. Rubbing at it, Annette pulled a face at Glenn. 'Anywhere has to be better than this!'

'Man, this is crazy tonight,' he said while pulling her close. 'Anyway, I was going to mention this later. One of the guys has a room . . .'

Annette was immediately suspicious. 'What kind of a room? I thought you all lived in the camp at Zehlendorf.' Rooms were hard to come by in the city so how had Glenn found one?

'Yeah, we do, but this guy knows someone who knows someone. Anyway, there's a key that gets passed around and . . .' Glenn put his hand inside his trouser pocket and pulled out a brass key. He grinned at her. 'So we played poker for it and I won it for the night.'

'Where is this room?'

'Not far from our camp – I have the address. You can guide me.' He took hold of her hand and kissed it. 'Come on, Annie, let's get out of this place.'

For a moment Annette felt a surge of delight – he'd found them a proper room. Surely a proposal couldn't be far away . . . ?

48

Berolina stood in the doorway, surveying the crush of dancing bodies in front of her. She was delighted with the uptick in business and all down to one clever idea. Monika, who was useless in very many ways, had a boyfriend who specialized in the packets of 'bonbons' that were flooding the dance halls of the city. Suddenly, from a handful of desperate girls searching for eligible men during the week, the Babylon Circus was inundated with crowds of people who within minutes of arriving thought that life was perfect and everything was beautiful.

She could tell that the little 'bonbons' were working by the amount of time her customers seemed to spend in front of Dieter's fairground mirror. In the beginning, customers had given it an occasional glance and maybe a mild giggle but lately both men and women stood in front of the mirror staring madly at themselves with silly smiles on their faces.

Whatever Monika's boyfriend was packaging up for them was bringing a rare moment of joy to the proceedings, and she wished for it to continue as money was rolling through her doors. There was barely room for another body on the dance floor tonight.

The orchestra was playing away madly in the corner while couples danced the hours away. Suddenly she frowned – that American soldier was back again dancing with the fair-haired girl. She was a pretty little thing but had an air of desperation about her that Berolina understood only too well. Playing her games and pretending that she was interested in the American. Berolina wasn't fooled for a minute but it wasn't her concern – she just didn't need them in her club.

Berolina was under increasing pressure from her Russian major to keep the Americans away from this place, and the boy was becoming a pest now. The girl was standing by the cloakroom draped in her fox-fur jacket while the soldier held on to her as if he were afraid that she might run away.

'Good evening,' Berolina said, her voice cool but not unfriendly.

'Hello,' the fair-haired girl replied, smiling as if they knew each other.

'You've been here a lot over the last few months and I need to tell you that you are upsetting certain people with your visits. This isn't your sector, soldier. I think you might find the American clubs more comfortable . . .'

The soldier looked taken aback and the girl opened her mouth to say something but the soldier just muttered, 'OK, ma'am . . . understood,' before turning back to the girl and murmuring, 'Let's go, Annie.'

'Good. I don't want to see you again,' Berolina shouted after them. At least she could get her Russian major off her back. Anyway, if she carried on making this much money every night, she wouldn't need him for much longer.

Taking a last satisfied look around the Babylon Circus, she walked slowly back to her office. Climbing the stairs to

Dieter's old rooms, she kicked off her shoes and flopped down on the old leather couch underneath the window.

She thought about the little 'bonbons' that were going to make her rich . . . as long as they were careful.

Then Berolina began to laugh – a loud, cackling roar of delight . . .

49

The room was a small basement with only a bed and a single chair. It smelled of sweat and mice. Annette stood in the doorway, looking at the grimy bedclothes as a single lightbulb swayed over her head.

She swallowed hard. Glenn seemed so pleased with himself, and yet she hated everything about this room. The main thing she hated was that it was just the kind of place the soldiers used to take their whores to.

She wanted to be his wife, not just some girl he wouldn't think twice about when he went back to the States.

'It's not so bad . . .' Glenn said, although Annette noted that he hadn't sat down on the bed either. Turning to embrace her, he pushed the door shut behind him. As he got closer, she felt entombed in the tiny room. Pulling her down on to the bed, he kissed her roughly on her mouth. She was crushed beneath his weight, unable to move. It was all going wrong: she wanted this man to propose to her, not bring her to this terrible room for sex. Maybe she'd played this all wrong – maybe he was the type to have preferred coyness and empty promises? The thoughts whirled around her mind as Glenn's hands moved up her skirt. His face loomed over her and she could see his freckles like tiny brown coins scattered over his skin. Her head was pushed to one side as Glenn kissed her neck. The pillow was dark yellow with grease and dirt. The stench of it made her feel sick.

A wave of revulsion rose up from deep inside her belly and Annette began pushing him away with both her hands.

'NO! Get off me . . . get off. I can't stay here . . .' she cried, staggering to her feet.

'Annie? What's wrong? Hey . . . come on. It's just a room.' He looked perplexed as she headed towards the door.

'It's not a room that . . . that . . . men bring girls they are serious about to . . .' She didn't know what else to say – she'd felt a grip of panic so great that she couldn't get her breath.

'Where else can I take you? There's nowhere for us to go! Hey, come on . . .' He didn't like being denied what he'd waited for. His voice grew petulant as he reluctantly got to his feet and tried to hold her.

'No, I won't stay in this room – and that's final.' Annette shrugged off his embrace and walked away.

'What the—' Glenn sounded irritated as he followed her out of the door. She was practically running back up the steps to the street, clambering into the jeep.

Breathing heavily, she tried to compose herself and by the time Glenn slid into the driver's seat, she managed a weak smile. 'I'm sorry . . . I can't stay in that room. Let's go to our usual place . . . it's better there,' whispering in his ear as she began caressing his face and down his shoulders.

'But it's freezing out there. It's not the nicest room, I'll grant you that, but it's better than being out in the cold.' The muscles of his face gave a slight twitch that told her he was angry with her. She'd ruined his surprise and spoilt his plans for the evening.

'Please . . . I'll make it up to you.' Annette curled into him, her arm sliding around his waist. He shook his head but fired up the engine and drove off, speeding through the deserted streets, driving recklessly and not caring that she was nervous about it. He knew that she hated going fast but she couldn't say a word about it. Annette suddenly pulled away from him, clinging to her own side of the dashboard to steady herself. He was never going to marry her. She was such a fool.

As he slammed the brakes on and pulled up in their usual spot, he took out a cigarette and lit it. He didn't offer her one and Annette felt as if she were a child being scolded.

She had not shown enough gratitude for her gift of a horrible dirty room that smelled of all the men who had taken their girls there. She could feel her eyes filling with tears and she turned her face away. He carried on smoking his cigarette, slowly inhaling and exhaling until she couldn't stand it for another minute. Leaping out of the jeep, she ran down the alleyway and into the abandoned courtyard, not caring whether he followed her or not.

Heading to their usual spot, she sat down on the bottom step and looked up at the crumbling walls that had once been somebody's room before putting her head in her hands. She could hear his boots crunching across the yard and then he was by her side. Kissing her tenderly and telling her he was sorry. She was shaking with cold and the fury of not being able to get what she wanted from this man.

'Hey, sugar, you're freezing. Let's at least go back inside the jeep. We'll be warmer in there than here.' His voice gentle now, coaxing her . . . All the anger was gone. He just wanted his reward.

The panic rose again as she lay back on the stairs, her

eyes pleading with him. 'Come here . . . let's not fight. Let's be friends again . . .' It was all going wrong.

'Not here. It's freezing cold,' he said sulkily.

'Please . . .' She blinked up at him but he didn't fall on her hungrily as he usually did. The panic was getting worse. Her stomach clenched and she began to tremble.

Glenn got to his feet and gazed down at her. 'What is it about this place? What's with you, Annie?'

'Nothing. It's just a place. Hold me, please.' She pleaded with him, needing to be held now – hoping that the wave of panic would subside.

'You know, maybe we should call it a night? Come on, I'll take you home.'

'No. Don't go.' Annette tugged at his hand, trying to get him to come back and sit on the stairs, but Glenn's eyes were full of pity not desire.

Her mind was racing. How could she have lost all of her advantages over one stupid room? She had to think of something quickly. She knew if he took her home now that she would never see him again.

'Let's go . . .' She smiled brightly and, seeing his confusion, offered up her hand so that he could pull her to her feet. Smoothing down the skirts of her dress, she tiptoed across the rubble and climbed back in the jeep. Glenn piled into the other seat and started up the engine but Annette put her hand on top of his until he switched it off again.

'Could I have a cigarette, please?' she asked politely as if they were strangers. She had let this man inside her without murmuring a complaint, yet she was begging for a cigarette.

A flash of hatred rose up from deep inside her. The

humiliation of it. Who did he think he was? Throwing around cigarettes like confetti yet making *her* beg for one.

'Here you are.' He took a cigarette from his Lucky Strike packet and lit it for her, passing it to her and then lighting another for himself.

She took a small drag and then let out a soft cloud of smoke. 'I'm sorry . . . I'm just upset this evening.'

She could feel Glenn softening towards her and she turned to look at him. Pleading with her eyes for him to understand and to offer her something, to say more than he had been willing to say up until that point.

'I thought we were having fun together. You know I'm crazy about you, Annie. You've been in a strange mood all evening . . . Did I do something wrong?' Annette noted that it was about him, not whether she was all right. But she gave a small mirthless laugh and then moved closer to him.

'No . . .'

'Then what is it? We usually have a lot of fun together, don't we? The other guys take their girls to that room and nobody minds. I didn't think it would upset you like that. I was just trying to do something nice.'

'I know you were. It's my fault.' Her voice cracked as she took a drag on her cigarette. 'It's just . . .'

'What is it, honey? Come here.' He held out his arms and she happily snuggled into him, breathing in the fresh- ness of his smell. Everything about Glenn reminded her of the way new things smelled. The rest of her life was dirty and used up – but this man seemed untarnished. Annette wanted some of it to rub off on her, although she knew it was too late. Slipping off her gloves, she stroked his knee and then let her hand casually wander up his thigh, resting her palm in his lap until she heard his breath catch in his throat.

'I want us to be together . . . I worry that you will go off me and find another girl.'

'Hey – you're my girl. The only girl that I want. I'm nuts about you . . .' He placed his hand over hers and pressed himself into her palm, breathing hard. She let him do what he needed to do. She had to regain her advantage somehow . . .

Afterwards, he was gentle. Stroking her hair and telling her how pretty she looked.

Annette couldn't help herself. She knew that she'd messed up earlier and there was only one way she could think of to make everything right.

'I've got something important to tell you and I've been so worried about it . . .' She hardly dared look at him as she pulled her gloves over her hands.

'What is it? I don't want you worrying about anything. Come on, tell me what the problem is.' He pulled her close to him, his arm slung around her shoulder as he placed kisses on top of her head as if she were a small child needing comfort.

'The thing is, Glenn . . . I'm pregnant. We're going to have a baby.' She could hear the sound of his breathing and the silence between them.

As soon as the words were out of her mouth, there was no way to pretend that she hadn't said them. His jaw went slack, and then he mouthed the words 'a baby' to himself. She sat upright, alert now for any signs whether good or bad.

'I know this is a shock . . . but if it's what we both want then there must be some way to be together?' Annette let the words hang there between them, watching his face register the meaning.

'Wow,' he said. She could see his mind racing, forming pictures of a future right in front of them. He sat back in his seat and put his hand to his forehead as if his thoughts were so tumultuous that he needed his hand to steady them.

Annette played her final card.

'Oh . . . you are not pleased. Maybe you don't love me. I see . . .'

Then she dabbed at her eyes with the back of her gloved hand – and waited.

50

Leni had finished her shift at Café Bauer earlier than usual. Customers were few and Herr Bauer had complained loudly to anyone who would listen about his money problems. She had two Lucky Strikes left in her handbag but Walter hadn't had a chance to go into the storeroom on his own.

Annette had not been out dancing for the last three nights, mooning around the apartment, doing as little as possible and generally annoying Karl with her presence. Leni was tired of being caught in the middle between her husband and her sister.

She hesitated on the stairs, wanting a moment for herself, before getting out her key and reluctantly opening the apartment door.

Karl was sitting at the kitchen table brooding, with the bedroom door tightly shut. Leni presumed that Annette and Thea were behind the closed door and the silence was no doubt the result of harsh words being spoken. Standing in the doorway of the kitchen, she felt her heart sink, and tried to look as if she were pleased to be home.

'Have you eaten dinner? There's soup – I can heat it up for you. There's no bread, I'm afraid. We go through food so quickly . . .' Leni placed her handbag down on the kitchen table and moved towards the stove, only for him to catch hold of her wrist.

'We would use less food if your sister moved out with that child. It's not our responsibility and I'm not going to carry on sleeping on the kitchen floor like a dog.' He let go of her arm and stood up.

'Let's not fight. You know how difficult it is to find accommodation. We need a little patience, that's all . . . Annette has her own ration coupons and she brings in extra things for us.'

'Yes, and how does she come by those extra things? Behaving like a whore . . .' he snarled. Karl's anger was white-hot and he marched to the bedroom, throwing open the door and demanding that Nette come into the kitchen immediately.

Leni stood by the stove, unsure of whether to heat the soup or try and intervene between them. This wasn't the same man who had always spoiled Nette when she was a child, treating her as if she were his own daughter.

There was nothing to be done. They couldn't just throw her sister out, and anyway, she didn't want to lose Thea. Annette, who had now skulked into the room, barely cared for her daughter as it was.

'Karl, I'm making dinner for you.'

'I don't want dinner. Annette, get your things and take your child out of this house.'

'What? Where can we go? We can't sleep on the streets! Leni, tell him. It's getting late; the child needs to be in bed. I was thinking of going out myself so I won't be in your way.'

Leni remained silent, aware that when her husband was in this mood it was best not to interfere.

'Well – what are you waiting for?' He fixed Annette with

a dark stare. 'Is it not enough that I fought for my country? That I fought to protect people like you and now you take my bed – and when you are not in my house, you are out dancing with the enemies of this country! You are nothing but a *whore* – a traitorous whore. Take your bastard and get out of my house.'

'It's not your house. Don't you dare speak to me like that. Leni, are you just going to stand there?'

She moved swiftly to stand between them.

'You're tired, Karl. Go and lie down on my bed. Nette, why don't you take Thea for a walk? Just for an hour . . .'

Her eyes pleaded with her sister to shut up and do as she was told. Annette marched angrily back into the bedroom and returned with Thea, shooting Karl a murderous glance and giving Leni a cold stare.

'I'll be back later . . .' And with that she was gone, slamming the door shut behind her.

Karl lay down on her bed and threw his boots on the floor. 'Come here.'

Leni's heart sank as she walked slowly into the bedroom and closed the door behind her.

'Annette is my sister. I know she can be difficult but you can't talk to her like that. I won't let you throw her out on the streets. If you do then I will go with her. Why did you say those things?' Leni sat down next to him.

He used to adore Annette. He was so angry and bitter now. The war had changed him – the war had changed them all.

'It's the truth – she's not a good woman. And what about you? What were you doing while I was away?' Karl grabbed hold of her arm, forcing her to look at him.

'Nothing! I haven't been with anyone since the day you left to go to the front. Are you calling *me* a whore now? I don't recognize you, Karl Müller. You were a kind man . . . you loved my sister. What's got into you?' Leni struggled for a moment and he loosened his grip on her.

'A "kind man". Well, at least I *was* a man when I left my house. I had pride. I was somebody. Now I have *nothing* . . . None of us have anything. We can only watch our women buying and selling themselves to the same men who were killing us. You expect me to be kind – where is your kindness?' Karl's voice was low and furious. He rolled over on to his side, making room for her.

'Now come – you're my wife. Lie down with me . . .'

51

Her feet began to ache as she trudged along. She did not want to be pushing an old pram through the streets of Berlin waiting until it was safe to go home again. And suppose Karl wouldn't let her back in the house? Annette looked at Thea nestled under her blankets and imagined a life where she was stuck in Berlin on her own with this child to feed.

She had never wanted her – that was the truth. She wished that she'd gone to one of the army clinics with the lines of other women in the same position. It was the child that was holding her back.

By the time she'd discovered that she was pregnant it was too late – she had missed the signs until there was nothing that she could do about it. The night she was born, Annette had howled in pain for hours with only her sister to comfort her. She grimaced as she looked down at the sleeping child in her pram – her tiny rosebud lips parted and her black eyes tightly closed.

The first time she'd seen her little face, it was red with anger. Thea had fixed her with those knowing black eyes, and she couldn't bear to look at her. Annette had turned her face to the wall. But when Leni picked her up, Thea had stopped crying straight away – as if she knew that her sister was the only one who could love her.

Annette hadn't mentioned her to Glenn, and she wasn't

planning to, until the time was right. Of course, the time never seemed to be right. It was a delicate matter and she wasn't at all sure how he might feel about taking on another man's child. That's if she ever heard from him again. It had been four days since she'd told Glenn that she was pregnant and there had been no sign of him. He'd dropped her off at home without saying a word or making plans for another date. It occurred to her that she might never see him again – that she might have to start over with another American soldier.

'I'll think about that tomorrow,' Annette murmured to herself, remembering the movie with Scarlett O' Hara. What would *she* do about these things?

If the child had never existed – if the child didn't exist now . . .

Her feet had led her to the river, and she stood for a moment watching the water. Rippling dark water. Annette looked at the child, and for a moment she wondered . . . It was barely a second, but it terrified her. *What was she thinking?* She turned the pram around and pushed it back towards the apartment, her footsteps hurrying, running away from her thoughts. She stumbled over some stones on the road, nearly losing her balance but clinging on to the handle of the pram to keep herself upright. They were silly thoughts – she would never hurt Thea. Annette just wanted more than she had. She wondered if it was such a crime, to want more . . .

She needed to get home to Leni. Her sister would know what to do. She would solve it all. A madness had overtaken her caused by too much hunger and worry. She couldn't even trust herself with her own child now. That's what had become of her. She was a savage – no longer civilized.

An old woman scurried past – a thin coat clutched at the neck to keep out the cold. She could hear a strange series of whistling sounds from a bombed-out house – probably the children who lived amongst the rubble. Annette hurried on, eager to get back to Leni.

As she turned the corner into their street, she saw an American jeep parked across from their building. Glenn was leaning against it with a Lucky Strike hanging from his lips. She tried to work out why he'd come here. Was it good news or bad?

She couldn't see his face as he was looking in the other direction. She just needed to see him clearly – and she would know instantly. 'Glenn . . .' she called out softly.

He turned and saw her walking towards him. His face lit up. And she knew he was hers.

52

Leni lay silently on her bed, her legs parted, resigned to her fate. Yet it didn't happen, and after a few minutes she began to wonder if it was going to happen at all. Karl didn't speak a word to her. He'd grunted as he parted her legs and removed her underwear but since then not a sound had escaped his lips. He hadn't looked at her or bothered to undress her. Either her body was of very little interest to him, or he'd forgotten what was expected.

Perhaps he had lived in a world of killing for so long that he could not remember any other world.

He fumbled around more urgently but there was only softness where there should be hardness. The time that had elapsed between his rough parting of Leni's legs and his silent fumbles were now making it obvious that there was a problem.

Leni lay there watching Karl's hand twitching inside his long underwear. She knew that he would not want her help – that her place was just to lie there and wait patiently. She gazed up at the ceiling, and then tried to see the sky through the bedroom window, but she couldn't. It was dark and cold outside. She worried about Annette and Thea. Where would they go?

In the distance she heard knocking on the street door below but Leni wasn't in any position to get up and answer it. She felt faintly ridiculous now. Her skirt bundled up to her thighs and her underwear wrapped around one ankle. She stifled her laughter – a childlike giggle that had burst up from inside her like a spring stream splitting through rock. Leni bit down on her bottom lip and tried not to look at Karl.

It occurred to her that she didn't really know this man although she'd lived with him for many years before he went to war. She'd cooked him meals: adding more salt when instructed, and leaving out the salt when necessary. She'd washed his clothes – removed his intimate stains. Dressed nicely for him and spoken politely to his friends: offering them a beer or something she'd baked with a cup of coffee. She'd polished his floors and wiped his windows, yet Leni didn't know what his favourite colour was or his deepest wish.

She couldn't recall one significant conversation with him. Even when he'd gone off to war, their parting was that of two strangers wishing each other well.

Karl had not cared about children and so neither had she. It was only when Annette announced she was pregnant that Leni had felt a burning jealousy. For a time, she couldn't be in the same room as her sister.

A quiet sigh escaped her lips and inevitably her mind turned to Paul. The night they'd spent tangled up in each other. It was so long ago. He was a ghost that haunted her.

Leni closed her eyes, imagining his bed . . . their arms wrapped around each other . . . the way he had loved her.

Suddenly there was a peculiar choking sound. Blinking her eyes open, she saw that Karl was sitting back on his haunches, his face screwed up in agony. It was impossible to ignore the strange noise he was making and yet she felt nervous about offering her husband consolation. Wriggling her legs free, Leni put her arms around his heaving shoulders, whispering, 'Oh, Karl . . . Karl . . . we are none of us the same . . .'

Then he crumpled into her lap, and wept.

53

Annette felt a surge of joy swell up inside her at the sight of Glenn leaning against his jeep. Her plan had worked out perfectly. She could cast off her past like her old clothes. She would be an American wife – fresh and clean. A new life beckoned and all she had to do was agree to whatever was needed.

'So, you're getting an early start on buying things for the baby?' Glenn gestured towards the pram and her smile froze. She was so stupid. How could she have thought that she would get away with this?

Annette was just about to speak when Thea pushed off her blanket and let out a hearty roar. Glenn stared down into the pram, his face puzzled. 'Is this . . . *your* baby?' he asked.

Her heart skipped a beat yet a peculiar sense of calm enveloped her. Taking a long breath, she smiled up at him. 'This is my sister's child. I like to look after her sometimes . . .'

As she spoke the words, she almost believed them herself. After all, Thea did really belong to Leni . . . she was nothing to do with her. It was her sister who loved Thea and cared for her. It would be better for all of them if that were the truth.

The coolness of the lie – on top of the lie – so many lies now, like knots in a thread, they couldn't be undone. There was no explanation: she couldn't wipe it away with a girlish giggle, or say that she hadn't meant that at all and he must have misunderstood.

'Oh,' was all he said, but she could tell that he was relieved by the way his arm tightened around her shoulder. 'Hey, that reminds me . . . I brought you something.' Glenn reached down to the side of the driver's seat and pulled up a brown paper bag which he handed to her.

Grinning as if he was pleased with himself, he said, 'You need vitamins for the baby.'

Annette peeked inside to find that he'd brought her two oranges. The sharp tang made her want to press them to her nose. She hadn't eaten an orange in so long.

'Thank you.' Annette looked up at him pointedly: 'I've missed you the last few days . . .' urging him with her eyes to say why he'd come to see her.

He was nervous, running his hand through his neat strawberry-blonde hair. She watched the little muscle under his freckled cheek twitch as he swallowed. *Just say it*, she thought as he cleared his throat.

'The thing is . . . I want us to get married. That's if you want to?' He said the words so definitely she knew that he'd been rehearsing them.

Thea lay in the pram between them, her black eyes curious. Annette took a deep breath. She would worry about it all tomorrow. She would ask Leni to help her. There had to be a way.

'Of course, it's not so easy getting married when you're in the army – there's bound to be a lot of paperwork . . .' He shrugged as if none of this could be helped.

'So how do we begin this paperwork?' Her tone was soft, beguiling but also quite businesslike.

'Is that a yes?' Glenn's smile beamed out at her. The little muscle was still twitching in the hollow of his cheek.

Annette put on her broadest smile. She would have everything that she'd ever wanted. There wasn't anything that could stop her now.

'Yes. I will marry you.'

Taking a step forward he plucked her right off the ground, twirling her around and around until she squealed to be put down. 'That's great news, Annie. I can't wait to show you New York City!'

Everything in life seemed to require papers and official stamps these days but that was all right. She would get everything they needed, and by Christmas they could be living in New York as a married couple. Her heart soared at the thought of her escape – a new city, a land of plenty . . .

'So . . . I have to ask my commanding officer for permission, there's a bunch of forms to fill out, but then three months later we can get married.' He looked so pleased with himself now that he'd asked and been answered. She could feel a pulse of fear inside her.

'Three months? But that's a long time to wait.' *How could she pretend that she was pregnant for another three months?* She hadn't really thought it through – only imagining a quick wedding and then an unfortunate miscarriage.

'That's how it works – the army has its rules. I don't pretend to understand why. It'll all work out fine, Annie. I'll put in my request first thing tomorrow – after that, it's up to them.'

Annette's mind churned over this new and unexpected set of problems. She had only thought as far as getting this man to want to marry her. She had not understood that she was marrying the entire US army . . .

54

Leni felt a rare moment of peace as she darned an old sock while sitting on her bed. Breathing in the silence, she exhaled the days of worry that she'd been keeping inside. She was so rarely alone these days.

Karl was at work, having eaten his breakfast and slammed out of the house at first light. As soon as he had registered his return from the prisoner-of-war camp with the authorities, he'd been told to report for rubble-clearing duties. He hated the humiliation of standing in the streets shovelling bricks on to trucks, and returned home in a foul mood each evening.

Leni was relieved by his absence, spending the hours they were apart praying there would be some change in their situation. Something that might put him in a better humour or at least return him to the man she had married. She had never loved him but she had recognized him as a caring man. Now she wasn't sure what Karl was any longer.

To her relief, there had been no repeat of his attempts to throw Annette and Thea out but, all the same, Nette was quick to avoid him these days. Leni appreciated her efforts but she knew the day of reckoning was fast approaching as there just wasn't enough space for them all.

She had managed to beg another mattress from a neighbour so at least Karl could have some comfort as he slept on the kitchen floor. But Frau Knopf tutted and rolled her eyes every time she came in there and found him fast asleep in the corner.

Leni put her darning in her lap. Stifling a yawn, she looked around her as she handed Thea a ball of wool to play with. Her thoughts drifted to a small, white-washed Spanish house with red geraniums at every window. She saw this house in her dreams and had become convinced it was the place that she would have lived in with Paul. A home filled with children and music. For a moment she imagined waking in his arms each morning. Cooking him breakfast with the sound of his piano echoing through the house.

Opening the drawer of the bedside table, Leni reached inside for the blue cotton handkerchief. Smoothing it across her lap, she ran her fingers over the edges.

She wondered where he was – if he was happy without her. If he regretted leaving her.

Mostly she wondered why . . . over and over again.

Thea began to bite down on the ball of wool so Leni took it off her, causing her little face to screw up into a fury. As she opened her mouth to wail the bedroom door opened and Annette stood in the doorway with an anguished look on her face.

'I need to talk to you. I've been waiting to catch you on your own. Can we ask Frau Knopf to take the child? It's very important. Please.' Her expression was deadly serious. There was no hint of her usual sulky demeanour or sarcastic tone.

'What's happened?' Leni was instantly alert, able to discern trouble coming her way. It wasn't like Annette to be like this. She struggled to take anything seriously most of the time.

'Please . . . let's go somewhere we can talk . . . just the two of us.' Nette was so unlike her usual self that Leni agreed at once even though she only had an hour before she needed to go to work.

Frau Knopf raised her price to three cigarettes, sniffing their desperation and taking the opportunity to voice her annoyance about Karl sleeping in the kitchen.

'He was a soldier, Frau Knopf. We have to take care of those who fought for our country,' Leni said adamantly, causing the old woman to clamp her mouth shut and pocket Annette's Lucky Strikes. Depositing Thea on to her lap, the sisters hurried down the stairs and out of the front door. Walking briskly down the street, they headed inside a café and ordered two cups of quite watery coffee without complaint.

'I know things have been very difficult since Karl came back . . . and I have a solution to all our problems. But I need your help.' Annette's speech sounded rehearsed and Leni put the coffee cup down and sat back in her seat, sure that she probably wasn't going to like it.

'What is this proposal?' she asked coolly, not quite trusting her sister to have anyone's best interests at heart except her own. Annette shuffled around in the seat opposite her, nervously picking at her fingernails.

Leni felt a flicker of irritation. 'Nette, say what you have come here to say.'

'I . . . I'm getting married.' Her sister glanced across at her furtively and then looked away again.

'You can't mean the American?' Leni tried to think how that would work. For a moment she couldn't quite put all the pieces of the puzzle together and then slowly it dawned on her . . . Nette would leave Berlin.

Leni's voice grew thick with emotion. 'And you would live in America? But it's so far away . . .' Her eyes filled with tears at the thought of it. 'We wouldn't see each other . . .' She thought of the times that she'd wanted nothing more than to be free of her sister but now the idea of losing her was more than she could bear.

'We could write letters – and you could come and visit one day.' Even as Nette spoke, Leni knew that would never happen. She felt a sharp longing for someone who cared enough about her to stay yet she knew it was too late to change Annette's mind.

'I can make a new life – not a life where I have to go out every night to get men to give me their cigarettes. Don't you see? If I don't go then what will become of me? Who is going to marry me? And what if Karl throws me out . . . ?'

'He won't throw you out. You're my sister – you're all I have left of my blood family. I won't let him do that.' Leni was trying to sound certain although inside she knew that if Karl got into a rage there wouldn't be much that she *could* do about it.

'Oh, Leni. It's time for me to go. I can't be happy here – you must see that.'

Leni sniffed loudly, raking her teeth over her bottom lip to hold back the tears. Then she slid her hand across the table. Annette wrapped her own palm around it and for a moment they sat there, silently holding on to each other.

'Do you remember how I would always make you tell me the story of when I was born?' Nette said.

'Yes – over and over again. You were so happy when I

told you the part about how we all cheered your arrival.' Leni squeezed her sister's hand, her throat tight with emotion.

'You've always looked after me – I'll miss you so much . . .' Their eyes met across the table and she was surprised to see that Annette's were filled with tears.

'Is he a good man?' she asked quietly.

'I think so.' Her sister let go of her hand and began tracing the outline of a stain next to her cup.

'I want you to be happy – more than anything. You know that.' The coffee grew cold in the cup as they sat staring miserably at the table.

Annette looked up nervously. 'There's . . . there's just one thing I need you to do for me . . .'

'What is it?' Leni wiped her hands across her face and put on a brave smile for her sister. She was resigned to losing her now. All she could do was offer her help even if it broke her heart – and it would.

'I told the American . . . that Thea was your child . . .' Annette's voice was so quiet that she could barely hear her.

She stared at Nette trying to understand what she wanted . . . And then, like daylight creeping across a window, she suddenly saw quite clearly. Of course she wasn't going to take Thea with her. She'd never wanted her in the first place.

'You want me to lie for you. To raise your child here.' Her voice faded away, leaving Nette staring dumbly across the table at her.

'You love her . . .' Annette said, but Leni could hear the little wheedling tone that she always employed to get her own way. In many ways she was still the baby sister who never took responsibility for anything.

'What about my job? Who will care for the child when I'm at work?' There were practical things to work out. She couldn't just take on Thea full-time. And what would Karl say?

'Frau Knopf could look after her, or you could pay a local girl. I'd send you the money. We would have money, Leni . . . I could get whatever we needed. They have everything in America . . . And you would hate to be parted from Thea . . .'

Leni watched Annette's face as she spoke. This woman she had cared for as a baby, helping their mother to feed and change her as if she were a new doll; the little girl she'd tried to keep safe and fed when there was just the two of them. Her sister that she loved with all her heart . . . and trusted with none of it.

But there was Thea to think about – and it was true she would hate to lose her. She did love her and couldn't imagine her days without seeing that little face and her beautiful dark eyes.

She sighed wearily. 'So now we come to it. You need me to lie for you – to collude with you to deceive the American . . . and to take care of your child.'

'Please, Leni. You have to help me. I can't stay here. I have to leave Berlin . . .' Annette's face was wretched and miserable.

Much as Leni hated the thought of losing Thea, she wanted the little girl to have a chance of a new life too. She could grow up in America with everything she needed.

'Why can't you tell him? If he loves you then, surely, he could accept the child. She's such a beautiful little girl. Why don't you try, Nette? See what he says?'

'No, I won't tell him. I have to get out of here. You don't understand what it's like for me.' Her sister's face darkened as she began to cry pitifully. Leni knew deep inside how this would unfold. She would give in and do whatever Annette wanted, because that's what she had always done. But she couldn't forgive her for wasting Thea's chance of a new life too. Leaving her child behind in the rubble of Berlin when she could live in a land of plenty.

Leni swallowed hard. 'All right then, make your plans. But I don't understand you, Nette. Don't you want Thea to have a new life too? You're her mother.'

She gathered her things and stood up but as she turned to walk away, Annette grabbed hold of her hand.

'I just can't do it. Please don't think badly of me.'

Leni pulled her hand free and walked away without saying a word.

55

Having been told that Glenn couldn't return to the Baby-lon Circus, Annette and Marta had instantly transferred their efforts back to Clärchens Ballroom. They'd already danced with seven different men each, although Annette was keeping them at a respectable distance as she was expecting Glenn any minute. They had collected up almost a dozen cigarettes between them, although Annette was less interested in spare cigarettes these days when she could get as many as she wanted from Glenn. She happily handed over her stack to Marta and waved away her grate-ful thanks.

'I'm celebrating,' she said, hoping that it was still true.

'Celebrating . . . ? Tell me everything. Are you getting married? Is it really happening?' Marta was so excited that she carried on for several minutes, voicing endless ques-tions that Annette couldn't answer. 'And I'll be your maid of honour? Please say yes . . .' The girl twirled around, fin-ishing off with a playful curtsey.

Annette laughed along. 'He's asked me, but we're wait-ing for permission.'

Marta's face fell, her excitement suddenly quenched. 'Oh, that is too bad. I know girls who couldn't get permission – either the Americans said no, or for some of them their parents were in the Party . . . or even the

Communist Party, and they won't take you then . . . but you don't have anything like that, do you?'

'No, we've never been political. It's all fine, I'm sure. We just have to wait,' Annette said, feeling anxious even as she tried to reassure her friend.

'And what about Thea?' Marta said quite loudly over the blast of the orchestra.

'Hush . . .' Annette pulled Marta to one side. 'My sister will keep Thea here. He doesn't know. Nobody knows except you and Leni. You mustn't say a word, Marta – promise me!' She trusted her friend with her life but sometimes Marta spoke without thinking and she needed to impress upon her that she had to be quiet.

'Not a word, I swear. Oh, Nette, imagine you in America . . . you will write, won't you?'

'Of course I'll write. You're my best friend in the whole world.' Annette embraced Marta and the two women began their premature celebrations once more.

Suddenly, there was a hand on her shoulder and she turned to find Glenn standing there grinning at her.

'Hey, there's my girl – I've been looking for you. It's busy in this place.'

Annette flung herself into his embrace. 'Any news?' she said hopefully.

'We're getting married, Annie!'

She squealed with joy, throwing her arms around his neck and kissing him all over his face. Suddenly there was a group of girls surrounding them, all shaking their hands as if they'd achieved something magical.

Marta hugged Annette tight, whispering in her ear, 'You

did it, Nette . . . you're getting out of here. I'm so proud of you.' The two women held on to each other, crying and then laughing at the same time.

Annette looked around her, at the tall American soldier by her side, at her best friend wiping away her tears in front of her, and felt as if she'd never been happier.

56

Leni bundled Thea up against the bitter November chill and covered her with a scruffy blue blanket. It was so old now that it was fraying at the edges. Thea's black eyes stared up at her. The child wore a red woollen hat with matching mittens on her hands and Leni's heart swelled as she looked at her little face. How could Nette leave her behind?

The morning had begun with yet another argument. Annette had used too much hot water again. Leni was so tired of listening to other people shouting about what they needed. She had needs too and nobody cared about them. She felt like screaming – listening to the same rows, day in and day out. If it wasn't the hot water, it was the food – there wasn't enough of anything to go around.

Leni buttoned up her coat and slipped her hands into her gloves. She needed to walk, to get away from the apartment . . . and particularly from Karl. He had sunk into a pool of despair that she couldn't rescue him from. When he wasn't at work, he sat alone at the kitchen table staring at nothing. If anyone entered the kitchen and greeted him, he didn't respond. Most of the time, he didn't even look at whoever was speaking to him.

After the sobbing incident, she had created a makeshift barrier across her room by attaching an old washing line with a blanket draped over it in the hope of some privacy for them. She hoped it would appease him, yet he carried on sleeping in the kitchen. Blaming her for his inability to feel like a man. She was tired of it.

Turning out of the front door, she walked briskly, stopping only to make sure that the child was still wrapped up warmly.

Leni had no plan or direction that she needed to follow. She had exactly two hours before she would have to return Thea to Annette and report for duty at Café Bauer. And so, she walked wherever her feet might lead her.

She passed feral gangs of children clambering over the broken ruins of houses – most of them without parents or anyone who cared about them. They made their own way in the city, stealing or trading on the black market, doing what they needed to do to survive, eyeing Leni suspiciously as she walked past, then waiting until they thought she could no longer see their hide-out before returning to it. She felt sorry for them but she had nothing to offer them that would make a difference.

Further along the street she could see a large line of 'rubble women' shivering in the cold, waiting for another truck to arrive so they could begin removing stones from the road. It had been two years since the war ended and yet everywhere she looked, the city was still in ruins. She wondered whether it might always be this way – whether the soldiers might leave it like this as a lesson to them all.

So many piles of stones, and the more they cleared, the more there seemed to be. As she walked past, a cry went up. They'd found the remains of a body. Even two years on they were still uncovering the bodies that were buried under the rubble. At least some family might get to hold a funeral, she thought.

On she walked, passing two young women waiting for the tramcar to arrive. It was full of neatly dressed men and women going about their day. On the corner some shifty-looking characters were buying and selling in hushed whispers – a small crowd of desperate people gathered around them clutching their family heirlooms. From time to time one of them would walk away with a disappointed look on their face.

Leni crossed the street, ignoring a group of Russian soldiers gathered around a military vehicle. They took no notice of her, only carried on smoking cigarettes and eyeing passers-by. She walked on, finding herself on Friedrichstrasse – yet it wasn't an accident. She knew her feet always led her back to the same place.

Lately, no matter which direction she started off in, she would always end up outside the street door of the Babylon Circus. She would re-enact her last conversation with Paul in her mind. Searching for clues. Then came the regrets – that she'd foolishly told him the silly lie about her family. Leni couldn't understand why she hadn't just said that they were dead. She was young and so easily shamed. It had seemed so important that he didn't think badly of her.

Leni formulated her regrets, counted them up and then pushed them to the back of her mind. It was too late. She began her journey home and all the way she imagined herself arm in arm with Paul, talking softly about their dreams of the future. Every day she told herself it was the last time she would allow herself to think about him. But the next day she would do it all again . . .

She wondered what would become of her when Annette left. How would she bear sitting in silence with Karl night after night? Would she live to see this city being rebuilt or spend the rest of her days in the ruins – washing dishes, living on rations and trading cigarettes to live?

Thea slept peacefully in the pram and for a moment Leni felt desolate at the idea that Annette might send for the child – for then she would have nothing and nobody to love. Yet the thought of this little girl growing up amongst the rubble was so much worse.

She walked past the feral children again. A boy of around ten years old sat on the very top of a pile of bricks smoking a cigarette – like a little prince surveying his kingdom. She was dragging her feet now – reluctant to go back to her apartment. Yet Thea would need feeding soon and Leni had to go to work.

Unlocking the front door, she wrestled the pram into the hallway, parking it under the stairs and bundling Thea into her arms. The child smelled milky-sweet nestling against her neck and she kissed her little rosy cheeks.

Climbing the stairs, she opened their front door, shutting it quietly behind her, not wanting to disturb anyone with her comings and goings. As she did so, Annette appeared in the doorway of the kitchen, gesturing wildly.

'What's the matter now?' Leni asked wearily.

Nette pulled her into the kitchen and closed the door behind them so that the Knopfs couldn't overhear their conversation. 'It's Karl – he's gone . . .' she hissed.

'Gone where?' Leni asked uncomprehendingly.

'He packed his things in his knapsack and he just left. He's taken all the money you kept in your sewing box and all my spare cigarettes.'

'But where's he gone? I don't understand . . .' Leni

sat down at the kitchen table, putting Thea on the floor. She blinked up at Annette, confused and then suddenly comprehending . . .

Karl has left me . . .

She felt curiously numb. He'd just walked out on her after all these years, as if she was nothing at all. Leni was tired of people leaving her behind as if she didn't matter to them and a ball of anger flared in her belly.

Yet at the same time there was a tiny leap of something else. A strange happiness igniting deep inside her. Because now she was free.

57

Annette ran as fast as she could. She'd spent so long consoling Leni that now she was late. She was meeting Glenn for coffee to discuss the progress on their marriage. His commanding officer had said yes and now the rules stated that they had three months to arrange everything.

She was feeling particularly pleased with herself, having used a carton of Lucky Strikes to get a glowing character reference from the pastor of a church that she had never set foot in. Glenn had been a little suspicious when she'd asked him for a whole carton of Lucky's but she'd managed to explain that Berlin was very bureaucratic and cigarettes would make everything a little easier. He had accepted her explanation without saying another word and brought her the cigarettes the very next day.

Annette folded the paper carefully into an envelope and tucked it safely away in her handbag. She was taking it to Glenn and then he would pass it on to the authorities. It was another tick in the box.

They had pored over the paperwork, writing out endless sections on her family history and swearing to their lack of interest in political matters. There were no records of any affiliation to any political party so that was one thing she didn't need to lie about. Now she had the character reference, all that was left for them to do was to set a date and organize the wedding ceremony. She'd always wanted a church wedding with a beautiful dress but it was better to just have the simple legal ceremony and forgo the rest.

All Annette needed was the gold band on her finger and some kind of transport to get her out of the city. That might be difficult to arrange, but at least she would be married by then.

Glenn was already sitting at a table near the window when she arrived at the café. Annette slid into the chair opposite him and let him fuss over her, ordering two cups of coffee in his terrible German.

'Here – I have the reference signed by the local pastor.' She pushed the envelope across the table towards him. 'Now you know your future wife is of good character . . .' Annette giggled a little at her joke. Nothing could spoil her good mood these days.

'Oh, that's great, Annie! It's all coming together now. It won't be long before we'll be having coffee in New York – imagine that.'

Annette could imagine it; she imagined it so clearly that some days she was surprised to wake and find herself still in Berlin.

The waiter brought them their coffee, setting the cups down in front of them carefully. She glanced up to thank him but the man just scowled at her and muttered something under his breath, making it clear what he thought of her for sitting with an American. Flushing with embarrassment, she remembered Karl's furious accusations of betrayal.

She didn't care about any of them. She was leaving them all behind. It wasn't her fault they'd been fooled into another war.

'So, I guess I'll need to buy a ring pretty soon!' Glenn sat there smiling sweetly. He was completely oblivious to the dirty looks or the muttered insults. Annette reached across the table and took his hand.

'Yes, you will. I can't believe we'll be married in just a few months. It's such a relief to have completed all the paperwork. Now we can finally set a date and plan the ceremony.'

'Sure – we can pick a date right now, then as soon as you've had your medical, we can arrange everything.'

'Medical . . .' The smile froze on her face. She could feel a raw terror building inside her. 'What do you mean, a medical?'

'Oh, it's nothing to worry about. The army always needs a medical. It will just be a quick exam. You're fit and healthy. I had to tell them about the baby when I asked for permission so they'll be able to carry out checks to make sure everything is all right. It's just a formality.' Glenn sipped at his cup of coffee and gave her a reassuring grin.

Annette swallowed hard. Of course the army would want to examine her. She'd been sure that she could fool Glenn for the next few months – after all, plenty of women barely show at all and then she could pad out her skirt with something. Beyond that Annette didn't really have a grand plan. But an army medical was entirely different – her lies would collapse like a pack of cards and she'd be stuck here forever.

Once Glenn found out that she'd lied to him then it would be over. She gnawed at the inside of her cheek, unable to say a word.

58

Leni was taking all of her frustrations out on the grease-stained pans at Café Bauer. She scrubbed and scraped at the blackened pans as if cleaning them would offer her some kind of redemption. She'd barely spoken a word to Walter all evening, just accepting another load of dishes and filling the sink with hot, soapy water over and over until she was done.

When she'd first arrived for her shift that morning, Walter had asked if she had anything that she wished to trade as he was about to pay a visit to the storeroom. But as Karl had taken all their spare cigarettes with him, Leni had nothing to offer Walter until Annette could replenish their supplies.

He didn't seem to mind, focusing instead on his cooking, the two of them working side by side without saying a word. From time to time, Walter would hum a little tune that Leni remembered from before the war. She liked to listen to him as he stood just a few feet away from her, chopping and frying, boiling and stirring. The café was busy, but whatever the customers wanted, Walter was perfectly calm. Walking slowly to collect the dishes that Leni had dried, and then assembling his food on the plates, all the time he carried on humming his little tunes. Leni wondered how he could be so happy in his job. The only time she'd ever felt happy at work was the brief period when she'd got to see Paul every night at the Babylon Circus.

Walter was always content – as long as he had food to cook, a tune to hum and a cigarette to smoke.

Having prepared the final meal for the last table of customers, Walter turned off the cooker and leaned back against the cupboard, smoking a cigarette. Leni was aware of him there but she could only carry on scrubbing angrily at the dishes before wiping them carefully and putting them away. It was so quiet in the kitchen that she could hear Walter gently exhaling the smoke from his cigarette. Leni wondered if he was waiting for her to say something as he did nothing but stand there, puffing away and watching her scrubbing the pots.

The door to the kitchen opened and Herr Bauer came in looking quite agitated. 'Walter, you lock up tonight. I'm not feeling well.'

'Yes, Herr Bauer, of course. What's the problem?' he asked without sounding as if he particularly cared about hearing the answer.

'I think I've got a fever . . . Just make sure and lock the doors. I need to go home to my bed. I don't feel well at all.' Herr Bauer grimaced slightly and put his hand to his belly before handing over the keys. He walked gingerly towards the front door, stopping every so often to rub his hands over his face and his stomach while Walter and Leni watched him go.

Walter jangled the keys in his hands and resumed humming his little tune. 'You might as well go home too, Leni. I'll sort out everything here.'

'If you're sure . . .' She hesitated, not wanting to stay any longer but not wanting to return to the apartment either.

'Yes, why not?' Walter took off his apron and walked into the café to escort the last customer as he ambled out of the door. When the locks were firmly slid across the door at the top and bottom, Walter returned to the kitchen, surprised to find Leni standing by the sink.

Her coat was still hanging in its usual spot behind the kitchen door. Walter grew suspicious. 'What's wrong? You usually can't wait to get out of here.' He gave a laugh but stared at her curiously. 'You want me to get something from the storeroom for you? I thought you didn't have any cigarettes this evening.'

'No – I don't need anything. I'm going home.' Yet her feet stayed rooted to the spot.

'Leni, you are going without going . . .' He sighed. 'Would you like something to drink before you go?'

She wanted to say no, but having something to drink would at least delay the inevitable return home to Nette's sulks or the Knopfs' endless complaints. She nodded and Walter searched through his kitchen cupboards before retrieving a bottle of brandy. He poured two glasses and handed one to Leni. She couldn't bring herself to move from the kitchen sink but she sipped at the brandy and wished that she was alone.

Walter offered a toast but she wasn't in the mood for toasting. Her hands clutched at the glass and then before he could say another word, she emptied the contents down her throat. She knew that he was watching but the warmth that was flooding through her made her feel instantly better. She held out the glass, intending only to give it back to Walter but instead he refilled it. Not a word was said but, somehow, he had sensed a need that she had to feel something other than misery. She lifted the glass, hesitated for a moment and then downed it.

'Take it easy . . .' Walter sounded slightly alarmed at her behaviour. She could feel him watching her closely, assessing her, finding her puzzling. Leni slammed the glass down on the side of the sink and took a deep breath.

'Thank you,' she murmured. Leni took a step away from the sink, intending to walk over to the door and put on her winter coat but for some reason she halted and looked up at Walter.

He took a step towards her, his arm slipped around her waist and the weight of him pressed her back against the wall. She could feel his breath on her face, the smell of brandy and then his mouth was on hers. She was being kissed.

It had been so long since she had been kissed that Leni was quite stunned. The feeling of it was not so much unpleasant as surprising.

Leni stood quite rigidly, her hip nudging at the kitchen sink, wondering what she should do. It must have only been a few moments while she tried to clear her mind for long enough to construct a sentence. For a second the warmth of his lips ignited something inside her until the fog of the brandy lifted and Leni wriggled away from him.

The moment she had resisted, Walter had stopped kissing her and moved away. The two of them stood in the kitchen, staring at each other in a mixture of shock and horror.

'My apologies . . .' he stammered, dragging his eyes away from her face.

'Good evening, Walter. I'll be going now . . .' Leni

danced past him, only stopping to grab her coat from its peg, before dashing red-faced through the back door.

The cold night air stung her cheeks as she stood outside Café Bauer, buttoning her coat, watching Walter through the windows slowly turning off the lights.

Leni studied him for a long moment and then walked briskly away.

59

The next morning, Leni felt sick. She'd slept feverishly, unsure at times if she was really awake or if it was yet another strange dream. The last time she'd been this ill was during the final days of the war. She'd had such terrible dreams, and was barely conscious while the entire city had fallen to the Russians. Then her fever had broken and Leni woke to find that the war was over. When she opened her eyes, Annette was sitting by her bed, sobbing desperately and looking as if she hadn't slept for days.

Now, Leni lay back in her bed feeling hot and sleepy. Opening her eyes, she squinted up at the light. Her head was splitting and her throat parched.

'Nette . . .' she whispered but there was no reply. Trying to raise her head from the pillow, she called out again. 'NETTE . . .'

Then her sister came running over to her bed. Standing there with such a horrified look on her face. Maybe I'm dying, Leni thought for a moment.

'Water,' she gasped as her throat felt thick and raw. Still Annette stood there with that strange look on her face.

Then there was a cup of water – cool and delicious. She was drinking it so quickly that it dribbled down her chin.

Closing her eyes, she slumped back against her pillows, hoping that the fever would break. In the distance there were voices and doors slamming shut. She couldn't keep track of them. It hurt to swallow her own spit. Eventually she found herself drifting into a feverish sleep.

When Leni awoke again, she was all alone. Someone was knocking on the door – not the street door, but the door to her apartment. The knocking went on and on. She tried to call out to Frau Knopf but there was no answer and no sign of Nette at all.

Stumbling to her feet, Leni staggered out of her bedroom, clutching her old red dressing gown around her, her naked feet causing her to shiver as they touched the cold floor. The knocking grew louder and more persistent.

Pulling the front door open a crack, Leni peeked out to see Walter standing there, clutching a small metal pot in his hands. For the life of her she couldn't think of one reason why this man was at her door. Had she sent for him in her fevered state? Did she tell Annette to bring him to her?

She shook her head, puzzled. 'Walter, what are you doing here?'

'Your sister came to the café to tell us you were sick. You must have picked up something from Herr Bauer as he's taken to his bed today too. I brought you some soup. I made it fresh this morning.' He seemed uncomfortable now that he was faced with her. She thought how terrible she must look, with her tangled hair and flushed skin, and felt strange that he should witness it. This large grizzly bear of a man held out his little metal pail of soup. Leni suddenly remembered the night before and his kiss. She felt embarrassed that he was at her door as she stood there burning with fever, the smell of her own sweat disgusting her.

'That's very kind. I would ask you to come in but I . . .'

She had barely got her words out when Walter interrupted her:

'Oh no ... you need to rest. I hope you feel better tomorrow, Leni.'

He held out the little pot again and she took it from him, feeling the warmth between her hands. 'Thank you, Walter,' she whispered, each word feeling like a razor blade in her throat.

He nodded. 'The soup is warm so you can eat it now, or heat it later. Anyway ...' His face lit up with a kind of hopeful embarrassment and he nodded again before walking away, his left leg dragging slightly behind him, and his head bowed.

Leni watched him walk back down the stairs and found that, in spite of it all, she was smiling ...

60

The sign on the door said 'Medical Officer'. Annette had read it several times as she sat nervously on a steel-legged chair in a cold and unwelcoming corridor. It smelled strongly of disinfectant. From time to time, men and women in uniform bustled past her, carrying clipboards. Everyone seemed to have something important to do or some place to be – everyone except Annette, who sat neatly with her knees together, waiting.

Glenn had met her outside the army base in Zehlendorf and escorted her to the medical wing, patting her hand to reassure her. Yet she wasn't reassured at all.

She'd left Leni at home feverish and ill – the sight of her being so helpless sent Annette to her darkest memories of the war, when she'd been sure that her sister would die and she'd be left all alone. Annette had given Frau Knopf strict instructions to look after Leni and Thea before she'd left – now all she could do was focus on her medical.

Annette had chosen Saturday 7 February as the wedding date. Everything was arranged. She'd bought some blue wool material with several packs of Lucky Strikes so that Leni could make her a new dress to go with the old stolen fox fur. There wouldn't be a party or anything but then there was only a handful of guests. The entire list comprised Leni, Marta, Glenn and his best man, Bennie. It wasn't the wedding she had planned in her dreams but there would be plenty of time for celebrations once she was living in America . . . *if* she was allowed to live there . . .

She studied the sign on the door again. The door had opened only once and that was to admit another Berliner, a stout, dark-haired young woman who had given her a nervous smile. She'd been inside for several minutes now, and a lot longer than Annette had been led to believe this process should take. She wondered what could be taking so much time.

When she'd had medicals in the past, they were always just a matter of being weighed and sticking out your tongue. Whatever was happening behind the tightly closed door was evidently a lot more complicated than that. The thought plagued her. She was petrified that everyone would find out she wasn't pregnant, but Glenn had assured her that this was merely a routine check-up. Simply listening to her chest and taking her vitals.

'They just want to make sure you don't have any diseases.' He'd laughed but Annette didn't think it was funny.

Glenn could be very casual about their fate sometimes, as if it had never occurred to him that he wouldn't get his own way – because he always had.

Annette shuffled her feet on the grey-tiled floor and looked down at her hands. She was trembling, partly with cold and partly with the sheer terror of being exposed as a liar and left behind in Berlin. Glenn was being shipped back home soon and this was their only chance to get married. She wasn't even sure that she'd be allowed to travel with him, after hearing stories about other 'war brides' who hadn't been able to get themselves out of Germany, even though they'd passed all the tests and were legally married.

She would have two months to make her way to America – Glenn was sure he could find her a seat on a cargo plane or pull some strings but that was assuming he would still want to after this medical.

Suddenly the door opened and the young woman came out of the room rather hurriedly. She didn't make eye contact with Annette but instead walked briskly through the double doors at the end of the corridor. Then a man in a white coat appeared in the doorway, a stethoscope draped casually around his neck. In his hands he carried a clipboard of notes. Flipping through the pages, he peered over his spectacles and gestured towards her: 'Annette Taube? Come in, please.'

Her legs had become quite jelly-like when she tried to stand on them. She felt slightly dizzy as she walked towards this man and his clipboard. Gulping down anxious breaths, she went into the room and glanced around to see what might be in store for her.

In one corner was a wooden desk. Either side of it were two of the same steel-legged chairs that she'd been sitting on in the corridor, and in the other corner was a small examination table covered in a white sheet. There was a set of metal screens erected on one side of the table and two smaller tables, one at the side with a number of steel instruments laid neatly on a white cloth, and one at the bottom of the bed, on which stood a lamp that could be moved to any angle.

Annette couldn't take her eyes off the instruments, trying to work out what each metal object was for or what might be done to her. There was a strange smell in the room that she couldn't quite place for a minute, and then realized that it was the smell of oranges. Glancing at his desk, she noticed a peeled orange sitting in a dish, half-eaten.

'You speak English, Fräulein?' the doctor said without looking up from his notes.

'Yes ... I speak English,' Annette replied, trying to sound confident and clear but coming across as neither. The trembling had thankfully subsided but now she waited to be asked to sit down on one of the steel-legged chairs, or offered a thermometer to place in her mouth.

She gripped at her handbag tightly, and stood rigidly to attention waiting for the man to stop reading and tell her what was expected.

'Go behind the screens and get undressed, please. There's a gown just on the wall there.' The doctor still had not looked up at her and she stood rooted to the spot, praying for someone to rescue her from this situation. He must have sensed her disobedience and, being unused to having his orders ignored, lifted his eyes, puzzled. 'Did you understand what I said, Fräulein?' he said brusquely.

It was clear to Annette that he just wanted her to get on with it now. He was probably ready for his lunch – maybe he even had his favourite sandwich in the drawer of his wooden desk and only she, and her reluctance to move, was holding him up.

'Yes ...' Only compliance would allow her to escape this room. There was nothing to be done except submit to the examination and let the results speak for themselves.

She exhaled – a resigned sigh of desperation – before walking over to the screens and unfastening her clothes.

Annette peeled away her layers, taking the time to fold each item neatly. The man could think many things about her but she would not allow him to think of her as slovenly.

The gown tied in two places, one at the neck and the other at the waist. Annette had never worn one before and wasn't sure whether she should put it on to tie at the front or the back. She felt tears filling her eyes and gave herself a little shake to gather herself. She would not cry in front of this man. She would not beg Glenn for forgiveness. She would keep her dignity above everything else.

She was a liar, that was true, but Annette would not demean herself by weeping. She guessed at which way round the gown should go on and lay back on the examination bed with her feet together and her arms fixed by her sides.

After a few moments, the doctor pushed the screens to one side and stood over the bed. She had guessed wrongly with the gown and the man tutted as he had to untie the front and pull it down at the back so he could listen to her breathing. The metal tip of the stethoscope felt cold against her skin.

He listened for a few seconds – asked her to breathe in and out before hanging the tube back around his neck. Taking a pen out of the pocket of his white coat, he scribbled something on his notes. Then he asked her to stick out her tongue. Putting his hands on either side of her face, he pulled her cheeks apart so that he could peer inside her mouth, his thumbs bruising her mouth as they tugged at her. Her body turned rigid with fear.

'Say aaaah,' he said and Annette obliged with a silent fury, longing to pull his hands away from her face. Then he let her go, and once again wrote in his notes. His handwriting curled large and spidery over the white paper. Her mouth felt sore and a small wave of panic began to rise from the bottom of her belly.

When nothing happened immediately, for a blissful few seconds Annette thought it was over and she was free to leave. She sat up on the bed and was about to swing her legs over the side and stand up, when the doctor walked down to the bottom of the bed and switched on the lamp.

'Lie back down, please. You're pregnant, I understand?' His tone implied the fact of her pregnancy had displeased him in some way. Annette's breathing became shallow and uneven as she lay back against the bed.

'Yes,' she whispered, dreading what would surely happen next.

'How many months?' He gazed at her over the top of his glasses.

'I don't know . . . exactly . . .' She lay there, staring up at the ceiling, praying for it to be over.

'Raise your knees, please . . .' As he spoke, he adjusted the lamp so that it shone between her legs and with one hand he parted her knees.

Annette couldn't breathe . . . She felt his hands between her legs and the cold metal of some instrument pulling her apart. Pain rippled through her and she clenched her teeth and waited. His hands were feeling her abdomen, pushing and prodding at her. Then the metal instrument was removed and he put his hand inside her, making efficient little noises as he did so. She swallowed a scream.

You're leaving Berlin ... she repeated silently to herself like a prayer, willing it to be true.

Then it was over and he snapped off his rubber gloves, throwing them into a bucket on the floor. The lamp was switched off and he clicked on the top of his pen several times before writing more spidery words on her notes.

Finally, he walked away. 'You can get dressed now, Fräulein.' And this time, Annette did sit up and swing her legs over the side of the bed.

The doctor was done with her. Somehow, she had passed her test ... surely there was nothing else to come? Annette stood up, pulling at the knots on the gown to untie it and struggling back into her own clothes. When she was fully dressed, she stepped out from behind the metal screens and attempted a brave smile at the doctor as if everything was under control.

'You can go. I'll send in my report.' He dismissed her without even a glance.

'Thank you ...' Annette wanted to say something – to ask what the outcome might be but she didn't dare. A few seconds passed. He stared up at her, surprised to find her still in the room after he'd told her to go. He took off his glasses and sighed.

'I see a lot of women like you, Fräulein. You're in good health. I would say around eight weeks pregnant, if that. My report will be ready by the end of the week. Good day.'

She couldn't believe what he was saying. *It couldn't be true.* Her feet were rooted to the spot. He stared at her, obviously wondering why on earth she was still standing there bothering him.

'That will be all, Fräulein.' The tone of his voice was

ice-cold, and Annette felt a deep burning humiliation spreading over her. This man despised her. She hurried out of the room and down the corridor. One thought rang through her mind over and over again. *She was pregnant.*

Annette stopped moving and leaned against the wall, taking a deep breath. She'd had no need to lie. Shaking her head from side to side in disbelief, she muttered to herself, 'My God . . . oh my God . . .' over and over. Her hand clamped across her mouth as she clenched her teeth. She had to pull herself together.

Seconds later, she stepped out of the medical wing into an icy wind. There were American soldiers everywhere she looked. Tall and crisp in their uniforms. And then she saw him leaning against the wall of the next block. Glenn was waiting for her.

The minute she saw his face, Annette knew that she could never love this man. She told herself that it didn't matter because she was getting out of Berlin, but then she began to cry – great violent sobs.

'What's wrong? Hey . . . hey now . . . tell me what happened?' He held her tight, allowing Annette to bury her face in his chest so he couldn't look at her.

'It was awful. The doctor was so horrible to me . . .' Her chest dry-heaved several times as she tried to speak.

'Oh, honey – hey, don't get upset. Hush now.' Glenn continued holding her, offering tiny pats of comfort on her back.

She couldn't help herself. The shock of finding out that she was pregnant together with the humiliation of the medical and the scathing tone of the doctor's words made her cry harder.

'Annie, sweetheart, don't cry. Everything is going to be all right, you'll see . . .'

Annette heard the words but all she could think about was that she didn't want to marry this man and she didn't want to have another baby. But it was too late . . .

Berlin, February 1948

61

It was a bitterly cold February day, with molten-steel skies threatening rain. Annette had woken up early and now lay in her bed, thinking about the day ahead of her. Behind the bedroom door hung her blue wool dress. Leni had taken great care making it, carefully fitting it to Annette's body, and hand-sewing every seam and dart in the gloomy bedroom light until it was finished.

It felt tight now as her belly had expanded, although nobody could really tell that she was pregnant yet. It was just over two months since she'd suffered through that awful medical exam and Leni had got sick again, when the sight of her lying there flushed with fever had cast Annette back to those long dark days at the end of the war.

Things were more strained between them than ever. She felt miserable and trapped by the thought of this marriage. She told herself that she had to marry Glenn now for there was no way to explain to her sister that there was another baby on the way. Leni wouldn't be able support them all. They were barely managing as it was. Yet some days the prospect of the wedding filled her with gloom.

Across the room, Thea was wide awake, her arms stretching out towards her. The child was quietly babbling. Leni was still asleep – curled into a small ball as if she were a tiny animal in hibernation.

Annette looked at Thea – the black eyes staring back at

her. She was doing the right thing. Reluctantly she got out of her bed, shivering with cold and reaching for her dressing gown. Tying the belt tightly around her waist, she pushed her feet into her old wool slippers. Ignoring the child begging for her attention, she quietly slipped out of the bedroom and into the kitchen.

Other than the dress hanging on the door, there really wasn't very much else to suggest that this was her wedding day. No flowers, or cake. None of the things she might have hoped for as a child.

Yet today she would become Mrs Glenn Forester Junior. It was the beginning of a new life.

She was sitting at the kitchen table drinking a cup of Maxwell House coffee that had been generously supplied by her future husband when the bedroom door opened and Leni came out clutching Thea.

'Ah, the happy bride – you're up early,' she said, trying to pour herself a cup of coffee while jiggling Thea on her hip.

Annette could feel Leni's eyes searching her face.

''Nette, you are sure about this, aren't you?' Leni picked up her cup of coffee and took an anxious gulp while she waited for an answer.

'Please don't . . . not today. We've been over it so many times.' There was nothing left to say and she wanted to get into the bathroom before the Knopfs began their daily litany of complaints. Her voice sounded miserable and flat as she went on: 'I just want to make a new life in America and that's all there is to it.' Getting to her feet would bring an end to this conversation she hoped as she stood up – but her sister wasn't done.

'But you don't love him . . . and marriage is very hard without love. You'll be in a strange land with nobody to help you.'

'Well, you didn't love Karl,' Annette snapped and instantly regretted it. She planted a kiss on Leni's cheek and gently squeezed her shoulder. 'I'm sorry. I shouldn't have said that. I'm just nervous today. Let's not quarrel.'

'Oh, Nette . . . it's just that you seem so unhappy. It shouldn't be this way,' Leni pleaded.

A beat of anger drummed inside her until she couldn't stop herself. 'Then how should it be? You and I . . . we've sat here with death all around us. We've lost everyone we've ever loved. Our city is in ruins. Am I supposed to wait for the kind of fairy tales that you tell Thea? Do you think someone will come and rescue us? That's not for women like us. You can only dream of that kind of love if you have food in your belly and a comfortable bed at night. I don't need love, Leni – I need a life.'

Annette had not intended to make a speech but now that she had, she realized that it was exactly how she felt. All that mattered was getting a seat on that cargo plane out of this city.

In America she would have a new life and she chose that over the kind of love that made her dizzy. She'd read about such love in books but had never experienced it. Her heart had sealed itself shut a long time ago and now she was unable to open it, no matter how hard she tried. She'd watched other girls make fools of themselves but that wasn't for her.

'We all need love . . .' Leni looked up at her with such pity on her face that she couldn't stand to see it.

'No, we don't. *You* need it, maybe – I've made my choice. I'm going to have a brand-new life, Leni, with everything that I've ever wanted and nothing is going to stop me.' It was probably their last argument, Annette thought as she walked out of the room. Soon there would be an ocean between them.

Running the bath, she studied herself in the mirror over the sink. Her face had lost that wide-eyed girlish look. She looked so very weary.

But she had survived it all. So what if she didn't love Glenn?

Annette jutted out her chin. She didn't feel proud of what she saw reflected back at her – but she didn't feel ashamed, either.

At exactly eleven o'clock, they were standing outside a rather bleak-looking temporary government building where she was to be married. The previous government building had been turned to dust in the final days of the war.

The bride was wearing her blue dress with her hair pinned up and the stolen fox fur carefully draped around her shoulders. She dabbed some face powder over her nose and chin, and smoothed away any stray hairs that might have escaped their hairgrips.

Marta gave her a reassuring smile as she squeezed her hand. Leni stood to one side, giving off an air of disapproval, but when Annette caught her eye, she did at least manage a friendly nod. Thea was at home with Frau Knopf. As far as the child was concerned, it was better not to take any chances at this point.

Marta looked elegant in her rust-coloured suit while

Leni was wearing a well-worn but still presentable bottle-green dress with her usual grey winter coat and headscarf over the top. By her side stood her friend Walter, who was becoming a regular fixture these days.

In some ways, Annette was glad that she wasn't leaving Leni completely alone although she found Walter quite intimidating. He was a large man with a brusque manner, and when he'd stepped inside their apartment, he seemed to fill so much space that she found herself creeping around him.

A blast of icy wind sent them all scuttling towards the door, Annette rubbing her hands together to keep warm as she'd forgotten her gloves. Pushing open the wooden door, she caught sight of Glenn waiting nervously just inside the hallway with his best man, Bennie. His face broke into a relieved smile when he saw her standing there.

As she moved towards him, Annette caught a glimpse of Leni's face – a worried frown on her forehead and an anxious smile on her lips. For a moment she wanted to run back to her, hoping she would make it all better.

Except there were some things that Leni could never make better.

She tried to give her a comforting glance, praying that her sister wouldn't cry. It suddenly occurred to her that they had never been apart. Every day of Annette's life she'd woken up and seen Leni's face over breakfast. The more she thought about it, the faster a ripple of fear flowed through her. How would she cope on her own in a strange country? What would she do without Leni?

Her mouth opened as she felt the need to say something to Leni but the words wouldn't come. Instead, her sister gave her a reassuring nod from across the hallway.

'Are you ready, Annie?' Looking up, she was almost surprised to see Glenn standing next to her.

She smiled up at him and then, with a final glance over at her sister, Annette took a long deep breath and said, 'Yes, I'm ready.'

Everything about the room was cold and uninviting. The floor was bare, the walls were bare, the windows were bare. The furniture in the room was cobbled together from the remnants of other rooms: a strange mixture of mismatching wooden chairs and a wooden table in front of two large curtainless windows. Annette and Glenn walked slowly into the room and took their places. Their loyal band of witnesses followed behind, Marta clinging lovingly to Bennie while Leni stood next to Walter, a tight smile on her face.

Annette tried to take in what was happening, but the ceremony had no sooner begun than it was over. Official words were spoken haltingly in both German and English, a gold ring was hastily pushed on to her finger before Glenn gathered her up in his arms and kissed her for so long that their witnesses began to make polite coughing noises.

Afterwards, she twisted the gold band around her finger until the skin turned red. Allowing herself to be congratulated – shaking hands or accepting polite kisses on her cheek. The smile on her face did not falter for one second. Annette would not let anyone think that she regretted any of it.

She was married. And she was leaving Berlin.

PART THREE
Berlin, June 1961

62

Leni surveyed the tragedy of her ankles, puffy and slightly livid in colour, as if her misery had slid all the way down her body and pooled at her feet. The worst of it was hidden under a pair of thick beige-coloured stockings but Leni knew, and in that knowing felt all of her fifty-four years of age.

Stretching out her aching big toe against the cheap leather of her left shoe, Leni grimaced. She regretted buying the cheaper pair now that she was standing in them. Her big toe pushed itself up against the inside, desperate to find just a little more space but there was none. The good leather shoes had cost more than she had wanted to pay but it was a false economy as these shoes pinched whenever she stood up for any length of time.

She had been standing and waiting for at least thirty minutes now. She'd got to the airport early, although when Leni thought about it, she had immediately realized that was a pointless thing to do – as if the fact of her early arrival would make an aeroplane arrive any sooner. Embarrassed by her waiting, Leni stood to one side just in front of a small shop that sold cameras and pretended to be looking in the window at them. Out of the corner of her eye she could see two large black boards with yellow stripes displaying all the comings and goings that day.

Suddenly the boards made a strange clattering noise,

and showed that the Pan Am flight she was waiting for was delayed by an hour. Leni sighed, unsure now what to do with herself. She continued pointlessly staring at the different models of cameras behind the glass – all the time wishing that she hadn't come.

Leni had never flown in an aeroplane and couldn't imagine how it must feel. A large white bird so high up in the sky you could barely see it with the naked eye. She wondered about clouds, and what they might look like from up there. She didn't expect that she would ever find out. The blonde woman working in the camera store saw her looking and smiled politely, trying to encourage her to enter the shop, but Leni had no wish to buy a camera, or anything else for that matter. She just wanted to get this waiting over with, and so turned away from the cameras and tried to fix her stare on some other part of the airport.

The arrivals hall at Templehof was an enormous, cavernous space. When Leni had first arrived, it was not so busy, but now strangers flooded past her, suitcases of all shapes and sizes being heaved along. She lifted her aching left foot out of her shoe, at last finding some relief but feeling decidedly off balance. There were so many people around her that she worried about being knocked down. It was as if she were the only person trying to walk in the wrong direction. Hastily shoving her foot back inside its cheap leather case, Leni moved to the side, away from the herd of passengers.

An announcement echoed across the large hall as a woman repeated the arrival of the flight from London. Leni tried to stretch out her big toe once more and rubbed at the small of her back, which had begun to ache. The waiting was making her nervous. What would she say? How would they greet each other? They had once been so familiar but now, after so many years, Leni wasn't even sure they would recognize each other.

She was old now. Her hair was greying; her face had lost the hopeful girl and gained a stranger. Lately she'd caught herself unable to stand completely upright, as if her body wanted to fold itself over. Leni straightened her spine, hoping to relieve the pain in her back and feet. She'd caught a glimpse of her reflection in the glass of the small camera shop, her face puzzled as if she weren't quite sure what she was doing there. She hadn't expected to be waiting at an airport today, or any day if she were honest. Up until now her life had been a series of departures, waving goodbye in a crowd of strangers. Arrivals were a different kind of occasion, Leni thought: an occasion requiring better shoes, good wine and a rich chocolate cake. She had none of these things.

Above the two black boards was a sign for a restaurant and Leni wondered if she might consider a cup of coffee, or a bowl of soup perhaps, but her stomach felt sour and full of acid. She hadn't felt able to eat breakfast that morning and now she regretted it, along with the cheap leather shoes. Everything felt wrong. Her stomach rumbled with hunger, her back ached, her toes pinched and her mind . . . oh, her mind was the worst of all. Suppose . . . there were so many 'supposes' that Leni tried to focus on the people around her. The dark grey uniforms of the customs officials; the impatient passengers being asked to open their suitcases for inspection. For a short while, she amused herself by watching the greetings as passengers searched out those wating for them. Polite handshakes or long, yearning embraces. The chatter in her mind began again . . . Suppose . . . well, which would it be?

The London flight landed, and suddenly the hall was buzzing with people. Men in dark hats, women in light coats, children with wide eyes. Leni watched as they began to disappear through the glass doors and into the bright June sunshine. She didn't know why she'd come here. Leni took a deep breath and then let out a long complaining sigh. It really would have been much better to meet at her apartment. She could have waited in her old brown slippers and her rose-pink day dress. She might have sat on her little brown settee, drinking a small cup of strong black coffee or listened to the radio talking about the news to distract her. It was too late for such distractions now. Her mind could think of nothing else but the arrival of the Pan Am flight. She had no choice but to wait . . .

The same woman's voice announced the late arrival of the Pan Am flight. She seemed irritated, as if the people waiting were responsible for the delay, rather than an unusual weather pattern in the middle of the Atlantic Ocean.

Leni sniffed and then licked her lips. They felt chapped, her mouth was dry and she wished that she really had gone upstairs to the restaurant for a cup of coffee, but it was too late now. She tried to focus on the strange faces surrounding her. A little boy was crying, the bustle of the crowd suddenly all too much for him. A handsome young man stumbled into her and apologized profusely but without even looking at her. There were so many people that Leni began to worry she wouldn't be able to see anyone in this crush.

A swell of panic rose up from deep inside her. If she couldn't see then there was no point being here . . . there really was no point meeting someone at the airport if you then failed to actually meet them. Leni couldn't understand why she suddenly felt so nervous as she stared accusingly at her cheap, ill-fitting shoes. She would be found wanting – too old, too shabbily dressed, too . . . Her list was incomplete yet she knew that she would be inspected and that she would fail that inspection. The thought made her anxious.

Suddenly the crowd parted as passengers began to get their bearings and spot the beige taxis parked outside. Leni scanned each passenger: too short, too tall, too young or too old. Enormous piles of luggage were wheeled past her. People ran into the arms of their loved ones with high-pitched squeals of delight. Other passengers carried small suitcases and walked solemnly, arriving and leaving alone. Leni took a deep breath as another bubble of passengers arrived. She ran a hand through her hair, patting it down, smoothing it over nervously. Her foot slipped in and then out of her shoe without her thinking about it. And still she waited . . .

In the distance, she could see an elegant woman in a pale blue skirt and jacket carrying a small cream vanity case in her left hand. A white handbag swung from the crook of her elbow as she pulled a large grey suitcase behind her. Her hair was painted an unnatural shade of silver-blonde. Her clothes were not expensive, but neither were they cheap, and her shoes looked as if they fitted her perfectly.

Leni watched as the woman drew closer to her. The click of her perfect heels on the tiled floor, the setting down of the cream vanity case. A flicker of recognition, then a smile . . . The woman's mouth opened as she prepared to say something but Leni was too quick for her.

'Hello, Nette . . .'

63

Annette stood in the doorway of Leni's living room, trying to get a sense of the life that her sister had been living. It was much smaller than her own accommodation back in Brooklyn. Leni only had one floor of the building, containing two bedrooms and a kitchen, all off the tiny living room. There was a balcony outside the window but Annette couldn't see any way to get out there. The furnishings were typical of Leni, she thought: plain and well cared for. There was very little colour in the rooms, unlike Annette's house, which she'd filled with bright colours and the latest things when they could afford them. Her days were spent flicking through weekly magazines searching for the latest fashions. Annette was not wealthy but she lived in a land of plenty. And she liked to look nice – buying two-piece suits in good fabrics to wear with silk blouses.

Leni's home was that of a woman who still darned her clothes, only replacing them when the old ones were too worn to be repaired. Her life seemed frugal, as if she would not allow herself anything that might bring pleasure. Even today, she had come all the way to the airport wearing an old navy cotton skirt and a dull pink blouse. Her life was making do with sturdy old furniture and faded clothes with cheap shoes.

Annette pursed her lips in disapproval. They had always been different, but the years apart had only made their differences more acute, it seemed. She'd expected something else but quite what, Annette couldn't put into words.

The walls were covered in a selection of black and white photographs, mostly of Leni with Walter. There was Leni at the lake, and Walter waving to the camera, then the two of them sitting in a restaurant alongside another couple, with wine-induced smiles and a stained tablecloth where some of the wine had spilt. A decade of companionship laid out in casual snaps of outings and celebrations.

Underneath the photographs of Leni and Walter was a whole row dedicated to photographs of Thea. There were no photographs of her, Annette noted. She was excluded from the wall of family portraits. Most of their old family photographs were lost when a bomb had fallen on their house, but still it stung that Leni had never asked her to send a recent photograph of her and Glenn, or their boys, Jimmy and Glenn Junior. Of course, Annette had never offered to send the pictures, either.

She'd sent perfunctory letters by airmail. Polite scratchings on the page, talking about nothing. She'd hidden herself away from her sister, unable to confide the truth about her new life. When Annette finally picked up the telephone and dialled long distance to speak to Leni, the sound of her sister's voice evoked such a sharp pain inside her that she'd briefly considered not going through with her trip to Berlin.

While Leni bustled around in the kitchen, Annette stood in front of the wall of photographs, barely recognizing the child she'd left behind. There she was with a gap-toothed smile, riding a red bicycle – and another sprawled on the rug in front of a Christmas tree, grinning over a neat pile of boxes, beautifully wrapped with ribboned bows. Annette chewed at the inside of her cheek until it felt sore. She felt no connection to this girl and yet she had lain down on her bed and screamed in pain until the tiny body had separated from her own. She remembered Leni placing the baby in her arms, and turning her face to the wall, refusing motherhood. She wondered about the girl now and how she might feel seeing her. When Annette had pushed her two sons out of her body just five months after leaving Berlin, it had been in a sterile hospital room and she'd loved them on sight. Their tiny noses, their fingers and toes; Glenn bounding in from the waiting room with his fearful, ecstatic face. Annette had felt she'd pleased him. Twin boys – one for each of them to love.

She walked to the end of Leni's gallery. The most recent photograph was of a moody teenager, unsmiling, her eyes demonstrating her unwillingness to be photographed. Thea's black eyes blazed out of the wooden frame at her and Annette took a deep jagged breath before wandering away from the photographs and leaning against the kitchen doorway, watching as Leni scuttled about fetching cups and coffee.

'I should have bought a cake to have with our coffee . . .' She smiled apologetically and Annette smiled back at her. She was trying so hard – they were both trying so hard.

'It doesn't matter. You've got a nice apartment here,' she said while searching in her white handbag for her pack of Chesterfields.

'Thank you. At least there is no more sharing with the Knopfs.' Leni gave a bitter chuckle as she poured out two cups of coffee. 'Walter always liked it here . . .' Her voice faded away, leaving Annette wondering what to say to her. She'd only met Walter once or twice before her wedding and hardly knew the man at all.

'I ... I ... was sorry to hear about Walter ... D'you mind?' It felt strange to be speaking German again, and she hesitated, stumbling over her words. She pointed to the cigarette pack and Leni shook her head. Annette flicked the top of her silver lighter and directed her cigarette at the tiny flame, before exhaling a cloud of smoke out of the corner of her mouth. 'Thank you. Shall we sit down?'

Leni gestured to the living room, leaving Annette to retrace her steps and find a place to sit, reluctantly choosing a narrow, rust-coloured armchair. Her sister placed a cup of coffee on a low table between the chair and a dark brown settee with wooden arms. In the centre of the table was a fruit bowl filled with oranges. Annette leaned back in the armchair and looked across the table at Leni, taking her in. Trying to make sense of this new Leni who had grown old without her.

It was the first time she'd set eyes on her sister since that crisp winter's day in 1948 when she'd waved goodbye and got on an uncomfortable US cargo plane that had rattled her bones all the way across the Atlantic Ocean, leaving her feeling terribly sick.

Leni was fifty-four years old now and she looked every one of her years. Her hair was still fair but if you looked closely, you could see strands of white-grey. Her eyes were lined and her lips tugged downwards, giving her the look of a woman who was unhappy with her lot. There were tiny clusters of spidery veins on her cheeks. Her face was scrubbed clean and her hair brushed but it was typical of

Leni that she made so little of herself. Annette tried to imagine her sister living in Brooklyn in a world where they might meet at the beauty parlour once a week and then go on for lunch. She couldn't see her there, no matter how hard she tried.

Her sister belonged to Berlin in a way that Annette could not. She wasn't sure that she belonged to Brooklyn either – yet it was what she'd chosen, and she was comfortable there. Berlin felt like an ill-fitting shoe and she suddenly regretted her journey. She couldn't imagine what she was thinking of coming back here, yet it had made perfect sense when she'd booked her ticket. All it had taken was a sharp note of longing for her sister one morning after a fight with Glenn, and the next thing she was packing her suitcase without any real thought or plan.

'You didn't marry him,' Annette said out of the blue. It had just occurred to her, and the words flew out of her mouth before she could stop them.

Leni gave her a sharp look. 'I never found out what happened to Karl – I might still be married to him for all I know. It didn't matter. We made a life together that suited us.'

'Of course. I didn't mean . . . anything . . .' She could have kicked herself for not giving a thought to the situation that Leni had been left in. 'You look well.'

'What are you doing here, Nette?' Leni hadn't touched her cup of coffee. She sat with her knees together and her hands placed neatly in her lap, staring at Annette. She wanted to look away but there was something about Leni's stare that stopped her. She felt like a child again, being scolded by her mother.

'I wanted to visit. It's been a long time.' She knew she sounded defensive, but she wasn't ready to tell Leni the truth – not yet.

'Just a visit . . .' Leni eyed her suspiciously. She was waiting for something. Annette shifted uncomfortably in her seat.

'How's Thea?' she asked tentatively.

Her sister gave her a furious glare. 'What do you care?'

'Leni, don't be cross with me. I did what I could.' She knew they would argue about Thea in the same way she knew the sun would rise in the morning. Annette didn't want to explain. She didn't want to think about the girl at all. It was a mistake – *she* was a mistake.

'She was better off with you . . . Please, let's not fight.' Annette put her head down, searching for her cigarette pack in her handbag once again, trying to avoid Leni's scornful stare.

'Thea is no longer a child. She's a young woman who lives in the world we created for her. Sometimes she is angry about that, as you will see. She doesn't know you're her mother. I thought it best to not mention you and over time she started calling me Mamma. I didn't correct her because I *was* her mother. I didn't leave her behind.' Leni got to her feet and walked over to the window where she stared out at the buildings across the street and shook her head as if she were holding an imaginary argument with someone.

Annette knew that the someone was her.

64

Thea had been kissing Rainer for at least forty minutes against the only uncharred walls of an old dance hall on Jägerstrasse. The street door had been boarded up but after a long evening of scraping and pulling, Rainer and his friends had managed to break inside, finding a wonderland of rooms untouched by the fire to bring their girlfriends to.

The first time Thea had walked through the burnt-out dance hall, seeing the blackened walls and broken remains, she'd imagined all the young women who might have kissed inside its walls. She'd waltzed around what was once the dance floor and finished off with a silly curtsey. They'd laughed and Rainer had wrapped his arms around her and begun kissing her. Discovering a strange mirror propped against a wall, they'd amused themselves by making grotesque shapes – laughing hysterically at their reflections. He'd told her that a woman had burnt the dance hall to the ground for the insurance money and now she was in prison, so there was nobody to bother them.

Then they'd raced around the building, inspecting the undamaged rooms, finding an old office with a staircase leading up to a set of rooms that seemed strangely abandoned, as if the person who'd lived there had just stepped out for a walk.

There was a living room full of furniture, a number of comfortable armchairs with small tables beside them and a leather couch pushed up against the window. Books and papers were scattered about on every surface and small figurines of cats decorated a sideboard. In the bedroom, there was a large closet at one end, with a small wooden bed pushed against the wall. Both the bed and the armchairs were full of damp and insects that crawled in and out of them. It smelled musty and stale but Thea loved their secret place and the things they did there.

She knew that her mother would be angry about her being in this part of the city, but it fascinated her. It was so different from the western part with its freshly painted buildings and glass-fronted shops full of expensive goods. The Soviet sector had a lot of old buildings that were either blackened and crumbling or left as piles of bricks after the war. For Thea, it was a peek into another world – one that she had no knowledge of and she couldn't stay away from.

She'd stolen a blanket from her own bed to cover the leather couch so they could lie down together. It was yellow wool made up of knitted squares. Her mother had made it for her. Thea left it draped across the leather couch as a way of marking her territory, both the old dance hall and Rainer.

Rainer was tall and dark-haired, with an easy smile and a rangy yet muscular build. He liked Thea because she didn't fawn over him like the other girls he knew. She was a loner, except when Rainer offered her the prospect of exploring his warm mouth.

Each day, Thea met him after school, telling her mother that she was staying late for some drama group. Her mother had not questioned her about what plays they were working on and that left Thea free to be pressed up against the wall of this derelict building whenever she felt like it. Lately she'd extended her drama hours to include most Saturday afternoons as kissing Rainer on school days was proving to be not nearly enough.

'Wait . . . Rainer, I can't stay long. My aunt is coming to stay and I promised that I'd go straight home today.'

Rainer's hand was riding up her skirt and had just reached the band of elastic separating her underpants from her thigh. Her hand quickly followed his, putting a stop to his progress.

'Five more minutes . . .' he murmured into her neck but Thea pulled away.

'No more minutes.' She smiled as she watched his face fall into a slight sulk over not getting his own way. Planting a fat kiss on his cheek, she smiled at him. 'Don't be cross.'

Rainer sighed and then gathered her to him. 'OK. Will I see you tomorrow?'

'I'll try but my mother is driving me crazy about her sister coming to stay. She's coming from America.'

'Oh, this is not fair. We always meet on Saturday afternoons. Tell your aunt you have a boyfriend who needs to kiss you . . .' Rainer leaned forward and began planting kisses on Thea's face, making her squeal with laughter.

'Be here at three o'clock and I'll try to get away. I don't want to upset my mother. She's been so sad since Walter died – but once I've said hello and they're gossiping, they'll forget all about me and I'll come here.' Thea wrapped her arms around Rainer's neck, nuzzling into him.

'I'll be here at three. I don't see why you don't just tell them that you have a boyfriend. Are you ashamed of me?

Am I such a terrible boyfriend that you have to keep me hidden?'

Thea playfully slapped him on his arm and retrieved her school bag from the floor. 'Yes, you are.'

Rainer dropped his arms to his sides and stood back to look at her. 'I'm serious, Thea. Why don't you tell her about me?'

'Because I like you better as a secret. Now, kiss me goodbye . . .'

65

Leni heard the key turn in the front door and got to her feet. 'It's Thea.'

Annette looked nervous, she thought, as she listened for the familiar thud of a school bag hitting the floor. 'Come and say hello to your Aunt Annette,' Leni called, although the girl could hardly avoid them as she had to walk through the living room to get anywhere in this apartment. While Leni waited for Thea to appear, a deep frown gathered between her eyes as she realized that she hadn't told the girl they would have to share a room while Annette was staying with them. She'd been building up to having the conversation but lately Thea was always moody and it never seemed like the right time.

But there were only two bedrooms, and it was either that or Annette would have to share with Leni, and she couldn't face that. Thea, like most fifteen-year-olds, was precious about her privacy and her own bedroom. Leni sighed, wishing she'd had this conversation before Annette had arrived. She could only hope that her presence might make Thea less likely to have one of her sulks.

'Hello . . . You're late. You were supposed to come straight home.' She moved to kiss Thea, which the girl allowed reluctantly before shrugging her off. Leni watched as Annette stood up and offered her hand.

'It's very nice to see you again, Thea. You've grown up!'

Thea gave a weak smile in return but didn't seem interested in investigating Annette further. Watching the two of them engaged in a formal handshake gave Leni a peculiar feeling but she busied herself by worrying about dinner.

'If we get changed now, we could go out for dinner. Wouldn't that be nice?' Leni sounded as if she was trying to convince herself that it might be. Neither her sister nor Thea responded with much enthusiasm to her offer.

'I'm really not very hungry – I ate on the plane.' Annette sat back down in the armchair and lit another of her cigarettes. The entire living room was developing a stuffy airless atmosphere and Leni longed to throw open all the windows. Thea took the opportunity to flop down on the settee, stretching out her legs and placing her feet on top of the coffee table.

'Well, I'm starving.'

Leni sighed. She could already see how the next few weeks would go, trying to keep both Thea and Annette happy. 'I'll make something for us, then.'

She was about to go into the kitchen and start cooking when Annette suddenly got to her feet. 'I'm really feeling the jet lag now – it's been a long day. Would you mind showing me where I'm sleeping? I really can't keep my eyes open.'

Leni hesitated, catching sight of Thea's black eyes gazing at her first in curiosity and then in horror as she realized what Leni was about to say.

'I've put you in Thea's room. We can share, can't we, Thea? It won't be for long . . .' Leni could tell that Thea was about to start an argument. It was a regular occurrence these days. The sweet-natured child who would crawl on to her lap seeking comfort at all hours of the day or night had turned into a young woman who would not let anything pass without demanding to know why things were this way. Never satisfied with the answers and often only relenting when she saw that Leni couldn't take any more. From time to time, Leni would wistfully catch a fleeting glimpse of the child Thea had been but mostly she felt stunned to find this furious dark-eyed stranger who lived alongside her. She hoped it was merely a teenage phase and the sweet-natured girl would eventually return to her.

'All right . . . but I have to go out tomorrow afternoon. I'm meeting my drama group.' Thea's black eyes bargained with Leni. They were supposed to take Annette out for the day. Leni had thought it might be nice to show her sister some of the new things in Berlin and had begged Thea to come along with her.

Leni sighed. 'Fine . . . Get your night things and show your aunt where she can put her clothes. You can move some things into my wardrobe if you need to.'

Thea, having got what she wanted, leapt to her feet, stopping to kiss her mother on her cheek as she ran past her. 'Thank you, Mamma,' she said with an impish grin.

Leni was grateful not to have a row in front of Annette. She had been looking forward to a nice dinner at a local café, and maybe a glass of wine, but it looked as if she would be serving cold meats and salad, which they would be eating on their laps.

66

Leni was up early, even though it was a Saturday. She'd left Thea fast asleep, strewn across the bed that they'd been forced into sharing by Annette's presence. Standing at the kitchen counter, holding her cup of coffee between the palms of her hands, Leni stared out of the window at a row of anonymous buildings in the distance. The coffee was the way she liked it – strong and black – but she was barely sipping it. Her mind was entirely occupied with how she was going to keep the peace with both Annette and Thea to take care of. She wasn't good with difficult situations requiring diplomacy. Leni could never find the right words.

She missed Walter – he had been good with people where she was shy. Although physically imposing and slightly gruff in his manners, he had a way of making everyone feel relaxed around him. He would have found a way to talk to Annette where Leni could only think of polite questions as if they were strangers. She didn't know when things had gone wrong between them. They were once so close, but their relationship had splintered during the war. Leni looked back to 1945, with the city in ruins. She had been sick for several weeks, leaving her younger sister in charge of caring for her. Annette had done so – keeping them fed and looked after. However, once Leni was well again, Annette had seemed colder, harder and more determined to leave her behind and make a new life elsewhere.

Leni sighed and put the cup down next to the sink while she rubbed the sleep out of her eyes. She felt old today – weary in a way she had never experienced when she was young. Not just physically weary but tired of life. She felt as if she'd seen the worst of people and now she couldn't find the best in them. It made her jaded and Leni hated the feeling. There was a kind of hopelessness that greeted her the minute she opened her eyes and stayed with her all day long. When Thea was younger, Leni had felt happy watching her thrive, and after she'd found Walter she wasn't lonely any more. He'd proved himself a faithful companion and allowed her space to exhale – to put her burden down as he shared the load willingly. These days, with Walter gone and Thea so busy with her own plans, she'd begun to realize that her life was not at all as she had wanted it.

She missed the young Leni – the girl who could walk miles across the city without tiring, who could dance for hours without stopping and who felt such love that she was prepared to pack her things and leave everything behind. She envied Thea her passion for life – the energy to fight for every tiny scrap of independence: from what clothes she would wear to what she might eat for breakfast. Leni didn't have any energy left for such fights.

In the distance she heard a bedroom door open and braced herself for company, hoping it was Thea as she wanted to make peace before her sister got up.

'Morning. Is that coffee fresh?' Annette yawned. Her first cigarette of the day was already lit and Leni wrinkled her nose at the smell so early in the morning.

'Yes, I just made a pot.' Leni poured a cup and handed it over to her sister, wafting away a cloud of smoke that engulfed her. She cracked open the window and let the noise of the city distract her. Tramcars rumbled down below in the street. It was another fine day and Leni stared up at the deep blue sky for a moment.

'Thea's still asleep?' Annette asked. She seemed nervous around the subject of the child and Leni found herself strangely pleased by her sister's discomfort.

'Yes, it's all she does these days – sleep, eat and run out of the door to her drama group.'

'At least she has an interest – that's good . . .' Annette wandered into the living room, switching the radio on while she sat down in the armchair to drink her coffee.

Leni bristled slightly at being told what was good for Thea. Surely she was the judge of that? She poured herself a fresh cup of coffee and reluctantly followed Annette into the living room where she opened all the windows to let fresh air replace the stench of stale cigarettes.

The radio announcer was reading the news. There were more rumours that the Russians were about to divide the city in two, although the officials denied them. It was the same thing every few months – threats and nonsense. Leni got up to switch it off.

'Don't you worry about it?' Annette asked.

'What? Oh, take no notice of that. We're used to the threats. It will all blow over.'

'I can't say I'd want to get used to it . . .' She exhaled a cloud of smoke and drained her coffee cup.

'So how is life in America?' There was a sarcastic tone to Leni's question that she regretted instantly but it was too late.

Annette raised an eyebrow. 'It was difficult in the

beginning. We moved to Brooklyn because Glenn's family live there – and they didn't like me. I thought they would accept me because he loved me . . . I didn't understand. They just didn't like the fact that I was German.'

'None of us can choose where we're born.'

'Oh, they didn't say it of course, and they were mostly polite, but I could tell from the way they looked at me sometimes. There were questions about what we knew – about the camps, about the things that happened. They couldn't understand why we let it happen. What could I say? We were just women trying to live our lives. So, for a long time I didn't have any friends, but over the years that's got better . . .'

'And Glenn? Has he been good to you?' Leni asked softly.

'Yes. He works hard. We have a nice home and enough of everything. The boys are well cared for. He loves them very much.' Annette's hands were clasped nervously as she spoke and for a moment Leni felt a wave of pity towards her sister. She could see the same bravado as when she was a little girl. In many ways she was still that same child. Courageous yet still needing someone to cling to.

'And does he love you?'

'He's been very good to me.' Annette glanced at her and then quickly looked away. Leni was about to say something when the bedroom door flew open and Thea appeared in her pale blue pyjamas. Her dark hair was tousled and her face still childlike with sleep.

'Ahh, the sleeping princess arrives for her coffee,' Leni teased as the girl sat down heavily and put her sleepy head on her shoulder.

'I'm so tired – I don't like sleeping in your bed. How long will this go on for?' Thea demanded.

'Don't be rude. Your aunt has come to see us.' She stroked Thea's hair while chastising her to soften the blow but the girl shrugged her off. She wouldn't be touched or consoled and Leni missed the days when she was the only source of comfort in Thea's life. She got to her feet and went into the kitchen to fetch the coffee and think about breakfast now everyone was up.

By mid-afternoon, Annette was still chain-smoking in the armchair, but her possessions seemed to be everywhere that Leni turned. Her suitcase was dumped in the small space behind the front door where Thea liked to drop her school bag; her cardigan was hanging over the corner of the chair, her shoes cast aside on the rug. On the table in front of the armchair lay a series of empty cups containing coffee dregs, a full pack of Chesterfields and an empty crumpled pack. Annette just abandoned things as she used them and never seemed to notice them again. Leni felt her lips tighten as she looked around the living room. They had run out of conversation some hours ago, or at least Leni had run out of questions. Her sister did not seem even remotely curious about Leni's life or that of her daughter. She declined the opportunity to go out and see Berlin – how it had changed in her absence. Leni had wondered if Annette had kept in touch with Marta as they'd always seemed so close but she'd just shrugged and shaken her head. Her sister only wanted to sit and to smoke in silence.

It seemed rude to ask how long she was planning on staying, but Leni wanted to know if this was just for a week or for months. Part of her wondered if it might be forever, but to dwell on the feeling made her feel sick inside. She hated conflict of any kind and hoped that they wouldn't reach the point where Leni would need to ask her to leave.

Thea spent an hour inside the bathroom before suddenly appearing wearing her favourite summer dress – a white cotton shift that made her look older than her fifteen years. Leni worried about her growing up too quickly – or was she worried that Thea would turn out to be reckless like her mother? She didn't want to fight with her, yet she couldn't stop herself nagging at the girl. There had been nobody else to do that for Thea and Leni wanted so much for her – mostly that she did not live a life of regret.

'You haven't forgotten I'm going to drama club this afternoon have you, Mamma?' Thea's face held her usual sulky pout as if she was already preparing the battleground. It wasn't necessary as Leni had already conceded.

'I haven't forgotten. Have you done your revision?' Leni fixed her with a steely glance as a little tell-tale frown appeared between Thea's black eyes.

'Most of it. I'll finish it tomorrow.'

'Thea, you have to focus on your schoolwork and not just this drama club. If you don't do your other work then you'll have to stop going. You have exams to complete.'

Thea gave an anguished cry. 'I won't stop going and you can't make me. It's my life and if I don't pass my exams, it doesn't affect you.'

'Of course it affects me, I'm your—' Leni caught sight of Annette watching them argue and couldn't finish her sentence.

'I have to go, or I'll be late. I'll do it later.' Thea was already at the front door before Leni could open her mouth. As she started to say 'Be home by—' the front door slammed shut and Leni was left standing there under Annette's reproachful gaze.

67

Rainer was already outside the old dance hall when Thea turned the corner on to Jägerstrasse. He lifted his hand in a wave and she waved back. He was wearing a loose blue shirt and a pair of dark trousers that were slightly too short for him. He had grown so tall this year that all his clothes seemed not to fit him properly. Thea thought it made him look as if he were limitless. There was so much of him that not even his clothes could contain him.

She thought about Rainer constantly. The way his legs were too long for his trousers – the way his arms felt so much stronger than hers. He was a subject she was studying: taking in his details and remembering them all. There had been so many days of her young life that Thea had not spent wondering when she might get to kiss Rainer again, yet now she believed that they were all a waste of time. All that mattered was him – the way he held her, his smell, the way he tasted on her tongue, his lingering kisses. He had infiltrated her mind and it seemed to Thea these days that she had no other thoughts than him. Nothing else interested her. Still, she was wary of giving herself over completely to him, and found that at times she deliberately held herself back.

Rainer began grinning at her but Thea didn't smile until she got closer to the spot where he was standing – each step bringing them to the point where they would stand in front of each other, and wait . . . Then Rainer would open his arms and gather Thea into him. She wondered what she might do the day that he didn't open his arms to her and hoped she wouldn't have to find out. She breathed in the smell of him, his nervous sweat and the sun-kissed scent of his skin. Thea let herself be held, which she rarely allowed from anyone else these days. She liked the warmth of his arms around her and the way her breathing seemed to slow, as if she knew that all was well and she was safe there.

After greeting each other, they slipped down the alley-way, checking to see if there was anyone around and then, when they were both satisfied that the coast was clear, Rainer gently wrestled the street door open and in they went. Today, there was no dancing in the charred remains of the dance floor, for Rainer took Thea's hand and they crept in through the office and went straight up the stairs to their little room, sitting down on the leather couch with their hands entwined before Rainer leaned against her.

'So, you escaped, then?' he said while playing with her fingers, gently pulling them one at a time. He picked up her hand and inspected her fingernails, kissing the tips, and then finally reached his hand across to turn her face towards him. Thea liked to look at his face – the soft expressions in his dark eyes as he watched her. Sometimes, Rainer looked as if he was searching for clues, as if she were some great unsolvable puzzle. Thea didn't feel she was difficult to understand, and yet nobody did seem to understand her.

'Yes, I escaped.' She sighed, thinking of her mother and the fight she knew they'd have when Thea finally returned home. She loved her mother desperately but couldn't stop herself fighting for every inch of freedom these days even when she didn't particularly want it.

Rainer kissed her softly; his mouth tasted of fresh apples. The taste of him, the smell of him, lit a small flame deep inside her that made her feel afraid. She feared that one day that flame would turn into something that would take her over.

She let him kiss her for a few moments and then, when he pulled away to lie back on the leather couch, Thea stood up, pretending to inspect the room. She could feel Rainer watching her as she walked from one end to the other, opening drawers they'd already searched or pulling open cupboards. There wasn't much to find. A few more discarded books and dusty papers. Thea ran her fingertips over the wings of the armchair and wondered about who had sat there and what they had thought about.

She couldn't imagine being old and the thought of her own home being abandoned made her shiver. A burst of fury exploded inside her chest at the frustration of her life. Thea felt as if she were a wild animal contained in a small box. She wanted to escape from the cramped apartment she shared with her mother, to be free of petty rules and the demands of school. She thirsted after experiences because that was the only way she could feel things – not just reading about them in a book. The frustration built up a wild fury inside her and she wanted to pound her fists on the walls until the feeling went away.

'I want to run away . . .' she announced dramatically but Rainer was already bored watching her inspecting the room. He sat up and held out his hands to her. Thea began walking slowly back towards the leather couch. Her fury subsided, replaced by her need to be held. Thea stood in front of Rainer, sliding between his legs and putting her hands either side of his head, her knees pressing against the edges of the leather couch. She stroked his hair, laughing as she showed her crooked little white teeth.

'Where will you go?' Rainer kissed the waist of her white shift dress and then moved his hand to the edge of her hem.

'I don't care where I go . . . I just want to be free from rules.' Thea watched his hand inching up her leg as she made decisions about what to allow and what to refuse.

'What about me?' he asked, pressing her close to him as his hand proceeded to inch upwards.

'You can run away with me . . .' Thea made a small gasp as his fingers reached her underwear.

'What will we live on?' He lifted her dress but she brushed his hands away and settled herself on his lap, wrapping her arms around his neck and offering her mouth. They kissed until they needed to resurface, both panting and gazing at the other.

In one movement Rainer lifted her off his lap as he lay down on the leather couch. Then he pulled her down beside him. Thea nestled under his arm as they both stretched out.

She shivered a little; a row of goosebumps appeared on her arms. Rainer pulled her yellow blanket from the top of the couch and wrapped her in it. It reminded Thea of being a child, feeling safe and warm – and loved. Sometimes she just wanted to be held like a little girl again.

'We will live on kisses . . .' She giggled as Rainer rolled on top of her, his hand beginning its journey up her thigh once again as Thea's black eyes flickered shut.

68

Annette heard the doorbell ring while she was in the bathroom. She could hear the tone of Leni's voice change and then came the fixed polite words. 'Oh yes – I'll get her now.' Annette smoothed down her hair and ran the rim of her fingernail around her mouth to remove any excess lipstick.

'Nette! There's a long-distance telephone call for you,' Leni called out but it took several seconds before she could bring herself to respond 'I'm coming' and leave the safety of the bathroom.

'You have to go downstairs. I'll show you—'

'It's all right. I'll find it.' Annette knew it would be Glenn and she had no wish to have Leni hovering over her as she talked to him.

The telephone was kept in a special booth just outside the building supervisor's office. The apartment block rarely received calls for the residents, and Herr Stoller did not look particularly happy to have had to run up two flights of stairs. Annette quickly ran down and slid inside the small booth, pulling the wooden folding door shut behind her. One or two of the residents were gathered in the lobby, curious about who might be making or receiving telephone calls.

'Hello?' Her voice sounded casual, she thought, as if she were at home waiting for a call from one of those endless committees that she'd volunteered for in order to fit in.

She flicked the lighter and let the flame catch the tip of her cigarette.

'Hi, Annie. I just wanted to check that you got there.' She knew he was sitting at the kitchen table, with the telephone cord stretched to the middle of the room. She pictured him with his morning coffee and bowl of cereal. He was probably wearing his green bathrobe, loosely tied around the middle. His feet would be bare, even though he had perfectly good slippers lying under his side of the bed. Annette even knew how he would smell – that same fresh soapy scent he'd always had.

'Obviously I am here,' she said, instantly regretting snapping at him. It had become a habit she couldn't break.

'OK . . . I just wanted to make sure you were all right.' There was a pause. He was waiting for her to reassure him now.

'I'm fine, Glenn. No need to worry about me. Are the boys there?' Her tone was softer but still not particularly friendly.

'The boys are sleeping over at my sister's house this weekend. They're going to some party with their cousins. I did tell you.'

'Right, you did.' She was the one hesitating now – waiting for him to get to the point.

Annette raked her teeth over her bottom lip. She was aware of Herr Stoller standing just outside the booth with two of the residents. She really didn't want to have an argument in public.

'Is that all?' she said. There was a long silence and then Glenn spoke.

'Annie . . . I think we should talk about getting a divorce

when you come back. We can't go on like this.' His voice cracked a little as he spoke the words and Annette wondered what had prompted him to call right at that moment when he was still eating breakfast and rubbing the sleep from his eyes. It felt rehearsed. How long had it taken him to pluck up the courage to call her?

She took a deep lungful of smoke, and hung up.

69

The air in the city seemed to crackle with the electricity of fear today. A taut rope of rumour and gossip. Leni could see people standing around in the street chattering like little birds as she ran down the steps of the U-Bahn station and walked briskly in the direction of Oranienstrasse.

She was late, having had to deal with a last-minute emergency at the hotel where she was employed. Leni had been working as a housekeeper for the past three years. She'd begun by working as a chambermaid but soon made an impression owing to her willing nature and reliability. Now she was in charge of a team of chambermaids and took pride in making sure the rooms were clean and welcoming.

Monday was her favourite day, as new guests arrived and the old guests packed up their belongings and went back to their lives. She often tried to imagine what their lives must be like. They seemed so different from her own.

She was a woman who had never left the country she was born in. For all her youthful dreams, Leni had never travelled or worked in anything but quite ordinary jobs. She had no special skills or qualities that she could think of. She was, however, reliable and proud of that fact. The weekend had taken its toll on her and she'd felt distracted all day, hardly able to focus on her work as she worried about Annette and Thea.

Suddenly she felt weary. Her legs were aching, and all she

wanted was to sit quietly drinking a cup of coffee or even a glass of chilled white wine. It was a hot day and the thought of returning home to an awkward silence with Annette made her sigh as she absent-mindedly greeted a neighbour who was walking her puppy on the other side of the street. Leni waved as she reached the front door of her building, taking out her key with her other hand and raising it to put in the lock.

From somewhere inside her there was a stubborn refusal to go through with it. She couldn't do it. She couldn't bear the thought of sitting across from her sister. Of choking on her cigarette smoke. She just wanted a moment of peace for herself.

Instead of going inside, Leni turned around and carried on walking. At the corner of the street, she turned left and walked a little further along, past the new dress shops with their summer pinks and yellows. On past the grocery store with its Coca-Cola signs in the window, until finally she crossed the street to a café with a throng of smartly dressed people sitting outside enjoying the early-evening sunshine.

Leni wasn't in the mood for conversation and as she approached the café, she hesitated for a moment to inspect the crowd, making sure there was nobody there that she knew. Once she was satisfied that she could enjoy a glass of wine in peace and quiet, she slipped into a vacant seat at a small table in the corner where she could be perfectly alone.

Leni had been on her feet since early that morning and barely had time to stop for a break. The hotel had a conference taking place and there had been endless requests for clean towels or fresh cups for the rooms. She rubbed at the back of her aching legs before taking a cool sip of her wine. Her shoulders relaxed and she felt the pressure of the city dissolve around her.

She let go of the tension over the fractious weekend she'd spent with Annette and Thea, over the irritations she'd felt at work that day when things had not gone to plan. After the second sip, she closed her eyes for a moment and sat back in her chair. The late-afternoon sun was on her face and Leni could have curled up like a cat and happily slept.

The people surrounding her were all in couples or groups – old friends chatting; boisterous youngsters – yet she didn't mind being alone. Leni smiled, quietly observing the clientele and the passers-by.

Glancing around at the other tables, she saw two young women talking quietly in the corner. From time to time one of them burst out laughing as her friend told her a funny story. Leni couldn't hear what they were saying but, judging by their giggles, she was sure that the story was about a young man.

A few tables away sat an older couple. The woman wore a red hat with a blue feather in the brim while the man squinted uncomfortably into the sun. Both of them stared blankly out at the street without saying a word to the other. From time to time, they lifted their glasses, taking tiny sips – only to place them back down on the table and carry on staring in silence. A group of men in the far corner were talking too loudly about what the Russians might do next – droning on and on about the West and the East. Leni turned away, bored with all their stupid talk.

On a table behind her was a man with his back to her.

He was engrossed in the book that he was reading. Leni couldn't make out the title from where she was sitting.

A waiter approached the man and he hastily looked up from his book, as though rather irritated to be dragged away from it. Then, seeming to realize where he was, he quickly ordered a glass of beer.

Shielding his face from the sun, he scraped his chair further around the table so that he no longer had his back to Leni.

She had moved her own chair a little to accommodate the waiter as he returned with a frothing glass of cold beer on a silver tray, setting it down in front of the man. He leaned back in his chair, closing the pages of his book and placing it carefully to one side.

Leni took another sip of her wine, bored with inspecting the people around her. Out of the corner of her eye she saw that the man was staring at her. A flicker of annoyance crossed her face. She was unused to being stared at by men and in no mood for company. She turned her head, hoping that a stern glance might dissuade this man from starting a conversation.

As she did so, their eyes met, and Leni suddenly felt her heart leap. A strange tingle of shock ran through her. His eyes were fixed on her now, but all she could do was sit there clasping her wine glass. Her fingers became clumsy and stupid, trembling as she set her glass down in front of her.

Her breath quickened as she tried to make sense of it. Her mouth opened to say something but no words came out.

The man spoke first. 'Leni . . .'

Leni got to her feet, almost overturning her table as she

did so. She felt a strange and awful fluttering in her chest – like a bird's wings beating wildly against her ribs.

His voice sounded so familiar . . . but it was not possible. She must be dreaming – the heat of the day had sent her quite mad. Yet the man was still sitting there with his glass of beer, staring back at her. His dark eyes wet with tears, his soft, full lips parted.

Her mouth opened, and this time she was able to speak . . .

70

Annette had washed out her underwear and hung it all over Leni's bathroom. Then she had stood at the window smoking her Chesterfields and wondering what to do with her day. Leni wouldn't be back from work until later that evening and Thea had gone to school so she felt quite abandoned.

It struck her how she seemed to be surrounded by people when she was back in America – there were always friends or well-meaning neighbours telephoning or tapping on her door for some reason. This was the first day that she'd been left completely to her own devices and Annette didn't like the feeling at all. She was becoming tangled in the weeds of her own miserable thoughts.

Every time she envisioned a future without Glenn, she began to worry about their boys, Jimmy and Glenn Junior, and what they might think of her. She also worried about money as Annette had never held down a job in America, choosing instead to turn herself into the perfect housewife. Even that she did with the help of other women she paid to clean and do laundry for her. She wasn't wealthy, but Annette preferred to do without fancy holidays and spend any extra cash on making her life easier. Once someone else was scrubbing her floors clean, she could relax and go to the beauty parlour for a manicure or a shampoo.

If she was no longer going to be married to Glenn, it

occurred to Annette that she might have to move out of her house and find somewhere cheap to rent.

Thoughts darted in and out of her mind as she stared blankly through the window at Berlin. She hadn't been outside since she'd arrived at Leni's apartment, even when her sister had tried to persuade her to go out for dinner or take a stroll. Annette had resisted, pleading jet lag.

The truth was that all the feelings she'd left behind when she'd stepped on to that US cargo plane on a freezing February night had been waiting for her on her return. She'd found it hard to sleep, tossing and turning until dawn in Thea's little bed. She couldn't bear being surrounded by the mementoes of the child she'd left behind.

She was driving herself crazy with her own thoughts, made worse by surviving on a diet of coffee and packs of cigarettes. Before she'd left America, Annette had imagined her and Leni sharing confidences until the early hours – falling back into their sisterly bond. Yet Leni had little to say to her. They had become strangers and lately Annette was a stranger to herself. After years of grasping at a life she'd thought she wanted, her insides seemed to be fracturing and letting in all the emotions she didn't want to feel.

Crushing out her cigarette in the ashtray, she cracked open a window to let out the smoke, knowing that Leni would complain about it. She made a fist, placing it against the glass and resting her head on it.

She didn't belong in Brooklyn any longer and she couldn't stand to be in Berlin. She felt untethered, as though she were floating away from herself. Lost and unable to find her way back . . .

Turning away from the window, Annette took a deep

breath and grabbed the door keys and her cigarettes off the table. She couldn't stand herself for a minute longer – she would go out for a walk.

Standing outside on the pavement, Annette wasn't sure where to go. She hesitated, turning first one way and then the other. 'Just choose . . .' she muttered to herself and crossed the street.

Her feet found their own rhythm but she barely recognized any of the buildings. Everything seemed strange and new to her. Even the old familiar shops were somehow not the same. Freshly painted, or with fancy new glass in the windows. Products she'd never seen before. A lot of it reminded her of America: high-rise buildings and brightly coloured advertising wherever she looked.

It seemed as if she had never lived here. This wasn't the Berlin she remembered as a child – nor was it the devastation she'd left behind. There was a new city growing out of the dust of the old and Annette wasn't a part of it. There were so many new apartment blocks and they were so very neat: a rebuke to the chaos that had caused them to be built.

Her breathing quickened as she turned into more familiar streets. Ahead of her lay the abandoned courtyard. Her pace slowed as her feet lost their purpose. Annette felt light-headed and queasy. Her stomach churned from the acidic combination of coffee and cigarettes. She thought of turning back but something stopped her from doing so – she had to see it again. Just once more . . . to see if it looked the same. Or perhaps to see if she was the same.

She passed by a small grocery shop she remembered from before the war and a well of emotion exploded deep inside her chest. The dark wood interior, the women in their headscarves and white coats serving behind the counter. She could almost see herself tapping at Leni's elbow, wanting a pink sugar mouse as a treat. Memories of her childhood engulfed her and for a minute Annette could barely breathe, gasping at the warm air trying to fill her lungs.

The palms of her hands grew sweaty and she wiped them on the sides of her skirt. The bow of her white silk blouse caught on a breeze and slapped against her neck. Annette took small steps as she passed the final building in the row – preparing herself for what she was about to see.

Her hands were trembling as she stopped to light a cigarette, not caring that she was in the middle of the street. She sucked in two deep comforting gasps of tobacco into her lungs and calmed herself enough to walk on.

Another step. And as she braced herself, Annette slowly realized that she'd arrived at the place where the old, abandoned courtyard should have been – except that it wasn't there.

The bird shop and the apothecary were long gone – smashed to rubble by the shells of an invading army. The courtyard had been razed to the ground along with everything else. The corner she'd slept in with Leni. The hard cobblestones underneath their thin blankets. The shattered buildings; the steps she'd lain down on with Glenn, staring up at the night sky through the broken roof.

Now there was just a large dusty grey-brown patch of dry earth waiting to be made into something new.

71

Leni could hardly believe what she was doing as she followed Paul up the stairs and into his apartment. He only
lived a few streets away from her, and yet she had never
seen him. She didn't know if he'd been here for days or
years but his proximity made her feel peculiar. Her breath
came in little gasps as if she'd forgotten how to breathe.

His apartment was in a new block. Leni remembered
when this street used to house a barber's shop and a kosher
bakery. Things had changed so rapidly – new buildings
covering over the dust of the dead.

Everything seemed clean and freshly painted. As he
unlocked the door, Paul turned and smiled at her. 'Please,
come in.' He gestured to her to go first and Leni walked
timidly into his home, feeling as if she were in some sort
of dream.

There was a small entrance hall with his winter coat hanging on the wall. To one side of the hallway was a small
bathroom with the door ajar. Leni could see sparkling white-
tiled walls and a basin with a mirror hanging over the top of
it. A few paces off the entrance hall was the living room. The
apartment was really just this one large room with a kitchen-
ette in one corner. There was a closed door that Leni
assumed led to a bedroom and directly in front of her was a
wide window with a view of the buildings across the street.

For a moment they both stood nervously.

Paul was looking at her so tenderly that she couldn't bear it. The silence expanded around them until Leni could hear only her own breathing and nothing else. She felt as if she were falling from a tall building and where she might land was a mystery.

'Would you like something to drink? I have coffee . . . or beer? There may be a bottle of wine somewhere . . .' His eyes did not leave her face, not even for a second. Leni shook her head. The formality of making coffee or watching him pour her a drink would take away from this endless moment where there was only waiting – and once the waiting was over, her life would be different. Leni realized that she had wished for this – for her life to be different. Every day she'd uttered a silent prayer for it and only knew it at that moment.

She had loved this man since that first night when they'd walked home from the Babylon Circus. She'd married Karl and struggled to survive war and hunger. She'd found a companion in Walter. She'd put away her dreams of Paul.

Now, standing in front of him, Leni knew that she'd never stopped loving him. She'd buried her love away so deeply that she could no longer feel it, but as she gazed up at him she could sense it flooding back through her. Yet it could not be. She didn't know Paul – they had spent such a short period of time together and a lifetime apart. Leni felt stupidly shy. What was she thinking of coming back here? Yet she'd followed him without question, her heart unable to say no.

'Maybe a glass of water . . .' She wasn't thirsty, but she couldn't stand the silence of the nothingness between them. It felt painful to see this man standing so close to her. Leni had sealed her feelings for Paul away a long time ago and now she could feel the seal cracking like ice inside her. It was unbearable.

Yet he'd left without her, after the things they'd done together in his bed. He hadn't waited for her. She had so many unanswered questions – and, suddenly, her belly pooled with anger at the thought of them.

Paul nodded. 'Water, of course . . .' He walked over to the kitchen, filling a glass for her. Leni followed him into the living room and stood there looking around.

The apartment was very neat – everything was in its place. Cups wiped and put away on a kitchen shelf; a small brown radio on a tall sideboard by the window; a dark blue sofa placed in the centre of the room with a coffee table to one side. A plant with yellowing leaves drooped miserably on the windowsill. A blue-grey rug covered most of the wooden floor and a tall grey lamp took up much of one corner of the room. Leni's overall impression was of a man who lived alone, and had done so for a long time.

'Please, sit down.' He placed the glass of water on the coffee table, nervously spilling a little over the sides as he did so.

Leni sat on the very edge of the sofa, keeping her spine rigidly straight. She reached for the glass and took a long gulp. Tiny drips of water landed on her dress and she scrubbed at them with her fingers.

She looked at Paul out of the corner of her eye. His face was weathered. He had a small scar over his right eye that wasn't there when she'd known him. A reminder that life had changed them; that there were so many things they didn't know about each other.

He sat down at the other end of the sofa. A small, inviting space lay between them. She could feel the weight of him – the reality of his flesh and blood. He wasn't a dream any longer; he was sitting by her side. If she reached out a hand, she could touch him, but the consequences of that would be too much. She couldn't imagine doing such a thing.

Leni gripped the glass of water tightly, staring down at her cheap shoes and the tiny stains on her dress, trying to think of something to say. He was watching her – inspecting her maybe. She hoped not. For a moment Leni wanted to shield herself – to run away from his gaze.

'It's been a long time,' he said shyly.

'A lifetime,' Leni whispered and then sat dumbly again, clutching the glass. She felt his eyes searching her – drinking her in. Leni didn't like the feeling. She wished to be nineteen again – to have some future self to offer this man. She could only disappoint him now. All she could think to ask were things she didn't need to know.

'It's a nice apartment. Have you lived here long?' Leni posed the question cautiously although her mind was whirling with unasked questions.

'Not so long. I lived in another place when I first moved back here.'

She took another anxious gulp of her water and then put the glass back down on the coffee table. Leni instantly regretted doing so as her hands lay vacant in her lap.

She'd thought of Paul so often over the years and now they were so close she could smell the familiar scent of his skin. It couldn't be real. Leni refused to believe that he existed beyond her imagination yet she was sure that she could almost feel his breath on her cheek as he sat beside her.

The world had taken so much from her: her family and Paul; even Annette had left her for another life. Leni thought fleetingly about Karl and then Walter – different men with varying degrees of kindness. All her life she'd wished for this moment. To see Paul again.

But he'd left her behind when he ran away. She told herself that it was a long time ago. Today, they were just two old acquaintances saying hello.

But it didn't work. The angry thoughts pulsed away inside her even as she desperately wanted to reach out her fingers and touch him.

She should leave. There would only be more heartbreak for her if she stayed now.

'I should really be going – it's getting late,' she said. But Leni didn't move.

'Please don't go yet,' Paul said.

The silence was agonizing. She tried to think of some conversation she could start that wouldn't end up being difficult, because she was unable to ask him the questions she really wanted the answers to.

'Do you still play the piano?' she enquired timidly.

'I teach music now.' He was raking his teeth over his bottom lip. She decided he looked nervous and the thought made her feel a little better. Then another thought floated into her mind: maybe he'd never loved her and she was a fool. Her mouth grew tight as she continued with her dull, polite questions.

'Oh. Do you work in a school?'

'No. I have private clients. I go to their homes. Wealthy

people, mostly. I teach scales and nursery songs to bored children.' He gave her a weak smile and then stared down at the floor.

'Oh . . .' she said, picking at her fingernails. She reached forward for the glass of water again – picking it up and then putting it back down without taking a sip. It was all too much – the awkwardness of two people without anything to say to each other. She didn't know why she'd followed him back here. She'd dreamt about this man for years, and now . . .

'I really should be going.' Leni watched his face sag a little with disappointment. It reminded her of that first night he'd walked her home. Then the second night she'd kissed him even though she knew nothing about him except that he played the piano in a nightclub. She wouldn't dream of doing such a thing now. How young and stupid she had been.

'Leni . . .' was all he said. 'I never thought I would see your face again in this life.' He reached out his hand, placing it awkwardly on the sofa – filling the space between them. Waiting.

'I am not that young girl – I am not the same.' She wasn't sure exactly what she meant to warn him against. It was obvious that she was not the same. Her greying hair, the softness of her body where there used to be firmness. Did she think he might be disappointed?

'Neither of us is young,' he replied.

'I don't know how to be with you. I . . .' Leni couldn't think what she was trying to say except she was afraid to be loved. She had only felt this passion once in her life but she'd kept the thought of it alive in her dreams of him. Taking out his blue cotton handkerchief and putting it away again. Now he was sitting there, possibly offering himself to her.

'We barely know each other now.' Her voice sounded sharp and she regretted it. He hadn't moved his hand away but he didn't attempt to touch her.

She looked at his fingers. How easy it would be to fold her hand inside his and forget all her questions. To wipe out the past hurts and think only of today. Leni wanted to inch forward and take what she needed from this man and yet she didn't want to ruin her memories of him. She didn't want him to see her as she was.

When she looked at him, she saw only shadows of the boy she'd loved and not the man he had grown into.

'Oh, Leni. Does it matter?' His voice was soft in contrast to her own. Patiently waiting for her . . . to do what? She couldn't imagine. He would not be able to love her. Indeed, it was possible that he never had, otherwise he would have waited, all those years ago.

'I never expected to see you again. I have so many questions.' In reality only one question remained buzzing inside her mind: *Why did you leave me?*

But did she want to know the answer, after all these years? What difference would it make?

'We have time to answer all our questions later. I've found you. That's all that matters.' He reached his fingers closer to her hand but they didn't touch. His eyes were still so soft and brown. Somewhere inside him was the same Paul that she'd dreamt of.

'It's not that easy.' She would not give in. Why hadn't he waited for her? She'd loved him enough to sacrifice everything.

Leni was silent. When she had dreamt of seeing Paul again, it wasn't like this. Her dreams contained none of this nervousness. They slotted effortlessly together in her imagination but in reality, sitting on this sofa, they were just two people with their sharp edges intact. Another bite of anger wormed its way to her surface.

'I know it won't be easy. I wouldn't expect anything from you.' His hand moved closer – his fingers grasping for hers but she would not reach for him. She would not.

'I don't have anything to give anyone . . .' Leni could feel tears begin to spill down her cheeks. *Ridiculous to cry . . . you silly woman.*

'Could we just sit here together? Will that be enough for now?'

The light was fading inside the apartment as dusk fell outside. Paul's face was clouded by shadows. He seemed miserable and awkward as they sat side by side. Perhaps he'd been hoping too.

Leni felt so tired of reasoning with herself. She had always been the sensible one – caring for others not herself. She wanted something for her – for the young girl who had lost her first love and for the woman who was so very tired of being strong.

She should stop and ask questions about his life. Lay down rules. She was after all a grown woman. She hadn't laid eyes on this man in thirty-five years. She knew nothing about his life. Yet the comfort of sitting next to him as dusk fell made her feel more alive than she had in years. What did it matter about her stupid questions? What did anything matter but this moment?

Leni took a deep aching breath. If she was a fool, then let it be worthwhile, she pleaded with the Fates – while not believing that they listened to her.

She placed her hand delicately on top of Paul's hand. She held it there, feeling the warmth of his skin and remembering his touch. His fingers threaded through hers, pulling her towards him.

'Yes,' she whispered. 'It's enough.'

Leni moved as if she were underwater. There was only the sound of their breathing as their lips met. A flicker of recognition ignited inside her and then his arm wrapped around her waist and she clung to him. She was drowning and unable to save herself. His lips pressed so soft and warm against hers.

The kiss was fleeting and then they drew apart from each other. Paul reached out his hand, placing it gently on the side of her face. His thumb stroked her cheek. She wanted to fall into his arms – yet at the same time she still couldn't trust that he loved her.

'What are you thinking about?' he asked.

Leni wasn't sure what to say and so she said nothing.

'Tell me . . .' he whispered.

'I need to know why you didn't wait for me.' Leni knew as soon as she'd asked that it wouldn't matter what the answer was. She could not walk away from him now and yet she needed to know. Her curiosity burned inside her. Had he not loved her? And if he hadn't loved her at that point when they had their whole lives ahead of them then what could they possibly offer each other now?

'But I did wait for you.' Paul sat alongside her, their shoulders touching, his fingers tenderly stroking her face.

'That's not possible . . . I sent my sister to tell you that I'd had an accident.'

How could it be that she was finding out, after all this

time, that Paul had waited? That Annette must have got it wrong? To discover, all these years later, that it had been no more than a horrible mistake. He hadn't left her behind . . . the knowledge of it sang inside her.

Yet there was something nagging at her. Annette's eyes flitting glances at her from under her eyelashes, unable to look at her directly. Leni had imagined her sister was upset about the accident, but maybe it was something else entirely . . .

'Didn't you see Annette? She told me that you weren't there.' Leni turned to face him, afraid of what he was going to say.

'Yes, I saw her. I asked her where you were and she told me that you weren't coming because you'd changed your mind. Isn't that what happened? All this time, I wondered why.'

'I don't understand . . .'

But she did understand. And the cold stab of anger that came with understanding made her gasp.

Berlin, August 1961

72

Annette sat on the edge of her bed, running her fingers over the rough edges of her aeroplane ticket. She'd been in Berlin for nearly eight weeks and now she was forced to decide whether or not she was going to use the return portion of her ticket. There didn't seem to be much to return home to – her boys were away at summer camp for the whole of August somewhere in upstate New York, while conversations between her and Glenn were reduced to mere formalities over the ending of their relationship.

She put her head in her hands. There might not be much to return home to, but equally there wasn't much of a life for her in Berlin any longer. For a second, Annette wondered what kind of a life she might have made here if she hadn't gone to America. Would she be like Leni with her new apartment and her faded old clothes reliving her memories every time she turned a corner?

A jumble of thoughts and images flashed through her mind. What if she hadn't married Glenn?

The day they'd moved in with his family, Glenn's mother had welcomed her but her eyes were flinty and cold. Family dinner was filled with the chatter of his brother Wes and his sister Shirley. Glenn kept shooting sharp looks at his brother across the table. He'd brought his girlfriend to their family dinner. Mona had flaming red hair and a face dotted with freckles. She spoke loudly and at length, from time to time dissolving into fits of laughter over some family joke, usually at Wes's expense. Annette had envied the easy, familiar way that Mona was able to talk to the rest of the family and doubted that she'd ever enjoy the same relationship with them.

Glenn's mother had asked about Leni and her family back in Berlin. Annette had given brief details, but no more than that. Then Mona had said something about always wanting a sister and Glenn had made a joke about Shirley that made them all laugh again.

'Do you have any brothers?' Annette had asked Mona. She was only trying to join in but the table descended into a stony silence. The girl blinked up at her with her large brown eyes and said, 'My brother Danny died fighting the Germans in Normandy.'

The shame that engulfed Annette made her whisper, 'I'm sorry . . .' yet she wasn't sure why she was apologizing. It wasn't her fault. She hadn't started any war.

After that she knew that although they were polite to her the real conversations were taking place without her.

She tried to fit in – offering to help clean up or go to the grocery store if necessary but Glenn's mother had merely given her a disappointed smile and said, 'No, thank you, dear.'

One day Annette had gone into Manhattan alone, even though she was heavily pregnant at the time. She wanted to see the city for herself and had made Glenn write down which train she needed to get. Her English was much more fluent now than when she'd first arrived and she'd felt confident after finding her way to Macy's department store.

She'd taken her time going around each floor looking at all the beautiful things. There'd been some perfume in an elegant glass bottle. It had a gold stopper and a tiny velvet ribbon tied around the top. Annette wanted to buy it. If it wasn't too expensive, she thought that she might send one to Leni to show her the lovely things they could have now. To prove that she was right to come here and leave them all behind.

Standing at the counter, she was eager to try the perfume. In her mind she was already imagining her sister opening the package in front of the horrible Knopf family, delighting in dabbing it on her wrists and neck.

The sales assistant was a tall brunette with a bright smile and dark red nail polish on her fingers. Annette rehearsed what she needed to say but somehow the words came out wrong and the girl didn't seem to understand her.

'I can't understand you, honey?' the woman said loudly, and so Annette had repeated herself but to no avail. She couldn't remember the correct words in English and got herself flustered. It was so simple when she was at home with Glenn but standing here with this girl looking down her nose at her was a different matter.

She tried again but to her horror the sales girl called over a friend from another perfume counter. 'Hey, Maisie, can you see if you can help this customer? I think she's foreign.'

Maisie was short with black hair and bright red lipstick. She wore large gold hooped earrings and her blouse gaped a little across the bust.

'Do you speak French?' Maisie asked, pronouncing her words very slowly as if Annette were an idiot.

'NO! I am German,' she snapped at the two women, putting the perfume bottle back down on the glass counter, her face flushing crimson with embarrassment.

'Oh . . . well now,' Maisie said and the two women exchanged a look between them. Annette knew what the look meant. She was being blamed for something – found unacceptable to them. They didn't want to sell her perfume, and she no longer wanted to buy it.

She'd seen the same look at the dinner table with Glenn's family and again at the grocery store on the corner of their street. Everywhere she went, she saw it, the minute she opened her mouth to speak. The warm greetings fading to steely glares.

Annette was so lonely in those early days. She missed Leni and being able to speak her own language. Talking in English all day long gave her a headache. By the time they were all gathered around the dinner table at night, she could only smile and nod like a child – pretending to listen to words that she could no longer understand as she was too tired to care.

In the end, she'd made a life for herself and her boys. She'd won them all round. But the woman who had won the battle was not the same woman who had begun it.

Outside the bedroom door, she could hear Leni getting ready for work. Annette couldn't understand why she'd fallen out of her good graces, but Leni had returned home one evening with an icy stare and a tight smile. She'd muttered something about how the hotel had a very busy summer season and Annette had barely seen her sister since. Leni was out all hours of the day and night now, and when she was home, she barely spoke to Annette at all.

Some days, she was polite, but no more than that. Other days, her sister looked at her with such fury that she was afraid to ask what she'd done to deserve it. So, they went on together with forced politeness and a barely constrained rage under the surface.

Annette had come to the conclusion that Leni was unhappy with her life and so she tried her best to stay out of her way – and the same went for Thea although that was proving more difficult as school had finished for the summer vacation.

All she needed was a few more days to decide what to do – her aeroplane ticket would need to be changed by the end of the week if she wasn't going to use it. It seemed an impossible choice: two cities and neither one offered her any kind of happiness. Glenn's telephone calls were now brief and perfunctory; he shared news on the boys, but she noted that he'd stopped asking her when she was coming home.

The apartment door slammed shut as Leni went off to work, leaving Annette and Thea alone together. The girl usually spent hours getting ready, before disappearing to her drama club. Although surprised that a school club carried on meeting right through the summer, Annette was grateful for it, as she had nothing to say to the girl and found her presence unnerving.

She would have liked the apartment to herself so that she could sit and think. Her thinking had not produced very much action so far because she remained as confused as ever about what she should do with the rest of her life. Even her boys were getting to the age where they needed her less except to feed them and to do their endless amounts of laundry. They were always rushing out of the door these days. Within a few years, they wouldn't need her at all and then what would she do?

The apartment was eerily silent as Annette wandered out of her bedroom and into the kitchen to make some coffee. It was a warm morning although it was still early and she knew that by lunchtime it would be unbearably hot in these rooms, with only one small electrical fan to bring some respite.

Thea was leaning against the top of the kitchen counter eating a bowl of cereal while staring dreamily out of the window.

'Oh . . .' Annette said, surprised to see the girl standing in front of her wearing a pair of thin pink pyjamas. She'd grown tall – her legs were long and thin. The hems of her pyjamas exposed her pale ankles and bare feet. For the past couple of months, she'd tried to avoid the girl as much as possible, but here she was, yawning and chewing on her breakfast.

'Good morning,' Thea said sullenly as if Annette had greeted her instead of just standing in the doorway staring uncomfortably at her. 'There's coffee . . .'

Taking a small white cup from the shelf, Annette quickly poured herself some. Now the two of them were standing together in the kitchen, the room felt entirely too small. The girl finished her cereal before abandoning her bowl in the sink. The spoon hit the steel with a clatter.

'What's it like in America?' Thea hoisted herself up so that she was sitting on the kitchen counter, swinging her bare feet back and forth. She had such an intense way of looking at her – searching her face for information.

'It's not so different from here. People get up and eat

breakfast, drink coffee and go to work.' Annette flicked open her lighter and lit a cigarette, trying to bring the conversation to a close. She had no wish to discuss her life with Thea – or to discuss anything with her, come to that.

'I'd like to go there one day. I want to travel.' The girl spoke with the same restless energy that Annette had had at her age.

'Yes, it's good to see some of the world,' she muttered while walking back into the living room. She sank down into her usual armchair and began flicking through a fashion magazine that she'd brought with her. The pages were worn and creased now. It was a signal that their conversation was at a close but the girl followed her into the living room and flopped down on the settee. She tucked her legs underneath her and fixed Annette with her fierce black eyes.

'What was my mother like when she was young?'

Annette took an anxious gasp of her cigarette. 'Why do you ask?'

'She's always so serious. I can't imagine her being my age. I've never seen a photograph of her as a girl and she doesn't really talk about it. You're the only person who knows.' Thea flashed a pleading smile at her.

'She's always been the same way – a little shy, responsible and too serious. I don't have any stories about her doing terrible things, I'm afraid . . .' Even as she spoke Annette thought back to watching her sister kissing that man in the street and wondered if she was right. Leni had always seemed so serious, but then she was a lot older than Annette and had taken over as her mother in some ways. The thought of watching Leni kissing Paul made her feel uncomfortable; for a moment she wondered if her sister would have been different had she gone away with him. Happier, perhaps – but it wasn't something Annette wished to dwell on and so she pushed it to one side.

She glanced at the girl sprawled over the settee. She seemed so childlike, yet Leni was only a few years older than her when they'd been sleeping on the streets. Annette sighed.

'Was she ever in love with a boy?' Thea grinned at her wickedly, her eyes shining with mischief.

'Oh, you should ask her about such things. Anyway, I must go and write a letter to my sons.' Annette stood up to leave but the girl seemed reluctant to let her go.

'She must have had a boyfriend when she was my age?'

'I was very young – I really don't know. Maybe she did.'

'Did you know my father? She never talks about him.' Annette flinched as a guilty thought flashed across her mind, but she swatted it away.

'Not really. So, do you have a boyfriend?'

Thea looked away shiftily. 'No . . . I . . . I was just asking about Mamma,' she stammered. Annette knew she was lying – there was a boy. The girl's cheeks flushed a little under her gaze but she soon recovered her composure and began rattling out more questions.

'Why did you leave Berlin? Don't you miss your sister?'

Annette hesitated by the bedroom door for a second and then looked at the girl. 'I left because there was no life for me here. My sister and I are very different people. That's enough questions for today, I think – I'll miss the post if I don't get on with my letter.'

And with that she went inside Thea's bedroom and shut the door on the girl and her interrogation.

73

'I only have an hour,' Leni whispered apologetically. Paul was already unbuttoning her blue cotton dress as she slipped off her shoes. Their lips met and for a moment they stood entwined in the centre of his apartment.

She had waited all day for this moment, unable to believe her good fortune. She was not the same woman who had walked into this apartment two months earlier. Any shyness or worry had dissipated and Leni felt nothing except the warmth of Paul's kisses and the tender exploration of his fingers on her skin.

She shrugged off her summer dress, allowing him to remove her underwear until she was standing completely naked in his living room. Leni felt alive in a way that she hadn't in years. Her body was full of hope and possibilities. All that mattered was the hunger they felt for each other and the many ways they found to satisfy that.

She could not stop herself smiling, even at work when dealing with a difficult customer. Her thoughts were full of Paul. She fizzed with energy, finding that little songs were on her lips more often than not.

Her days had a new structure to them. She would wake and make breakfast for Thea before heading off to work. Then, once her day was done, Leni would meet Paul at their little café and return to his apartment. The hours she spent lying next to him passed in a blur of pleasure.

They spoke very little about the past, as neither of them wanted to spoil the hours ahead of them. Paul had never heard from Otto and thought he was probably dead. Leni had no wish to question him further. Nothing that had happened before their reunion mattered – only that moment and then the next. Even when she had finally brought herself to tell him everything about her family, he'd merely put his finger to her lips to quiet her confession, before planting slow kisses on her throat. Nothing mattered except this.

The unwillingness to ruin things had stopped Leni from confronting Annette. Having walked all the way home in a furious rage about it, she'd found herself icily calm by the time she'd slid her key in the lock of the apartment door.

To tell Annette that she knew was to confess that Paul was back in her life. Leni would not risk that. And so she remained silent, making sure that she was scrupulously polite in all their dealings while her fury still burned bright.

Her skin tingled under Paul's mouth. She tugged at his clothes until he too was naked. His kisses slipped down her neck and on to her breasts, while his fingers moved between her legs, stroking her gently. Only a few weeks before, Leni had been a woman who needed to be covered in sheets, but now she felt brazen and triumphant. Time had changed her.

There were the days before being reunited with Paul and the days following it. Before Paul, her mind had ached with cares about so many things, but now there was only the dusty sunlight making patterns on the wooden floor . . . and this man greedy for her body.

Their kissing became more urgent, yet they didn't move towards the bedroom. She allowed herself to be pulled down on to the rug in the middle of the living room. She felt the thrill of it racing through her veins. Paul pressing himself inside her right there on the floor. Leni wrapped her legs around his hips and wondered at the kind of woman she had become. One who allowed herself to be taken on the floor.

Clinging to him . . . urging him on . . . whispering words in his ear . . . Leni found herself making guttural noises against her will. She couldn't help herself. The woman who had felt so weary and beaten down by life was gone. The Leni who couldn't feel anything for anyone had disappeared.

Every part of her was alive and crying out for this man. She loved Paul – she had always loved him, and nothing else mattered to her.

'Tell me about your life in Spain,' she said as they lay in each other's arms.

'I worked in some clubs. I couldn't settle so I moved on to Lisbon. I stayed there throughout the war and for several years afterwards . . .' His voice tailed off as if there was something that he didn't wish to talk about.

Leni ran her fingers up his arm. 'There was a woman?' she offered. She wanted him to tell her everything – to have no secrets between them any longer. Only truth. She had offered him up all her secrets, revealing herself to him for all that she was.

'Yes, there was a woman. It ended badly. It was my fault. I had nothing to give her. I wanted to come back to Berlin. I didn't expect to find you again. But part of me always hoped.'

'What happened to the woman?' Leni covered up her anxious thoughts by planting kisses on Paul's chest, not wanting him to see that she couldn't bear the thought of him with someone else. Yet she'd married Karl and then gone on to live with Walter. Leni satisfied herself that it wasn't the same thing at all. She'd never loved them this way.

'She left me for someone else. I was glad for her.'

'You didn't love her?'

'I cared for her . . .'

'But you didn't love her.'

Paul wrapped his arms around her. 'I loved you. I still love you . . .'

Leni offered her mouth to his. Their lips ignited their need once again. She lay back on the floor and drew him towards her.

Afterwards there were only her clumsy fingers trying to do up buttons and straighten her crumpled clothes. Leni felt the memory of Paul's kisses on her skin as she walked along the street towards her apartment.

The thought of sitting across the room, watching her sister chain-smoking the evening away, made her slow her footsteps. Leni wanted to sit alone and think about Paul. She glanced at her watch, knowing that someone had to cook supper for Thea but still she couldn't make her feet go any faster.

The café where they'd met was just across the street and she wondered if she could take a few moments to sit and drink a cup of coffee. She craved the peace of being alone where she could replay her meeting with Paul. It was only now that she could examine his declarations of love and think of all the ways he'd kissed her. Her skin was alive at the thought of it. Her head filled with him as if she were a young girl again – except now there were no more lies.

Leni smiled to herself. She was the keeper of the most delicious secret. Anyone passing her on the street would think she was just another middle-aged woman in her faded summer dress. They would not know the gentle exhaustion of her body or the passionate thoughts that filled her mind.

Let Annette cook supper, or let them go without entirely. She wanted a few minutes alone to savour her thoughts of Paul, Leni thought as she crossed the street towards the café.

Sitting down at a small table at the front of the terrace, she ordered a cup of coffee. The waiter greeted her as if she were an old friend now.

Leni closed her eyes for a moment, picturing Paul's face. When she opened them again, she was distracted by noisy laughter coming from across the street, where a tall, athletic young man was teasing a young girl. He was holding something just out of reach. The girl was laughing and then he let her take whatever it was from his hand. They embraced and as they did so, Leni gave a confused gasp as she recognized Thea.

So, this was the drama club, she thought to herself, suddenly realizing that Thea had been lying to her for months about her whereabouts. She knew nothing about this boy other than that the girl was greedily kissing him in the middle of the street. All the time they kissed the boy had his hand under her blouse.

Leni hurriedly got to her feet, scrabbling in her purse for the money to pay her bill. She hastily left some coins on the table as she rushed out of the café. Shielding her face from the sun, she searched the street to see where Thea had gone.

In the distance she caught sight of them strolling aimlessly along before turning the corner. Leni began to walk briskly after them. She wasn't quite sure what she was going to do but at the same time felt afraid of what might happen if she lost sight of them. Maybe the girl was just like her mother.

She worried about what might already have happened, all this time she was so blissfully ignorant. All summer long Thea had been so sweet about sharing their bedroom and stubbornly polite to Annette. Apart from the girl's occasional teenage moods, Leni had had no reason to suspect anything was going on. Yet Thea had been lying to her. The ease of those lies stunned her. How often had she smiled and chattered away about the drama club and how much fun she was having that summer. Leni felt such a fool.

Almost thirty minutes had passed with Leni feeling increasingly stupid and thinking about turning back home. She could deal with the girl when she came home rather than spying on her. Coming to a halt, she watched Thea and her boyfriend carry on across the street and into the Russian sector. Leni sighed . . . it really wasn't a good idea for her to be seeing a boy from the other side of the city at the moment. Things were so easily inflamed these days.

She decided to carry on following them for a little while to make sure that Thea was all right. The streets became increasingly familiar to Leni and then suddenly the pair of them turned on to Jägerstrasse.

She hung back a little with shock as Thea and the boy approached the Babylon Circus. *What was Thea doing here, of all places?* The couple slipped quietly down the alley at the side of the club towards the street door and Leni felt as if the air were being squeezed out of her lungs.

She took a deep breath before slinking down the alley-way and arriving at the boarded-up street door.

There was no sign of Thea and her boyfriend. Leni pushed at the door until she was finally inside. It gave way easily – swinging open to reveal the charred walls of the passageway. The floor was covered with ash and debris. A sour smell filled her nostrils as she stepped further inside.

Leni stood for a moment taking it all in. Here was the door to the office, and there was the door into the night-club. Everything was tarry and black. She edged her way slowly along the floor and pushed open the door.

Where there had been silver and gold mirrors, now there were only burnt walls. The dance floor was filled with ashes and dust. The piano that Paul had played was gone and so too was the stage. The stairs that had once led down to Dieter's mysterious basement rooms had collapsed, the wood blistered and scorched.

She couldn't see any sign of Thea and the boy and so she gingerly retraced her steps back out into the passage-way, broken glass and burnt wood crunching under her feet. Once she was back outside, Leni quietly opened the door to the office. Inching her way forwards, she could hear Thea's voice. Her laughter tinkled in the distance.

Creeping up the stairs, she followed the sound of muf-fled voices . . . and then an alarmingly long silence. Leni had never been upstairs to what used to be Dieter's private rooms and she wasn't quite sure what she might find up there. She tried to think how the girl might have heard about this place. She was sure that she'd never mentioned working here or anything about it . . . but how was it possible that she'd discovered it for herself?

Leni uttered a quiet groan. The glorious pleasure of her earlier meeting with Paul was now a distant memory and she'd been forced back down to earth. Thea was her responsibility and, clearly, she'd got so carried away with her own life that she'd forgotten about her. She'd believed her stories of a drama club and all the time the girl was coming here.

As she got to the top of the staircase, Leni placed her hand on the door handle and twisted it open.

It took her a moment to understand what she was looking at. Thea and the boy were lying on a leather couch under the window, their limbs entangled – and Thea's skirt was bundled up to her waist.

74

Thea was not allowed out until she had proved that she could be trusted, although this felt like more of a punishment for Leni at the moment, as the girl moved from room to room with a sullen look on her face – silent and miserable.

Leni moved a pile of Annette's folded laundry off her kitchen counter and sighed. There was still no sign of her sister leaving. All she did was mope around the apartment, leaving mess everywhere and never offering to help clean up. It was beginning to feel as if she could do nothing to please either of them at the moment, and if it hadn't been for Paul, Leni would have been in a much worse mood than she was.

The place stank of stale cigarette smoke as her sister chain-smoked all day long. Occasionally Leni had dropped hints that maybe Annette could clear up or do some ironing while Leni was at work, but at the end of the day she would come home to find her apartment was just as she'd left it that morning, apart from a glass ashtray overflowing with cigarette ends and an empty coffee cup left on the table or Thea's dishes in the sink.

She bustled about, placing the folded laundry on Annette's bed, before adding fresh towels to the bathroom. Catching sight of her reflection in the mirror as she passed the sink, Leni paused for a moment. 'Fool!' she muttered to herself and sighed.

She had considered throwing Annette out – in fact she'd

held long imaginary conversations in which she presented Paul as evidence of her sister's crimes. One day she'd almost done it too, but there was part of her that somehow couldn't go through with it. After all, Nette had only been a child at the time. She'd lost her mother and Leni still remembered how upset she'd been at the thought of being left with Frau Vogel. When it came down to it, she was still her sister and Leni loved her, although she couldn't say that she liked her very much at the moment. There was another deeper reason too – Leni didn't want to share her secret. Keeping Paul to herself was the only way to safeguard their relationship. For now, she would pretend that all was well between her and Nette.

There was a sharp rap on the apartment door and Thea raced to open it. Leni could hear Herr Stoller, who had made the onerous journey up the stairs once again. 'There is a telephone call for Fräulein Thea.' He seemed rather out of breath. She was about to ask who it was but before she could say a word, Thea was already halfway down the stairs.

'Thank you, Herr Stoller,' Leni said.

'You're getting a lot of telephone calls at the moment . . .' He frowned at her and Leni felt she should apologize for his trouble. She walked down the stairs just behind him, wanting to check what Thea was up to. By the time she reached the lobby, Leni could see Thea smiling as she gripped the telephone receiver tightly, the soft giggling and whispers making it clear who she was talking to.

The girl seemed determined to make up for her lack of freedom by chattering over the telephone while shooting Leni dirty looks as she stood there watching her.

Annette, on the other hand, was hardly using the

telephone at all these days. Leni worried about it and wondered if she would ever get rid of her. She couldn't stand being stuck inside the apartment with the two of them for much longer, both silent and sulking in their own way. *Like mother, like daughter*, she thought, and found that the idea shocked her. She had long ago ceased to think of Thea as having anything to do with Annette at all. Leni gestured to her to get off the telephone and began trudging back up the stairs towards her apartment.

A few minutes later Thea burst through the door in an excited mood. Her face was flushed and her black eyes filled with hope.

'Mamma, can I go out this evening?' The girl was now standing in front of Leni with a pleading look.

'No! I told you that you couldn't go out to meet that boy until I was satisfied that you were responsible, and I meant it.' Leni pursed her lips and tried to ignore the fact that Annette was watching her from her usual spot in the armchair.

'But I promised you that I wouldn't go back to the dance hall. Please, Mamma, it's Saturday and I haven't seen Rainer properly since that night. Please . . . say yes . . .' Thea was standing inches away from Leni's face now and she felt her heart soften a little.

'No – and that's final.' Her lips pursed as she clenched her jaw to stop herself smiling at Thea.

'But, Mamma . . . It's been a whole week.'

'I said NO!'

'I hate you! You're ruining everything . . . I'm fifteen. I'm supposed to have a boyfriend and go out having fun. Aunt Annette would let me go out, wouldn't you?'

Leni raised her eyebrows as her breath caught in her throat. She could see that Nette was about to say something and she couldn't bear it.

'Aunt Annette is not responsible for you. And this will teach you to lie to me, won't it?' she said sharply before walking away so that Thea couldn't see that she was weakening.

The bedroom door slammed shut as the girl threw one of her sulks and Leni felt a sharp blade of hurt that she was being compared to her sister and coming off worse. But although she'd had days of this behaviour she had no intention of letting Thea end up like Nette. The girl needed to learn to be responsible and Leni would make sure that she did. She would not let Thea ruin her own life, even if the girl was angry with her.

Annette's mouth snapped shut and she didn't say a word. Out of the corner of her eye Leni saw her lighting yet another cigarette but there was just another awkward silence.

'It's a lovely evening – I think I'm going to go for a nice long walk,' Leni said, hoping that she sounded casual but fearing that she would make her sister suspicious. She desperately wanted to keep Paul to herself for as long as possible.

'I think I might go and lie down for a bit. I've got a terrible headache.' Annette stood up and put her hand to her head as if to emphasize the point. Leni shrugged.

'There's aspirin in the kitchen drawer. I won't be long. Please make sure Thea stays where she is.'

Leni glanced at her watch. If she hurried then she could spend an hour or maybe even two with Paul before returning to Thea's awful cold sulks and Annette's silence. She couldn't wait to wrap her arms around him and feel his kisses on her skin. The thought of being with him made a half-smile creep on to her lips until she noticed her sister eyeing her curiously. Leni fussed a little with her hair and smoothed down the collar on her white blouse.

'Would it really be the end of the world if she went out to meet her boyfriend?' Annette said sternly.

Leni sighed. The last thing she wanted was a row with her.

'I don't want them hanging around in the Babylon Circus. It's dangerous. And she has to learn not to lie to me. It's not open for discussion. I would have thought that you of all people would know the trouble she could get into ... I can't bring up another baby at my age,' Leni hissed and before her sister could say another word, she turned on her heel and walked out of the front door.

75

The moment Leni slammed the front door shut, Annette sat back in the armchair and crushed out her cigarette. She could hear the sound of music coming from the bedroom as Thea took refuge in sad love songs. Her sister was so exasperating sometimes. Annette couldn't understand why she had come down so hard on Thea. After all, she was only kissing a boy, which was perfectly normal at her age. But by all accounts Leni had practically dragged the poor girl out of that dance hall and now she wouldn't allow her out without knowing exactly where she was going and who she was meeting.

Her sons were thirteen now – an age where they too would start hiding things from her. But she convinced herself that when the time came for them to have girlfriends, she would react with understanding, and not at all as Leni had behaved.

Annette tapped on the bedroom door before opening it a crack. 'Do you know if Leni has a nail file? Mine has snapped.' She took a long drag on the cigarette in her hand and stared at Thea.

The girl was lying on her belly – her thin legs dangling over the end of the bed. A small record player was blasting out a German pop song that she didn't recognize. Thea raised her face from her pillow. 'I don't know . . . You can look if you want.' The girl buried her head in her arms again.

Annette took a step towards the chest of drawers but there was no sign of a nail file, and she didn't want to root through Leni's things. It would be typical of her sister not to possess something so very basic.

'I can't see one. I'll leave you alone.' She was about to back out of the bedroom door when the girl raised her head again and glowered at her.

'It's not fair. I've been locked up here all week. It's Saturday night – I should be able to go out. I promised not to go near that dance hall again.' Thea pouted.

Annette couldn't help a sly smile crossing her lips. For the first time she found herself wondering what she would have done if Thea had been her sole responsibility. Being fifteen was such a terrible age. She tried to recall the urgency of her own feelings back then but, like all things, it had faded from her memory and what she recalled was merely a blunt version of youthful flirtations.

The girl's face was a picture of agony. Her keen desperation to be allowed to go out melted Annette's resolve to try and keep in Leni's good graces. Thea must have felt her weakening. She sat up eagerly, hugging her knees to her chest. 'I just want to see Rainer . . . I wouldn't be long at all.' Her eyes pleading with her to understand.

'It won't be forever. You'll be allowed to see him again,' Annette offered but the girl wouldn't be consoled so easily. Thea's cheeks flushed red as her face screwed up into an anguished mask – and then tears began to flow.

'Don't cry,' Annette said, feeling inadequate to this task. It occurred to her that she'd rarely had to console anyone showing emotion. It wasn't a skill she possessed. Annette was usually the person requiring a little comfort in life.

'She doesn't understand . . . She's never had any fun and so she doesn't want me to have any . . .' Thea wailed.

'She means well. You shouldn't have lied to her.' But Annette found herself agreeing with the girl in her heart – after all, Leni was always so serious about everything. The girl had been punished for a whole week now and secretly she thought it was too much to carry on with it. Yes, Thea had lied, but it wasn't the end of the world.

'I wouldn't have lied to her if she was different. Some of the girls tell their mothers that they are meeting boys and they don't mind at all. I know it was wrong to break into that old dance hall but we had nowhere else to go. We just wanted to be alone. We weren't doing anything except kissing.' Thea fixed her watery black eyes on Annette's face, recognizing the faint possibility of clemency.

Annette took a long, thoughtful drag of her cigarette. 'I am going to have a nice long bath. For at least an hour, let's say. Of course, I imagine that you'll be in your room.'

The girl's face lit up. 'You mean I can go out?'

'I didn't say a word. Now, I must get ready for my bath. I'm sure you have things to do.' Annette walked back into the living room to stub out her cigarette before going into the bathroom.

Before she'd leaned over to run the hot water tap, she heard the determined click of the front door as it slammed shut.

76

Thea practically skipped along the street as she raced towards Rainer's house. She hadn't even waited to telephone him to say that she was coming over – not wanting to take a chance on her aunt changing her mind. Thea didn't even want to think about what might happen if her mother were to find out about her disobedience. She was free – and that's all that mattered.

Rainer lived in a large cream house with a black front door. To the side of the door was a brass bell button and she rang it enthusiastically. It wasn't Rainer who came to the door but his sister, Lottie. She was a studious ten-year-old with little time for her big brother or his girlfriends. Her round, sullen face was completely overshadowed by large wire-rimmed spectacles; she kept having to push them back on to her nose as they slipped forward when she spoke.

'Oh, hello. Rainer's gone out to a party.'

Thea felt her heart drop. When she'd spoken to him earlier, he hadn't said anything about a party, but Thea put that down to the fact that he'd known she wouldn't be able to make it.

'A party? Do you know where he's gone, Lottie?'

'I think I heard him say it was at Max's house. I wasn't eavesdropping though!' The child's voice became defensive although Thea was quick to reassure her.

'It's all right, I wasn't accusing you.'

Lottie pushed her spectacles back on to the bridge of her nose and frowned. 'Don't tell him I told you . . .'

'I won't, I promise.' Thea was about to smile at the child but Lottie had already closed the front door on her.

She didn't know exactly where Max lived. Thea remembered the street but not which house so she began walking in the general direction, cursing her luck as she would need to be back home in less than an hour.

It turned out it was impossible to miss Max's house, because she could hear music blasting from the second house she came to. Thea walked up to the front door and hammered loudly on the door knocker. It took a long time before someone bothered to answer but eventually a girl that she recognized from school pulled the door open and let her inside. The girl gave her a funny look and Thea realized that in her haste to get to see Rainer she'd given no thought at all to what she was wearing. Her tatty old shorts and faded shirt suddenly felt as if they were entirely wrong for barging into a party that she hadn't been invited to.

Inside the hallway, Thea was surprised to see crowds of people that she didn't know sitting all over the stairs. A girl was smoking with a bored expression on her face while a boy stood behind her kissing the back of her neck. There was no sign of Rainer or Max so Thea pressed on through the crush of bodies to get into the living room. The music was particularly loud there as Thea tried to make herself heard.

'Have you seen Rainer?'

She was greeted by a shake of the head, or just ignored, but Thea squeezed through the throng to reach the kitchen.

Inside the sink and all over the counters were buckets of beer bottles stacked on top of ice. The ice was melting so there were pools of water over the worktops and the floor. People were pushing forward to grab their beers and then shoving the same people to get back out of the kitchen again.

Thea found herself pressed up against the wall with two buckets of beer at her feet. She couldn't move until a crowd of boys had got their drinks. They were loud and singing a football chant at the top of their voices. One of the boys picked up the entire bucket of beer, giving Thea enough room to slip out of the back door into the garden.

The sun was going down and there were people kissing in the shadowy corners of two tall trees. Thea nearly turned to walk back inside the house but something caught her eye. A familiar outline – or maybe it was the red shirt. Either way, Thea knew it was Rainer with his long rangy body pressing a girl against a tree in the far corner.

She wanted to run away, but at the same time she wanted Rainer to know that she'd seen him. Her mind raced with possibilities but she couldn't decide on a course of action. Thea wouldn't let him see her cry. She took a deep breath and walked towards the tree where Rainer and the girl were kissing, completely oblivious to her presence.

'Hello, Rainer . . . remember me?' Thea said coldly.

Rainer turned around, his face registering shock at seeing her standing there.

'Thea! What are you doing here?' He was trying to remain calm but she could hear the slight panic in his voice. He'd been caught red-handed and they both knew it.

'Well, enjoy this lovely party . . .' Thea spun around and

began walking away before the tears fell, pushing frantically through the crowds until she was back out on the street. Only then did she begin to cry. It wasn't until Thea turned the corner of the street that she realized Rainer had carried on holding the girl he'd been kissing all the time she was standing there.

A blaze of anger rose from deep inside her belly. Her chest felt tight and she wanted to scream. All the time she'd been telephoning him he'd probably been seeing some other girl. Her mother had ruined everything. Or else maybe Rainer *hadn't* really cared about her. Could it be possible that all those hours spent lying in his arms at the old dance hall had meant nothing to him?

She felt deflated – as if all the hope had leaked out of her. She walked aimlessly through the streets, thinking miserable thoughts, not caring that it was getting late and she would be in trouble. Thea only cared about Rainer and he didn't care about her. She was humiliated by his betrayal. Everything in her life felt flat and gloomy.

She walked until darkness fell and she finally stopped picturing Rainer kissing another girl. Only then did she turn in the direction of home.

Thea turned the key in the apartment door and crept inside. Softly closing the door behind her, she waited to be sure the coast was clear. She had no idea what time it was, yet it occurred to her that she'd been missing a lot longer than she'd intended. As she took a step towards the living room, to her horror she heard her mother screaming at her Aunt Annette.

77

The minute Leni had left Thea and Annette behind in the apartment, safe in the knowledge that she was free for an hour or so, her frown had softened and her lips turned upwards in anticipation of seeing Paul. As she approached the café where they liked to meet, Leni could see him sitting at their favourite table with a glass of wine waiting for her. He stood up to greet her, kissing her full on the lips and holding her hand even as they sat back down together.

She sat close to him, sipping at her wine as they chatted idly. She loved the way he looked at her even when talking about nothing in particular: as if she were important and precious. Leni had never felt important or precious to anyone before.

'I was thinking about a vacation. It's already the middle of August and soon summer will be over. What do you think?' Paul looked at her eagerly.

'You mean ... a vacation together?' Leni had never thought about such a thing before but the moment he mentioned it, she began to imagine spending all day and all night alone with Paul. She wanted a life where that was possible. To travel with him and see all the things she'd dreamt of since her youth.

'Yes. Maybe we could go to Spain? I'd like to show it to you. It would be nice to be alone for a little while. Just a few days, if that's all you could manage.' He squeezed her hand affectionately and Leni smiled back at him.

'It's just that . . . I have Thea to think about. She's at that awkward age. I can't leave her alone.' Leni fretted over it for a moment and took another sip of her wine. The thought of being with him and finally seeing some of the world made her heart start racing with excitement.

'Well, isn't your sister here? Surely she could look after her for a few days?' Paul leaned closer, planting a soft kiss on her cheek. 'If you can't get away it really doesn't matter – I just got the idea into my head and then once I'd thought of it—'

'I'll see what I can do. Leave it with me.' She drank more of her wine and nestled closer to Paul, holding his hand under the table as if they were teenagers in love.

As they stood up to leave, he whispered to her, 'Do you have to get back?' She could feel his warm breath on her neck and wished she had the freedom to spend the night with him.

'I should, really . . . It's getting late and I only said that I was going for a walk.'

'Come back to the apartment. Your sister is home, isn't she?' Paul pulled her into a doorway next door to the café, knowing that nobody could see them in the evening shadows.

Some nights she found herself pinned against that doorway for several minutes as they refused to let go of each other. As he pressed her to him and kissed her greedily, she weighed up what she might say to Annette if she came home much later.

Maybe she'd bumped into an old friend . . . Paul's mouth brushed against her neck and Leni made her decision.

'All right – just for an hour.'

'Where *have* you been?' Annette exclaimed as Leni walked into her living room. For once her sister wasn't flopped in the armchair smoking cigarettes but instead was coming out of the bedroom dressed in a pretty yellow cotton robe with her hair pinned up in pink rollers.

'Just walking – it's such a lovely evening. Then I ran into an old work colleague right by the Tiergarten and we had a glass of wine to catch up.' Leni lied effortlessly as she dropped her handbag on to the sideboard and opened the window to feel the night air on her face.

She could smell Paul's musky odour on her skin and feel the memory of his touch all over her body. Leni turned away for a moment so her sister didn't see the secret smile on her lips.

Annette didn't move from the bedroom doorway.

'There's something I have to tell you . . .' she said with a strained look on her face.

It took a moment before Leni realized that something was very wrong. Glancing at her bedroom door, she was surprised to see it wide open – and the room was empty.

A combination of panic and anger began to flood through her veins.

'Nette . . . where's Thea?' she asked sternly.

'Please don't be cross with me. I told her she could go out, but only for an hour. I was very clear about that . . . But she hasn't come home. And it got so late and then of course I realized that I don't know where she might have gone . . .

and I didn't know where you were either.' Her sister gave a helpless little shrug of her shoulders that infuriated Leni.

A flare of anger exploded inside her. 'What do you mean, you told her that she could go out? It's nearly midnight! She's never stayed out this late.'

Leni began to pace around the living room. She wanted to shake her sister until her teeth rattled. Standing there looking pathetic as if it wasn't all her fault to begin with.

'How on earth could you do this? I don't suppose you even asked where she was going?'

Annette's face twisted in anguish as she tried to excuse herself. 'The girl was upset. It's Saturday night . . . and she just wanted to see that boy. God, Leni, you must remember what it was like to be that age. Everything seems like the end of the world. I told her it was only for an hour—'

'You had no right to tell her anything. Who do you think you are?' Leni could feel years of volcanic rage bubbling up from beneath the surface, combining with her genuine fear that something terrible could have happened to Thea. Her hands flew to her face, fingers lightly clawing at her cheeks. She didn't know what to do . . . She would have to go to her school friends' houses and knock their mothers out of their warm beds to try and explain.

It suddenly occurred to Leni that she had no idea who the boyfriend was or where he lived. She'd never even asked his full name.

She'd been so busy loving Paul that she had thought of nothing else . . . and now Thea was gone.

Letting loose a desperate roar of pain, she muttered, 'How could I have been so stupid? I should never have left her alone with you.'

Annette's eyes flashed angrily as she snapped back, 'I'm sure she'll be home soon and then you can impose your rigid little rules again.'

Leni clenched her fists. The anger inside her began folding and expanding until she was sure it would take over her.

'There you go, interfering with people's lives again. You don't care who you hurt or what damage you do to the rest of us.' Spitting the words at Annette – Leni was white-knuckled with rage now.

'I haven't *done* anything to you – I just felt sorry for the girl. You went out and left her. What was I supposed to do?' Nette stalked into the bedroom, slamming the door behind her. Leni felt a wild fury possess her as she burst through the door without bothering to knock.

'Who do you think you are? I didn't invite you here. You don't bother with us for years on end, and then you turn up and begin undermining me. You're so selfish – you always have been. You *ruined* my life, and I will never forgive you for it.' The words hung in the air between them as they glowered at each other.

'I . . . I don't know what you mean,' Nette stuttered.

'I think you do! That day I fell down the stairs– you told Paul that I didn't want to go away with him, didn't you? DIDN'T YOU?'

She couldn't stop herself screaming at Annette. Her rage was consuming her as she faced her sister with her hands curled into little fists and her eyes black with hatred.

Nette's guilty face told her all that she needed to know.

'But how . . . how do you know all this?' Her sister's voice began to crack but Leni would not, could not stop screaming at her.

'Because Paul is *here* . . . in Berlin. We've been seeing each other again. I know everything, Nette. I know what you did.'

Her eyes blazed with fury but now she stood there with her lips trembling, barely able to speak. 'All those years I was without him. I was so miserable, and it was all *your* fault. You knew what you'd done and you didn't say a word.'

Annette flinched as if she'd been struck. 'I was a child . . . a baby. I thought you were going to leave me forever . . . You didn't give me a second thought. I was only six years old. You were like a mother to me . . .'

'But I wasn't your mother, Nette. I had my own life, and you ruined it.'

Leni eyed her sister coldly. She couldn't forgive her for any of it. She'd expected Annette to beg for her forgiveness but she did not. Instead, she rolled her eyes while heaving an irritated sigh. A burst of fury bubbled inside her; then, taking a deep breath, Leni said icily, 'You had no right to interfere – and you had no right to tell Thea that she could go out when I told her she couldn't.'

A deep red flushed over Annette's neck as her temper rose, and then she screamed at her: 'I HAVE EVERY RIGHT. YOU'RE NOT HER MOTHER!'

'I'm more of a mother than you ever were!' The moment Leni slapped back the words in retaliation, the room became deathly quiet as the two women stared at each other.

Suddenly there was the sound of the apartment door slamming shut and Leni felt a sharp stab of panic. 'Oh no . . .' she cried, running out to the hall, but by the time she'd opened the apartment door Thea was already gone.

78

Leni pounded on the grey metal door with her fists. Standing in the street, she saw a light go on upstairs and then Paul's face at the window staring down at her. The door opened and she flew into his arms.

'I need to find Thea. She's run away.' Leni was breathing hard as she spoke.

'What happened?' Paul was buttoning up his shirt as he stood there, his face heavy with sleep.

'I'm sorry . . . I woke you. I didn't know where else to go.'

'It's all right. Leni, calm down. Tell me what happened.' He put his hands on her arms as she blinked back furious tears.

'Annette and I were fighting – we said such terrible things to each other. Screaming like mad women . . . Thea must have come home and overheard us. She knows that Annette is her mother. She ran off before I could talk to her – and I don't know where she's gone.' Leni could feel her anxiety palpitating in her chest as she explained.

'OK. What can I do?' Paul was always so calm that she instantly felt better.

'There's a boy she likes but I don't know where he lives. They've been hanging out at the old Babylon Circus. It's all boarded up now but they broke in there . . . I don't know where to start.'

'I'll go to the Babylon Circus and see if she's there. You try her school friends – see if they know where the boy lives. Where's Annette now?'

'I told her to stay in the apartment in case Thea comes back. It's all my fault. I shouldn't have let her believe that I was her mother. It just seemed easier at the time. Suppose something happens to her?'

Paul gave her arm a reassuring squeeze. 'We'll find her. Don't worry. I'll go right away. You go and ask her friends what they know and I'll meet you back at your apartment. It will be all right – she won't have gone far.'

Leni looked up at him, desperate to believe him. Thea had to be all right.

She nodded. 'I'll see you back there.'

An hour later she was no closer to finding Thea. She'd tracked down several of her friends but none of them knew where she was, or had any idea where her boyfriend lived. Leni began to imagine grim scenarios and her mind raced with awful possibilities. She told herself that Paul was right, Thea wouldn't have gone far, but then she knocked on another door only to find that there was no sign of her.

Turning the corner, Leni walked up to a large brick house with a neatly painted grey front door. She sighed a long exhale and lifted her hand. This was her last hope.

Gerta had been friends with Thea since they were tiny children but lately Leni hadn't seen her around so much. Thea seemed to prefer the company of other girls. Even as Leni thought about it, she realized that she'd been so wrapped up in Paul that she didn't really know what Thea was doing lately, or who she'd been hanging around with.

She felt selfish and stupid. She'd always thought that she was a far superior mother than Annette, but it just wasn't true.

The lights were still on at the top of the house and Leni took a deep breath. Pressing her finger to the doorbell, she let it ring for the longest time. Eventually Gerta's mother Susanne opened the door, wearing a purple dressing gown.

'Oh, Leni, I was just about to telephone. Thea is here. She was so upset that I couldn't get her to tell me what was going on. She's upstairs with Gerta.'

Leni clamped her hand to her mouth as she tried to stop the tears from flowing down her cheeks.

'She's here? Oh, thank God . . .'

'She turned up about fifteen minutes ago. I don't know where she's been but she won't stop crying. I was so worried about her. After all, it's the middle of the night. Is it a boy? What's happened?' Susanne ushered her inside.

'We had some family drama . . . Yes, I think there's a boy involved.' Leni had no particular wish to tell her their business but some explanation seemed necessary.

The two women climbed the stairs until they reached the top floor. Susanne tapped on the bedroom door and then opened it. 'Gerta, take your quilt and go sleep in with your sister. Leni needs to talk to Thea.'

Gerta reluctantly gathered up her things and scooted past her mother, giving Thea an apologetic look as she did so.

Thea was lying on top of a small single bed, her face smudged with tears. She scowled as Leni walked into the room behind Susanne. 'I don't want to talk to you.'

Waiting until both Gerta and her mother had left them alone, Leni sat down on the bed next to Thea and for a moment the two of them sat silently, wiping away the remnants of their tears.

'I was so worried about you,' Leni said eventually.

'Why? I'm not your daughter.' Thea's black eyes blazed with anger as she crawled away to the furthest corner of the bed.

'Maybe I didn't give birth to you, but you have been my daughter for a long time. Since you were a baby. I love you just the same as if you were all mine.'

'You LIED to me!' The girl's face was flushed with torment.

'Yes – I'm so sorry that I did that. I thought it was the right thing to do. I didn't know how to explain the things that had happened. You were just a baby, and it seemed easier to let you believe that I was your mother. I never meant to hurt you, my beautiful girl.'

Her voice cracked as she spoke. Reaching out a hand, she tried to stroke Thea's hair but the girl slapped her hand away. She curled up in the corner of the bed, refusing to meet Leni's gaze.

'Say something, Thea, please . . .'

'I don't want to talk to you. Go away!'

Leni gulped down an anxious breath. 'We have to talk about it. Please, let me explain.'

'NO!' Thea buried her face in her hands and began to weep. Leni felt her heart breaking as she tried in vain to reach out and say something that might make it better.

'I love you, Thea! You need to know that. I have always loved you . . . that's what matters. I know it's been a horrible shock. It was a very difficult time after the war and it was just easier to let you think that you were mine. I always thought of you that way. I made a mistake, Thea – that's all it was. A terrible mistake.' Leni's voice broke as she looked at the girl curled away from her. 'We can talk about things – maybe I was too hard on you about that boy. You could bring him to the apartment and I could get to know him.'

'He's got another girl. You wouldn't let me go out and he found someone else. It's all your fault . . .' She kept her face averted as Leni stared at her helplessly.

'I'm sorry, Thea. Please look at me.' But the girl wouldn't.

'You can stay here with Gerta tonight . . . and then tomorrow everything will seem better. It's very late. Try and get some sleep, and we'll talk when you come home.' Leni felt so weary and broken that she just wanted to go home and crawl under the covers. She stood up and walked towards the door. Maybe everything would look better in the morning but, somehow, she very much doubted it.

The girl didn't even bother to look up as she left the bedroom. Leni's heart splintered with every step. She'd ruined everything. Thea was right – it was all her fault.

Susanne smiled weakly as Leni walked back out on to the landing. She presumed that Gerta's mother had overheard their conversation but it was too late to worry about such things now.

'She can stay here – I'll take care of her.' The woman gave Leni a sympathetic look, which just made her feel more ashamed and embarrassed.

'Thank you. She's so angry with me.' She worried that Thea would never forgive her.

'It will pass. They're so dramatic at that age but I'm sure

when she calms down . . .' Susanne gave her a reassuring smile and the kindness made her eyes fill with tears.

'I'm so sorry to have disturbed you. What must you think of me?' Leni wiped her eyes with the palm of her hand.

'Oh, please don't worry about that. You go on home. I'll make sure that Thea gets some rest, and then I'll bring her home in the morning. It will all look better after a good night's sleep.'

Leni couldn't trust herself to speak so she nodded dumbly and made her way back down the stairs and on to the pavement. She felt bone weary as she trudged back through the streets to her building, hoping that Paul was waiting for her. She couldn't bear to face Annette alone, and the thought of lying in his arms made it seem possible that things would indeed look brighter in the morning.

79

As Leni unlocked the apartment door she was puzzled as to why Paul wasn't outside waiting for her. It was after one o'clock, and there was no sign of him. Maybe he'd given up and gone home to get some sleep, although that wasn't like him. She crept into the living room hoping that her sister had gone to bed but Annette was sitting right there in the armchair with a cigarette burning away in her hand as if nothing had happened between them.

'Did you find her? Is she all right?' Nette asked anxiously.

'Yes, I found her – she's staying at a friend's house. I talked to her for a little while but she's very upset. She heard everything ... I hope you're satisfied,' Leni said sharply.

'I didn't know she was there, or I wouldn't have said a word. I didn't mean to make things difficult, I swear.'

Leni wasn't interested in hearing her sister's pleas. She was worried sick about Thea and what on earth she might say to the girl to make things better between them. She told herself that the girl would forgive her – they loved each other deeply. Yet Leni tortured herself with the thought that the betrayal was too huge ever to be forgiven.

Rubbing at her face with her hands, she walked wearily over to the window to look down into the street. There was no sign of Paul.

'Did anyone come by here while I was out?' she asked anxiously.

'No, I haven't seen a soul.'

'I was expecting Paul. He only went to the Babylon Circus – he should be back by now.'

'Maybe he went home?'

Leni chewed on her bottom lip. He wouldn't have just gone home without making sure that she was all right. Ignoring Annette, she opened the window and began searching the street below hoping to see him.

'I'm sure he's fine,' her sister said casually.

She turned and looked at Nette chain-smoking – cluttering up her apartment as she had done for the last two months. She was nothing but trouble and Leni was done with her.

'I think it would be better if you went back to America. There's nothing more for us to say. As usual I will have to pick up the pieces of your mess.'

'If that's what you want. But . . .' Annette started to say something but Leni wasn't listening. Out of the corner of her eye, she'd caught a glimpse of people running down the street.

'What's going on out there? Why are there people shouting at this time of night?'

Her first thought was some kind of an accident – and she imagined Paul lifeless in the road. Leni hesitated for a split second, and then she began to run as fast as she could. Clattering down the stairs, she raced out of her front door and into the street. There was no sign of anyone close to her building now.

In the distance a small crowd had gathered. She could hear their voices but couldn't make out what they were saying.

Leni ran until she reached the corner, panting for breath. The crowd had grown bigger – they were talking animatedly. A tall man was waving his arms around and pointing along the street.

'What's happening?' she gasped. Her only thought now was of Paul. A cold hand of fear gripped her insides as some of the crowd turned to look at her. She could tell by their faces that something terrible had happened. One of the women was sobbing desperately and Leni felt her heart slam against her ribs with fear.

'They've *done* it. Those bastards have done it,' the tall man said urgently.

Leni's eyes became wide. 'Done what?' she asked, not understanding why these people were so upset.

The sobbing woman turned to her. 'The Russians . . . they've closed the border. They've split the city in half.' She made a breaking gesture with her fingers.

'But it's just temporary? They'll open it again?' Leni couldn't believe that an entire city could be divided in two just like that. There must be some mistake. But more people joined the crowd – each of them babbling, agitated and distraught.

'No, they've rolled out barbed wire everywhere. I asked one of the guards and he told me that's it now. Nobody can get in or out. It's done!' an old man told her.

'But they can't . . .' Leni couldn't believe what she was hearing. The sobbing woman clutched at her arm.

'My son lives in Alexanderplatz . . . how will I see him again? The Russians won't let anybody leave . . .' She rocked with despair as her fingers dug into Leni's arm.

Shaking her head, Leni suddenly thought about the

Babylon Circus over in the Russian sector ... and she began to run.

'Paul!' she cried as she ran until her lungs hurt and she had to double over in the street to get her breath. As soon as she managed to gasp a few breaths, Leni took off running again and didn't stop until she reached the edge of the Russian sector. All the times she'd casually walked through these streets without giving it a thought. Even if a policeman stopped her, they usually waved her through. It had never occurred to her that the idle threats of the past few months would turn into this ...

She came to a screeching halt.

The first thing Leni noticed was that it was pitch black – the street lamps were all turned off. The only lights were the icy-blue glare of searchlights sweeping across the border. As she reached Zimmerstrasse, there were soldiers standing at two-metre intervals along the street carrying guns.

In front of them were enormous coils of barbed wire that lay twisted and tangled across the road. There were rows and rows of it. So much wire that it was impossible to step around it or over it. As she edged closer to the barbed wire, a policeman held up a red light and shone it in her face.

'I need to get through ... I have to get to Jägerstrasse.' Leni took two steps forward but the policeman put his arm out to stop her.

'No entry. Get back,' he said, half pushing her with his outstretched hand.

For a moment she was blinded by the light shining in her eyes and put her fingers up to shield them from the glare.

'I have to find my friend. Please, let me through,' Leni pleaded but the man waved her away.

'The sector is closed. Nobody comes in and nobody leaves.' He moved his light and began to walk away.

She was about to plead her case but just behind the policeman she saw a dog barking ferociously, yanking on its metal chain as a guard struggled to hold it back.

The icy blue of the searchlight swept over them and, to the side of her, she saw another soldier raise his gun at a crowd who were starting to gather. Like her they were desperate to get to their loved ones. She could see the man's determined stare as he picked out his targets.

Leni tried to see further down the street but it was dark – other than the blinding searchlights. She began to run again.

There must be a gap somewhere. They couldn't have closed the border so quickly. There were miles of streets dividing east from west. Her mouth turned dry with fear. Blood pulsing in her ears as the sound of her heels clipping against the concrete echoed through the night air.

Leni had to stop again, leaning against a street lamp to get her breath, her lungs raw with the effort of racing through the blacked-out streets. A faint sheen of sweat glistened on her forehead. She had to find him. There must be a way.

There were buildings for several blocks with no way to get through them but then right in front of her was another gap in the road, where it might be possible to cross over to the other sector. Leni took a long, wheezing breath and ran towards it. Her heart hammered inside her chest as she did so.

All she could see were soldiers in a row, lined up with their guns slung across their shoulders. But then a large grey truck drew up alongside them and began unloading more coils of barbed wire. Behind it another group of soldiers raced into position and started to take concrete blocks from the back of the lorry.

There was no sign of the Americans, anywhere. The only soldiers to be seen were Russian.

Leni tried to walk towards the coils of barbed wire, searching for a way around them.

'Please – I need to get through . . .' she shouted at the young soldier who was standing closest to her. He was just a boy, his skin pitted with pimples. His mouth opened wide as he laughed and shook his head. Rows of crooked teeth grinned at her.

The boy soldier shouted one word.

'NO!'

Leni didn't know what to do next. Maybe if she tried back the other way – maybe they wouldn't have got to the smaller streets to close them off? She spun around on the pavement, overwhelmed with panic.

Then a thought struck her – the trains. She could get a U-Bahn to Friedrichstrasse. She took off towards the nearest station, praying that it wasn't too late, running until she felt a sharp pain in her side and her breath came in great juddering bursts.

As Leni turned the corner, she could see people gathered outside the U-Bahn station. Filled with a desperate hope, she shoved her way past the crowd and tried to get on to the steps but there was no way through.

A young woman next to her was screaming hysterically while a boy tried to pacify her.

'Are the trains running?' Leni demanded. The girl carried on screaming and rubbing her eyes with her balled-up fists.

The thought of Paul being trapped and it all being her fault made her stomach churn with fear. She had to find him . . . Leni gripped the young woman by her shoulders. 'THE TRAINS . . . are the trains running?'

The girl didn't answer her but a young man who was standing close by shouted, 'Leave her alone. There are no trains. It's all shut down. You can't get in there.'

Leni glared at him. 'I have to get through . . . I have to . . .'

She took off again – this time racing back the other way. She didn't even know where she was running to. In the dark she was losing her bearings. All she needed was a tiny gap – the smallest street. A chink in the armour.

She had to find a way to get to Paul. She couldn't lose him – not after everything they'd been through. Why hadn't she listened to the news broadcasts, taken the rumours seriously? Every street she ran down came to another dead end.

There were only soldiers and barbed wire everywhere she looked. Another policeman shone his torch in her face as she walked up to him.

'Please . . .' Leni panted but he pushed her away so violently that she almost fell over.

'Why are you doing this? It's all Berlin . . . You have to let us in, please . . .' A group of men began shouting at the Russian soldiers. Throwing stones or whatever they could lay their hands on. The soldiers fired a warning shot into the air making the crowd move back quickly, a wave of terror sweeping through them.

Leni couldn't run any further. She struggled to get her breath.

Maybe tomorrow they would change their minds. It

was just a show of strength – not a permanent fixture. The Americans wouldn't allow this to happen. But where were they?

Leni stared blankly at the soldiers moving their concrete blocks. 'What are they doing?' she cried.

An old man looked at her through watery eyes. 'They're building a wall . . .' he said.

Leni didn't know what time it was when she finally arrived back at the apartment, her lungs bursting and her mind dazed. It couldn't be true – it couldn't be. Yet she knew that it was.

Climbing wearily up the stairs, she scrabbled about in her pocket for her key. As she opened the door, Annette called out to her.

'Leni – is that you?'

The sound of her voice set Leni's teeth on edge.

Her sister stood to greet her.

'Did you find Paul? The radio said they've closed the border. Is it true? What are the Americans doing? They have to do something about this.'

'Yes, it's true.' Leni had no tears left to cry as she looked at her sister sitting there like a scolded child. Her jaw clenched as her hands twisted together. 'I could have gone away with Paul when I was young. We could have been happy. But you had to come between us with your lies.'

Leni shook her head. 'I took care of you . . . first you and then Thea. I tried to make a decent life for us. We were doing all right on our own. But you couldn't leave us in peace. You've never cared for anybody except yourself. You wouldn't even care for your own child.'

'You don't understand, Leni – you don't know what it was like for me . . .' Annette stood up in the centre of the living room with her arms by her sides. Her face was ashen.

Leni was too furious to care about the effect her words were having. 'I know *you*! I know what a selfish bitch you are. You don't care about me at all.'

'You would have died without me. I looked after you when you got sick, when the Russians were invading. There was nobody else to take care of you and I did that all by myself.'

Annette began to weep. Tears streamed down her cheeks but Leni was unmoved by the sight of her.

'Fetching me a cold towel for my fever doesn't make up for the mess you've made of my life.' She felt so exhausted that she could have fallen to the floor right there but something pushed her across the room until she was standing in front of her sister. 'I'll never forgive you for what you did tonight. Never.'

'You have to understand. There's something I need to tell you—' But before Annette could finish her sentence, Leni drew back her hand and smacked her hard across her face.

The sound of the slap echoed like the crack of a pistol around the room. The two women stood there, shocked into silence by the blow. Annette put her hand to her cheek as she stared wildly back at her sister.

Leni couldn't believe what she'd done. She'd wanted to hurt her sister as she'd been hurt. She could see Nette's cheek turn red as her eyes filled with tears, and for a moment she felt a deep shame.

'I didn't mean to . . .' she mumbled. Yet part of her felt

that Annette deserved it. A mixture of anger and grief churned inside her.

The doorbell suddenly split the air with a shrill ring, startling both women. Leni felt a surge of hope where only moments before there had been the darkest despair. Leaving Annette standing clutching her cheek, she turned and ran out of the apartment.

Racing down the stairs as fast as she could and pulling open the front door. Her fingers clumsy with nerves as the blood pulsed in her ears. Praying it was him – and as the door flew open, standing there on the pavement was Paul. He was out of breath from running and panting heavily as he spoke.

'I couldn't get through – they've blocked off all the streets. I tried everything to find Thea, but there's no way to get there. I'm so sorry, Leni.'

'Oh, Paul . . .' She flew into his arms, clinging to his neck. Crying and kissing him at the same time. 'Thea is safe. She was at her friend's house. I've been going crazy worrying that you were trapped.' Leni could barely speak through her sobs. 'I . . . I thought I'd lost you.'

Paul wrapped his arms around her. 'I'm here. I'm right here.'

80

Annette was sitting in the dark, smoking a cigarette. She could barely make out the hands of the clock on top of the sideboard, but she could hear it ticking. Outside was a violet sky and the promise of a new day. She hadn't slept at all. She wasn't sure that Leni had either. The apartment was still draped in a bitter silence – but the dull yellowish glow of a bedside lamp shone from under the bedroom door, and Annette thought that she could hear her sister moving around: the gentle tread of her footsteps and the creak of the floor.

Paul had eventually gone home about an hour ago. Leni had refused to speak to Annette when she'd shown him to the door. Once he'd gone, she'd simply given her a furious glare before slamming the bedroom door, and she'd remained inside ever since.

Crushing out her cigarette in the glass ashtray she walked over to the window. Outside, the streets were empty and she felt completely alone. Running her fingertips across the side of her face, Annette winced. It felt sore and tender – a bruising reminder of just how much her sister hated her.

She had nobody now. She'd lost everyone she'd ever cared for. Annette felt sorry for herself, even as she realized that it was probably her own fault. Hot tears spilled down her face as she contemplated her future. Where could she go? There was nobody waiting for her. Wiping away her tears, she cast a glance towards the tiny pool of light.

There was something she should have done years ago. It was probably too late to make any difference now. But Annette needed to at least try and explain things.

She took a tentative step towards the bedroom door before hesitating just outside with her hand raised. Finally, inhaling a deep breath, Annette gently tapped on the door with her knuckles.

There was no answer, yet she was sure that her sister was awake. She waited for a few more seconds, her hand hovering in the air, unsure of what to do. Then, Annette knocked again – and, this time, she didn't wait for an invitation.

Leni was sitting up in bed with the covers thrown to one side. Her face looked weary and pale – the product of a sleepless night. Thea's records were still strewn over the floor where she'd left them earlier. Brightly coloured sleeves of songs from young American singers.

Annette nervously entered the room. Her voice quivered as she began to speak.

'I know you're angry with me, but I need to tell you something. Then you'll never have to see me again if you don't want to . . .' She took a tentative step towards the bed.

'I don't want your apologies. Get out.' Leni turned her face away but Annette couldn't leave without saying what she'd come to say. Now that she'd finally found the courage to speak up, she had to go through with it.

'I am really sorry that I hurt you – and Thea. I know that you hate me right now but there's something I need to tell you. I should have told you before . . . It's just that I've never told anyone . . .'

Leni glared up at Annette – her face tear-stained and furious.

'Well, say what you have to say and then get out.'

Berlin, May 1945

81

Annette placed the back of her hand on her sister's fore-head. Her temperature must have gone up again in the night. She was burning with fever. Nette took the flannel from Leni's head and went to wet it again in their only bucket of water but it was nearly empty.

'Leni . . .' she whispered but her sister didn't open her eyes. People were moving around in the streets outside. Across the road was a long queue for the water pump. The fighting had stopped just days before – the peace was signed. The building had been hit by a bomb – most of the rooms were unusable now. They'd taken refuge in the base-ment but then Leni had got sick and she didn't seem to be getting any better.

Whispering silent prayers to a God she no longer believed in, Annette mumbled, 'Please don't let her die . . .' over and over. She knew that she'd have to go and join the queue for water but Annette was afraid to leave Leni. There was nobody to stay with her. She was so alone now. They only had each other and if Leni died then Annette had no idea what she would do. She whispered her little prayer again. 'Please don't let her die . . .' Choking back her tears, she used the last of the water in their bucket to force some between Leni's lips by wringing out the flannel on to her mouth. The water wasn't even cold any longer. She wiped her sister's face carefully and then placed the cool flannel on her brow.

Then Annette picked up the bucket and clambered up the stairs to go outside.

'What a life we have now . . . standing around for hours to fill a bucket with water.' The woman in front of her wouldn't stop talking. Nobody wanted to hear it, but her mouth kept moving. Words spilling out – the life they'd lost. Defeat meant living in rubble like animals – no food or water. Annette couldn't move away from the woman, yet she longed to tell her to shut up. The queue shuffled forward slowly. Eventually she was able to fill her bucket and carry it back to the basement.

Leni was moaning softly in her sleep, her face covered in sweat. Annette placed a kiss on her forehead and wet the flannel again.

'You can't leave me, Leni . . .' she cried, but there was no response.

It was dusk now; outside, the streets were eerily quiet. The lines for food or water were all gone. Annette felt as if they were the last two people left on earth. She sat on the edge of the bed and held her sister's hand. It felt cold and lifeless although her face glistened with fever. Annette felt tears choking her yet she couldn't cry. She had relied on her sister for everything. She was always so strong, but now, looking at her lying there . . .

'There must be something I can do . . .' She tried to think of someone who might help them. The city was devastated – she didn't even know if people were still in their houses in the next street. Rumours were rife but there was no real information available to them. The women at the water pump told stories of things they'd heard, yet so far nobody had set eyes on a soldier. They just knew that the fighting had stopped and the war was over.

Leni needed help – she couldn't just let her die. Annette soaked the flannel again, trying to force a little more water between her lips. She gave Leni's hand a reassuring squeeze. 'I'm not going to let you die . . . I'm going to get help.'

Keeping to the shadows, Annette hurried through the deserted streets. There had been an old apothecary where they'd lived before the war, by the abandoned courtyard. She didn't know if it would still be there but she had no idea where else she could go. Slipping in and out of doorways if she heard a noise, Annette made it to the end of the street. All the shops and houses that had been so familiar to her were broken piles of rubble and bricks. She couldn't stop to think about it. Pressing on, she turned the corner, clambering over a pile of rubble until she could see the faded sign for the apothecary in the distance. It was still there. Breathing a sigh of relief, Annette began to run towards it, past the entrance to the old abandoned courtyard where she'd slept out with Leni. The bird shop and the apothecary had both been hit by shells, with their walls blown apart. The building was in darkness but that didn't mean anything. There was no power. Anyone inside could be hiding in the dark or sitting in the cellar burning a candle.

Suddenly she saw the flash of a light at the corner of the street. In a split second she realized that it was Russian soldiers patrolling. Annette's heart began to race and she looked for somewhere to hide. There was no way to get around to the back of the apothecary's, but then she remembered the courtyard. She knew it like the back of her hand: each corner and crevice that she'd played in as a child, exploring when Leni was at work.

Hardly daring to breathe, Annette slowly crept down the alleyway and into the courtyard, sliding into the darkness and pressing herself against the wall. Using her fingers to feel her way, she made her way around the courtyard until she came to a stairwell. The building was no longer there and, as she hid inside, Annette looked up to see the night sky where there had once been flights of stairs. Her breath became juddery and terrified as she saw a flash of light enter the courtyard. She could hear voices coming closer.

She looked around for somewhere else to hide – but there was nowhere to go except back out into the court-yard. Annette was trapped. All she could do was stay as still as possible and pray they wouldn't find her. One of the soldiers stood at the entrance to the stairwell and lit a cig-arette. The match flared into a tiny orange flame and Annette caught a glimpse of the soldier's face – his fierce black eyes looking straight at her.

A wild fear clenched her insides. She began to shake so violently that she thought she would die. The man said something to his companion and then a flashlight blinded her. Annette backed away along the wall but the soldiers just laughed. She couldn't understand what they were saying, yet she knew what it meant for her.

The man with the black eyes gripped her arm so tightly she thought he might break it. She tried to say something – to plead, but no words came out of her mouth. Annette pulled away from him but he was too strong for her. A fist came out of nowhere and punched the side of her face until she felt sick and dizzy. The other soldier held a flashlight and shone it on to the stairs. He seemed to be urging the man with the black eyes to hurry up.

Annette felt her body slam on to the staircase and her legs forced apart. Then his hand was around her throat and she couldn't breathe. She was shaking with a raw terror and she knew these men would kill her. The smell of him made her feel sick – thick engine oil and sweat. She felt her stomach churn and vomit start to rise. Then she heard his companion shout something and all she could see was those hateful black eyes looming over her as her head hit the staircase.

The flashlight made shadows of them on the wall. Annette watched them move as if it were a strange creature with no name. His hands were clutching at her – ripping her clothes. Then his fingers pushed inside her and he said something to his companion. The pair of them laughed.

Annette felt dizzy but as she looked up all she could see was those piercing black eyes staring back at her. His fingers hurting her. His hand squeezing her throat as he pushed himself into her. Then his penis was thrusting inside her and she prayed for it to be over. She hoped they would kill her quickly. The stink of oil on his skin made her retch as his thrusting became frenzied. His black eyes closed as he took two shuddering breaths and collapsed on to her body. In the distance she could hear a truck revving and the other soldier yelled something. The black-eyed man released his grip on her and began to get to his feet.

He grinned at her: a malicious, gap-toothed smile. Leaning over, he tweaked her cheek hard, pulling it until she cried out. Then he adjusted his trousers with one hand and bent down. Annette gasped – for a split second she thought he was going to do it again. Instead, the black-eyed man cleared his throat and spat on to her face. Then he was gone.

She lay there trembling violently, her legs wide apart and her clothes torn away, his saliva dribbling down her face. The taste of him on her mouth. Her thighs wet. She thought she was bleeding but she couldn't see anything in the dark.

Wiping the spit from her face, Annette glanced up through the broken roof at the night sky, and saw the stars looking down on her.

Berlin, August 1961

82

Leni put her hand to her mouth remembering all the times she had chastised Annette for her behaviour.

'All these years I thought you'd had some fling with a soldier. But that's why you couldn't bear to be around Thea. All the times I called you selfish or made comments about her father . . .'

Nette's face caved and she began to sob, 'I . . . I don't want you to hate me. I know I've hurt everyone but I can't stand it if *you* hate me, Leni.'

'I don't hate you.' She wrapped her arms around her sister and held her as she wept. She'd rarely seen her sister cry since she was a child but now Annette seemed unable to stop as the pain poured out of her.

'I'm so sorry, Nette,' Leni whispered. 'Why didn't you tell me?'

'At first, I . . . I couldn't tell you because you were so sick – and then afterwards, I didn't know how . . . I tried to find the words . . .'

Leni stroked Annette's hair back off her face. 'I wish I'd known. You shouldn't have had to bear this all alone.'

'I just wanted to carry on living. Everything was different afterwards and then when I found out I was pregnant, you were so angry with me. So I decided that I would never tell a soul what happened.' Annette wiped her hands over her face, taking quivering breaths.

Leni could feel the thin blades of her sister's back as she hugged her. 'I'm glad you've told me.'

'I wanted you to understand that's why I couldn't take care of Thea. She looks like him . . . *those black eyes*. I know it's not her fault but for a long time I couldn't even stand to look at her. It reminded me of that night. Of what he did to me.'

'What about Glenn? Did you tell him?' she asked quietly.

Annette shook her head. 'No. You're the only person I've told. I used to take Glenn to that same place. I don't know why I did it . . . I couldn't stop going back there. It was as if I'd lost something and I couldn't find it again. Maybe I thought I would be like I was before . . .'

'There have been too many secrets and lies between us. From now on let's always tell each other the truth.' Leni reached out her fingers and took hold of Annette's hand.

The two sisters clutched at each other as they gazed through tear-stained smiles.

'I promise we will. Now, let's get some sleep. Tomorrow, I'll talk to Thea. This is all my fault and I have to put it right.'

'It's not your fault, Nette, but it's not Thea's either. She's a good girl. Bright and loving. She's like you in so many ways.'

'You did that.' Annette wiped her eyes. 'You've taken such good care of her. I'll talk to Thea when she comes back. I need to tell her why I left her behind. She deserves an explanation. It's time I faced up to that.'

Leni watched her sister's face open with the relief of having told her the truth.

'What will you say?'

'I'll tell her what happened.' Annette fixed her with a determined look. 'She needs to understand why I left her behind. I don't want her to hate me forever. You're right – none of this is her fault, but it's not my fault either.' She parroted the words in a way that made Leni alarmed.

'She won't hate you. But what will you tell her?'

'I'll explain to her what happened. I have to – or she will go on thinking of me as this horrible person who abandoned her, and that's not fair on either of us.'

Leni sat up on the bed and looked anxiously at her sister.

'You can't tell her what happened to you. She's only fifteen – how is she supposed to understand that you left her behind because she reminded you of the man who raped you? You can't tell her, Nette . . .'

'I won't say it like that. Of course I won't. But I don't want to lie to people any more. I'm tired of keeping this secret.'

'No . . . no . . . Nette, I won't let you do this. I'm sorry for what happened to you. You're my sister and I love you dearly – but I won't let you destroy this child.'

'But it's not fair if my own child ends up despising me. I'll find some way to explain it.'

'There is no way to explain it that won't hurt her. Please, don't do this. Let me talk to her.' Leni clasped hold of her arm but her sister gently shook her off and stood up.

'No, I'll talk to her in the morning. I'm her mother. I'll make things all right between us.' Annette looked wrung out and exhausted but Leni couldn't take the chance that she might actually go through with it.

'Nette – I'm begging you not to do it,' she cried but the bedroom door had already closed behind her.

83

Annette crushed out her cigarette in the ashtray and took a long nervous gulp of her coffee. Leni gestured towards the closed bedroom door with her eyes.

'You can't do this to her, Nette . . .'

Taking a deep breath, Annette brushed her sister's arm away and tapped on the bedroom door. There was no response. Thea hadn't left her bedroom in hours or said one word to either of them since she'd returned home earlier that morning.

Annette could feel Leni's eyes burning into her back, but she was determined to explain everything properly. She had no wish to hurt the girl. She would find the right way to explain everything – the words would come to her. There must be some way to say everything gently so Thea would know that she hadn't been abandoned for no reason. And yet when she thought of the reason she couldn't think of what she might say.

'Please . . .' Leni whispered but Annette couldn't stop now. She opened the bedroom door and stepped inside.

'Thea, there . . . there are some things that I need to explain to you.' A sharp jolt of anxiety made her voice tremble.

The girl was curled up on the bed, facing the wall. She looked much younger than her fifteen years and all her usual bravado was gone. Her face was pinched and etched with misery.

Annette edged towards her, feeling nervous, her hands clasping and unclasping. They trembled slightly and she wished for a cigarette to calm her nerves.

'Thea?' she called softly but the girl didn't turn around. Her body tensed against the intrusion.

This was not how Annette had envisaged their conversation going. In her imagined explanations the girl was sitting up, alert and curious about what she had to say. Instead, Thea lay there staring blankly at the wall, sullen and uncommunicative.

Walking across the room to the bedroom window, Annette stared out at the grey buildings. The little windows with other anonymous lives going on behind closed blinds. None of this had been built the last time she was here. It made her feel more of a stranger than ever.

She glanced at the girl, hoping for some way to begin a conversation but Thea didn't even look up at her. Releasing a shallow breath, Annette began to speak.

'I know you're very angry. What you overheard last night must have come as a terrible shock. If you'll let me, I want to try and explain what happened, and why we didn't tell you before.' She was talking to the girl as if she'd submitted her homework late but Annette couldn't find the right tone for this particular occasion.

Again, there was no response. Thea flung an arm over her head, and buried her face in the pillow. Annette sighed.

Moving closer to the bed, she wondered if she dared to sit down next to Thea. She didn't know this girl at all, although she remembered the cold February dawn when she'd entered the world. She remembered how the baby had cried for hours. How she wouldn't be comforted, until Leni had picked her up and settled her.

It was as if some part of Thea knew right from the start that Annette didn't want to take care of her.

'Do you mind if I sit here?' she asked softly. Thea shrugged her shoulders, her face still hidden in the pillow. Annette sat down gingerly, smoothing over the pale green quilt with her fingers.

'All right then. I'll just talk and if you need to ask me things then you can.' She blew out a tiny nervous breath. She didn't know where to start or what to say. There were no words to describe what she'd been through, but she had to try.

'There was a very good reason why I left you here with Leni. Do you want me to tell you?' Annette put her hand out and gently patted the girl on her arm. Her skin felt hot under her fingers. Thea moved away from her touch, shielding herself with her arm, but Annette could see her black eyes staring up at her. She could hardly bear to look at them.

Yet she only looked curious, and hurt.

'The truth is . . . Well, the truth is . . .' Annette cleared her throat. Thea was still watching her with those eyes, wary but interested now. And they weren't *his* eyes. She was just a child.

'The truth is I left you here because . . . I met an American soldier. He wanted to marry me but I worried that he wouldn't want me if I told him about you. So, I didn't tell him . . . I lied to him. You see, I've always been a selfish person, Thea. I've always done exactly what I wanted to do. None of this was ever your fault. It was all my doing.'

The words hung there in the air between them. The girl didn't move, but Annette could tell that she was listening. 'Leni *is* your mother – she's more of a mother than I could ever hope to be. She loved you from the minute you were born, and you would only ever stop crying if she was holding you. I knew then that she would care for you as if you were her own daughter – in a way that I never could. I did what I thought was best for all of us at the time but I am so very sorry that you found out like this.'

There was a long period of silence as the girl digested what she'd said. Thea rolled over on to her back and then sat up.

'But you didn't want me? You have other children.'

'Yes, I have other children . . . but I'm here feeling sorry for myself instead of spending the summer with them. The truth is that I don't think I'm cut out to be a mother. Some women aren't made that way. Maybe I'm one of them.'

Thea gave her a hard stare.

'So that's it. "Sorry, I can't be your mother. Find another one." You can't choose not to be my mother!' Her voice became shrill as she spoke.

'I am sorry . . .' Annette felt a rush of strange emotion as she gazed down at her. This girl was part of her – and yet she wasn't hers at all. She'd never wanted her. She hadn't asked to be in this situation. It was impossible for all of them.

As she spoke, she saw two bright pink spots of anger appear on Thea's cheeks.

'YOU'RE SORRY! What good is that? Is that all you can say?' Her face darkened as her anger spilled out.

'Thea, please try to understand. I did the best I could,' she offered weakly.

'You didn't even try. The first chance you got, you left me. And what about my father? DO YOU EVEN KNOW WHO HE WAS?' Thea screamed at her.

Annette opened her mouth and then closed it again. She was so out of her depth. What could she possibly say to make this better? She couldn't tell her the truth – she saw that now. There was only one thing for it.

'He died. He was a soldier and he was killed at the end of the war,' she muttered softly.

'Did you even know his name?' the girl hissed at her.

'No, I didn't know his name,' Annette whispered as her heart shattered into a million pieces.

The two of them sat there on the bed in silence for a few seconds. Thea's face was a picture of fury.

'I can't undo the past. But everything that happened to you was my fault. You shouldn't blame Leni. She didn't do anything to hurt you. She loves you very much.'

'But she LIED to me,' the girl protested angrily.

'*I* lied to you. She just picked up the pieces. You have to forgive her. She's a wonderful mother, Thea. That's all that really matters.'

Annette could feel her throat tightening as she stood up. She'd been stupid to think that there was any way to explain this. 'I'll be leaving Berlin soon. That's all I wanted to say.'

'And that's it? I'll *never* see you again?' Thea cried out furiously.

The girl was watching her as Annette walked over to the door, feeling those black eyes judging her with every step.

Reaching out her hand she twisted the handle – but then stopped. Turning around, she took a last look at the girl.

'Forget about me, Thea.'

'Forget about you! You walk in here and say you're my mother but I should just forget all about you?' Her lips began to quiver. She looked utterly wretched and Annette couldn't bear it.

'Yes . . . forget about me. You have your whole life ahead of you. Don't waste it thinking about me. You have a wonderful mother, and she loves you very much.'

With that she closed the bedroom door behind her and walked slowly into the kitchen where Leni was staring out of the window. At the sound of her footsteps her sister turned around, her face showing the torment of waiting.

'Did you . . .'

'I didn't tell her,' Annette said as tears began trickling down her face. She allowed herself to be wrapped up in her sister's arms, Leni wiping away her tears as if she were a child again.

Holding on to each other in the morning light, Annette caught a glimpse of their reflection in the kitchen window as Leni whispered 'Thank you' over and over again.

Epilogue

Annette glanced out of the window at the comings and goings outside the aircraft. Settling back in her seat, she thought about Leni – their goodbyes had been sweet but tinged with sadness. She wondered if they would ever see each other again.

Thea had chosen not to come out of her bedroom and, in some ways, Annette was all right with that. It was better for her to be hated so that Leni could be loved.

The final passengers boarded the plane: men in smart suits and a woman carrying a baby. It was a busy flight, stopping in London before carrying on to New York.

Fastening her seatbelt, she tried to think about Glenn. She would tell him the truth about how she'd only married him because she was so desperate to leave Berlin. How she'd plotted and lied to get her own way. Then divorce, and after that Annette didn't know, and of course there were the boys to think of. Whatever was ahead of her, she was determined to face it truthfully. She would make a new life – an honest life.

The aircraft door closed just as the final passenger boarded. An elderly gentleman with silver hair limped down the aisle and sat down in the seat next to her. He was juggling a walking stick and a brightly wrapped gift box tied with blue ribbons which he placed on his lap.

As the plane began to roll forwards, his walking stick fell to the floor between them. Annette bent down to retrieve it, handing it back to him with a polite nod.

As he turned his face, she could see that a thin, flesh-coloured mask covered half of it, leaving his one good eye staring out at her.

'Thank you,' the man said, taking the silver-topped cane from her and settling it at his side. 'So, we are to be fellow travellers. Are you going to London, or on to New York?'

His mouth moved in a peculiar lop-sided way as he spoke.

'I'm going to New York,' she replied, trying not to stare at his face, but the man just carried on smiling at her.

'Ahh . . . New York. And do you have family there?' he asked.

Annette thought for a long moment and then she glanced up at him.

'Yes, I do . . .' she said. She thought of her two boys – who needed her now in the same way that Thea needed Leni, and sighed. The old man continued to look at her with his peculiar lop-sided face. He reminded her of some-one, but she couldn't quite place him.

'And where are you travelling to?' she asked, feeling obliged to say something.

'Oh, London for me. That's my home.'

As he spoke the pretty ribboned box lurched to the side and ended up lodged between the two of them. Annette stopped it from slipping on to the floor and returned it to him.

'Oh . . . your gift,' she said with a tight smile.

'Thank you. I mustn't lose this. It's for my friend, you see. He's a pianist.'

As he spoke, the engines burst into life as they roared along the runway and lifted high up into the clouds.

The lights of Berlin below them – and above them, only sky.

Acknowledgements

Writing a book can mean long hours sitting in a chair trying to commune with imaginary people. It can be a lonely and frustrating process when it's not going well but it is the best feeling in the world when it flows. At the end of all that chair sitting I have a manuscript filled with a story. I have invented characters and they are living their imaginary lives on the page. A book, however, is a very different thing and this book would not be possible without the creative genius and input of so many people.

Firstly, a huge debt of gratitude is owed to my favourite editor, Clio Cornish, who always believes that I have just a little more to give when we're editing and is always proved right. She makes my work better and gives me endless support and encouragement along the way.

Thanks also to Maddy for her wonderful editorial support and to Jessie, Liv and Gabby for their creativity and brilliance in looking after and promoting my work.

This book would be riddled with errors and wouldn't make it to a bookshelf without the careful eyes of Nick, Richenda and the proofreaders who save my blushes on a regular basis. Enormous thanks to the sales and production teams and to everyone in audio for always finding the perfect voice.

Thank you once again to the brilliant Lauren Wakefield for the beautiful cover design and *grazie mille* to the Balbusso twins, Anna and Elena, for the gorgeous illustration.

Forever grateful to my early readers, Frances Quinn and Anna Mazzola, who read this over Christmas and came back with such lovely words that I cried with relief.

This book took a lot to write. Three different time periods with a cast of characters at different ages is a challenge, and one I would not have survived if it hadn't been for my husband Sean making sure that I was fed and had clean clothes through the endless months of writing. He kept me going when I was sure that I had bitten off much more than I could chew until eventually I could actually call it a book. Love you always.

The idea for this book came partly from my endless fascination with the Weimar period and also from a tiny spark in *73 Dove Street* where the landlady Phyllis remarks that 'We all had a war didn't we?' Sometimes the smallest detail grows in your mind, and during events I spoke with readers about the fact that women who are often civilians and bystanders in conflicts usually end up bearing the brunt of those economic or political decisions.

Often when or where a woman is born can determine the course of her entire life and that is very much what I wanted to explore through the lives of the sisters Leni and Annette. They are, of course, entirely fictional, but their lives reflect how women have to adapt to their circumstances, caring for their families regardless of what happens around them. We see this in action every day in our world. Nobody gives women a service medal for surviving and this book is my tribute to women everywhere who struggle to overcome their circumstances every single day.

Finally, my thanks to you, the reader, for supporting my

work. I've so enjoyed hearing from you and meeting some of you at events. I love the way you feel so strongly about my imaginary women, and when I am sitting in my writing chair struggling to create, it is the thought of my book being read many months from now that keeps me going.

I hope you enjoy *Circus of Mirrors* and being part of the lives of Leni and Annette as much as I enjoyed writing them.

Julie x